THE
BONE
STARMADA

THE
BONE
STARMADA

by

WYATT   HARVEY

terebinth tree publications

ISBN : 978-0-578-79281-1

Published by Terebinth Tree Publications
"A place of true inspiration."
Terebinth Tree is committed to publishing truly inspired, uplifting works
of literature. It draws its name and fundamental belief from the
Scriptures, **Genesis 18:1**
"Then the LORD appeared to him by the terebinth trees of Mamre..."
It was near those trees that God appeared to Abraham and it was there
Abraham would be given great promise and inspiration.

Printed in the USA

The Book of John, Chapter 1, Verses 1-5
New King James Version (NKJV)

The Eternal Word

1 In the beginning was the Word, and the Word was with God, and the Word was God. ²He was in the beginning with God. ³All things were made through Him, and without Him nothing was made that was made. ⁴In Him was life, and the life was the light of men. ⁵And the light shines in the darkness, and the darkness did not comprehend it.

Jesus Christ

The living Word of God, and the Son of God, and One with God

My fervent hope is that all who hear of Him would come to Him and accept His forgiveness and find Salvation in His Love.

I did, and I have never been the same.

My thanks go to God,
for it is from Him that all true blessings flow.

To my wife, Tara, who is also
my best friend, my confidant, my adviser, and my lover.
Life here would not be the same without you.

To my family. I believe I could publish
a grocery list and you would herald it as
great literature.

To all of my friends who enjoy science fiction with me.
Ray, Jake, my Union Chapel Tribe, you know who you are.

To Dr. Franklin Baggett,
a real inspiration and a true man of God.
When I grow up I want to be just like you.

PROLOGUE

"Captain, you are needed."

She rose from her sleep with a gasp. Sweat bathed her, though she was only dressed in little silk wrappings that wound from her hips to her left shoulder in tight bands. Her lower lip quivered.

The dream. Always the dream.

Bright green eyes searched her dark quarters. Her hair fell about her face in a loose golden frame, strands attached to her full lips and the tear trail over her cheek.

"Captain Garriton, this is-" the communique chimed again.

"I heard you, Mr. Shoka," she barked then shook her head for no one in particular. "I'm en route. Garriton out."

The shapely captain reluctantly slid across the bed, rolled off the side and strolled toward her closet. The closet doors swished aside at the wave of her hand and two racks of clothing rolled out for easy extraction.

She began to dress, reminding herself that nightmares had to wait. Her bridge needed her. Her starship, the *Vindicator*, needed her.

Her fitted uniform consisted of cargo pants and an officious, double breasted jacket. They were royal blue and silver, colors for a captain.

"Mr. Shoka," she muttered. Tapping the communicator earpiece as she adorned it, she asked, "Why am I on a path for the bridge on my first rest break in two days?"

Mr. Shoka returned on the communicator.

"My apologies. I need your input on something of importance. You must make the decision."

Garriton acknowledged him somewhat ruefully.

Though quite young, she had seen a lot in her career. Her trip to her own Command had been difficult and controversial. She had given up a lot to get there, always making the tough decisions.

In a corridor she passed a Greylik tech repairing a gravlift door.

"Captain," the technician nodded, saluting in the acceptable manner.

Samara Garriton smiled, slowing, then stopped. Hands on her hips, she nodded to the door and said, "Frozen? Like deck four?"

The technician agreed, brushing the fleshy tendrils of her scalp back from her face. The Greylik bore those instead of hair and the plenteous blood vessels within them aided in cooling their hot blooded natures.

"Precisely," the female tech answered. "Most...frustrating."

"I agree. But I'd be happy with the sticking doors if we could get all the decks working with their environmental controls."

The Greylik nodded, managing a shy smile for the captain.

"In the meantime, you're doing fine. As you were," Garriton finished and strode away.

Her ship had seemed to be cursed for weeks. One system after another failed. She had asked her first officer, Chief Security Officer T'Leah, if she believed in curses. The tall, lovely Chabron had scoffed at the idea.

Garriton trembled with a chill as she remembered the dream. She had helped commit mutiny once. That had to be grounds for a curse.

On the way to the command gravlift, the one that went to the bridge, she nodded to an approaching security officer. He was a Toran. The people of Torana had a somewhat notorious reputation for being bloodthirsty in battle. She had been advised not to accept the Toran's application to security but she had trusted her gut and he had been a valued member of that service.

As they spoke briefly in passing, she was proud of herself. Proud of her instinct. That famous gut instinct.

The gravlift doors opened and she peered inside. She hated gravlifts.

It was not the indigo light that bathed the shaft. That seemed quite relaxing. It was the fact that she would have to step out and only that light would be there to catch her in the shaft. Gravity manipulation forged a thick, moving light for carrying the crew, floating as if in a graviton beam outside a starship, but she never could seem to trust it.

She locked her jaw and told the open shaft her destined deck through clenched teeth. Then she stepped off into what was, in her opinion, nothingness. The nothingness caught her, however, and she floated upward rapidly.

Samara Garriton stepped onto the bridge after a brief lift.

Her ship bridge was not large, not like the ship she had once helped overtake from her former captain. No, her bridge was humble compared to the Reaper class ship for which she had been First Officer. The *Judgment*. That had been a dominating craft.

Her *Vindicator* was smaller and more agile, an ArcAngel class.

One time First Officer Samara Garriton had become a captain on the much smaller ship after helping overthrow Captain Bordin Mo on the *Judgment*. He had lost his mind, too many missions and years in space, they said. Whatever the cause, she had led a handful of the crew in a necessary mutiny and that very loyal band had accompanied her to the new assignment on the *Vindicator*. They had fallen in love with the small craft, accepting it as home.

Garriton strode onto the command deck with confidence, saluting the Security Officer by the lift.

"Report," she snapped and dropped into her seat in the center.

"Captain on the bridge."

The announcement came from a quickly spinning Graystalker Shoka, her head Weapons Officer. He sat at the Weapons Station, his usual post. Beside him was half of the Helm Station, on his right, for the head Navigator. On his left rested the main flight and pilot controls, the other half of the Helm, for the lead Helmswoman.

The Navigator, a young Oriental woman, stood and saluted then worked furiously at buttoning the loose flap of her double breasted jacket. Her uniform, like all below the rank of Captain, wrapped her in white and gray.

The only color exception to that standard was the security uniform.

The lead Helm Officer, their Pilot, was a very slender reptilian woman. She stood up beside Shoka as he rose, neither of them suffering from the heat. Their respective peoples were fond of more intense climates. Both saluted.

"As you were," she sighed, though her peripheral vision watched the Communications Officer, stationed to her far right, and the Chief Science Officer, at the far left, stand anyway. Both men were human and were quickly trying to close their jackets.

"As you were, people," she insisted and all dropped to a seat again.

The exception was the Security Officer. The Security Officer assigned to bridge duty during any shift stood at all times by the gravlift, adorned in black, like space itself.

"And all of you stop tightening up your uniform jackets," she growled, unbuttoning her own down one side. "If we don't get some better air going on this ship, we'll all just take them off. Silkens are enough for this heat."

Silkens were the shirt and footed pants that the starship crew wore beneath their uniforms. Made of a highly stretchable, skin tight silk polymer, they were very adept at protection from the cold and were, within a reasonable degree, fireproof. They were not very cool, however.

"I take it you did not wake T'Leah?" Garriton asked Shoka. "Since Mr. Penrose is here," she added and gestured at the Officer by the lift.

Shoka agreed then gestured to the communications officer.

"I did not know if you would want T'Leah for this. Mr. Respra has intercepted a communication, Captain."

He gestured for the man to play the audio, reveling in his status as second in command in the absence of the First Officer.

"I disbelieved its very existence at the start," the Jamaican accented man announced. "It's confusing, at best."

Garriton scowled with, "You? Confused?"

The man prided himself on knowledge and intelligence about communication. He had learned more than twenty languages and forty-four dialects and that was without the aide of his translation equipment. With that, he could decode and program a translation function for nearly any language.

The mystery at hand, however, had nothing to do with translations.

Niles Respra arched his shoulders and looked at his console.

"I can play it for you, Captain, but I can't explain it. I don't think anyone can."

Garriton waved away his bewildered glance, rolling her eyes.

"It's too hot for theatrics. Play it, Mr. Respra."

The message began. Terrible interference separated the distorted words.

"... broken ..." a crackling, electronic voice creaked. "... power is ... not ... from weapons are ... somehow survived the initial ... unknown ... casualties ... too much damage ... Captain Mo ... *Judgme* ... eaper Class..."

Then the recording became an automated distress signal made by the comsystem of a starship. It begged response for the disabled ship in question.

Garriton slid out to the edge of her seat, her long nails digging into the pads of her armrests. Her mouth hung agape, her eyes stretched wide.

Those who had served alongside her on the *Judgment* also took on a haunted look, staring back at the captain. Weapons Officer Shoka, Pilot Vissk, Navigator Chu and Communications Officer Respra all watched the captain for a cue as to response.

Garriton's legs felt weak. Her stomach rolled as her skin flushed.

What was out there? The communique was impossible.

16

On Captain Bordin Mo's last run with the *Judgment*, the day he decided to raze a settlement on Operatis Seven, from orbit, with the ominous firepower of the *Judgment*, he had died.

Samara Garriton, then his First Officer, had led the mutiny, disabled his ship...and, when it all went terribly wrong, she and the others abandoned ship in a shuttle craft. So many blindly chose to stay and support the madman, struggling to stop the decompression and the draining life support...and it killed them. All three hundred and ninety-one.

Tears filled her green eyes as she stared at the viewscreen. An incredibly massive asteroid was before them, a field of others behind it.

"Where is that transmission coming from?" she demanded of Respra.

"Behind that vanguard 'roid. It's the size of a moon; plenty of room to hide a Reaper class vessel-"

"It's not. It can't be," Garriton interrupted.

She seemed to be telling herself, not Respra.

"Actually, Captain, you could park a small fleet behind that thing," the Science Officer said flatly. "Asteroid makeup is somewhat typical, which means lots of ferrous materials, but also some rayonnix particles, so we couldn't sensor sweep behind it with ten times the sensor array we have now. All the following asteroids in the field have it, too, so ships could be lurking all through that field and we-"

"I know what rayonnix particles do, Mr. Boatwright. Every captain in the fleet does."

Rayonnix, a natural product in asteroids and asteroid fields, was a low level radiation used in starship shielding and masking from sensors. An asteroid field was naturally masked from detailed detection; a captain always knew an asteroid field was on the scopes by the massive reading of nothingness, which is how asteroid fields scanned.

Garriton seemed to break her trance. Whatever it was, it could not be the *Judgment*, so she shook off the mesmerizing moment and snapped back into her captain role.

"Mr. Penrose, go to deck three and get my First Officer out of bed," she growled at the Security Officer by the gravlift, though she never looked away from the viewscreen.

T'Leah was a Chabron, a quite humanoid race from the planet Chabrose. As such, she was two feet taller than the average human woman, she did not grow hair on her body, and her golden complexion had pigmentation spots on her shoulders, back, and thighs that reminded the captain of a leopard.

One other distinction of the Chabron was that they slept with programmed intent. When they went to sleep, they set in mind how long they would sleep, and the only way to wake them before that time was to physically touch them.

"Mr. Shoka, bring our Rayzon Mask online. Then establish Gravstar defenses, as well as our shields," she ordered.

"Captain, that's a lot of energy output if-"

"Do it," she added lowly. "I want the Chamber cannons online, the missile bays loaded and I want it yesterday."

"Captain, we don't even know-"

"Until we do, follow my orders to the letter, Mr. Shoka," she warned. "Now, Mr. Respra, return a message. Hail that transmitter, whatever or wherever it is. Tell them Captain Samara Garriton of the starship *Vindicator*, an ArcAngel class vessel in the Unity Starmada of Allied Planets, wants to know their identity and location."

Respra keyed his console and began to initiate transmission.

"Ms. Chu, plot us a course closer to the 'roid field. Ms. Vissk, try to angle our approach so that we might get a sensor peek behind that big rock in front."

"Captain, a return transmission is being sent and it's not a programmed distress signal. It's live."

"On screen," Garriton ordered.

"I'll try but the visuals are really dilapidated. Mainly audio is available."

"Do what you can but don't sing me a song about it," Garriton said.

For a split second, the bridge crew thought an image was coming up on the screen. It seemed to resemble a humanoid figure, flickering and inconsistent in the poor relay.

Whatever the reason, everyone shivered, frightened by the face they could not see.

Then the transmission turned to static and interference almost immediately, the video gone. The audio then came out insistently. It was a low, droning hum, digging into the senses and vibrating the bridge with its tone, not its volume.

"What isst thisst?" hissed the reptilian Helmswoman.

"The groan of death!" T'Leah shouted as she emerged from the lift and onto the bridge. "We have to pull back! Back from this 'roid field, back from this sector!"

The captain spun her seat to look at her second in command.

"Captain, trust me! My people have encountered this before," T'Leah urged.

The reptilian, Vissk, hissed at her console and keyed it rapidly.

"What? Report!" Captain Garriton snapped.

"I am reading a power ssurge, Grekbil," Vissk addressed the Captain. "But, I am not acsselerating! It isst asst if the sship ansswerss thisst death call and goess toward it…"

"Stop calling it that!" Garriton growled then stormed from her seat to the communications station. "Respra, shut that noise down!"

"He cannot!" T'Leah interrupted, joining the captain. "We must turn back!"

"We can't seem to do that, either," Garriton muttered.

"Then we will destroy it!" Graystalker Shoka roared.

The Weapons Officer slammed his fist down upon his console. His normally salt and pepper hair, cut short, grew a sudden four vins in length and turned a blazing white. His eyes shifted to a glowing green fury and his roar revealed fangs in the top and bottom rows of his teeth. He growled as he prepped a series of sequences into his controls.

"We have to find it to destroy it, Shoka," the captain chided. "Calm yourself!"

Shoka tilted his head and popped his shoulder. His body had grown in sinewy muscle.

"T'Leah, how did your people fare against this sound? What did they do?" Garriton demanded. Her face was desperate, her eyes fevered.

"The one ship, one of so many that have encountered this…they escaped because they ran, Captain…ran as fast and as far as they could…" The First Officer trailed off, staring at the blank viewscreen, her big, powerful body trembling.

"Your people?" the captain exploded. "Ships of you crazy space amazons actually ran from something?"

"One ship!" T'Leah shouted, turning furious eyes to her captain. "Chabron run from nothing! Nothing! But no ship had ever survived pursuing the death call-"

"Stop calling it that!" Garriton yelled.

"-until, to her eternal shame, Von'mar, captain of our Dreadship L'Oran, turned and ran."

"What a plan!" Shoka growled, his eyes burning as he turned to the Chabron. "Running!"

"One ship! One captain!" T'Leah railed angrily. Her left hand flew to the hilt sticking up above her right shoulder. Her uniform was different than the others by the addition of a permanently attached scabbard to her back and an open shoulder at the side where the handle rose to view. "Watch your tongue, Starstalker. Make no mistake; this Chabron is no coward."

"Stop it, both of you!" Garriton ordered. "No one here is a coward. We proved that a long time ago."

Both turned to view the captain then both nodded. T'Leah drew her family blade and placed the hilt over her right breast, blade pointed toward the flooring.

"I was wrong, Captain Garriton. We should not run. I was…beside myself."

"Yeah? Well, I wouldn't feel bad about running myself, since it seems we're caught in something. I don't feel like playing fly to some unknown spider."

"Spy dir?" the somewhat transformed Shoka growled.

"F'Lie?" T'Leah asked.

The humans on deck rolled their eyes as the captain waved it away.

"I need ideas, people! Now!" Garriton snapped.

"I will blow it up! Whatever it is…wherever it is…" Shoka announced.

"The sound won't be shut down," Respra said flatly. "I've tried everything."

"I tried but I cannot sshut down the engines," Vissk said. "We are moving in."

"I plotted several escape routes," Chu added. "It can't help if we can't use them."

Science Officer Boatwright sighed, "This coded transmission is overriding our systems, bringing us to the transmitter. I say we just go in for the ride, find out who's behind the invitation. I mean, we all know it isn't Captain Mo of the *Judgment*. Can't be. I mean, he died when most of you-"

Garriton flashed a look that silenced him immediately.

No one spoke of the mutiny on the *Judgment*. Even if it was condoned, even if it was cleared as justified. Even if it was taught in the training camps of the USAP. The Starmada couldn't ease her conscience. An officer just simply did not commit mutiny.

"Your plan is flawed," the captain snapped, angry at his reference, not his science. "If we're powerless here, how powerless will we be when we get to the transmitter?"

Then Captain Garriton got 'the look' for which she was known. The discovery look, the look of the woman with the plan, the solution.

The look she had just before she had arranged a mutiny.

"Captain?" T'Leah urged.

"Grekbil," Vissk pressed.

"This cursed coded transmission is pirating our systems, using our propulsion, using our communications to link to us, driving us crazy with the drone over our own interior audio systems. Well, take away their toys, everyone!"

20

She rushed back to her seat and dropped into it. There she triggered the earpiece she wore and then touched her seat's console.

"Engineering," she said. "I need you to-"

An unintelligible response squarbled over her seat com.

"I don't care, Wobble! I need you to kill the power! All of it!"

The bridge crew spun to her. What was she doing, their eyes asked.

The racket over the com was garbled and random for anyone who did not speak Octoviod. The captain was one of the few humans in the USAP who could.

"I don't care, Wobble! You've got eight hands; get it done!"

"Captain?" the Science Officer began.

Garriton triggered the ship wide intercom.

"All hands, this is Captain Garriton. We are about to go blackout. I repeat, we're going blackout. Arm yourselves and take up stationary positions. Those of you with control posts, remain there and be prepared to reinitialize power on my command."

"Captain, with no power-"

"Mr. Shoka, with no power in our ship, our special message will cease to use our propulsion, our communications and our own systems to manipulate our ship. You have a better idea, shout it out."

No one said anything, though several smiles broke on the bridge faces. The captain had come through again.

"Good. Vissk, shut us down on this end. As the power dies out, all of you switch your systems to manual initialization so that none try to come back online until we ask them to." Then Garriton turned and locked eyes with her First Officer, her Chief Security Officer. "T'Leah, we don't know that our host won't come to find us. Put your department on defensive edge against hostile boarding. Arm them to the teeth, T'Leah."

T'Leah whipped her family blade from her scabbard and nodded. She left Mr. Penrose on the bridge with orders to protect the bridge crew with extreme prejudice.

Slowly, lights began to go out a few at a time. Several warnings ignited new lights and sounds, until their power was stolen as well, and they faded away like all the others. Finally, the drone, or the death call, was silent again as communications powered down. Everyone sighed at once, relieved for the respite from the brutal tone.

In a few moments, the *Vindicator* was dead in space. It would be a long time before anyone spoke. Time would pass painfully slowly. No ships would come to get them. No adversaries slipped free of the passing asteroid field. No ghosts rattled the chains of the past and called for revenge.

Finally, at a half an hour in the darkness, a voice broke the silence.

"Captain," Shoka said from the darkness.

"Mr. Shoka?"

"If this should go poorly, I routed power to one of the escape shuttles and severed it from our power down procedures. You will still have a means of-"

"You what?" Garriton exploded, lifting from her seat in the darkness. "What shuttle? What bay?"

"Captain?" the Science Officer eased.

"What bay?" Garriton demanded.

"Bay three, Captain," Shoka answered, his voice hesitant. "What is-"

Garriton triggered her earpiece and spoke.

"T'Leah! Get down to docking bay three! Pull the manual releases and let the shuttle bay open to space!"

She was too late.

The explosion echoed through every deck and every hall. With gravity systems offline along with everything else, every Starmada officer and crewman left the deck when the ship lurched upward and sideways, tumbling back through space. No one was able to stay at a post, save those quick enough to grab onto a seat, a banister or a rail someplace. The ship listed afterward, still drifting with momentum garnered in the blast.

Earpieces lit across the bridge. Each department was reporting in to their supervising bridge officers the carnage and its effects.

"The shuttle in bay three exploded!" the Science Officer shouted over the echoes of the blast.

Then his face dropped. They were not echoes.

"Captain, without shields, the ship couldn't fill the gap in hull integrity! The smaller blasts aren't all echoes; some are the blasts of pressure tearing through other nearby decks!"

Without shielding, made of the gravitonic energies designed to repel assaults, and without power to the Gravstar defenses, which used extreme magnetism to strengthen hull plating by locking it together and charging it electromagnetically, a hole being punched in the belly of a pressurized starship wreaked true havoc. The first blast was like having a balloon pop in one spot inside a larger balloon, beside other balloons. There would be chain reactions.

"Depressurize all the decks surrounding the points of hull breach! Right now!" the captain screamed into her earpiece. "I don't care how, just do it! Manually if you have to!" she answered someone's question.

"All lower communications chambers and equipment have been destroyed, Captain," Respra said, holding his earpiece.

"Wobble, you okay in engineering?" the captain howled.

The octovoid answered erratically.

"Captain, all sstarboard propulssion isst offline," the Helmswoman hissed. "The damage isst obviouss. Port damage hasst yet to be reported."

"Wobble, put the fire out and get me power back on, now!" the captain shouted. "No, no, I don't care about lightspeed! Any power! Cruising propulsion, lights, weapons, even the gravity would be an improvement now!"

"We won't be able to get Chamber cannons back online!" Shoka howled. "The eruptions opened up the matter chambers and released our energies! Reports are suggesting we might have missile bay capabilities, if repair crews can get the collapsed corridors opened up enough to load-"

"Get them loaded, Mr. Shoka, even if you have to go down there and help them!" The captain grabbed at her earpiece again. "I know that, Wobble! Just give me what you can! Prime Reactor aside, you can give me something!"

Power flickered across the bridge, panels lighting here and there, then all went black.

"Don't toy with me, Wobble!" Captain Garriton yelled.

"We lost five entire decks," the Science Officer reported, listening to his earpiece. "Twelve sections over four other decks have collapsed or become impassible. Chamber cannons are lost, long range sensors are lost, almost all communications are lost and shield generators are lost."

The bridge lit up again and the viewscreen came to life. Several bridge officers gave a relieved breath.

The captain took no moment to celebrate.

"Doing good, Wobble! Now I need whatever propulsion you can manage and I need it right now! Stabilizers, docking thrusters, whatever! Get us moving!"

"Captain, central navigation and our chart index were lost in the fourth breach," Navigator Chu informed. "I can't plot-"

"Away! Away is all we need! I'm sure Vissk can manage to aim us away!" the captain said. "Vissk, before our propulsion and controls are hijacked again, as soon as you get power, aim us away from this 'roid field and this sector and give it all you've got!"

The last of the lighting kicked in and a familiar hum of star drive engines rattled to life then smoothed out. Simultaneously, the crew felt the pull of generated gravity.

"I've activated Cruisse propulssion, port sside only," Vissk said. "Port and sstarboard docking thrussterss engaged and port sstabilizerss are erratic but working. We have control."

"Short range sensor array has come back online," Boatwright said. "Looks like…wait a minute…"

"We need good news, Mr. Boatwright," Garriton said.

"Captain!" First Officer T'Leah cried over the earpiece. "We've been boarded!"

"What?" Garriton shouted.

"Sensors agree," Boatwright muttered, then added, "There's a band of small fighter craft attached to our underside! Bipedal humanoids entered our breach and have infiltrated all the levels you depressurized!"

"What race are they? Human? What?"

"I get no life signs at all, Captain…" the Science Officer said breathlessly. "I only know they're there because of motion sensors still working on the hull and on the breached decks…imaging is fuzzy, probably damaged-"

"T'Leah, who boarded us?" Garriton demanded suddenly.

The Chabron's voice was very calm.

"Not who, Captain…what…"

"Say again, T'Leah. Where did you see them?"

"I can see them through the visor panels in the blast doors that closed after deck depressurization…they drift in lifelessly but then grab onto the ship and begin trying to get deeper inside…"

"Captain," Mr. Boatwright said hesitantly.

"T'Leah!" Garriton pressed. "Who are they?"

"Captain," Boatwright insisted, "the fighter design matches one in our database. It's a Unity fighter, Scorpion class. They match the call numbers assigned to many lost when the Reaper class carrier, the *Judgment,* was destroyed…"

Garriton spun on him just as T'Leah answered her.

"Captain…they are no one. We are being boarded…by the dead…"

"Not possible…" Garriton muttered.

"I can't understand it!" Boatwright answered lowly. "But the boarders have no life signs! I read energy weapon signatures and diffuser bands but no signs of life, whatsoever!"

"T'Leah!" the captain shouted over the com. "What can you see?"

"The end, Captain. I see the end."

CHAPTER ONE : *Drifting*

*T*he chamber was some twenty milvins high on the inside. Hand carved over ages from the very stone of the mountain, it was more elegantly designed than any would guess from outside. Purple and gold tapestries draped above isles passing under the etched, stone archways. Hewn anglewood pews lined the chamber, adorned with carved Scripture along all the handrails. Similarly carved timbers, bound in engraved, meleth iron bands, formed the front doors.

Most beautiful of all stood the anglewood Cross at the face of the chamber.

To the right chanted the choir of Anglewood Chamber Church, all of them monks in the brotherhood who cared for the Church and the travelers who visited from all over the sector. They sang a soothing, dreamy, choral call to all listening.

One woman sat in the very back, just one soul in a mass of well over a hundred. Her cloak covered her attire and the hood covered her head. Her face was down, hidden in the shadow. She trembled, though it was not cold.

A much older man, white haired and white bearded, watched her for a time. Eventually, he looked to another older man. The little that remained of that man's hair grew gray like the mustache and goatee he wore. The two nodded at each other. Then the second man turned toward someone on the back row and nodded.

When the service was over and the Messenger had spoken his farewell, all stood to leave. The woman in the cloak stood slowly, her hand on the back of the pew before her, but she kept the cloak pulled snugly around her form.

To the eyes of two aging men and their watcher in the rear, however, the glove on her hand was more than identifying. Nods exchanged again, they moved quickly to exit before her.

Outside the intricately hewn doors, just outside the open mouth of the cave foyer, the mountain face looked down into the valley with no telltale signs of a cavern Church. There was a path that wound down from the height but it was barely that.

The woman in the cloak thought about that as she traversed the decline with all the others going back to the valley. She had studied the locale quite a bit before venturing there, too.

Reconnaissance, she mused.

Wisdom was a valuable counselor and information a potent drink, her former tactics trainer had taught at the academy. Most often it had to be sought and found, not found by chance.

Just like that Church.

The valley held a town in its gentle grasp, much like cradling a small child. The valley had no name of its own, nor did the mountain watching over it. The planet bore much animal and plant life but no sentient beings to name things. That came later, when the area had the planet's one and only town built by Sabb travelers.

The town, a little outpost without so much as law enforcement, was called Eppla. The name was a Sabb word for *drifting*. A docking station, built half underground and half in a cliff overhang, offered ships rest and refueling but no security. There was a grounder fueling station and a grounder rental post, too, but it saw little business. Roads were a rarity on the continental height, as most of it was uncharted forest and rocky mountain terrain. Mostly, the town was a way station between more active and traveled worlds, offering rest and recuperation with its hundreds of rustic inns for the chart weary spacefarer.

The town also hid pathways to the industrial processing plants established by the Sabb settlers. There they reaped the monetary and resource rewards of laying claim to the unnamed world and its most valuable commodity, the angleory tree.

Outsiders were not allowed there. Those places did have Sabb security.

The planet, later named Sabbor Two after the Sabb's home world, was two-thirds water. The water was undrinkable to most sentients who visited, its rich mineral content toxic to many. However, on the one land continent, called by most the continental height, the angleory trees grew oddly strong and resilient from the waters of the planet.

Anglewood, processed from those trees, became the Sabb fortune. The wood did not rot, did not bow and would not burn. And no less than diamond or energy tools could cut it. The wood was in high demand in nearly every sector and made the Sabbs very rich, as well as quite influential. That was how they could have the lasting peace they enjoyed;

no one would violate Sabb law for fear of losing trade in the anglewood business.

It made Eppla very peaceful. There was nothing to steal but the anglewood industry and to even attempt to take that would be to war with the Sabb home world. Though they were predominantly peace loving, no one wanted to war with them. No one.

The cloaked and hooded woman slipped in a bit of loose rock scattered along the dirt and vine growth on the path. Beside her, a man caught her arm, jostling her out of her review of Sabb history.

"Easy," the man said, his voice low. "Rolling all the way back to Eppla would be uncomfortable."

She cast a glance up at him when she retracted her arm.

"Thank you. I can manage," she informed flatly.

She watched him from the angled cover of her hood. Her keen, bright eyes examined her chivalrous companion.

"Oh, to be sure," he nodded. "Been here before?"

He turned his face back to the path, though her stare lingered. She ran her eyes over his long, black hair, gathered into a 'samurai', and she scoured his face for any trace of his motives. All she discovered were handsome brown eyes and a couple of days of unshaven scruff.

"No," she admitted. "Why?"

The stranger turned directly at her, smiling.

"Just curious, for the most part. I've never seen you here. And I'd remember a woman as lovely as you are."

Her face flushed a bright pink, though her hood shielded it from him. She whipped her face back toward the path ahead with a huff.

"Indeed," she muttered. "It's good to have my value in existence assessed so completely, so quickly. I'm 'lovely'. How quaint."

He laughed. His rock jawed countenance bore a strong allure, his features quite pleasing, though he had two scars on the left side of his face. His smile was quite disarming, quite charming.

"Well, I hope I haven't insulted you. I wasn't suggesting you bore no other values," he sighed. "I don't know you, yet. Your appearance is simply what I can see."

He tugged at the collarless, snap front, white shirt he wore. It was designed to be loose fitting but he filled it with a rather muscular frame. Below it he wore brown cargo pants and a tan utility belt that matched his tall, tan boots.

The woman watched him from the corner of her lovely eyes, curious and irritated at once.

"Can you be helpful as well as observant?" she asked brusquely.

"Sure. What do you need?"

"I'm looking for a pilot. He's supposed to be well known, so perhaps you can direct me to him. Gideon Ridge."

She angled her head to watch his eyes, looking for recognition.

Her companion rubbed the two day scruff along his jaw line then shook his head.

"I don't know…there are so many pilots here. What ship does he fly?"

"He doesn't just fly. He's the captain of his ship, the owner. The *Spoken Word.*"

He cut his keen eyes back at the woman, the smile back.

"Now I know who you mean. The man isn't so famous but everyone here knows that ship. But...are you sure you want that ship?"

"If you can't direct me, fine. Have a nice day."

She sped up her pace and moved away from the man.

"I can direct you, sure," he said, catching up to her stride. "They just say that guy's some sort of outlaw. I hate for you to get involved-"

"Do you think I'm stupid?" she snapped, turning on him.

They were at the first street in the town proper. Most of the other pedestrians around them had turned off for other locales. Few remained to witness anything that transpired, so she chose that moment to act.

She tossed back her cloak, revealing a Unity Starmada uniform, and shot her hand down to a low slung holster.

It was empty.

The woman did a double take at the empty belt attachment.

"No, not stupid," another man said from behind her.

"Just unarmed," the man before her replied, "and covered."

She looked over her shoulder and saw the older, balding man from the Church. Another old man with white hair and a white beard joined them, as well.

"I knew something was off," she muttered angrily.

"She ain't been around too much," the newcomer chuckled. "She didn't even feel you pull that 'bump-n-grab' routine when you caught her arm and steadied her, boy."

She snapped her face back to the man in the 'samurai' hairstyle.

"You stole my venter," she said.

He showed her the energy weapon, tucked into his pants on the side opposite her.

"I did. Venters make me nervous."

"You have no idea who you're-" she began royally.

"Actually, we do," one of the old men said.

"Captain Samara Garriton," the youngest man said, a gentle nod and smile offered. "Please, come with us. We've been expecting you."

Her eyes grew wide.

At Earth base command, one of many base commands for the Unity Starmada of Allied Planets, a holomeeting was taking place. In the holographic communications room, a holocom tech had set the imaging and audio emitters and recorders to action.

Two seats in the room had users; the others were place holders for the projected images of other seated officers from the other Starmada base stations.

The holographic projections were extremely lifelike. If not for the occasional blur, one would have never known the difference without touching the images. Touch always gave it away, however, as the physical structure to the light based forms always tingled to the hand, no matter the advancement in technology.

Perhaps the most fascinating advancement to date had been the addition of contact transfer. One could shake the hand of a transmitted image or pat a shoulder and the individual on the other end would feel the touch.

"Welcome," the head officer of Earth base command said. He looked around at the images of his counterparts around the planetary systems. "You all know me but let me introduce one of our fine officers from our sector's fleets, Commodore Wrigley Zeckinbridge."

The uniformed woman in the seat beside the base commander greeted the others. She brushed shoulder length brown hair back from her face and turned back to the commander.

"Commander Basnight," a Starstalker base commander growled lowly, "we appreciate the meeting. However, we are unsure just what it is you wish us to do."

"I agree," a Chabron commander echoed, her voice stern. "This seems a waste of time."

"It's never a waste of time to mount a rescue mission," Base Commander Walker Basnight countered. "One of our ships and a great number of her crew are still out there, someplace." He ran a hand over his bald, ebony scalp. "We cannot ignore that."

"I concur," a Greylik noted, brushing back thick tentacles. His image flickered.

"No one ignoress it, nor do they suggesst we do sso," an obese Vipon corrected. He was an unusual sight. Most of the reptilian race remained extremely slender. "We do not think there isst anything to ignore. We do not think the *Vindicator* still fliess."

"Our ship captain, Samara Garriton, does. She gave a full report when she was found adrift. She assured us the ship hadn't been destroyed completely but had instead been pirated. She didn't think the entire crew had been killed either, though the casualties were massive," Commander Basnight continued.

"Oh, we know all about the casualties!" a Toran commander snapped, her face flushed. "There were Torans on that ship!"

"We all had people on board. Just like all of our ships have a mix of crew. That is the point of the Unity alliance. We learn from each other, work together," the Greylik sighed.

"Odd that from the Human run ship, only its Human captain and a handful of Human survivors returned!" the Toran barked, her mouth twisted to a grimace.

"What is most odd is that, from what you just said yourself, the crew members missing are your own people but it is only our Human fleets who are interested in investigating," Commodore Wrigley Zeckinbridge remarked coolly.

"How dare you?" the Toran yelped, pride and integrity wounded. "Not even an admiral and you would sit in judgment of us?"

Basnight put his foot down.

"She's here as a qualified counselor. She is the Commodore of the specific fleet division Captain Garriton served with the *Vindicator*. After years of knowing the captain, she knows best if Garriton's perceptions of the events are to be taken to heart or if they are the impressions of trauma."

"We do not need a sspesscialisst," the Vipon hissed. "The dead do not pilot, nor do they navigate. The dead do not wander about, much less do they wander open sspasce. Her sstory isst either trauma, a nightmare, or a lie."

The Octovoid squarbled then, high and low pitches at once, a confused conglomeration of input. The urgency rose during the speech, the being's bulbous head changing colors. One of his eight arms crashed down on his chair arm at the end.

"I have heard of her honor as well," the Chabron admitted lowly. "I cannot believe she would make a lie of the deaths of our people, her own crew. Sadly, I cannot say I believe the tale of the dead. What are we to do with that? Embrace again the supernatural?"

"We leave it where it is, lost in that sector with the wreckage of the ship and bodies of the lost," the Starstalker growled again. "As for her honor, she did sabotage her previous ship, the *Judgment,* and mutinied."

"And received high praise and commendation," Basnight snapped. After gaining his composure, he added, "She had no choice. Her captain had gone mad. He was dangerous. She did her duty. That is not in question here. The question is what our response will be to her report."

"If she did not lie, fine. We cannot believe she is correct. It must be the strain of losing her people and her ship and her command," the grizzled Starstalker finished.

The Greylik seemed frustrated, insisting, "It would harm nothing to investigate the sector with a few ships. What could it harm?"

"To pay any attention to her delirious report is to propose the supernatural is reality," the Chabron said. "Are we ready to do that?"

"Long have we had a stand on religion and superstitions," the Starstalker said. "Recognizing none, endorsing none, none can be used to attain advantage. The stand of the Unity Starmada is that there is no supernatural. In that way, no belief can ever be used for gain."

"It was agreed long ago but I don't know if it best serves us," the Chabron admitted.

"Our peopless all have beliefss and traditionss," the Vipon said. "Acknowledge thiss Human captain'ss belief and we musst all be acknowledged equally. Who will be right? Will we war with each other to determine truth?"

"Of course not," Basnight said irritably, shaking his head. "But has our tolerance of each other become intolerance of each other? Are we saying that no beliefs can be acknowledged at all, to the point that we ignore what happens before our very eyes?"

"What are you saying?" the Toran shouted. "You want us to agree to your beliefs and let you run the Unity? Order our starships out to further your religious claims?"

"Are we this blind?" Commodore Zeckinbridge exploded. "Are you saying that if we can't agree on whose understanding of the rain is correct that we can't allow the rain to be understood as a reality? You want to tell our peoples that rain is a myth because we can't agree on its source, even while the rain pours down in the faces of those peoples?"

"She makes a good point," the Greylik nodded.

"She makes a speech for her father's cause," the Toran accused. "Her father was a Chaplain in the former Earth Starmada, before it joined the Unity."

"Your denial of the rain won't keep you dry," Zeckinbridge said and left the room.

"She cares greatly for her missing ship and crew," Basnight said flatly. "Frankly, she's also right. What do we do with this report? Do we acknowledge it, or do we put our heads into a hole and hide?"

"I stand with Commander Basnight," the Greylik said. "We cannot ignore this."

"I say we investigate," Basnight nodded, clarifying his position.

"Our position is torn," the battle scarred Chabron said. "We think it would be prudent to know what happened…but we question the wisdom of sending more ships to the Reaches. We already question why Captain Garriton was pushing beyond the boundaries." She sighed. "Our position is that we do not send ships. If something else happens, this side of the Reaches, then we send them. This instance must be-"

"Filed away, a mystery," the Toran said.

"A mystery," the Starstalker nodded.

"It isst a mysstery besst left unexplored. I am ssure it will reveal itsself ssomeday," the Vipon hissed in agreement.

The Octovoid squarbled yet again, changing colors and gesturing.

At the end, Basnight pursed his lips.

"So. Two of us say investigate. The Chabron and the Octovoids say wait and see what happens next. Three say to ignore it altogether. Is this our final vote?"

All nodded.

"Indeed. Well, I hope we do not have another occurrence. As much as you all fear religious sentimentality, you had all better pray it is not one of your ships next."

He turned to the holocom technician and gave a throat cutting gesture with one finger. Then he activated his earpiece with that finger.

"Baron, get me Commodore Zeckinbridge. While you're at it, get me a position on Captain Garriton."

The response did not warm his mood.

"She what?" he bellowed. "Baron, you're the Staff Commander here! Samara Garriton was confined to the base until a review could advise a course of action! Who gave Garriton clearance to shuttle out? And how many days did you say she's been gone?"

Again, a response that brought ire.

"Tell Zeckinbridge I want her in my office and now is not soon enough."

Samara Garriton sat down on an anglewood chair that was very ornately bent and shaped. Around her lay the most rustic room she had ever seen. There was a charm in its warmth but not for her.

"The authorities will find me," she bluffed. "The Sabbs know I'm on-world."

The old man with the white hair cackled, "Ain't no authorities out here. You left Unity space and the Sabbs don't police this area. 'Course, you know that. You were counting on that."

"What's that supposed to mean?" she demanded.

"It means you're trying to hire a man who's possibly a criminal and, at best, a smuggler. You didn't come here looking for law enforcement or officials. You came here incognito, Captain, and no story you tell is going to change that," the other old man said.

"Let it go," the younger man said and sat down before the woman. "Uncle Sun, would you take a walk down Terse Street and make sure we didn't pick up any followers?"

"You got it, boy," the balding man said and left the room.

"Pap, will you-"

"I taught you strategy, boy," the other old man snapped. "I know where to go. Where you going to be?"

"The captain and I are staying here," he said. "The dampening field we wired into the walls here will keep any tracking devices from working, and communicators will fail, too."

When the other man was gone, he looked into the eyes of Samara Garriton.

"Captain, I think it's time we got to know each other a lot better."

She narrowed her eyes and spat, "You're a kidnapper. Introductions made. I may as well tell you, the Unity Starmada isn't going to offer anything for me. We don't negotiate with terrorists."

He chuckled, saying, "Well, in the last few moments I've taken on two more titles. I gained kidnapper and terrorist and haven't even had lunch, yet. Speaking of, would you like anything?"

"Your head on a vibrofork?" she bantered, a snarl on her full lips.

"I can't say I've ever considered that. In the meantime, would you like some gibseed tea?"

"You brought me to an Inn room on the top floor of a building as low tech as a gombak's cave and now you offer tea? I don't know who you are but-"

"Oh, I'm sorry," he said suddenly, extending his hand. "Gideon Ridge. Smuggler, pirate, blockade runner, resistance fighter and, just recently added, kidnapper and terrorist."

Her mouth dropped a little.

"You're Ridge? Gideon Ridge?"

He nodded, his sideways smile engaged. His eyes sparkled as he lowered his hand.

"Show me," she ordered. "If you're Ridge, show me."

He extended his foldaway collar then, exposing it. On the right side was pinned a platinum Cross with a star field behind it. Then he again provided his hand.

She took his hand to shake but he turned it, bent her wrist then kissed her hand.

She snatched the hand free and stood from the seat.

"You've wasted so much time!" she barked. "Why didn't you tell me on the street who you were?"

"For obvious reasons, Captain," he said. "I'm not on the Unity Starmada's good side. You sent me an encrypted message days ago about needing to meet with me, so I arranged to meet you at Church-"

"And you didn't announce yourself!"

"No, that's pretty much the definition of a clandestine meeting," he said and chuckled. "We've been watching you since you hit the 'port. And we did our research before you got here. I'm not trying to be difficult but a man in my position has to be careful."

"What position?" she snapped, looking around. "Exile?"

He pointed and shook his finger at her.

"See, that's what living on a starship does to you. You start thinking everyone lives on their ship. This is my apartment. Don't you like it?"

"Are you crazed?" she asked.

"My dad thought I was when I agreed to meet with you. But I wanted to hear you out. I'll tell you what. We'll skip the tea and the lunch and get right to business." His demeanor changed somewhat, part of his jovial look fading. "I'm going to give you back your venter so you can be comfortable and we can be friends. Just let me be clear. Venters get their names because they vent charged plasma energies, in a bolt of light, projected at a target-"

"Everyone in the cosmos knows how a venter works!" she interrupted.

"Probably," he allowed. "But not everyone knows about the dampener we installed in these walls. It doesn't just kill transmissions. You fire off a venter in here, the blast is scattered, the cohesion lost. In other words, it becomes a game of chance. It could kill both of us, neither of us, or the wrong one of us...whoever that may be."

She took the weapon from him as he presented it and she holstered it.

"Now. What do you want with the *Spoken Word*...and her captain?"

"I want passage back to my starship, no questions asked."

He rubbed the scruff on his face.

"And this is the starship that was reported destroyed out beyond the edge of the Reaches?"

She paused then growled, "That sounded like a question."

"I have to know where I'm going."

"How did you hear about it?" she parried.

"Research, remember?" he answered. "Besides, a Unity vessel goes belly up in the Reaches, word gets out. Rumors, tales, campfire horror stories."

"If you're afraid to make passage, I can find another," she said and looked away from him.

His eyes sought hers.

"Not here, Captain Garriton. Pilots talk. Everybody's scared to touch your mission. They're scared to go after that ship."

"Are you?" she challenged, meeting his eyes.

He squinted at her, answering, "I'm a man of God, Captain. There's not much this side of the grave I fear. Problem is, the tales I hear say the grave itself is what took your ship."

"I want my ship back," she said then nodded. "I don't know how a criminal, a smuggler or a pirate is a man of God, a former chaplain in the Earth Starmada Services. But, if it's true, you know I need passage if there's any way at all I can rescue my missing crew. If I can save just one of them-"

"It has to be done," he finished. "I understand and agree. But I want to be up front with you. I'm going to share a bit with you about myself so we can trust each other. Why I do what I do…for that matter, what it is I do. The truth behind the reputation. Then I expect the same from you. All I know is what I've heard through blockade runner channels. I need the whole story. I'm not a 'no questions' kind of smuggler. I always ask a few questions. The first is this; what exactly happened to your ship?"

She eased back into her chair.

"Let's start with the dead."

"This is the starship *Firebringer*. On behalf of the Hunon Empire, we order you to respond," a short humanoid said again into the communications station.

The light battleship, one of the Hunon Empire's Corvette class, faced a space station designed for orbit around a planet or moon. It showed clear damage and system failures station wide, with a dwindling power core.

It was also adrift in open space, no body to orbit.

The Hunon captain, poised on his feet, glanced at his Communications Officer. Like the rest of the bridge officers, he was, by protocol, required to stand. The fact that the diminutive race rarely got above two valsics tall was good enough reason to stand.

"That is the third hail," the captain announced.

His saucer like blue eyes, a rarity among the predominantly green eyed race, blinked once. They glowed against his powder white skin, a race trait all bore.

"By Hunon Scavenging Ordinances we are cleared to board derelict vessels and stations after a third hail. Have security teams Dreg and Wahll prepare to shuttle over. Have four engineering teams accompany them for value assessment."

The Communications Officer keyed his console and gave the orders ship wide.

In moments, the efficiency of the Hunons had a shuttle already docked against a port on the station.

One security team went for the upper station, while the other went into the lower station. Both took a compliment of engineers and technicians with scanning gear. There was just enough residual power in the core to light emergency lighting, a pale, terribly inadequate glow that only illuminated a small alcove every seven to nine Hunon paces.

None of the Hunons were pleased with the reconnaissance.

From the time the teams split, each had the distinctive feeling of apprehension their people rarely experienced. For them to feel as though the hair was standing on the back of their thin necks was unusual; the Hunon were a hairless race.

Security Commander Dreg led his team into the upper station. Four armed tacticians accompanied him, watching everything, while five 'cobblers', what the security forces called the scavenger technicians, scanned for useful finds. The only sounds were those of the scuffing and clicking of their magboots and the hum of the scanners.

Commander Wahll took his company into the lower station.

Wahll was a veteran of the Hunon Empire's Starmada. He had led invasions. He had searched the wreckage of all kinds of ships and space stations. He had held front lines in the Blood War between the Chabron and the Starstalker races and he had fought on both sides at the whim of his fickle government. The Hunon believed he had seen it all and nothing in the bowels of a creaking, abandoned station held any danger for him.

"Dreg, this is Wahll," he called over his shoulder transmitter. "We are in the lower level. We are starting on the first floor and will go lower when we finish this one. My cobblers have already begun collection. It seems we emptied onto a medical floor."

"We are at the first of our floors as well," Dreg called. "We are scanning only. Nothing of value seems to have been left here; it looks to have been evacuated very rapidly but without much wasted resource."

Suddenly, a technician cried out behind Wahll. The veteran rolled to a crouch and spun his weapon, a medium sized particle rifle, to his rear. The entire unit followed suit and the technicians all jumped for cover.

The technician who had cried aloud turned, embarrassed, to the rest of the company.

She lifted an object to view in the sleeve of a medical laboratory coat. The object was a skeletal arm.

"Do you find value in that appendage?" Wahll asked bitterly.

"N-no, sir," she stuttered, her huge eyes flicking. "It startled me-"

"This place once housed hundreds of life forms. Did you think they all just moved away? We are sure to find remains." The security agent gestured for her to toss the arm. "Things of value only. I care not to see any more body parts."

She saluted and dropped the arm.

The decking creaked and a whine emanated from some hydraulics in the next chamber. Two of the technicians stopped scanning and stiffened completely. Their gasps made the security leader shake his head, though he never looked back at them.

"Dreg, my attachment is going to break down," he muttered lowly into his shoulder unit. He pressed into the next chamber alone. "A skeleton arm and some noises are going to stop the bilateral hearts of each of my company."

Though unafraid, he crept carefully.

Again, the hydraulics wheezed. The emergency lighting flickered.

He eased into a curve in the rear of his new chamber. The light on the fore grip of his weapon lit it a bit at the time as he made his turn. Slowly, the rear alcove revealed itself, the shadow gradually being stripped away.

"How is your company handling it, Dreg?" he whispered, almost completely around the curve. He paused when there was no response. With one white finger, he tapped the shoulder transmitter. "Dreg? Are you receiving me?"

Abruptly, a droning tone blared from his communicator and he snatched his head to the side to look at it. He slapped it several times then looked back at his unit in the other room. All of them were grappling with theirs as well, trying to drop the volume. Like his, they would not be silenced.

"Dreg!" he shouted, smacking the unit with his weapon grip.

That made his light go out.

"Commander Wahll," one of his underlings cried from the rear chamber. "Can we take them off, sir? They are deafening and we cannot turn them off!"

He had his back to the dark curve.

"Yes, take them off," he allowed, stripping his own from his uniform jacket. It fell to the floor from his shoulder…

…onto a pair of boots standing in the shadows beside him.

Blind in the shadow, he jostled his grip light and shook it then bumped it with his palm. It reignited almost instantly and cast a brilliant light on an open mouthed cadaver.

"By the Red Space!" he shouted and staggered backward. Then, with a deep breath, he turned to assure himself no one had seen him get startled. "Dead bodies everywhere," he muttered, turning back to the death before him. "No technological parts over here. Just body parts."

He looked beyond the cadaver. A doorway, hidden in the dark of the curved alcove, lurked behind the dead body. It rested open a few inches.

He turned back to the former chamber.

"You technicians see if you can find out what is causing the interference with our communications!" he shouted.

He noted immediately, however, that none of the others in the rear chamber were still in sight. Knowing he would have to backtrack and see where they had gone, he took one more glance back at the cadaver and the doorway he would have to wait to open.

However, the door was already open. There was a hall of dead bodies lined out before him where there had been only empty space.

"What in-"

The body in the front breathed out suddenly, a cloud of gas spewing from its open maw. Then it reached out, shuffling forward, gasping.

Wahll's particle weapon came to life just as suddenly. Ionized weapon fire ignited the mysterious hallway and the death within it. Wahll screamed for the first time since the very first battle of the Blood War. Also, for the first time since the Blood War, he ran as quickly as he could from a conflict.

Back on the *Firebringer,* things had also become complicated.

"I cannot explain it, Captain!" the lone Helmsman shouted over the inner comsystem. "I cannot kill propulsion! We are approaching the space station!"

The drone almost drowned out his words. It blared from the onboard communication system in a mind numbing tone that seemed to jar their very teeth and grow louder every moment.

"Kill that noise!" the captain roared. "We can worry about propulsion in a moment!"

"Communications is not responding!" the Communications Officer howled.

"Defensefield generator is offline," the Weapons Officer cried. "Our shielding is down!"

The captain strode to the Weapons Officer and literally threw him from his post.

"In total lack of defense," the captain shouted, triggering control after control, "an offense must be mounted."

Several pulsing red lights lit the board.

"Captain?" the Weapons Officer muttered from the floor.

"What I do, I would not ask another to do in my stead."

He looked through the open view before them. The station, with his people aboard it, drifted in front of him.

"Forgive me," he breathed.

Four forward missile bays deployed their full payloads.

Oddly, only one missile genuinely fired from the very first bay. Every one after flagged as a failure on the console and barely cleared the Hunon launch tubes before dying out into an aimless drift. None of the missiles from the other bays achieved true launch. The impotent thrust of deactivated warheads floated away harmlessly.

The captain swore and gripped the sides of the weapons station. The bridge crew watched the one lone missile streak away, propellant trailing from its tail.

On the space station, the dead were everywhere. Commander Wahll pressed by them at every turn, running for the shuttle through the maze of passages that had led to his first actual floor of investigation.

His company had been slain. He had found that quickly enough, running back to the first chamber to see them, lifeless, in the arms of broken, undead monsters. They had turned toward him as if on puppet's strings, no life and no intent of their own, but directed somehow.

The commander had let loose the particle rifle in all its destructive glory and made for the shuttle bay with extreme prejudice.

He ground his jaw shut, clenching his teeth and listening to the grit between them grind. The commander ran like he had never run before, even back when there had been Starstalkers on his heels. His understanding of reality had been torn asunder.

The particle rifle spoke again and again, its message of fury and violence very convincing. The projected ion beams blew the dead bodies apart effortlessly. If only they would stop coming, he thought several times. If only there were not so many.

Finally, he plowed through the air lock blast door that sealed off the lower station and he slammed it closed, spinning the airlock wheel.

The safety indicator did not light up, signifying a true seal. Wahll hit the magnetic lock switch on the bulkhead beside the door, staring intently at the indicator.

It still refused to light.

He turned to the other airlock door, the one that opened into the upper station. His side would not lock unless he locked that one as well.

He cursed and charged into that airlock passage. He would not leave Dreg and his company behind. Not even in the face of the dead. Commander Wahll had not been that kind of soldier; he certainly was not that kind of officer. Into the upper station he charged headlong, shouting for Commander Dreg.

A moment later, the station lurched to the side and shook violently. The power faltered and all went black as the missile from the *Firebringer* peeled into the metal skin of the lower station. It exploded exponentially, eradicating any hint of the lower level down to an atomic level. The remainder of the station first lurched and shook traumatically then spun around in a quick arc away from the starship.

On the bridge of the *Firebringer*, the droning died. The sound was canceled. The Helmsman noted that he had helm control again and threw on reverse thrusters immediately.

A sigh of relief rose from all on the bridge simultaneously.

"Back away to four times our previous distance," the captain ordered sternly. "Officer Kruhl, get my people on the com. I want to know if any of them survived that missile…and whatever was over there."

The Communications Officer began transmitting. Repeatedly, there was no reply. After some very long moments, the captain slapped his chair's back and sat down.

"Officer Kruhl, transmit a notice of lost crew to Hunon Command. Put their names in for commendations, their families in for lifetime provision. Also, post these coordinates as investigated and of no valuable content, as well as highly dangerous. Hunon Command will want to post this region as forbidden."

"What are we going to do?" a bridge officer asked from the rear.

"We are going to leave this place. Leave this place, glad to be alive. Then we will mourn the dead."

The captain had no idea that the dead drifting there had no desire for their mourning.

Captain Samara Garriton of the starship *Vindicator* told Gideon Ridge a very similar tale of horror. Her ArcAngel class, Unity Starmada vessel had faced a similar challenge and had been taken by the unknown…and the undead.

Though he had listened intently and given her every courtesy, he would still not promise he believed her.

"It's not that I think it's impossible," he assured, drinking his tea. "I just don't understand what the dead would want with a Unity ship. So, I wonder if trauma within your mind created this unbeatable enemy to explain how the ship was lost."

"I thought you were a smuggler, not a psychologist."

"I told you there's a bit more to me than flying fast and evading shipping authorities," he reminded as she drank a little of her own tea.

Gideon Ridge had elaborated far more on his past than she had expected. The honest truth was that she had begun to admire him, the man she had hoped would be criminal enough not to care why she wanted passage back to the Reaches. True to rumor, Ridge had served as a chaplain's assistant in the Earth Starmada Services, before the Earth had joined Unity Command.

How had a young Messenger and ship's chaplain turned to a life of smuggling and criminal liaisons, she had asked. The answer was simple.

"When you outlaw the good, the good are made outlaws," he had said flatly.

In short, the Earth had always been one of the few planets with wisdom enough to allow nations and cultures to remain individual and independent once space travel became commonplace. Perhaps they had learned that lesson from the years prior, when the age of political correctness and pseudo-tolerance stifled independent thought and autonomy. Once that stage of mankind's progress gave way to freedom of thought, speech and deed again, Earth was reluctant to hand it away in the name of being one government.

Many worlds tried to bring an umbrella government into place, usurping all power and control from that world's inhabitants and consolidating it all into one body of control. It often led to building one body of tyranny. Earth, in its early days of space faring, wanted none of that. Instead, each nation supplied crews and technology to aide in space travel and trade but all remained sovereign and independent, simply allies and partners, no one group or nation over another. Disagreements had to be settled between parties on their own, a thing not always easy but far better than having a 'big brother' step in and take choices away.

Proudly, the men and women of Earth called this the Earth Starmada Services. All cultures and nations were welcomed. All beliefs were met with equality, even when not met with agreement. Peace was found not through conformity but through allowance and understanding of differences.

This cooperative individuality would not last, however.

The end of the Earth Starmada Services, or the ESS, came when Earth joined the Unity Starmada of Allied Planets. The USAP consisted of many different sentient species from different star systems working together. In truth, Earth was honored to join. The goal had been to work together and learn from each other, keeping a greater peace and holding the ability to aide and protect each other in the event it was needed. That was a noble intent. The reality bore a darker tint, however, more a window to the past than a viewscreen to a better future.

In efforts to minimize differences and maximize cooperation, rules and ordinances began to tighten on members. Free thought and expression, the individuality of cultures and any relative sovereignty of worlds, began to feel suffocated, at best. Organization and regulation began to stifle the right of the individual for the *greater good*. No one seemed to realize there could be no greater good for a whole if there was no good for the individual.

Before long, recommendations and ordinances gave way to mandates and laws, set in place by the bureaucratic, crushing machine known as the Starmada, all for everyone's *own good*. Worlds no longer governed themselves, they were deemed inadequate and incapable of such. The Unity Starmada had to think for everyone.

Certain things were declared taboo in Starmada conversation, too. Behavior and speech with outside cultures were controlled, at first. The idea of sharing certain things with new civilizations was distasteful and could interfere with commerce and interaction.

Then regulatory commissions began to extend those prohibitions to behavior within the Starmada itself. Political views were prohibited. It was not long before sports team preferences and athletic admiration were banned from the Starmada, as were discussions of favorite historical subjects, entertainers, books, digireads, and more. The USAP quickly seemed to be attempting to initiate a mindless clone body, one capable of working as a massive unit but unwelcome to engage in singular thought.

Gideon Ridge reached his breaking point when the Starmada did away with Messenger positions and those of the chaplain's office. Faith was placed on the taboo list, whether shared with those outside the Starmada or others on the inside. He was unwilling to take a position as a ship's counselor and give secular counsel based in nothing more than human assumption.

And not only his Faith was targeted.

Chaplain work had originally been commonplace and available with many Faiths as the backbone, in the beginning. Suddenly, none of them were welcome...and none were tolerated.

He abandoned the Starmada. He knew there could be no true unity among people who were forced into losing all semblances of individuality; that was not unity, that was brainwashing. That was not unified. That was grooming controlled automatons.

Certain things were eventually declared nonexistent by the Starmada. The reasoning was because the belief in them might 'distress, distract, or disturb others'. After all, one could not have unity among members if the members were allowed to think or feel independently. Members, the command structure decided, could not be trusted to think on their own.

The supernatural was one of those things. If belief in it was allowed then the question would arise; what faith correctly identified the supernatural? That particular debate was one that the Starmada would not entertain. Why allow differing opinions and beliefs on a subject when they could just cancel the subject...

Since that time, the Starmada had taken on an arrogant, imperialistic view of itself. All knowing, all reaching, all powerful.

Gideon Ridge, former Messenger of the Christian Gospel, former Chaplain to the ESS, could certainly drop a pointed sermon. Captain Garriton knew he was right but she did not like thinking about it. It was not something she readily admitted to herself, much less others. Unity had been her life and she still believed it could do some good. She could do some good within it, at any rate.

Garriton snorted in her seat despite the denial she often embraced. What would the all powerful Starmada do against what waited in the Reaches, when they would not even admit it was there?

At any rate, Gideon Ridge had found a new calling. He had embraced his work sharing his Faith, spreading the Gospel of Christ in sectors that desperately wanted to learn of it...against the tyrannical will and control of their governments. So, faced with being an outlaw because of good being outlawed, he embraced it, making quite a scandalous reputation, though his work was one of peace and love. He had engaged in conflicts, however, aiding in defending the weak and downtrodden, giving rise to the idea that he was a mercenary. He had also taken a few ships that attempted to take his and he had been named a pirate.

If anyone had believed her without a thought, she had thought it would be him. She was quite surprised when he slowed the discussion.

"Nothing's impossible," he reiterated, jarring her out of her quiet contemplation. "I just wonder if you've considered that you could have been stressed beyond the normal scope of reason?"

"Look, Ridge, I appreciate your candor but I don't want to hire you to analyze me. I want to hire you to take me back to my ship."

"The dead, Captain Garriton. You want me to take you out to face the dead. Or, more to the point, the undead. Why do you need me? Honestly. What did the Starmada brass say-"

"They said I was either lying or crazy. Neither is true."

Her big, blue eyes softened.

"Ridge, I need someone to believe me. I can't tell this story for the rest of my life to flat, expressionless faces. That's why I came out here, to a sector outside Unity space."

He rubbed his jaw line then eased back again into his seat.

"Okay. You got out of your ship. You made it with a handful of your bridge crew to a shuttle."

"Yes, the dead were everywhere. They killed so many…some of my bridge crew, too, on the way to the shuttle. So precious few made it…"

"How did you make it," he asked, "when so many didn't?"

A tear broke from a bright, blue eye and streaked over her cheek.

"My Weapons Officer, Graystalker Shoka," she muttered with a crack in her voice. "He was the Starstalker assigned to my bridge. He had worked with me on the *Judgment,* helped me overthrow Captain Bordin Mo," she said, her throat tightening. "That catamorph was one of my best friends and he's the reason we made it, those of us who did. He morphed into his most felinious form and held the last band of dead at bay while we boarded the shuttle. I have never been so sick to my stomach as I was when I launched the shuttle and he wasn't with us."

"He must've been very brave," Ridge sighed. "He died rescuing his friends. No greater love does anyone have than to give his life for his friends."

She looked up at his ceiling, saying, "My Communications Officer, my Science Officer, one of my Security Officers, and my Navigator made it with me to the shuttle. The rest of my bridge crew was picked off one after another as we battled our way for the shuttle bays." She wiped her eyes. "When we left the ship, it was still intact, for the most part. I had a crew of one hundred and seventy-five. I can't leave it adrift out there if anyone survived the conflict. If they're holed up on some deck, locked away in safety, I need to get to them. Starmada won't let me, Ridge. They won't even let me tell anyone, anywhere, what happened. So, I shuttled out to a fleet of traders and bartered passage here."

"So, you didn't wait to see if your Base Commander could sway the Command Council?"

"Would you?"

"I'm not a Starmada captain."

"But you're a captain."

He smiled softly, saying, "I am, at that. I'm still curious, though. Won't your crew members back you in your witness?"

She paused, as if not certain of an answer in any totality.

"I don't know. I was told in debriefing that they can't remember any of it but I haven't been allowed to speak to them directly. That's the problem with other people deciding what you can and can't think, or say, or do. I don't know if they turned on me or it's all a lie."

"Captain-" he started.

"Call me Samara," she interrupted. "My captain days may be over."

"Samara, when do you want to leave?"

She snapped watery eyes back to his with, "What?"

He drank the rest of his tea and put the cup down.

"You're willing to go? To see?" she asked before he could elaborate.

"Of course," he chuckled. "If the Starmada says nothing's out there, that you can't talk about it or look into it, that you aren't allowed to believe anything happened out there, well, that's pretty much a polymer clad certainty that everything you say is true."

"You really are a scoundrel," she muttered, a sad, half smile breaking over her face.

"Yeah, maybe. But a scoundrel with the best intentions," he answered. "We'll go soon," he said. "I need to get my gear, tell Pap to come down from the roof and get Uncle Sun to go warm up the engines."

"Why did you send someone to the roof?" she demanded.

"I had to make sure you weren't followed, Cap…Samara. And, if you were, there's nobody who can compare to my dad with a long range weapon."

She gauged him anew.

"You really are full of surprises, Ridge. A Messenger putting a sniper on a rooftop-"

"With a stunning weapon," he interrupted sharply. "And you're in for a lot more surprises," he nodded.

"Oh?"

"Wait until you see my crew."

"Of course I knew! How could you not know she would go off planet?" Commodore Wrigley Zeckinbridge countered Base Commander

Walker Basnight. "She's upset about her command! Her ship and, most of all, her people!"

He slammed his hand down on his transparent holodesk. It fell far short of the dramatic effect a polymer or alloy, solid desk would have given. Instead of a loud thud or a ring of metal it simply gave a soft hum.

"I had to report her disappearance to the rest of the Command Council! They immediately put a holonotice out to every grid, at every port, from here to the Reaches! She won't be able to show her face in a port anywhere that's affiliated with any regulating body!"

"If she expected this sort of reaction, and she would, since we know how the Starmada tries to enforce its 'no talk' orders, who can blame her for her actions so far?" The woman threw her hands about, adding, "Who can blame me for rooting for her?"

"Well, congratulations," Basnight growled. "You rooted her into getting on the very bad side of the council; they also issued a bounty notice in all the 'questionable' systems for her."

"For live apprehension, I hope!" she snapped.

"That's one of the listed options," he said. "Guess what the other is."

"They've gone too far!" she shouted, her hands fisted. "They went too far a long time ago and, now, this is murder, just to control what someone says! This is tyrannical! This is…evil!"

"I don't agree with all the Starmada rules but what can we do? They've done such good work over the last ten years or so. It's extreme but-"

"What? But what? A life is a small price to pay for allegiance? What are we saying, Walker? What are we allowing? This has to be stopped!"

"Careful, Commodore," he warned, eyes wide. "She chose this chain of events."

"Really? Or is that what we tell ourselves every time the Starmada goes off the rails? You remember when Garriton led that mutiny on the *Judgment* to save that colony? There was a vast group within the Starmada even then who said she should be punished, no matter her reason for the mutiny. They said there was no reason for that, ever! She should have let him annihilate that whole colony full of Hunon settlers and then filed a complaint with the brass! Can you imagine?"

"I remember!" he yelled. "But we overturned that! We stood up for Garriton and got the mutiny filed away-"

"And things get worse and worse!" she said loudly. She propped her hands on slight hips. Her glistening eyes stared off at the afternoon sky through his skylights. "Anything to silence her. If she doesn't play ball with them, they'll let her be killed by a reckless bounty hunter."

"We all accept regulations in order to do the good we do, Wrigley."

She propped on his desk, her wrought face leaned close to his own.

"Not enough good to justify tyranny. We've watched this Starmada squeeze the good out of its people for a long while now. We can't just watch this."

She rose from the desk and walked for his door. Her all silver uniform shimmered with the colors of the skylight.

"Where are you going?" he demanded.

"If I told you, Walker, you'd have to put a bounty out on me."

"Wrigley!" he called after her but she was gone and down the corridor.

He reached up to his earpiece and activated it.

"Get me a holomeeting," he snapped but then his face sank and his brow furrowed. "No, no…" he answered the aide on the other end of the communiqué. "I…never mind. Cancel the holomeeting. Get me Cheyenne Winds." He tapped a light pen on the desk. "Yes, I know who she is and what she does for a living! I'm the one who got her put away last time!"

He clicked a button on the pen and its light beam splayed over the digifile pad on his desk. It beeped and triggered a flipping of holographic scenes from a file on his pad, playing out a three dimensional read atop his desk.

"Today, yes," he answered the earpiece. "Tell her it's life…or death."

CHAPTER TWO : *Exile*

A fter the tenth time Gideon Ridge stopped to converse with a passerby en route to his ship, Samara Garriton said something about it.

"For a smuggler lying low, you sure know a lot of people here," she said.

She wrapped the hooded cloak a bit tighter around herself and leaned her face downward into its concealment as he chuckled.

"Relax," he answered. "Everyone here is either purposely lying low, on the run or in exile of some kind. It creates this strange sort of kinship; no one can really contact a body of authorities because that may bring attention no one wants. Everyone here is in the same ship, so to speak."

"I'm only interested in your ship right now, Captain Ridge, and I hope not everyone on Sabbor Two is waiting in it."

"You may as well call me Gideon. I'm not very uppity about rank. Everyone here calls me Gideon, or Ridge, at the most formal."

"Indeed. I need to try to get used to forgetting ranks. The Unity Starmada isn't going to let me get away with this breach of protocol, even if they let me get away at all. I might end up in one of the prisons."

"For speaking," he added, casting a sharp look at the lovely woman. "I don't know how you work with that domination in the first place."

"They weren't always...I mean, things have changed..." she muttered, eyes distant.

The two captains strode around the curve in the last block of Eppla between them and the spaceport. The walk provided fresh air in the pleasant weather, neither too hot nor too cold, and the destination waited in a moderate distance. For lack of a better word, the walk was *nice*. It certainly could have been worse.

Samara Garriton still carried heavy concerns on her shoulders. She wondered how it would all work when Gideon Ridge brought the *Spoken Word* to life.

A wheeled ground vehicle rumbled to a stop beside them, jolting Samara from her pondering.

The grounder carried six seats in the rusty metal body above the six wheels. Smoke choked Garriton, evidence of the internal combustion engine so different to the magnetic exchange engines in use in most sectors. The grounder was ancient, a vehicle so old the roof had long since rotted away, leaving it uncovered. The only cover, a lid to the rear body area, a cargo space, popped open.

Garriton palmed the grip of her venter underneath the cloak.

Two old men sat in the middle two seats between the two front seats and the two farthest back. Those two farthest back were empty. The old men turned and greeted the captains.

"Give ya a lift, boy?" Sundar Ridge asked.

Gideon Ridge's father turned about, as well.

"Yeah, get in. Stow your stuff."

Gideon had been carrying a light gear bag and dropped it into the grounder. Garriton wondered if he had weapons inside it; the outlying world saw most inhabitants wearing sidearms slung low in holsters. Gideon Ridge, from what she could see, remained unarmed.

"What are you doing with these dust donkeys?" Gideon Ridge asked his father and uncle.

The driver and rider beside him, occupants of the two front seats, turned slowly to snarl at the youngest Ridge.

"Ridge..." Garriton warned in a hush.

The two men in the front slowly, deliberately exited the grounder and stood to their considerable heights.

The driver wore a pair of tattered black pants and low rise boots with an olive, sleeveless jacket, unzipped. No shirt peeked from within it, only tight, roping muscle. Big, bulging arms were displayed equally, their mocha skin tight with raw, undeniable power. His face, though strikingly steel jawed and handsome, gave a sneer to Ridge underneath a mustache and goatee.

The passenger, the driver's twin brother, looked identical with the exception of his lack of jacket and his skin tight, metallic silver shirt. The silver, short sleeved shirt glistened against the deep brown of the man's skin while it scarcely hid any of his musculature.

"Gideon Ridge," the driver said, his voice low and gutteral.

"What did you call us, Ridge?" the passenger asked in the same key.

Gideon opened his mouth but the driver interrupted.

"And where'd you get her?" he asked, eyeballing Garriton.

"I want one," the passenger added, also leering at the young woman.

"Yeahhhhhhhhh," the driver mewled lowly, "who doesn't?"

"Look, guys-" Gideon started.

"You also want a few new breathing ports?" Samara Garriton barked, her eyes no-nonsense and her venter leveled, clear of the cloak.

"Whoa!" the driver said quickly, hands raised.

"Easy, bombshell!" the twin exclaimed, hands in the air.

Gideon Ridge abruptly grabbed and lowered Garriton's venter hand.

"Samara, they're good," he insisted. "They're family."

"You keep clownin' around and somebody'll blow those empty heads off one day," Sun Ridge snapped.

"If he's told ya once he's told ya a thousand times," Gideon's father added. Then, to Samara Garriton, "Ignore them."

"Family?" she asked Gideon Ridge.

"Hey, we're just teasin' ya," the driver said.

Both twins replaced their false sneers with gentle smiles.

"But I admire that venter sweep," the passenger chuckled. "Never even saw her grab for it. Almost wet myself."

"Nice," Gideon noted sarcastically.

"We have time for this kind of thing?" Samara snapped.

"Sorry, Captain," the driver said and opened the door to the third seat in the grounder. "You two pile in. But lean down low."

"What? Why?" Samara Garriton demanded.

"You'll see," the passenger said.

In a moment, they were moving.

The port reached out expansively with a three story information center and fourteen wings sprouting from it like petals from a massive, metal and glass flower. Each wing offered fifteen bays of varying sizes for temporary or permanent housing of spaceships. Each and every bay was kept secure by graviton fields, digital lockdown facilities, optional emergency blast doors and a full time robot assigned to assist ship owners.

"We're in the northeast quadrant," Sylver Ridge said loosely, reminding the driver.

"I know," the young, built man said. "You're old and forgetful, not me. I know where we are and where we're going."

"You know what else, Kelvan?" the Ridge father growled lowly.

"I'm just kiddin' ya, Pap," the driver said quickly, smiling.

"Keep on," the twin warned. Then, turning to the man they called Pap, "Go on and bust him open, Pap. Might do him some good."

"Shut up, Kreden," the brother snapped.

"How 'bout you both shut up," Gideon's Uncle Sun barked.

The big twins, men of strikingly impressive size and shape, looked at each other sharply.

Garriton thought for a moment there might be trouble. The driver, however, surprised her again.

"Yeah," he said with a shrug, "that would probably work."

"Yeaahhhh," the twin said lowly. "Work pretty good, probably."

The grounder followed the illuminated rails working throughout the entire complex. Garriton and Gideon Ridge remained somewhat low in their seats but saw enough to take in the varied presence in the port.

Short range fighters from system after system slept in the bays. Some were older than the old men, the Ridge brothers. Some were as new as Samara Garriton's command ship.

Freighters, many with the markings obscured, fit the same sort of criteria. Owners and crews loaded them nonchalantly but Samara could tell they were watching everything and everyone while trying to look to be watching nothing and no one.

Robotic attendants fueled ships and waited by flight command consoles in the bays to lower fields and raise blast doors. Every color and alloy imaginable had been used to forge the automated aides.

The driver, the twin named Kelven, slowed them to a stop just outside the northeast quadrant, pulling the grounder into a group parking platform. The platforms were located along the railed roads here and there for parking vehicles that did not need to pull into an actual bay.

"What are we-" Gideon Ridge started.

"Hush, boy," Uncle Sun eased.

He purposely did not look in the direction of their bay but encouraged Gideon to do so with a faint twitch of a thumb.

There were four Starstalkers dressed in composite body armor standing right at the spaceport bay's ramp entrance. Each was armed to the long, fanged teeth.

"Those kitties are rabid," he muttered, sneaking a long look. "Trouble with a capital T."

"I take it you don't like Starstalkers. They remind you too much of Earth felines?" she groaned, rolling her eyes. "Am I to understand that I will be hearing vented prejudices on this trip?"

"I love cats," he informed. "I also have nothing against the Starstalker race. But I don't like those particular four Starstalkers. They never morph back into their completely humanoid state. Those guys leave the predatory side of their psyches engaged all the time, not just in battle. They're unstable."

"Again, the psychologist," she muttered.

"They ain't wired right," Kreden said in defense of Gideon.

"Their gravlifts don't reach the bridge, Captain," Kelvan added.

"All of you are biased against-"

"They're fleshhunters, Samara," Gideon said flatly.

She knew what that meant. Suddenly, like being in a dark chamber when the power returned, she understood. Fleshhunters.

The lowest of the Starstalker society, they remained in their most catlike form all the time, working as bounty hunters. They lived almost like animals, even tracking prey on all fours at times and eating the flesh of bounties they were allowed to take in dead. Their allegiance tied to only financial gain. Their god was flesh; for mindless, heartless sensual pleasure, for feed, for the hunt or for war. They had long ago embraced the animal and never came back.

The idea of fleshhunters so openly operating in a 'civilized' city tickled the hair on the back of her neck.

"You…know them, then? They live or operate from here?"

Uncle Sun perked.

"That they do. On the plus side, some of the best hunters you'll meet. On the down side, same thing."

"Who's that woman?" Samara Garriton asked.

Standing with the Starstalkers, a confident, animated woman carried on a conversation in a voice as loud as any of theirs. She wore lightweight, ripstop tactical gear wrapped in belts, straps and pouches. They light grays and reds still managed to show off quite a figure on the tall woman.

"Dalindrea Ridge," Sylver Ridge said. "My little girl."

Garriton saw the resemblance then, if in nothing else than the woman's long, wavy brown hair. It was a sure copy of the old man's wavy, long salt and pepper.

They watched for a few more moments in relative quiet, only because they stopped answering Garriton's inquisitive interview. Soon enough, the Starstalkers moved away from the bay ramp, more than one promising a quick return.

Kelvan made good use of an opportune moment. He fired the grounder to life and drove right over the rail boundaries and right up the ramp toward their destination. He slowed only long enough to let the Ridge woman hop onto the passenger door where Kreden balanced and secured her. Then they were motoring away again, up the ramp toward the bay of choice.

"Drea, are we primed and ready?" Gideon asked of his sister.

The wild, green eyes of the woman lifted in surprise.

"What do you think I've been doing? Picking ticks off your fuzzy friends?"

Ridge shook his head, saying, "Not my friends. You were the one talking to them."

The old grounder bounced and rumbled deeper into the facility.

"They were looking for you, Gideon," she growled.

The glare in her eyes rivaled some Gideon Ridge had seen in Starstalkers, a wild look she got from time to time as situations got intense.

"That bounty ain't going away, brother of mine. They told you before that they just didn't have time, at that time, to pursue you and they were giving you the chance to run. Some kind of good will since we all live here on the same planet."

"They're all heart," Gideon Ridge said.

"They just ran out of heart," she said. "They say they're officially looking for you, starting tomorrow. Apparently, your value went up."

"You have a bounty on your head?" Garriton blurted.

The grounder slowed to a stop with everyone chuckling except Gideon Ridge and Samara Garriton.

"Does he-" Kelvan started, laughing.

"-have a bounty on him?" Kreden finished, also laughing.

"What kind of a bounty do you have-" she tried once more.

"Well, technically he don't have a bounty on him," Sundar Ridge chuckled.

"Right. How many bounties is it nowadays, son?" Pap Ridge asked, laughing.

"I think we ought to take them out first. No need waiting to see what they're going to do. They told us. Tomorrow, they're blood enemies," Dalindrea Ridge warned. Then, giggling, she said, "And he was up to like twelve, last time I counted."

"Ridge, what kind of bounties-" Garriton tried.

"I'm not attacking anyone unprovoked," Gideon Ridge snapped.

He bailed out of the grounder, leaping over his door. Kelvan had stopped them at a palm reader by a field control console.

Samara Garriton, hot on his heels, grabbed his arm.

"What kind of bounties rest on your head?" she shouted.

Sun rolled his eyes, muttering about complications.

"I'm not appreciated in a lot of systems, Samara," Gideon Ridge said tersely. "I have no idea which bounty they've sniffed out-"

"What did you do?"

"Do we have time for this conversation?" Kreden asked the group, drawing more laughter. "I mean, the list is extensive."

The twins and the old Ridge brothers were unloading the cargo area when Gideon Ridge grasped Samara Garriton by her upper arms and held her still. His sister took his place at the power console as he spoke.

"Samara, you wanted a pirate, an outlaw. You got one."

"Ridge-" she tried, snatching free of him.

"I carry the Gospel to any and all systems I'm asked to. I told you, I've also gotten involved in more than one struggle for freedom. I've earned some enemies. I don't kill, Samara, but I'm never afraid to fight for what is right. That sort of behavior, something that used to be called honor, gets you noticed...by the good and the bad."

"Did you ever think that you shouldn't push your beliefs on everyone?" she asked. "And, for the systems that outlaw religion, don't you think you're violating their rights by flying in and stirring people up with teachings of-"

"Oh, here we go," Kreden said over her.

"Look, everybody," Kelvan pretended to announce to a crowd. "Here comes Unity to tell everybody how to think and feel."

"Some people need guidance on..." she started. Her own hypocrisy and the irony of her situation strangled her, however.

Gideon Ridge glowered at her.

"Before you keep subscribing to ideas like that, remember that's why you're here, asking my help. You want to know about something, look into something and talk about something your precious Starmada outlawed."

She opened her mouth but her voice failed her.

Sun Ridge was talking anyway as the Ridge sister palmed the console and finished code keying for access.

"Me and your pap could stay here while you take Miss High and Mighty out to see her skeleton ship," the older man remarked. "We could drop those hairballs and clean up this place for you."

"Miss High and Mighty?" Garriton shouted.

She huffed again when they both ignored her.

"No," Gideon Ridge said. "I may be gone long enough that they get disinterested. You can keep an ear out for me, though. I need to know what stories come down the line about the captain's ship. For that matter, I'll need you guys here holding this place down so I don't come back into an ambush."

Gideon Ridge led Garriton and the others into his docking bay. Once inside, he asked Dalindrea to reignite the defense fields with the interior palm reader.

Samara Garriton gasped when they crested the ramp incline and his ship fell into complete view.

"It's…" she trailed, slowing to a stop.

He turned back to her though the others kept moving.

"It's…beautiful," she muttered, her voice reflecting her level of genuine surprise.

Gideon Ridge nodded, stating, "I get that a lot."

It rose up before them in the bay as if crawling out of a gap in time. Time stood still in its structure, its shape. Admittedly old, it spoke of a time forgotten with a voice lost in the temporal winds. It was nevertheless immaculate.

"A TB7 Raindancer," she gushed as they moved again. "One of the first light fighter/freighter class ships produced by the Protoline starship yards, off the coast of Virginia, back on Earth. My grandfather flew one in the Palcappa Conflict, running behind enemy lines to drop food and supplies to refugees and allies. But this one…it could be brand new…"

The starship reached from a sharp nose backward to the two wings, almost at the very rear of the design, where the engines opened up behind them. The cockpit was the full width of the nose and stretched back from that nose for a span three times its width.

Several chambers inside took up the space between the cockpit and the wing location, seven chambers in length, but the outer beauty did not show that. The glaze on the outside was a brilliant, shining white, streaked along the fuselage with silver, gold and black stripes and bands. The body looked as though it had captured lightning itself.

The wings took up outside on the body where the engine room started inside. The engine compartment had a loading ramp of its own that matched the main ramp, open to the bay just behind the forward landing gear.

"It's perfect, Ridge," Garriton said. "A glorious piece of history."

He checked a couple of the cables running up the ramp into the ship. He eyeballed some gauges then turned back to her.

"Not just history, Samara. Don't fear its age. The weapons systems, the lightspeed and sublight engines, the shielding and the astronavigation have all been replaced with the most up to date equipment available."

Sun Ridge reemerged from the ship with the man Gideon called Pap. They strolled down the ramp, arms in hand.

"That's right," the man with the white beard and shaggy hair said.

Sylver 'Pap' Ridge had pulled a long, blood red coat over his other gear when he had reclaimed his arms from inside the ship. It had bandoleer pouches here and there.

"And," he continued, "we went through it and tuned it out." He gestured at his brother, Sun. "Once the Ridge brothers heat something up, it's hot, believe me. Can't nothing outrun it or outfight it, long as it's in the same basic weight class."

"Permission to board?" she asked Gideon Ridge. Her admiration of the classic craft seemed to cause her ire to wane, allowing her a grin.

He nodded with a smile of his own.

"Check it out, Samara. Make yourself at home."

The men let Garriton pass but they stopped the young Ridge.

"Be careful, boy," Sundar Ridge warned. "You don't know what you'll find out there."

He nodded, shaking his uncle's hand.

" I love you, boy," his father said. "You sure you don't need me?"

"I love you, too, Pap, and I need you more here," he answered, "making sure I have a place to come back to."

"Well, Kelvan and Kreden got ya set up. Ran all the starchart updates, preflight checklists, fueling protocols, the works. 'Course, ya got Grundy linin' up everything else."

"Okay," Gideon Ridge said and offered a smile. "It's all good, Pap. Just one more time around the Arendall Band and back again."

The two older Ridges both embraced him and left him.

Gideon Ridge checked the gauges on the lines going up the ramp again, tapping them, then nodded. He leaned downward on the ramp and looked at the bay's control console. Standing at the control station was a silver robot, humanoid in form.

"That's it," Ridge called. "Reel up the feed lines. Prepare to open the shielding. I'm lifting off."

The robot signaled an affirmative with a stiff hand.

Inside the ship, Ridge kicked the lines free of the ramp and closed it. He secured the belly cargo doors and their drop features then started toward the nose of the ship.

Garriton met him at the door to the cockpit.

The seats in the cockpit started with two at the piloting controls, facing forward, followed by two facing the sides, an astronavigation and a main systems console at those locations. Behind those two were four extra seats. Two were the farthest back, alone with no particular function. The two slightly forward of them had small consoles attached to the arms. One was clearly a weapons station and the other seemed to be a backup, catch all multi-use position.

"You met most of the crew, even if it was informal," Ridge told her, pointing to the copilot seat. "Once more, that's Dalindrea, my sister. We call her Drea."

Drea turned about in her chair and gave a wave.

"Hi, again," she said. "Food for thought; when Gideon says hold on, you hold on."

"Uh, hi....and okay," Garriton noted.

"Gideon, we got a course laid in for the Reaches, set to follow Unity records for the last flight of the *Vindicator*."

"Kreden Hotch," Gideon introduced the twin sitting at navigation. "My brother from another family."

"Engines at full capacity and fully energized; weapons ready," the other twin informed.

He nodded from his post at the main systems console, much like a chief engineer's position.

"Thanks, Kelvan." Ridge turned to Garriton, continuing with, "Kelvan Hotch, my other brother from-"

"Another family," she said. "Hello, again."

"I have one other person to introduce but it'll have to wait," he said. "He's back in the galley. He always wants to store up some good food before we start off."

She started to answer but he swept to the pilot's seat and fell into it.

"We've got quite a journey, Samara," he half shouted back to her. "There are two bed chambers with multiple bunks as you make your way back beyond the boarding bay. If you get bored, have a look around. You get tired, grab a bunk. No harm in resting. I'm not leaving this cockpit for the first few hours; I like to know if I'm being pursued when I leave a docking bay."

"I understand," she called. "You never told me about the bounties you have-"

The heavy vibration of the engines shuddered to life and a loud rumble echoed in the chambers, urging her to take a seat as well, though in the back where she stood.

"Okay," she muttered to herself, strapping into the seat.

"Captain Ridge," a proper, metallic voice chimed over the com.

Ridge reached above himself and pressed a switch.

"Go ahead, Baykeeper."

"While you are clear to launch, I would remind you of your proximity to the incoming trade routes. There is much more air traffic right now-"

"Thanks, Baykeeper."

"Why would he warn you about that when we're still approaching take off? Who takes off wildly enough to-"

Samara Garriton's voice broke into a scream as the engines plumed exhaust in a major thrust event. Take off pressures crushed her into her seat, heavy on her chest, as Gideon Ridge ignored take off pulsing altogether. He went straight into cruising engines from a dead stop, the engines roaring and drowning out her venomous screams.

Suddenly, the atmosphere was gone and the black velvet of space embraced them.

"He never said to hold on!" Garriton railed.

"I do not care what brought you out here!" a Starstalker shouted, tapping her credentials. The badges and stripes on her shoulder told it all but still she elaborated. "As the captain of the *Ferali 4*, I remind you that this area is off limits to outworlders! You are in our system, violating our planet's right to sacred burial territory! The dead moon you are orbiting is a part of that burial territory!"

"Captain, please," the quite tall Chabron commander nodded, her hands upturned passively. She towered at her desk, battle staff and pike ax crossed on the wall behind her. "Let our-"

"Don't try to brush me off! I have a genuine right to report this to Unity Command!" the Starstalker snapped.

Her long hair had grown longer and she had grown sideburns along her face in the moments she had been arguing. Her teeth lengthened, too, and her eyes glowed. Newly hairy hands shook slightly with aggravation.

"Captain Prentia, please be calm. We meant no harm. My Science Officer detected energy signatures around this dead moon and we came closer to investigate. When we did, we received a number of distress transmissions. Only then did we get close enough to orbit. We are Unity allies; if you had ailing or disabled ships here, should we not help?"

"You should not be in our space at all!" the lithe feline woman half snarled. "Neither of us is commanding an active Unity vessel; we are both leading two of our worlds' private military vessels! With neither of us wearing Unity call signs, you are fortunate I did not deploy our full compliment of fighters!"

The muscled Chabron put her hands on her desk calmly and leaned forward. Her dark eye, the one not covered by the cybernetic eye cover, glowered at the Starstalker. After a moment, during which the other felinious woman had time to take in the Chabron's staggering presence, she spoke again.

"Captain Prentia, as Unity allies, there are no borders between any of our peoples that ban any others of our peoples from passing through any space unannounced. We stopped to lend aide, nothing more," she said. Her voice betrayed her struggle to remain civil. "When you approached us and gave your misgivings about our presence, I invited you over here to make amends. I feel as though that is failing miserably."

Captain Prentia looked about the other leader's private study.

"Indeed. Perhaps it is," the catamorph said softly.

"It seems some memories are harder to lay to rest than others," the towering Chabron offered just as softly.

Captain Prentia asked, "Do you know how many humid jungle summers it has been since a Chabron Dreadship approached our burial space?"

"No. Do you know how many scorching summers it has been since a Chabron captain invited a Starstalker captain, in charge of a Starfighter Carrier, aboard one of our Dreadships?"

"No," Captain Prentia admitted. "If it happened ever."

"We should find out," the Chabron, Captain S'Nika, said wryly. "We could have just made history."

"It is the other history that bothers me," Captain Prentia said, even as her hair and fangs were shortening, her size dwindling.

"The Blood War was a long time ago, Captain. Until we leave it at rest, it will follow and haunt our peoples forever."

"Perhaps, Captain S'Nika, but to forget the past is to repeat the mistakes-"

The study doors swished apart and a red haired, somewhat shorter Chabron rushed in.

"Officer S'Reem, what is this? I told you I was not to be-"

"Every pardon, Captain, but the hails begin again!" the Communications Officer said.

The captain moved to follow her officer and the Starstalker fell into the chase, too. All three spilled onto the Dreadship bridge, the feline visitor garnering several stares.

"Put it on the com audio and give us a visual on the hologrid," S'Nika ordered.

"No holoprojection, Captain," S'Reem answered ruefully. "Audio is coming up now."

The transmission was broken, to say the very least. It was also flooded with others robbing its frequency and blurring its content. The voices spoke in a raw Starstalker language of the home world, Riista, and in native Chabron.

Neither language reordered itself into translation, despite the translation devices.

Starships had their translation matrix integrated into the communications systems; individuals wore portables integrated into their personal communications devices. None worked on the incoming transmissions in either fashion.

"That Riistan language," the Starstalker gasped. "Can you extract it from the others?"

"I am trying," Communications Officer S'Reem informed.

"It is badly mixed with a very old dialect of Chabron," Captain S'Nika said. "One never applied to the translation ciphers."

"Our world, Riista, has many languages," Captain Prentia added. "That one in the transmissions is one we never applied to translation. We used it exclusively in wars with other races, outworlders. As a language never translated, our transmissions were more secure. The tongue is called Nep."

Abruptly, the Science Console lit up like a landing beacon. Pinpoints of multiple colors and sizes of flashing lights danced throughout the three dimensional projection. The silver haired Chabron Officer watched her image of the dark side of the moon in disbelief.

"Captain, there are so many..."

The Communications Console suddenly blared wildly. Verbal transmissions stalled altogether and the automated, universal distress signals took over for all of them.

"...it is impossible how many..."

"Spit it out!" the Chabron captain shouted above the din.

"Energy signatures...there are hundreds of them."

The Communications Officer echoed the Science Officer's report.

"Literally hundreds of emergency distress calls incoming, Captain, all transmissions programmed."

"You...told the truth," Captain Prentia hissed. "What is this?"

"Another historical moment," Captain S'Nika nodded. "Take your fighter back to your Carrier ship, Captain. Let us work together to find the answers we want on the back side of your moon."

The Starstalker saluted the Chabron captain then followed one of the large female officers to the nearest bridge exit.

"Pilot L'Chessa, take us around the moon once Captain Prentia is on her way." The Chabron captain took her command seat and faced the open portals ahead of her, adding with a sneer, "No one toys with the Dreadship *Scythe* and walks away unscathed."

"*Ferali 4*, this is Captain Prentia," the Starstalker transmitted as she launched free of the offworlders' Dreadship. "Prepare to join the Dreadship en route to the back side of our moon."

"Captain," the return communiqué answered, "shall we wait for your return?"

"No, Commander Hosk," she told her First Officer. "You take control of the *Ferali 4*. I will accompany you in my fighter. Deploy two squadrons of fighters to fly free with me on approach."

"Captain, you should be-"

"In command, Commander Hosk! That is what I should be and it is what I am, as well!"

"Understood. Hosk out."

The Starstalker captain flew her crescent moon shaped fighter out ahead of both large starships, carving the route ahead out of the moonshadow.

Waiting in the darkness, drifting in utter stillness, a fleet of ragged, clearly damaged starfighters listed this way and that. Hundreds hung suspended against the black fabric of space, blocking out some of the stars like a swarm of insects partially blotting out the sun. Each was building in power, though all lighting was dark and dead. Engines and weapons were priming efficiently for a shattered fleet.

"*Ferali 4, Scythe*, are you reading this?"

"Affirmative, Captain Prentia," the Chabron captain answered.

"We are, as well," Commander Hosk answered from the Starstalker ship.

"My scans give a readout that is just impossible," Prentia continued. "Are all of our sensors reading the same thing?"

"No...it is impossible..." the Chabron captain announced then. "Impossible!"

"That is just what I said!" Captain Prentia snapped. "For all that is there, there are no life signs!"

Abruptly, the Dreadship veered off to one side and began coming about in totality.

"I'm reading some four hundred fighters, Captain," Commander Hosk said from aboard the Starfighter Carrier. "Some very old Chabron and Starstalker craft from the period of the Blood War!"

"And each one has weapons, engines, or both!" Captain Prentia howled. "Deploy my squadrons; six, not two!"

"Affirmative," Hosk returned.

Then the death call.

In every fighter cockpit, on the bridges of both starships, throughout all the unified crafts of the living Starstalkers and Chabron on the back side of that moon, the sound came. Mind numbing, droning, vibrating to the center of metal and bone, the sound permeated everything. It stole thought, courage, clarity and determination. It left the rallied allies afraid and yearning for an escape.

The Dreadship had already acted. It had turned back, leaving the Starstalkers. Sensors and communications had dropped dead almost immediately, however, so the Starstalkers were not even aware that the Chabron had attempted to turn and run. Neither was moving anymore, however, as ship systems failed one after another.

Then the relic fleet, adrift, surged and moved into action. Pieces of fuselage and hull floated in space where some came apart in the charge.

Long ago, the infamous captain of the Chabron ship, *L'Oran*, was a celebrated warrioress. However, Von'mar was not celebrated anymore after she ran from the death call. It mattered not that her ship was the only Chabron vessel to ever escape an encounter with the droning sound.

Apparently, Captain S'Nika had no qualms with being the next to be shamed. On her bridge, she screamed for retreat above the droning.

On came the swarm, junked and torn starfighters racing down on the struggling allied ships. Ninety one crescent starfighters, counting Captain Prentia's, listed randomly and out of formation as systems failed. The Starfighter Carrier drifted behind them, its defenses down, while the Dreadship was adrift as well, facing in the opposite direction.

"Get control back!" the *Ferali 4*'s commander howled. He was barely audible over the drone. "Captain Prentia is an open target out there! Someone shut down that noise!"

"Nothing is responding, Commander Hosk! We are all open targets!" the Weapons Officer shouted.

"We need those engines back online and I mean now!" the Chabron captain railed toward her bridge crew. "Give me anything! Thrust, pulse engines, whatever! That is the death call you hear! We must act!"

Captain Prentia, adrift in her fighter, looked back through the rear view of her cockpit. She and the other fighters had been utterly ignored by the ancient, skeletal fleet. Darker was the looming fate of her Carrier ship, however.

More than a hundred ghostly looking fightercraft from the past encircled the big ship then began blasting at it over the entire expanse of its massive fuselage. Long weakened energy weapons, coupled with the sheer mass and might of the Carrier, meant it would last quite a while, even defenseless. That while would not be long enough.

More than a hundred wrapped up the Dreadship in an energy onslaught as well, with the same prognosis. Commander Hosk and Captain S'Nika worked with their respective bridge crews to find a solution but none came to fruition. Like great Carda beasts on the plains, too clumsy to stay out of the Likron ants, their sheer mass would prolong an arduous and violent death but only prolong it. Eventually, only the skeletons would remain.

Worse still, the lifeless forms within the starfighters began to fly their ships into docking bays. There they blasted holes in the hull. The forms, the remains of Chabron and Starstalker dead, abandoned their crippled fighters and started boarding the bigger ships.

Finally, unsure of anything else to do, Captain Prentia killed her fighter's power cells entirely. All she knew was that she had to stop the sound. It was overriding all of her controls.

Her squadrons must have noted her lights flicker and die, because one after another they all followed suit. One by one, their lights went out, like lives extinguished. Each Starstalker reveled in the silence, the quiet of space, before looking around at their wingmen and nodding.

The captain acted first, unleashing part of the angst and the violent rage welling within her. She then showed her nearest allies what to do through her cockpit glass. She held up the communications array, torn by her own clawed hands from the operations console.

The squadron followed suit. They again followed her lead then as she rekindled her power cells. One by one, the power came back on in the drifting fighters and the power was thankfully under pilot control.

The last one hundred and fifty plus ragged fighters lost in time turned, sensing the surge of power coming back on in the Starstalker fighters. They began an attack run on the floating formation of the living, a cloud of the dead bringing more death.

The formation, however, was no longer helpless. Engines alive, the crescent fighters launched into evasive maneuvers. The battle was joined.

Ninety-one against one hundred fifty plus seemed a futile attempt but Captain Prentia's fighter crew was skilled. Even without audio links to communicate group maneuvers, they began tearing their ancient opponents to so much shrapnel and leaving them in clouds of discharging plasma. It was not long before the fighters nibbling away at the *Ferali 4* abandoned that action and attempted to bulwark their failing, ghostly allies. It still did not avail much. The outdated crafts were falling apart from just propulsion, much less battle.

Ghost ship after ghost ship erupted in a blaze of energy and floating metal. Captain Prentia swept in and out of their weak formations, evading loosely formed traps and igniting her bright green energy weapons time and again. Her crew did the same.

Clearly winning the engagement, Prentia and her fighters celebrated even further when the Dreadship *Scythe* came about yet again, bringing its forward end back toward the conflict. Though her Starfighter Carrier had not been able to break the death call's control, it seemed the Chabron vessel was about to show the dead just why their big crafts were called dreadships.

"Come, Captain S'Nika!" Prentia howled in her cockpit, feeling the heady rush of successful combat. "Show these ghouls what death the living can bring!"

She broke formation with four of her fellow fighters pulling back to watch the righteous carnage she knew was coming.

All nineteen forward Hammer Cannons of the Dreadship fired at once then began repeatedly firing great plumes of certain destruction. To the Starstalker captain's sheer horror, however, all across the expansive battle, her fellow crescent fighters were torn asunder. The Dreadship had not broken the death call's control; it had succumbed to it completely. The inhabitants had fallen to the boarding dead or had failed to keep the dead away from the controls. No matter what had transpired, the Hammer Cannons fell on the living.

Captain Prentia barely avoided a prolonged barrage, returning to her evasive maneuvers. She switched off her weapons entirely, rerouting all available power to her shielding, then put her fighter in a dead run for the moon's surface. With so much power to the shields, she would never be able to make a jump to light speed, so hiding became the next best idea.

Alongside her were four other crescent fighters, the ones from her previous formation, though one was trailing smoke and showing cracks all across the cockpit. Those four were the only ones who joined her. She wondered if those were the only survivors of the Dreadship's fire.

A long few moments later, Captain Prentia and her wingmen slipped into the dust clouds above her people's burial moon. She led them in and out of quite a few craters and moonscape shapes before she felt comfortable and slowed down.

Her crescent fighter dipped down below the dust clouds and she glanced to the left for her allies. She found no ship on her left wing at all. What had happened? Did they still have enemies on them? Had they crashed in the blind run? Her chest tightened.

She glanced over to make sure she still had allies on the right and found only one. His crescent fighter was still trailing smoke. Where were the others? She tapped her sensor array, trying to see if there was anything behind her.

There was.

Red particle beams ripped across her cockpit and her ship spun wildly. Her shields held but the dual engines of her starfighter faltered, one kicking out, then the other, then one kicking in again, and so on. Again, the particle beams pounded down on her, the shields flickering. Then the power died out altogether.

Captain Prentia lost control, going down in one of the mausoleum cities of her people, screaming all the way.

CHAPTER THREE : *Reaches*

"*I*'m saying what I saw, Sylver, nothing more, nothing less," Gill Bardoff pointed, eyes squinted.

"What you saw with your own eyes? Not them tavern stories you always bring home, either. What did you see with those squinty eyes of yours?"

The aging Gill Bardoff brushed a hand against his hip, casting dust about.

"Well...I might not have seen all of it but I've met the ones who did."

Sylver Ridge choked and fanned the dust away. He crouched by the landing bay 'bot, the Baykeeper automaton, sorting pieces.

"Do you mind, Gill? I'm working."

"You need to be working on getting someplace safe, not playin' with a landing 'bot."

"This robot landing system is our responsibility; you know how it works. You lease a bay, it comes with one of these!"

"What'd ya do to it, anyway?" Bardoff demanded.

"Me?" the Ridge father shouted. "Not me, you old dustbin! I found it like this a little while ago! Me and Sun went down to return that grounder rental and when we got back, here it was! And, if I don't fix it, my boy won't be able to land when he gets back! Besides, if what you say, Gill, is even remotely right, what place would you suppose would be safe, anyway?"

The tall, scrawny visitor pocketed his hands. His old face wore the lines of a lot of years but his eyes were still keen, their blue stare intense.

"Trekchatter has a lot of folks worked up. A lot of different starmadas, in an awful lot of different systems, have started upping patrol times and deploying ships that were retired from active duty."

Ridge snapped back around toward the scavenger. He put the seared Baykeeper's head down.

"I can't even begin to believe you still listen to trekchatter. As long as we've been around, as far as we've been and as much as we've seen… Rumors and fairy tales that traders and transports share over holocoms and long range audiocoms are just that! A bunch of imagination! Tall tales!"

"You think Hunon reclamation missions are a lot of smiles and jokes?" the scarecrow laughed sarcastically. "Even I don't cross them. They bring heat, Sylver."

"What are you-"

"A Hunon operation on a drifting space station went way wrong, Sylver. Way wrong. Those guys don't scare easy but they torpedoed the old derelict and left the wreckage."

Sylver frowned, licked his lips and picked up the head again.

"Hunons left the wreckage?" he asked, fidgeting with optronic relays, their photosensors and the associated wiring harness.

"Yep."

"And they put it out on travel transmissions that they'd seen the dead walking?"

Gill Bardoff chuckled, "Yep and yep."

Sylver Ridge pushed a photosensor back into the metal face.

The other old Ridge brother, Sun Ridge, sauntered onto the scene and propped his gloved hands on the docking bay's control console. He nudged the 'bot head with the toe of his high leather boot, a light brown suede, like the cargo vest he wore.

"I told the boy we should burn those bounty hunters," he growled. "Dirty fleshhunters. This bay 'bot ain't even ours. What would make them burn it down?"

"Maybe they didn't do it," Sylver muttered.

"How you been, Sundar?" Gill asked, hand extended.

"Oh, they did it," Sundar Ridge said, still talking while shaking hands with the old scavenger.

Gill Bardoff laughed, saying, "You ain't about to forget that fire you got in your gut for a catamorph, are you, Sun? Been a long time to carry that kind of widespread disgust."

Sundar took the toothpick from his mouth, considered the scavenger for a moment then flicked the 'pick into the distance. He brushed a gloved hand over his thick, white mustache.

"Nope," he said finally. "Not where the 'hunters are concerned. Animals. Pure and simple. Is what it is."

"Well, there are worse things out there than Starstalkers, even the feral flesh huntin' kind," Bardoff said.

He started his story over for the benefit of the other Ridge brother.

The dead were on the move, he swore. Reports from all over, from multiple systems and quadrants, swept down the communication lines like a brush fire on Corrin. It was widespread, whatever it was, and it was escalating. From organized starmadas to the smallest planetary security force, defenses all over known space seemed to be ramping up even if they didn't know for certain why. No one believed the dead were rallying…on the record…

"I don't think the dead are flying around in little spaceships, Gill," Sundar growled. "You watch what I say."

"So, where were you saying was safe?" Sylver Ridge teased Gill Bardoff.

"Only place you can hide from the dead. Got to find a Holy place."

The two Ridge brothers looked at each other.

Samara Garriton lifted her head slowly from her bunk, blinking harshly. Her eyes burned. Sleep was a difficult friend, often unwilling to cooperate until after she had remembered. Remembered and cried. The crew, in her mind, called out to her, protecting her and dying in the grasp of a horror too terrible for words.

She tossed back the blanket and swiveled, putting her feet onto the decking. The plate steel was cold to her through her silkens, prompting her to search about for her boots.

"You missed your dinner last night," a low, grating voice said.

It came from the corridor outside the bunk chamber.

Garriton snapped up her head. A tall, massive Rothidai stood just outside the door, blocking any view beyond into the corridor.

"I didn't mean to startle you," the speaker added. "I'm Grundy. I take it you're Captain Garriton?"

"Oh, no, it's okay. Yes, I'm...I'm Samara. Just Samara." She tried to shake the cobwebs as she asked, "How long have I slept?"

"Twelve Earth hours," that low, reverberating voice replied, "just in time for breakfast."

She half smiled, her eyes weary.

"Thank you but I...don't know. Maybe in a bit."

"You have to eat to live. What you and Gideon plan to face in the Reaches? He and you need to keep up your strength. My people know a little something about that. Fuel yourself, you fuel your mission."

She nodded somewhat absently, still remembering.

The Rothidai snorted upward from his lower lip, blowing the hair about that grew around his most prominent horn. He brushed at it, too, then brushed over the two smaller ones. He turned on his heel then and started toward the rear of the ship, going to the galley.

For long moments she could hear his massive footfalls on the decking. His feet were easily four times the size of her own. He was almost twice her height, with a chest, shoulders, neck and head above her. With arms and legs as big in diameter as her waist, she wondered just how much power resided in the Rothidai's form.

Down the corridor she followed, reveling in the aged ship's condition. She followed the passage while taking in the brilliant whites and silvers of the panels and deck plates. Engravings marked many panels in foreign, alien languages. She wondered why, since the ship was an Earth vessel.

"Morning, Samara," Gideon Ridge said when she reached the galley.

She sat opposite him at the brushed alloy table.

"Sleep okay?" he continued.

"A little cold," she admitted, "but okay."

"I wasn't sure how to dress you. I didn't know how much you were acclimated to low environmental settings, so I-"

"Dress me?" she snapped, her eyes fixed on his.

"You checked out in the cockpit," he informed.

His plate was empty. He was working on something in a mug.

"You snore," Grundy rumbled as he placed a plate before her.

"Oh?" she snapped. "Thank you so much!"

"You fell asleep shortly after I made takeoff," Gideon said. "After a few hours, when I was satisfied no one had clocked our trajectory in the jump to lightspeed, I let Drea take over. I moved back through the cockpit and you were asleep."

"Dress me?" she repeated, a dark ire in her eyes.

"I had to put you in a bunk," he said. "I didn't know how you liked to sleep, so I didn't know how to dress you for sleep. In the shirt, jacket and robe, or just the shirt and jacket, or just the shirt, or just-"

"Yes, I get it," she interrupted irritably.

"I removed your robe and your jacket," he said. "I thought if you weren't warm, the blanket would be help enough."

She looked down at herself, as if to remind herself that she was indeed dressed when she awoke.

"It was...kind of you. Thank you."

"You're very welcome. Now you have to eat."

He stood, retrieved another mug, steaming, and gave it to her. The liquid was a luminescent, pearly purple.

"I'll be back," Grundy said. "I'm checking on the payload."

"Payload?" she asked as Grundy left. "I thought he ran your galley."

"Well, when you're the galley commander, your idea of a payload is our supply chamber," he grinned.

She chuckled despite herself, taking a bite of her food. She quickly nodded, humming.

"Good?" he asked.

"Very," she allowed, shielding her mouth with her hand. Her mouth was still full. "It's some of the best flight food I've ever had."

"Grundy does a great job."

She agreed wordlessly with a lot of nodding and sounds.

"He's also one of the deadliest heavy weapons specialists I've ever known. He's just as good with the galley as he is with the Rayne Launchers, just as quick with a spatula as he is with that double headed halberd he has on his bunk's bulkhead."

"He hardly needs any more than his bare hands," she muttered.

"One of the gentlest souls I've ever known."

"Good to know," she smiled.

He rose from the table, drained his mug, then put it down.

"Back to the cockpit for me, Samara. Rest as long as you need."

"Don't you need to sleep?" she asked. "I was a starship captain, you know. I've flown before. I could hold the controls for a while."

"Maybe later. Rest now."

"I slept all night."

"Good...you'll need it."

She placed her bare palm on the palm reader. It gave the usual buzz, an angry warning that her identity was not verified and neither was it recognized. She used her other hand, still garbed in a black, technofiber glove, to touch two new nodes inside the open panel. A mild arc sounded between the posts, a new beep chimed from the palm reader and a swish of doors opening breathed from the new chamber.

In the total darkness of a command office, the woman slipped from the doorway to the humming energy desk. The seat behind it was an old world style leather swivel, an archaic anachronism in comparison. It squeaked loudly under her weight, under her pressure as she turned it.

She wondered how the owner could put up with the old chair, much less the squeak.

Atop the transparent desk rose mountainous stacks of digifiles, personal digireads, holodiscs and holoreaders. The visitor cared little for their worth and she kicked a few to the floor, propping up her feet. Thigh high black boots, soft and flat soled, crossed at the ankle.

The woman triggered a series of touch pads in the wrist of her technofiber glove, leaned back in the squeaky seat and waited.

Motionless, she only blinked again when the lights in the office ignited. In walked the Base Commander, Walker Basnight. Basnight's face dropped immediately.

"I saw the violated panel outside. I thought the technicians would be in here working on my climate control."

The woman smiled carnivorously.

"Do technicians normally break in, Walker?"

"Don't play with me," he barked. The big man stalked to the desk and leaned over it but did not reach for her. "Get out of my seat. Now."

"Relax. You called. I came. Does it matter where we sit?" She shifted, pushing more things from the desk. "It's a mess, anyway."

"You got no idea, no respect, no clue for the things that matter," he said through gritted teeth.

The tall, dark man grabbed up the fallen items from the floor as the woman pulled her wild, flowing hair back from her face. She ponytailed it, the length still reaching to the middle of her back. The cobalt blue tresses matched her black and blue striped outfit. Her white eyes studied him.

He could feel the stare without even looking at her.

"Time matters," she said. "Yours. Mine. Your good captain's."

"You have a lead?"

"No."

"When do you think you'll have one?"

"When someone slicks into the Unity Starmada's systems and removes all mention of my name…and the charges against me."

Basnight slammed his hand against the desk, quite a bit less than impressive in sound.

He shouted, "I told you it takes time!"

Like the strike of a king cobra, her body coiled slightly and she snapped out of the chair. She was inches above Basnight and in his face instantly, her breath sweet and warm.

"I told you it takes time, as well, slicking into the systems…yet, here we are, you rushing me and offering absolutely no progress. I'm hurt, Walker." She ran the index finger of her technofiber glove around his jaw. "You know how I can be when I'm hurt. I lash out."

He drew back from her in a jerk. Her hand was left in the open air.

"I want the captain found before any Council-hired bounty hunters do. I want her brought back here to me, unharmed, so that I can talk to her. When that happens, I promise you'll get what you asked."

"Captain Samara Garriton," she drawled in the soothing accent of her people. She ran a hand over her ponytail, the blue shimmering as if electrically charged. "She boarded a gibseed trader's freighter days ago. It was bound for Sabbor."

"Then you do have a lead," he said.

"As far as Sabbor. I haven't been there to verify it or to pursue it. And, Walker, I won't be going unless you can show me a little something for what I've brought you. I'm not going out there to get little Samara until, at the very least, you slick into your Unity files and make sure I can land like any other visitor in Starmada territories…not the wanted woman I am." She smiled a dazzling smile, adding, "You may not be able to fix my being a wanton woman but, as far as being a wanted woman, you need to get to work."

The tanned, smooth complexion. The oddly white eyes. The blue hair, long and straight. The smile, that leering, daring smile, blue lips pulsing. She was a wicked criminal, he reminded himself, wondering why he had ever gotten involved with her.

"With your race's inborn abilities, added to the taught skills of Wastasa Winds, you shouldn't have any troubles doing it yourself," he reminded.

"I don't talk about the Ton B'Gru, and you know that," she replied, her smile gone. "I may have been born into them but *my people* are those who cared for and raised me."

He stepped back at her distaste. She was nothing if not dangerous. Unstable was a good word for her, too, Walker Basnight reminded himself.

She had been Ton B'Gru by birth, with all the special physiology that went with it. But she had been left behind on a visit to Earth and her people had never come to find her, if they had ever missed her. The twelve year old child of alien traders from Tongru, she had been adopted by Native Americans on Earth and taught the ways of her new family. They gave her a new name and she added to her adoptive father's legacy.

Cheyenne Winds, child of Wastasa Winds.

"You're great at what you do," he said finally. "I'll do my best for you, so I hope I can expect the same. I don't want my captain harmed. I want her brought back here."

"And if she's on a ship, with travelers, or if she has allies already?" she pressed.

Basnight locked his jaw.

"No killing...my captain, Cheyenne. As for others..."

She licked over her blue lips, sneering, "You're all heart, Walker."

When the young Asian woman came into the office, Commodore Zeckinbridge did not look up from her work screen, even when the young officer saluted. Her short, black hair hung at the edges of her face.

"Navigator Chu," Zeckinbridge said, still not looking up at the woman. "Welcome. Please, have a seat."

"Thank you, Commodore," she answered and sat down.

"Officer Chu, let me be blunt."

Chu's eyes widened, her nervous hands wringing each other.

"Your captain, Samara Garriton, says the dead took over your ship and killed most of your crew. She said you, Officer Respra, Officer Boatwright, Officer Penrose and she were the only ones to escape, Penrose barely so. I've spoken to the others; now I want to hear from you. What took your ship? What happened to the crew?"

Chu opened her mouth to answer but faltered. Her mouth moved several times but only offered silence. Her eyes spoke volumes, however.

I am afraid, they said. *Terrified.*

"Chu, you can't lose here," the commodore said. "The truth, that's all. If the crew abandoned ship, if your captain killed them all one at a time, if they all took a spacewalk with no suits, whatever. It doesn't matter right now, as long as it's the truth."

"Commodore Zeckinbridge, we were directly told how impossible Captain Garriton's story is," Chu muttered. "It is the belief of the Command Council that we are suffering under some kind of impressionist perception because of our captain's orders, that we don't actually remember what we saw, only what Captain Garriton told us to remember."

"And you believe that to be true?"

Chu stared at her hands.

"The council was very specific-"

"Reje," Zeckinbridge said, using Chu's first name.

"Ma'am, the council-"

"Chu, I keep a disruptor wired into my desk. I turn it on when I need to have private conversations. No one else has to know about what you say here. This is between us."

"Captain Garriton saved our lives!" Chu gushed.

She barely had the assurance of secrecy from the commodore when she blurted it and began to cry.

"I don't understand everything…part of me hopes I never will…but the dead attacked us! The dead, Commodore! And we even received transmissions from the *Judgment*! It was there! Captain Bordin Mo…"

"I believe you, Reje," Wrigley Zeckinbridge said. Her eyes were soft, kind. "It's the same story each of you told, once you were off the record."

"What can we do, Commodore? For Captain Garriton?"

"Reje, I'm gathering a little crew together. A few specialist Officers, unassigned at the moment…"

"Commodore?"

"Patience, Navigator Chu," Zeckinbridge said. "Patience."

Samara Garriton had told herself, as well as Gideon Ridge, that she needed no more sleep.

I've already slept, she insisted, *slept well and slept all night.*

Rest, he had insisted. *You'll need it.*

The idea was ridiculous. She was a starship captain, not a damsel in distress. Samara Garriton was a fighter, a soldier, a commander. More sleep was for the weak.

When her eyes popped open and she realized she had indeed been asleep, she sighed. Above her prone position was the upper bunk she had not chosen. She barely remembered choosing the bottom one to sit on, thinking to herself how senseless it was for her to go back to the bed chambers.

Senseless. Ridiculous. Words now embarrassingly inaccurate as she awoke yet again.

She swept herself up from the bunk, stretched then sighed again.

Chalk one up to Gideon Ridge, she mused.

Garriton flipped a com switch on the wall. When the red light faded and the open channel blue light lit beside it, she spoke.

"Gideon, this is Samara. Where are we?"

Silence answered with an icy voice, chilling her.

"Ridge, where are we?" she asked again, just to hear her own voice.

Again, no one answered her. She resisted a chill that stamped its feet, ready to run down her spine. She shook her head against the imaginations of everything that could be wrong.

75

Her venter jumped into her grasp then and she strode out into the corridor, pausing outside the bunk rooms.

The *Vindicator* captain cautiously crept down the corridor, moving for the next chamber. The lights were down, unlike the bunk room. Shadow cloaked her walk. It danced about Garriton, whipping almost tangible tendrils of darkness before her eyes. The next break in the thick shade was a lowly glowing palm panel beside the corridor door ahead of her. The greenish ambiance was incredibly soft, offering little guidance.

Garriton swore under her breath. Would it have been so hard to just tell her what was going on? To have awakened her and prepared her?

She palmed the reader by the doorway. The door swished aside, the green light having indicated an unlocked barrier. Beyond it was another black chamber, small light sources here and there casting a scarcely adequate glow. She moved carefully, feeling her way along in the cargo chamber, hoping to neither trip nor make a lot of noise.

It was then that she noticed the com panel on the cargo wall. No lights burned at all, indicating it had been turned off. The hair raised on her neck yet again.

Finally navigating the cargo bay, she opened the next door. It had hardly swished aside when the light from the lowered loading ramp reached her eyes. The next chamber was like a spaceport's nighttime; she assumed immediately that they had docked someplace. She noticed the com panel there, also powered down.

Her fear was that they had not docked willingly.

Through the next chamber she pressed, stalking the loading ramp. Once she reached the lowering point she peeked down it then tried to angle her head so she could look off the sides. The flashing lights of some station's night life reflected against the metals of the ramp, letting her know they were definitely docked someplace in civilization. However, none of her peering revealed any details.

About to move back and head for the cockpit, a voice halted her.

"I still don't see what Garriton has to do with me," she heard Gideon Ridge saying, his voice drawing closer. "It isn't like I told her to go on the run from you guys. Besides, I told you where she was."

She stiffened, paralyzed for a moment. Had she been betrayed? She slipped back into the shadow and readied the plasma venter. If Ridge had betrayed her he would get the first shot. He sounded as close as the bottom of the ramp.

She tensed to move but abruptly could not. Very powerful arms wrapped about her and lifted her from the floor plating. Two other very strong hands pulled the venter from her grasp and covered her mouth.

Dalindrea Ridge eased into view and put a finger over her lips.

Eyes wide, straining to see in the darkness, her body straining to get free, Samara Garriton realized she was being held by the Hotch twins.

"Captain Ridge, we understand that," a return voice echoed metallically from someplace close to the ramp. "But we want you-"

"What I want,"Gideon snapped, irritated, "is for the dancing girl I picked up outside the Sunbrowser to get her rest. I told you she was sleeping off a long night. I have a couple of racy little outfits here I bought her, so I'm going to go wake her up in a little while and give them to her and I don't need chaperons. I'm sorry you guys can't keep up with the captains in your service but that's hardly any concern of mine."

One footfall hit the ramp.

Garriton waited with the twins and Drea Ridge.

"Ridge, you're well known around Unity space," the metallic voice challenged. "Your questionable...travel practices...are reason enough for us to detain you and your ship. All we want is to implant some holoimaging receivers and transmitters inside and outside your ship, so if you encounter her, we can be sure of your honesty in reporting it. After all, you didn't report her when you saw her on her way to Riista...if what you said is true. So, cooperate with us. Otherwise, the smuggling related to you might just catch up to you."

"Boys," Gideon Ridge laughed, "you're in Maximilian Station, in orbit around Dor Modo. Unity authority dies off way before the Dor Modros system. You're closer to the Reaches than you are Unity space."

"We know where we are. You believe that you're untouchable here, Captain Ridge?"

"The owners of Maximilian Station like smugglers and cutthroats more than they do the Unity Starmada, fellas. And, outside your own space, it'll take more than five Echoes to ruin my vacation."

Echoes, Samara Garriton thought to herself. *Echoes all the way out near Dor Modo.*

"Challenging us is dangerous business, Captain Ridge," a different male voice echoed under metal.

"I'll take that under advisement. In the meantime, I'm going aboard to give these gifts away. If you need me, I'll be here. I'm not leaving the station for a few days."

Again, a footfall on the ramp, followed by another. Another followed during the protests of the armored men, would be knights of the Unity Starmada of Allied Planets. Then two more steps and Gideon Ridge was aboard. The ramp lifted.

"We'll see you again, Ridge!" one of the men shouted.

"Not if I spot you first," Ridge shouted back at the closing breach.

"Dancing girl?" Samara whispered angrily.

Gideon Ridge spun suddenly at the voice in the dark.

Kreden, Kelvan and Drea released her and returned her venter.

"Samara?"

"You'd better not have skimpy little garments for me in that bag!"

"Samara-"

"How could you equate me with dancing girls? And from the Sunbrowser!"

"Wow," Kelvan said, wandering away with his brother.

Drea moved about, turning the com systems back on.

"Samara!" Gideon Ridge hushed through clenched teeth. "What did you want me to tell your friends? 'Oh, yeah, she's snoozing on one of my bunks?' Did you want me to sell you out?"

"I thought you had!" she railed then paused, drawing a deep breath and holding it, hands on her hips.

"Engage lights," Gideon said.

The lights in the chamber came on. The next room followed, then the corridors, then beyond.

"I'm sorry, Ridge. I didn't mean to question your integrity," she said softly. "Trust is hard right now."

He said, "You're in a bad spot. I understand. Forget about it." Suddenly, he smiled mischievously. "Besides, it makes us even."

"How?"

"You haven't seen the outfits I bought you at the BrowserBoutique."

"Ridge!" she barked.

He tossed her the bag.

"Take a peek. You can't wander around in a Starmada uniform."

"Wander? Where?" she demanded, though he was out of sight.

She looked inside the bag and gasped.

"I thought you were a Chaplain and a Messenger!"

Samara Garriton finally stole enough pieces from multiple ensembles to create a look that was, in her own mind's narration, the least 'provocative'.

Gideon Ridge redressed as well. He wore a black, turtleneck pullover, black cargo pants and tall brown boots to the loading ramp. Waiting for Garriton, he strapped bronze metal bracers onto both forearms and slid his hands into the brown, elastic gloves attached to them. Small touch panels were inlaid over the back of them and golden lines wound out designs over their entirety. Lastly, he put on a brown, leather long coat, the exact texture and color of his boots.

When he saw Samara Garriton, his breath left him. The plush curves of her form hypnotized him, mesmerized him momentarily, but he blinked and shook off the stupor.

If she caught his fleeting awe, she made no comment. The lady captain joined him at the ramp, tugging at her new, immodest attire. Red pants clung to her like skin, the material stretchy, while ice white boots started at her shapely thighs to run all the way to the floor. Her sleeveless top was woven of silver chain links over a thin, red wire fabric. A clear plastimold jacket with four wrap around belts warmed her but did nothing to hide the outrageous outfit. She was grateful part of that garment was hidden by the hip length, silver, straight haired wig. She wore lavender cosmetic lenses in her eyes.

"What, no body paint?" Ridge managed with a big grin.

"You only bought pink. It would have clashed with my outfit."

He met her sarcasm with a chuckle.

"That's because you tried to cross-match some of that stuff. If you had worn one of the three outfits as I bought them you-"

"Would have been bare in one or more unacceptable locations."

"But the colors would have been so mixed that the body paint wouldn't have clashed," he finished. Then, "And you exaggerate excessively."

"Nothing about this clothing is excessive," she sniped. "Let's get to it, Ridge, before I vent you. What are we doing here?"

"We're going to mix and mingle around the station, Samara. We'll check out the trekchatter, listen to whatever stories are getting around. When we're sure it's clear and no ships are lying in wait for either one of us, we'll streak for the Reaches. We just have to be certain. After here, there's no place to hide before the Reaches.

"Drea's waiting with the *Spoken Word*. Grundy's taking care of supplies and charging the systems, that sort of thing, and my Hotch brothers are going to mix and mingle on their own to cover more station. So, don't worry. We're most of the way there."

"Getting there wasn't the hard part…" she muttered.

Maximilian Station glistened with shining metals. Even from the docking bay, Garriton and Ridge could see the flashing neon lights in front of dance clubs, pleasure dens and cantinas lining both sides of the walk. The beaming spacestation had more view ports than most, see through panels everywhere. The light flared from inside it for all the system to see. Larger than some moons, the station stretched out into a massive orb.

Gideon Ridge walked close to Samara Garriton, at times wrapping an arm around her protectively. She almost balked once but saw an approaching band of particularly nasty looking Grievers. She let the arm stay.

There was always more to do in the place, always drawing back customers and enticing new visitors. Almost everything could be obtained there. Some outlets screamed of some kind of decadence. Others called to the more innocent of senses. From fleshly pleasures to consumables to technological supply to spiritual studies, the station offered at least what the traveler wanted, if not needed.

And the station never slept.

Thugs, mercenaries, outlaws and criminals from countless systems lined the walks and occupied every shadowy corner of the station. A lawless magnet, the station sucked in all on bad terms with galactic authorities of all kinds. Professional dates strolled the walks, often trying to lure Garriton or Ridge away from each other. Illegal transactions took place out in the open. Two weapon fire exchanges caused the pair to flinch along their travel. Still, they pushed on.

"We should've invited Grundy," Garriton said.

She turned her face into his chest, pretending to flirt when an Echo soldier marched by them.

"Grundy's busy," Ridge answered, nuzzling her forehead with his chin, playing along.

"Lucky him," she quipped. "Where are we going?"

"Be patient," he said.

It took quite a while for Ridge to slow and actually pick an establishment to enter. Finally, once he did, Garriton was less than thrilled.

The neons were faded outside, those that still worked, anyway. Inside was darker. The ambient light was no greater than a moonless night, like being adrift in starlit space with no glowing bodies to light the way. The air was thick with sanra smoke and the reek of too many intoxicants to define. And, though it was far less crowded than the walk, the characters inside presented a cross section of the galaxy's worst of the worst, packed into corners and shadows to sit, drink, plan and buy from the very dirty looking staff.

Gideon Ridge was no fonder of the open tables than the criminal element. He pushed to the rear of the establishment and planted his back against the wall at a small table. He pulled Samara Garriton's chair around to the wall, too, close by him.

"You certainly are protective," she mused, taking her seat.

She felt crowded, pressed side to side with him.

"I brought you here. Your safety is my responsibility."

"How romantic."

He eyed her curiously, answering, "Hey, I'm romantic. I bought you those nice outfits, didn't I?"

His sarcasm was not lost on her. She smiled ruefully at the grin tugging at his mouth.

Sudden, loud music replaced the more mellow sounds that had been playing. It left the feel of the Hunon love melodies for the clanging, raucous roar of the Tressla party songs.

"What do you want?" a barely dressed waitress asked sharply. Her tendrils fell from her head in tied bands of gold. "Drinks? Dancing? Private entertainment?"

"Two greskin rills," Ridge answered. "Drinks only."

"Flyboys these days. Always bringing their own entertainment," the waitress snorted and walked away, her nose upturned.

"I've never known a Greylik woman to dress that way," Samara said when they were alone again. "I can also say I've never known one to work in a place like this."

"No one race is perfect, Samara, nor is one immune to poverty, corruption, or darkness. I don't know how many places like this you've been to but you learn a lot about the depths sentients can sink to."

"I'm a starship captain. I've been all over, negotiated and met with all kinds of races. But I have to admit, when we approached zones like this, I deployed Echoes. I've never been this close."

The waitress returned with the drinks in smudged, dirty, plastimold beakers. She put down a pitcher cast in the same material, also no cleaner. Then, after a sharp glare at Samara Garriton, she was gone.

Garriton picked up her vessel.

Ridge caught her hand and eased it back to the table.

"Those are for looks, Samara. We're paying customers, we belong, that sort of image. Drinking them is not on the agenda."

"I'm thirsty," she said.

"We'll have something back on the *Spoken Word*."

"Look, I respect your beliefs, Ridge, but you can't force your convictions onto me. I happen to like a drink from time to time-"

"This ale would be like ten or eleven drinks you would probably just sip from time to time. We need the clearest heads we can have, Samara. Keep it clear. No sauce."

Her face twisted with the anger and the surprise of being ordered around by her hired hand. She opened her mouth to let him have a piece of her mind but her voice caught in her fear strangled throat. She snapped her head down and leaned it against her smuggler's shoulder.

On a table near them, glowing in gray, projected light, an image of Garriton rose out of a holocom. It was about three feet tall and it was extremely detailed. After it flickered out, another image appeared, this one a transmission, not a simple image.

"It's a big bounty," the hologram said to the individual at the table. "There are whole sectors on lock down right now but only in Unity space. Out in zones like yours, you got an edge. You see her, pick her up, I put you in touch with the best Unity contacts and we split the take."

The bar's patron paid grave attention. Gideon Ridge was listening, too, his head cocked a bit in the other table's direction.

The hologram, a very ugly, humanoid woman, broke into laughter when the resident at the table spewed something in an ancient Earth tongue never translated.

"So you think you got the contacts for yourself?" the hologram asked. "You're taking a real chance, old man, even if your daughter is on the hunt. But suit yourself."

The image faded. The man at the table got up, picked up his holocom and sidled away toward the bar.

Samara said, "He's looking for me."

Ridge followed the man with just his eyes.

"Yes, he is, Samara. Half this station probably is. And, if the other half knew how much you were worth, they would be, too. The difference about that guy is that I just don't know why he's looking."

The man propped against the bar, chatting with a Vipon and a Hunon. He was taller than both of them, even propped over on his elbows, though that was no great accomplishment where the Hunon was concerned. He was as tall as the Hunon when he was sitting down.

"You know him?" Garriton exhaled into his ear, keeping her face close to his neck, playing her part well. She did not want to be exposed.

Ridge looked at the ancient style leather boots, soft soled and laced up the shank. They protruded from beneath the overcoat the man wore, one made of the hide of a Carda beast. The coat was made of the whole thing; the leathery skin, thick, multicolored fur, and the four horns still intact. Two horns rose from each shoulder. Over the horns fell the man's very long, black and silver hair.

"I know him."

"Well?" she demanded in a strangled hush.

"He's no bounty hunter," the smuggler muttered, turning his face back to her. He angled his head downward, put his mouth against her cheek and let his lips drift there. "But I know who is and who's hunting you, if that man's involved."

"Who is he?"

"Later."

"Let's get out of here," she tried to say without moving her lips.

"You're in a good cover," he answered. "Besides, I haven't met my main contact, yet."

She felt like screaming at Ridge. The chances of being recognized multiplied by the moment.

He does smell wonderful, though, she thought to herself suddenly. *I know we showered before changing but I didn't take time to use any perfume -*

She abruptly screamed inside herself. What was wrong with her? She was so distracted that she had, for the barest, fleeting seconds, forgotten that her life was in danger.

Then she saw *him* as he came in through the open doors. Garriton was hardly the only one; far from it. It seemed that, despite the banging music, every soul stilled and every head turned to watch him.

A stark white, hooded cloak draped over him. It seemed to float about him. Under it was a boot length, double breasted, white cassock, just as bright, with shining steel buttons on the chest. They managed to find just enough light in the den to glint as he walked.

An Acolyte? In here? Is he lost? the mumbling came.

His cassock bore no buttons below the wide, attached belt that cinched around the waist. From the waist down it flared out over loose black pants and black boots, garments almost invisible in the dark locale. In the billowing sleeves, however, a glint of shining steel plates on black gauntlets revealed their presence as he moved. His gloved hands eased back the hood as he walked straight for Gideon Ridge and his charge.

Is that...? He's not just an Acolyte... others grumbled.

The official vestments of the Acolyte Temple Ambassador glowed in the place and glowed against his skin. The visitor's deep, dark complexion gave his stern features a mysterious distinction in the low light of the club. He seemed to be carved from ebony and set to life.

"Been a while, Gideon," the Human said, allowing himself a smile.

Samara Garriton tried to keep her head angled into Gideon Ridge's neck and only glanced at the newcomer with her eyes.

"I try to limit my visits to the Reaches," Ridge grinned, "so I don't get out this way much."

The men shook hands and the newcomer took a seat.

"Nobody does, unless they're running from something. These days, though, they're leaving out, running from something, too."

"I've heard stories," Ridge nodded.

"Who's your cargo, Gideon?" the man asked pointedly, turning his head at an angle to get a better look at Samara Garriton.

Cargo? she thought immediately. *Cargo? Not dancing girl, not professional date?*

The newcomer noticed the shift in her eyes and smiled.

"Gideon's a friend. A good friend. More like family. I know him too well to think he's here with a paid entertainer."

"Keep it to yourself, David," Gideon Ridge muttered. "We're under eyes and ears."

"I've heard the talk," the Ambassador acknowledged.

"Right now, I need to know about what's been chasing people out of the Reaches. Any other stories like them, too. I need to know if anyone's been skulking around after me, too, or any other people..."

David looked at Samara again with keen eyes.

"Samara Garriton, I presume," the man mouthed without sound.

She gave a scarce nod, running her hand over Gideon Ridge's chest.

"You're the craziest story I know," David said to Gideon Ridge. Then he looked back to his friend's 'cargo'. "I'm David Rule."

Again, she gave a nearly imperceptible nod.

"David, the stories?" Ridge pressed.

"So, you obviously know the rumor started around the *Vindicator* going missing. The United Starmada of Allied Planets doesn't like anything suggesting the supernatural. We all know that. Neither do most governments, as far as we know. In most organized, controlled systems, the rumor is laughed away...then squashed. But in remote, free systems, the story took on a life of its own. And it's funny, considering the story isn't even about life...it's about the dead coming back and taking ships."

Ridge felt Samara Garriton tremble under his arm.

"I know that rumor, clearly."

"Good. That'll make catching you up on the others a lot easier. They're all the same, only in different places and with different races," Rule answered him.

"There are more? More sightings of the..." Samara blurted, her first slip out of cover.

"Dead," Rule finished with a fierce glare in his eye.

Ridge pressed her head back to his neck and shoulder. He left his hand there to play in her wig's dangling length.

"Hunon people lost a cobbler crew to a spacestation they found adrift. They put missiles into the station and left it rather than scavenge it, so you know they were serious about what they encountered. Their ship was assaulted by some weird tone that overtook their systems."

Samara gasped.

"That was out near Red Space," Rule said, looked around then looked back at the two. "Other tales are spreading, coming in all the time. I don't believe them all but I know truth when I hear it. There's been some angry Starstalkers in here and some mad Chabron, too. Stories about one of the Riistan burial areas being taken over by the dead. A Chabron Dreadship taken. A Starstalker starfighter carrier being destroyed. The kind of anger involved tells me those tales aren't false."

"But no official authority is taking any of it seriously. So they don't have to actually face the reality of it."

Rule said, "Right. Total head in the moonsand syndrome."

"What do they say about the Unity ship? Anything else?" he asked.

Rule looked at Samara Garriton.

"The *Vindicator* still flies," he started, "and it isn't alone. The sentients that claim to have seen it say it's flying wing on wing with an older Unity vessel. The *Judgment*."

Garriton ground her teeth and squeezed her eyes closed.

"There's a small Unity Starmada ship docked here, a Transport class, called the *Corridor*. Put a lot of Echoes down here but they claim it's all training. I don't buy it, of course, since that ship is the very one that is supposed to fly backup for the *Vindicator* if it needs it. I think they've got the transport looking for the bigger ship."

Garriton grew sick to her stomach.

"Where?" she asked, once again the willful captain, not the fugitive.

Rule looked back at Ridge with wide eyes.

"You're not going after it. That's crazy."

"David, we need to know."

The black man rubbed at his mustache and goatee.

"Gideon, that transport's been looking and it keeps coming back here empty handed. The stories of what they actually have encountered..."

"David," Gideon Ridge pushed.

"A meteor shower passed into the Reaches just before the *Vindicator* went missing. Rumor is that the entire field stalled and stopped in place a few sectors into the Reaches."

"True enough," Garriton mumbled.

David Rule nodded, adding, "Rumor now is that both Unity ships are flying out in front of it, like a vanguard or an escort, and they've stalled with the field. It's like they're waiting on something."

"Someone," Garriton mumbled. "They're waiting for me..."

"You think it's funny that these happenings occur near some kind of spatial phenomena?" Ridge asked, changing the subject. "The gases and nebulous nature of Red Space, the effects of the Reaches on things, the burial sectors of the catamorphs? Old pilots have said for centuries that the burial moon of Riista played havoc with sensor arrays and whatnot."

Rule shrugged.

"Looks like a pattern. One you should avoid."

"I should avoid this kind of dive, too. So should you. But here we are. Sometimes the work of the holy takes us into unholy places," Gideon Ridge noted.

"I fear nothing. Living, dead, whatever. But one small ship, planning to challenge two unity battleships, inside the Reaches, knowing there's likely to be a lot more to deal with than you even know? Gideon, it's reckless to stab at it alone."

"Someone has to. So, I'll be off soon. But I could really use the eyes and ears of the Brethren, David."

"I understand. I just have to advise caution. It's the job of the Acolytes to protect and care for the Messengers."

"Like I said, you hear anything I should know," Gideon said, "send me a long range holo and give me warning."

David Rule nodded, answering, "The Acolyte Brethren can definitely handle that for us."

"Us?" Gideon Ridge echoed.

"You can't go alone. I've already declared my position on it. I'll follow you out and make sure you get back out of the Reaches. No one should fly a ship solo into that place."

So true, Garriton thought to herself but said nothing.

Gideon Ridge considered arguing but David Rule was a great friend and brother. He knew it would be useless to try to argue the point.

"I'll let you know when I make the run for the Reaches."

Rule stood then shook hands with Ridge.

"I can't wait," he said with a wink then left them.

Garriton spoke lowly once he was gone.

"I can't believe the Acolyte Ambassador to this station is your-"

Ridge nudged Samara as he eyeballed the bar, looking around.

"Time to go."

"What? Are we done?" she muttered.

"For now," he answered. He looked around again but could not find the man he had been watching at the bar. "Part of our party left and I want to be gone when he comes back."

With that, they abandoned the little 'hole in the bulkhead' dive.

To pass the time on their way back to the ship, as well as to reinforce their discretion and disguise, Gideon Ridge and Samara Garriton were careful to smile and talk while walking. Ridge kept his arm around her.

"So," she started once, in between topics, stalling and following up with silence.

"Yeah?"

"Your friend."

"You say that like I only have one friend," he chuckled.

"No, the one back there. David Rule."

"Okay."

"Not just a moral man or a Messenger of Faith. Not just an Acolyte."

Gideon Ridge watched the crowds as they passed.

"The Acolyte Temple Ambassador to this sector," she said in awe.

"David Rule. Great guy. Loyal friend."

"Well, yeah," she said, exasperated. "How did you make that kind of contact? Such a high ranking leader of a very influential religious order-"

"Okay, okay, hold it," Gideon openly laughed.

"What?"

"They're the Acolytes," he corrected. "They're not 'a religious order' of any kind."

"What? They're mysterious, secretive practitioners of-"

"No," Gideon said, shaking his head. "They're Christians, Samara. Plain and simple. They are followers of Jesus Christ."

She balked openly.

"Space faring Christians. Armed with weaponry, ships and intergalactic standing with honors among independent governments-"

"Samara," Gideon said.

"-while other governments fear them. They're zealots, sometimes believed to be dangerous to established-"

"That's a Unity Command description out of a digifile."

She gasped and said, "I do work for Unity Command!"

"How many Temples have you even been to?"

"Well...none."

"And how many Acolytes have you known?"

"None."

He sighed and said, "Samara, they're Christians with a very specific calling. They gather equipment and materials to help all around the cosmos with the hungry, the forgotten and the oppressed."

"Ridge, I know what-"

"Please, turn off your database for a second. Let me tell you who they really are. They are devout believers who specialize in protecting Messengers of the Faith, Churches, Temples and believers who are being targeted. Yes, they study combat techniques and have the weapons to back that up but they only use nonlethal force and only that when no other option is possible. They are not a mysterious sect of a religious order; they are Christians who protect and serve...like peacekeepers, law enforcement...whatever you choose to call them, depending on what system you-"

"On whose authority?" she asked smugly, thinking her point proven.

"On the authority of conscience," he answered flatly.

"Who gives them authority to involve themselves in galactic affairs, though? And why do Christians engage in any conflict? Should-"

"Do you believe any military, any authority, should exist? Anywhere? Any protectorates? Law enforcement?"

She rolled her eyes, growling, "Obviously, I do."

"Okay. Do you know what the Apostle Paul said about soldiers and law enforcement in the Bible?"

She opened her mouth, an answer ready, but realized she had not read it in the Bible. It was more teaching from Unity Starmada education.

Ridge explained, "Mainly soldiers enforced the laws at that time. In Paul's writings, the book of Romans, chapter thirteen, verse four says, 'For he is the minister of God to you for good. But if you do what is evil, fear him; because he bears not the sword in vain: for he is the minister of God, an avenger to execute wrath upon those doing evil.' There has to be an organized order to things for the greater good."

"Paul the Apostle, if I remember my Religion studies at the Academy, was imprisoned by those soldiers."

"He was. And he never blamed the soldiers. He knew it was the governmental move, the 'powers that be', so to speak. John the Baptist was imprisoned and beheaded by corruption in rule. When he was asked by soldiers what they had do to have eternal life in Heaven, he told them to not lie and not to rob the people they policed and to treat all fairly but he never said, 'Stop being a soldier' to anyone. Order is good, as long as the governing bodies are good. There has to be order or evil will overrun everything. Soldiers are called to protect and serve the good."

"But that involves government, Ridge," she argued. "I asked where the Acolytes get their authority-"

"All of us have the *duty* and the *right* to fight for good. When any organized body, government, whatever, begins to fall heavily upon its people, hurt its people, enslave its people, it's time to act."

"When tyranny becomes law, rebellion becomes duty," she muttered.

"What?" he asked.

"It's a quote from an old Earth leader...I can't remember which one."

"Well, let's pick up the pace while you search your databanks for it. I don't want the eyeballs that were on us catching up to us too soon."

"That's right!" she remembered. "Who was that man at the bar?"

Ridge and Garriton were all the way back inside their docking bay when he finally answered the question she had been asking. For the entire walk, all he would say was that he would tell her later.

Once he lowered the landing ramp to the *Spoken Word*, he chanced a glance over his own shoulder then spoke on it.

"The man at the bar," he started, "the older, long haired man from the table right in front of us, is some I knew. His name is Wastasa Winds, a Native American slicker from Earth."

"What?" she half exclaimed. "I know him, too! Or, I know of him, that is. He does a lot of work for the Unity Starmada. What's he doing out here? With a holo of me?"

"What he's always doing," Gideon Ridge said. "He slicks into the tech of whatever free zone he's in and monitors and records things for the Starmada. Only one thing I can think of he's watching for out here."

"Me?" she asked, knowing the answer already. "But how could he know we'd come here? How could he have beaten us here?"

"He didn't," Ridge answered, starting up the loading ramp. "He probably travels with that transport and they were already here when your image was posted all over the universe. Besides, it isn't the man who worries me. It's his daughter, a bounty hunter and all around killer. She's completely unhinged."

Samara started up the ramp behind him.

"Unity wouldn't send a killer after me, Ridge. Not until-"

"Every other effort was expended," a low, gritty voice finished for her. "Say hello to that effort."

At the top of the ramp into the *Spoken Word*, stepping from the dark of the interior cargo bay, Wastasa Winds opened his arms as if offering an embrace.

"Captain Samara Garriton, it's good to meet you."

At the far sides of the spacious bay, two access doors swished away. Through one poured the five man Echo squad, elite drop soldiers of the USAP. Through the other pressed the Vipon and the Hunon previously at the bar with Winds. All of them were still quite a distance away but advancing slowly, cautiously.

"Captain Arn Van Pelt will be very glad to be the commander to return you to Starmada Command," Winds said with a long breath. "I'd rather take the credit - and the bounty - for myself but I travel with Van Pelt's transport and I'm already contracted with the Starmada. So, it would be unfair. Like getting paid twice for the same thing."

"Your moral standards are overwhelming," Ridge growled.

"They aren't after you," Samara said suddenly, turning to Gideon Ridge. "I'll go with them. I appreciate all you've done but-"

Gideon Ridge slapped both of his hidden bracers in one deft flinch. The movement was so fast, so fluid, that Samara Garriton was standing within reach of him but never saw him move until a bluish energy shield ignited on his left arm and his right hand spewed blue energy bolts. The obviously conductive gloves flashed with energy as he acted.

Before she could speak, before anyone else could act at all, Wastasa Winds was on his back on the loading ramp, his body writhing and crackling, and Ridge had pointed his right hand in the direction of the Hunon and the Vipon. More arcing, crackling energy ripped from his hand, the underside of the ship blued in the reflection of his assault.

The Vipon went down in a heap. He had not out drawn the Vipon; he had rolled the energy shield of his left bracer about and absorbed the Vipon's much faster shots. The Hunon and the Echoes scurried for cover behind cargo crates and the like, lamenting the fact that all scouting reports had indicated Ridge was unarmed.

Unarmed, they swore at each other.

"What are those things?" Garriton demanded.

Gideon Ridge stormed the ramp, dragging her in a full charge upward into the ship. He shouted into one of his bracers.

"Drea!" Ridge roared. "Clean the bay! Hostiles in the bay!"

The ship shuddered as underbelly cannons dropped from the fuselage and opened fire. The Echo soldiers and the Hunon cried out as cover exploded and toppled away from them.

Then Kelvan and Kreden Hotch barreled into the bay through the door the Echo Unit had used. Both had heavy assault weapons, fully automatic, slung by their sides. They spewed the blue energies throughout the bay, leveling cover and dropping enemies in a wave.

Only the Hunon escaped, slipping from the far door and fleeing.

Garriton pulled free of Ridge, trying to straighten the clingy clothes she wore, all the while demanding an explanation for his violence. She shouted things like 'wholesale slaughter' and 'merciless abandon', tossing the terminology around as if giving a speech at a Unity Command dinner.

"Go change your clothes," he shouted back as he ran for the cockpit. "I don't take criticism from dancing girls!"

She ground her teeth together, swearing under her breath. Her eyes landed on the body of Wastasa Winds, still on the ramp where it had lifted and closed with him on it. His eyes were wide open.

"Drea, get ready to tear out of here," Ridge said to his sister.

"You got it," she answered, getting up from the weapons station and dropping into the copilot seat.

Ridge flipped a switch, shouting, "Grundy! Grundy, you read me?"

"On my way, Gideon," the low voice rolled over the com system. "I got delayed picking up the Barra Scopes. I'll get them installed as soon as I get in there."

"No, no, no!" Ridge howled, checking instruments in front of him and overhead. "You did *not* do a full shut down on lightspeed systems! You did *not* plan to rescope here on this station! *Please* tell me you didn't!"

"You said you wanted her ready to run, just in case we had to rip out of the Reaches," Grundy said. "She's needed rescoping for a while, Gideon. Now is better than then, right?"

Gideon laughed frantically as he continued flipping switches and hitting buttons that lit and beeped at him.

"I don't know, big guy! Depends on how quickly you get here! I'd hate to die alone!"

An orange display began to flash on his console. It showed the loading ramp opening.

"Gideon, I'm here already," Grundy said over his mobile com. "Kelvan and Kreden are coming in with me, too. But why is there a dead guy on our ramp? And why are there all those-"

"Just get inside!" Gideon snapped, pulling a headset free of the seat arm and putting it on. "Everyone, hold on," he said over the ship's intercom.

"Docking bay doors opening," Drea said.

"Good job. Now keep your eyes open for a Unity ship!"

"Gideon, spatial transmission incoming," Kelvan interrupted, taking a seat and flipping several switches at his console.

"Oh, by all means, patch it through," Gideon Ridge snorted.

The others, all but Samara Garriton, piled into the cockpit and began strapping into seats.

"Captain of powering vessel," a very formal voice addressed. "This is Captain Arn Van Pelt of the USAP Vessel *Corridor*. On behalf of the United Starmada of Allied Planets, I order you to power down your engines. You are in direct violation-"

Ridge fired a maneuvering thruster then a propulsion thruster. The ship began to move.

"Captain Van Pelt, have you not scanned my ship to see who I am?"

The other captain hesitated.

"I don't have that option. My vessel is a Transport class, not a bigger vessel with mass sensors. I cannot read or detect ship call signs or access pilot records. I only admit that because that doesn't matter. I am the authority here. And, if you will not yield to authority, you must yield to logic. As you know, we are both powering at the same time. You cannot elude us. We are willing to forgive your conflict with my Echo soldiers but you must-"

"Captain, have you ever tried to run down the *Spoken Word*?" Ridge asked then nodded at Drea.

She engaged all three engine chambers. The ship leaped forward from its landing gear, roaring upward as the gear was still retracting. The silver nose rose into the star studded black of space.

A shriek came from the room where Captain Garriton was dressing, after which all that could be heard was the fierce thrust of the *Spoken Word*.

CHAPTER FOUR : *Darkness*

L ittle light splayed into the cracks in the vessel's hull. Not much light permeated the Reaches at all, as was the nature of the phenomenon. But, on the inside of a depowered ship, adrift, with only splits in the outer plating to offer the very limited, dim light outside it, the best word for the environment was darkness.

That would have been the best description regardless, considering what went on inside it.

The Reaches; an odd name for an expanse, considering no one knew its real reach. It lay in wait beyond the regular patrol and boundaries of all the sentient races on the Earth side of the location. No sentient race had made contact from beyond the Reaches, as far as anyone could tell. No one had mapped the Reaches, either, so no one could actually be certain of their full expanse. All that was known was that they seemed to shift sometimes, to drift, and no one wanted to be inside the stretch most called cursed.

No active starmada would venture inside. Too many ships had been lost in the attempts. Most records of the starmadas, empires and organized explorers that had previously tried painted a horrid, terrorizing portrait of a phenomenon vast in unknown power.

Ships lost their way with no reason. Navigation and power fluctuations and malfunction were the beginning of the helmsman's curse within the expanse. Getting too close, too, was an early curse; curiosity led too many to the edges of the black pool of gaseous nothingness, at which time the ships involved would be drawn in, as if by graviton beam.

Once inside, the malfunctions were all biological. The crews would go mad with sudden abandon, no rhyme or reason known. The deeper the exploration, the worse the conditions…

A man put his finger up to his lips and shushed himself then cackled wildly. He bent with laughter, staggered then leaned against the helm of a humongous and ancient craft. His tired eyes, wide and wild, fixed onto a split in the bridge wall plating, one through which the darkness of space could be felt crawling in. For what felt like a millionth time, in what seemed like a million years he had been in the expanse, drifting and alone, he wondered how he was alive.

No. He wondered why.

"You already know why," the voice said inside his mind.

The man literally trembled when the voice spoke, his weak body leaning further onto the navigation helm station. His fingers clawed at the console, his nails dragging over dark displays and powerless keys.

"How can I know? I don't even understand how! I don't understand any of it!" the man cried but his voice made no sound, other than in his own mind. There was no atmosphere and no place for the sound to carry once birthed. He shouted in silence and frustration. "I'm not dead but I'm not alive! I'm here but I don't know where here is!"

The man collapsed to the floor, his face twisted into a mask of tortured insanity. He howled as if in pain, eyes squinted and lips twitching, but a second later he burst into manic laughing.

"You are alive to gather a starmada," that booming, ominous voice said.

"You mean…we have to get more?" the man asked, eyes wide like a child in trouble.

The silence answered the man and he began to weep on the decking of the bridge…

…while that crying was echoed thousands of times in nearby derelict ships, all powered down, all adrift in the expanse, drawn toward the ancient craft with the voice…

"I'm telling you; they just lifted off," Pap Ridge said to Uncle Sun.

They had fixed the Baykeeper robot and had gone home for some sleep. When they had returned to the spaceport, Gill Bardoff had handed Pap a key piece of reconnaissance discovery.

"Well, what are we waiting for?" Sun Ridge grinned bitterly.

"We don't have a ship, Sundar, if what you want is a chase," Sylver Ridge answered. "I sent a couple of encrypted holos but I don't know where Gideon is or if he can receive them right now. In the meantime, we got no transport to go rushing off in hot pursuit of anybody."

"You know, that right there is insulting," Gill Bardoff snarled at his two old friends.

"What?" Sundar asked.

Sylver shook his head, saying, "Something always insults him."

"I got a ship, boys," Bardoff insisted, hands on his hips.

A torn and weathered belt and holster hung from his old bones, barely able to find a perch.

Sylver and Sundar looked at each other.

"What?" Gill asked, noting their expressions.

"Gill, no offense," Sylver started.

"Too late," Sun said flatly. "Gill, it's junk. It's the kind of ship that most prestigious ports would try to confiscate and burn."

"What're you getting at?" Gill asked.

Sylver shook his head at Gill's lack of comprehension.

"That statement says it all, Gill," Sundar shouted. "It's a Hunon designed junk freighter, designed to collect space scrap, 'cause that's what the Hunon race does! But considering you got it dirt cheap from the people who made it, it was worn out when you got it!"

Bardoff gasped.

"That don't count all the 'repairs' you've made," Sun added snidely. "I mean, you've got more hull patches and engine rebuilds than the whole Hunon Empire's starmada, and that's saying something. How many colors are on that hull now?"

Gill Bardoff bowed up at them like a Lofta cockerel pushed too far. His voice cracked when he hollered at them and his neck stretched emphatically.

"Let me tell you something!" he started. "My old girl might not be a Raindancer but she's still the fastest thing in this spaceport!"

Sylver turned his head and covered his mouth, obviously trying not to respond.

Sundar Ridge had no such control.

"Fastest rusting," he snorted.

"What?" Bardoff railed. "That's it! Prepare to defend yourself!" the old man barked.

"Stop it," old Pap growled at Bardoff as he began bouncing around with his bony fists in the air. "Stop it, Gill. Sun's just pushing your buttons and you're letting him."

Sundar rolled up one sleeve.

Confused, Gill Bardoff stopped his dance and stared.

"What'd you roll up one sleeve for?" he demanded, fuzzy brows furrowed on his lined countenance.

"It won't take more than one arm to put you out," Sundar remarked.

"That's really it!" Bardoff shouted, his voice a little winded. He began his dance again.

"Shut up, Sun!" Pap warned, a sharp finger shaken his way. Then he turned back to Gill. "Stop peacocking all over! Act your age!"

"I'm eighty-six! I figure at this age I can act however I want!"

"If you ever want to see eighty-seven, you better stop dancing around me," Sundar said.

"Hold it!" Pap finally yelled. The other two stilled, looking at him. "This is about helping my boy. Gill, what was your ship's name again?"

Gill tucked his skinny thumbs into the top of his pants and leaned back in pride. He raised his face a bit, staring at the roof line of the bay.

"The *Belly Rub*, gentlemen, the fastest little-"

"That's disgusting," Sun Ridge grimaced.

"What? What do you know?" Bardoff exploded again.

"I know the idea of a bunch of little hairless Hunons dancing around me, trying to rub my stomach, is just disgusting!" Sun bellowed.

"Stop it!" Sylver snapped again at both of them. He gave Sun a hot, cutting glare then looked back to Gill. "Gill, you think the...the *Rub*... could get us on the trail of those fleshhunters?"

"Oh boy," Sundar sighed.

"Sylver, you'd never be able to find a better way to catch up to them!" Bardoff said.

"Then go get prepped," Pap said. "We'll grab some gear and meet you in your bay."

The other old man clapped his hands together and spun about. He scurried along, slowing to pull his holster and belt back up but stopped at the Ridges' bay exit.

"Hey, Sylver?" he called.

"Here we go," Sun muttered.

"Yeah, Gill?" Sylver answered.

"You suppose you could front me the fuels we'll need? I'm a little short after the way the Hunon devils keep raking in my scrap..."

Sylver waved him away, nodding.

When Gill Bardoff was gone, Sylver Ridge turned to his brother.

"Some of the things you say sure can be offensive."

"Offensive is a bunch of little, pale rascals trying to grope my belly."

"Shut up, Sun," Sylver sighed.

"Haven't you even gone to sleep, Gideon?" Dalindrea groaned as she stood up from the table.

"I'm fine, Drea. I slept a little. Besides, I'm taking turns babysitting with Grundy."

His sister shook her head, finishing off her Capitulan Tea.

"I thought nobody could suffer from insomnia the way I do, after losing Dandru the way I did," she shrugged. "You, brother, come close."

Gideon smiled sadly, considering her meaning. Her husband had been lost in the Forroweld Web, a sector of space known for brightly colored nebulae and the wild assertion of temporal disturbances. Dandru had been part of a Starstalker expedition; a Starstalker himself, he was the science officer aboard the exploration craft, *Rogan*.

"Grab a bunk, Sis," Gideon suggested.

"Maybe you should get a robot. Or an android. Someone you can put on the flight team who won't need sleep."

He curled up a lip.

"Me? No way." He waved her away, adding, "Now get some rest. I'm going to spell the brothers soon."

Manufacturers sure wanted people to feel connected to 'droids, even more so than to the 'bots. It was common practice to have both make small talk and mimic human actions as they conversed. They were designed to have varying volumes and tones to their audio projectors.

If a person let themselves, they could completely forget the 'bots and 'droids were just machines. The truth was simply that, however, and there was no 'life' in them. Clever programming, maybe. Dedicated database servers, definitely. But the spark of life? Not even close. That was fiction. Sometimes, that willing imagination got people in trouble.

"I bet you could make a 'droid do some impressive things, behave in convincing ways," Ridge said suddenly to the man sitting across the galley table from him.

Wastasa Winds cut his dark brown eyes at him.

Ridge shrugged in return.

"Do we have to talk?" Winds growled. "I mean, whatever you plan to do with me, do we have to be friends?" Wild, bushy eyebrows waved at Ridge above the man's scars and age lines when the man added, "We never have been friends in all the years we been bumping elbows."

"Humor me," Ridge smiled. "Why slick yourself into my ship but greet me at my ramp, unarmed?"

"I've told you repeatedly, Captain, ever since you woke me, that I am not your enemy."

"And, yet, you brought two known bounty hunters with you to the docking bay, along with an Echo unit from the starship *Corridor*. Tell me the truth, Wastasa. What gives? You weren't giving your 'A game', so you either find me and my ship a B'ronda walk, or your heart just wasn't in your work, or something else is going on."

Wastasa Winds leaned back in the table's metal chair, letting his long hair fall back.

Gideon just stared patiently.

Samara Garriton passed the open doorway and stopped, backing up in the hall.

"Still at it?" she asked Ridge.

"We had some breakfast," Gideon answered her. "We're bonding."

"How are the engines coming?" she asked.

"I have no idea."

"Um...okay...you do know how cold it is outside, right?"

The Native American, tied with pulsar cording to the chair where it was bolted to the decking, snapped up his head.

"I do," he said with a grin and a chuckle. "Records have this little planet pegged as the coldest ever inhabited by sentients, even temporarily. Temperatures, if you can call them that, dip well below-"

"Drop it," Garriton barked. "I don't need an elementary school definition of Dor Modo's temperatures. I don't want a spatial history lesson about where we are, either. I know all of that." She looked back to Ridge. "So? Does Grundy have any idea on the engines?"

"That's a big negative," Ridge smirked.

Garriton smiled sarcastically and left the room, heading for the cockpit.

Winds gestured with his head as Garriton walked out.

"Good looking woman, Ridge. You sure you're thinking all this through clearly? You're not...distracted, are you?"

Gideon Ridge sat forward in his chair, saying, "Let's stay on topic."

"She is the topic. Everybody wants her, you got her; now everybody wants you."

"What's your play, Winds?"

The captive stared deeply into Ridge's eyes.

"I want the truth, Ridge. First hand, not trekchatter."

"Funny. That's exactly what I want. Now."

His dark eyes were almost black when he answered again.

"I want to know what she saw. From her own mouth. First hand account. She's seen what so many people always wonder about. The afterlife...of some kind. I want to hear her account, to know what she saw, to sense her fear. You get that lovely lady to share, Ridge, I tell you whatever you want."

Gideon Ridge stood up from the table.

"Grundy, where are we on the engines?" Ridge queried, holding the wall switch.

Samara Garriton propped her booted feet on the command console in the cockpit. She leaned the pilot's seat back, listening to the coil springs beneath it creak and grind. The blanket Gideon Ridge had wrapped about her shoulders previously still lay on the floor, so she retrieved it and draped it over herself. Her breath lingered in the air before her, its message of the dire, coming cold communicated well even without a voice.

The cold. Lessons over a lifetime about the known cosmos paraded through her mind. The truth and the legends about the planet on which they had hidden collided and she wondered which part was actually which. Where had the cold come from on the planet nearest the Reaches? What had really led to the ice age on Dor Modo, the frozen planet around which Maximilian Station orbited? Her mind raced.

Nothing grew there. No animals could survive the cold and the lack of vegetation. No sentient species had been able to maintain any kind of settlements. Between the distance from supply worlds and the impossibility of attaining sustenance on the ice world, no settlement had been viable, nor had one been profitable. And the only sign of any previous sentients to later explorers was the ancient, forty-five mile stretch of subterranean tombs. Those were located in the northern hemisphere near that pole. No one had deciphered the language of the carvings. Frankly, no one had ever been paid enough to try hard enough. What was known was that Dor Modo was a deathbed.

Samara Garriton did not want to die there.

Her ire rose. Gideon Ridge had pointed the nose of the *Spoken Word* straight down into the snowstorms of the ice world, no thought to their chances of survival. When she had shouted that at him, his ship diving into the atmosphere too boldly for words, he had asked if she had a better plan.

The lightspeed engines are depowered, he had shouted over the scream of the ship ripping through the atmosphere. *We can't outrun your Unity friends. We have to hide.*

Hide. Deep in a frozen tomb world, cradled in snowstorms and the sculptures of nature's ice. *Hide,* he had said.

Die, she was hearing. *Die cold and alone.*

Oddly, she felt a pause in herself. Alone…but she had not felt nearly so alone since she had teamed with Gideon Ridge. Not until he had marooned them on the planet of death, anyway.

Grundy was on a life and death mission to recharge the light engines. Until they were ready to jump, Gideon had said flatly he was not going to emerge from the atmosphere. The Unity ship after them was in orbit around the planet, patterning themselves at angles to be able to intercept any trajectory emerging from Dor Modo. The troop transport was far more heavily armed than their ship. Without outrunning them, Ridge did not like their chances.

All of the rayonnix particles in the atmosphere masked them perfectly from the Unity ship. Unity craft were forbidden to fly down into the atmosphere for that reason. Flight was sensorially and technologically blind in the atmosphere.

One would have to be crazy to go in manually in all the storms, she mused. Gideon Ridge could fly well, however, and he did it manually from the viewports. Was it admiration for him she was feeling? The suddenness of it gave her pause…again.

"The main systems override is over there," Ridge was saying as he stormed the cockpit.

Wastasa Winds was close on his heels. He pulled on technofiber gloves as he turned to approach the console Kelvan usually monitored.

Drea and the Hotch twins were eating in the galley, however.

"What is he-" Samara shouted on the way to her feet, that venter aimed level.

"Whoa, Quickdraw! Put that down!" Gideon cried.

She looked back to Ridge.

"Wastasa is going to help us push the lightspeed online," Ridge continued. He pressed by her as he spoke, maneuvering into the foremost part of the cockpit, then flipped a switch. "Grundy, get ready to process a little extra input."

"Are you crazy?" Samara Garriton demanded.

She had not put the venter away, so Winds was still frozen to his spot, rolling his eyes.

Ridge glanced back at her and shrugged.

"Depends on who you ask…wait…whom you ask. Depends on whom-"

"That man has a Unity digifile longer than the tomb stretch on this planet!"

"So do I!" Ridge laughed out loud. "Besides, doesn't he work for you guys?"

"It's off and on," Wastasa Winds interrupted.

"Ridge," Samara started again.

"It's a 'keep your enemies closer' sort of relationship," Winds continued. "I started working with the Starmada the first time they impounded my ship."

Ridge cut him a sharp look.

"Wastasa, no offense, but I don't care. I need engines."

Samara put her weapon away at Gideon's gesture. Winds went about the business of slicking into the propulsion.

"He can't be trusted," Samara said confidentially, leaning close to Gideon Ridge.

"I know," Ridge laughed.

Wastasa looked over his shoulder and grinned at Gideon Ridge.

"Captain," she started again, emphasizing his title, raising her voice. "I'm not dying down here. Now you keep him leashed, for all our sakes."

Ridge flipped several other switches and adjusted a few slide bars.

"Ridge-"

"What is your problem?" he asked her finally. "You were upset when you thought I had cut him down permanently on the station, talking about my 'wholesale slaughter' and my violence. All because you had no clue that I, my crew and even my ship are armed with Neuropulsars and concussion blasters, all nonlethal energies. And you didn't bother to ask. Now you're upset because I let him off his leash. Make up your mind, Samara."

"She's not sure how to feel without the Starmada telling her. You can't run around feeling just however you want. You might have a feeling or a thought that offends someone," Wastasa Winds muttered.

"Shut up, Winds!" Garriton ordered.

"You're mad when I shoot him down, you're mad when I bring his 'dead' body up on the loading ramp. You're mad when I put him in a chair, tied up, while he recovered from my stuns and now you're mad that I let him loose."

She snorted at Gideon Ridge.

"First of all, as I've already said, I didn't know you were using Neuropulsars! I had no idea your ship was wired to use them, too! For that matter, I had no idea you could power up stunning energies to a level that could be used to disable the systems in entire vessels, so how could I possibly know you had converted your shipwide defenses to neuropulse energy? All I knew was that a Chaplain, a Messenger, had drawn and fired faster than I had ever seen and cut down multiple people-"

"I believe that."

"-with some kind of armbands and gloves you still haven't identified-"

"That's true."

"-so, I didn't know he wasn't dead!"

"Indeed."

"Lastly, I don't trust him, even if I don't want him dead, carried around or trussed up like an animal!" she finished loudly.

Ridge nodded, noting, "That's been clearly established."

"Will you stop agreeing with me?" she yelled.

"Yes," he said, taking her shoulders. Then he frowned. "Wait...no. You said don't agree with you, so no, I will not stop agreeing with you...no, wait, that's still not right..."

Wastasa Winds laughed lightly in the background.

"Captain Ridge!" she snapped.

"Look, Samara, I have to go help Grundy," he sighed his interruption. "Stay here. Point that venter at Winds if you feel it's necessary. But we have technical and electrical problems in the ship and I'm not going to leave a slicker locked in a cargo area. He's going to help us. And, before you ask, the reason to trust him is the fact that he's going to die down here with us, in the cold, if he doesn't help, and I'm pretty sure he'll do the right thing."

She stared at him, mouth open.

"He also wants to understand what we're doing out here, why everyone is after you. He wants to understand. Take a little while, take a deep breath and explain it to him."

"I don't owe him anything!"

"Then do it for me."

She opened her mouth quickly. Her eyes were narrowed in fury.

"Please," he added then trotted back out of the cockpit.

"You still haven't told me about the armbands!" she railed after him.

"Commodore on the bridge," a handsome young captain announced. He rose from his position in the center of the bridge and saluted properly.

"As you were," Commodore Zeckinbridge replied, her eyes jumping from station to station, most of them unmanned. "What is our status?"

He stared at her, clearly confused, as she rounded the rail in the room and stepped down onto the lower platforms, near the helm.

"I'm...I'm sorry, Commodore Zeckinbridge, but what status? I don't understand-"

"Our status!" she shouted. "Our departure status!"

"Departure?" he echoed again.

"A commodore comes on a bridge, asking about the status, during a retrofit and mission prep, to which you reply, *what status*?"

"But I wasn't told you were even coming," he defended. "I didn't know to expect you until your shuttle notified your arrival. We have a mission planned by Base Commander Basnight but he hasn't briefed me and we aren't ready to embark, anyway."

"Captain Brent, do you think that the role of captain comes with a manual for all unexpected situations? Do you believe you will be apprised of every problem you will ever face? Do you think you will be able to schedule every duty that lies before you? You are a captain; always be ready to act and improvise."

"We have most of our crew aboard the docking station and some of them have gone down to say farewell to Earth before we set out for the mission. We can't-"

"There is no can't, Captain Brent!" she barked angrily. "Ready your present crew and yourself. If you have to, go to Engineering and start prepping the engines yourself."

"Aye, Commodore," he said, snapping back to attention and saluting again.

"I have some fill in crew for this very reason; I have them boarding now. Tell me who you're missing," Zeckinbridge ordered.

In no time, she had populated most of the bridge with handpicked replacements.

Deep in the Reaches, a fleet gathered. It was drawn, tied together by the center ship and the darkness emanating from it. The faint starlight ambient in the expanse twinkled straight through some of the terribly damaged starships, their hulls open in places. Winged vessels had shattered and missing wings. Cockpit viewports were shattered and gone. Engine chambers lay open, compromised. Larger ships, using digitally projected viewscreen images to interior, protected bridges, often had entire hull plates missing where the bridge areas had been targeted...and penetrated.

And there were indeed some large ships gathering. Very large.

Pulling up the back of the fleet was the *Ferali 4*, a Starstalker vessel only recently taken by the dark of death. With it drifted the massive *Scythe*, a Chabron Dreadship overrun by the dead at the same time as the

Starstalker fighter base ship. Both wore enough damage to have killed mortal crews…and it had in fact had done so. The dead were not so strict on requirements such as life support and environmental control.

The starmada of bones, nearly fifty starships strong, wrapped the center ship in broken allies. About them, like moths attached to the flame, several hundred individual starfighters floated and followed. They came from many races and many sectors, all with one thing in common. They had each been wrecked or assaulted and left in destruction.

The center ship, however, was so massive one would wonder if it needed any allies.

The gargantuan defied reality. Oddly, it stretched out linearly for more than a hundred Dreadships in length but it curved at intervals, taking a snaking pattern down its fuselage. The curving occurred at joints that flexed, allowing the tremendous shape to further its snaking motion as it flew. Here and there were wings, or more likely, stabilizers and cargo holds, all along both sides. Atop the vessel ran a ridge, or a spine, of metal fins, most likely sensor and communication, or other technological posts. The nose was only as wide as a Reaper class Unity ship, and though that was the largest of the Unity ships, it was only a third as wide as the rest of the serpentine ship. The entire nose was an open maw of offensive weaponry, while open ports all along the face of the vessel looked to be missile or torpedo bays. The bridge looked over the back of the creature craft, from one third of its length back. It lifted within some of the spinework, well hidden and well armored.

Like the other starships, it bore the damage of wars and rumors of wars.

On the bridge, one mind, tortured and long lost, absorbed the intent of the bone starmada.

A lone man lay on the decking of that bridge. He stared out the long destroyed and vacant viewports through eyes just as vacant. The color had faded from those eyes, as had the life. Like his skin and hair, the orbs had gone gray.

"Captain on the bridge…" he whispered, only in his mind. Then, with a cackle and a twitch, he silently, manically laughed inside himself.

The serpentine starship floated along, swaying like a snake, bringing a starmada with it.

"Captain…of the Leviathan."

"You want to know what I saw," Samara said finally.

Ridge had been gone from the cockpit for some time, time that Winds worked feverishly on the ship's lightspeed systems. He slowed when Samara Garriton broke the silence. Looking over his shoulder, he stared at her.

"I do."

"Are you sure?" she pressed.

"Maybe you're one of those people who has their spiritual reservations. Or maybe you're well grounded in a Faith. Or maybe you have no belief either way. Me? I'm clueless about anything beyond this life. I never learned about my own heritage and the beliefs of my people and I haven't ever studied anyone else's. I'm...searching. I want to know."

"Fine," she grumbled. "Work while I tell you. And don't blame me if your nightmares won't leave you."

His fierce eyes read her honesty. Then he went back to work.

The lady captain dropped into a seat in the cockpit, lowering the venter but not putting it away. She fiddled with the blanket, pushing against the seat in front of her with her feet.

"We were on a skirting run around the Reaches," she started, her throat tight. She cleared it. "We received a distress call in some nearby 'roid field. Problem is...it was coming from the *Judgment*."

"That's the ship you-"

"Skip reading me my digifile. Anyway, it was more than just the automated distress call. We actually heard the recorded distress call that Captain Bordin Mo personally made back when...that ship was lost.

"Mo was dead, of course. That didn't matter. There his message was, echoing over our com systems, scaring the life out of all of us who remembered. Then the call turned into a droning sound, a hollow resonance. It numbed our minds, interfered with the thought process. It then began to shut down or take over our ship's systems."

He turned about and frowned.

"Undead techies? Ghost slickers?"

"I don't know, Winds. I'm just telling you what happened. It went very bad from there."

He went back to work.

"The ship was being pulled along, systems following the tone's command. I gave the order to kill all power, a full power drop."

"Didn't work?"

"Almost. My Weapons Officer...my friend, Mr. Shoka, made a decision to leave power available to a shuttle. He did it for me. Loyalty. Bravery. But the tone took the shuttle controls and detonated it. The carnage started right after."

"Too much damage?" he asked, grimacing at his demanding work.

"Damage? That was the least of it. We ignited power again in a last ditch effort to survive but the ship was overrun."

"By what?" Winds asked, intensely focused.

She shuddered, her voice low as she said, "Undead corpses...the dead, Winds. Dead bodies still moving, still chasing. Fighter pilots from the *Judgment*, Security Officers, too, brought by the Scorpion starfighters from the mother ship...from the 'roid field."

"What..." he uttered, his eyes wide, his attention fully hers. "What did you do? Did you communicate with them? Did you try to-"

"They engaged our Security forces with side arms and diffuser bands. Our people didn't have time to equip their own bands, so it was a one sided battle. We got cut down quickly. I..." she choked and cleared her throat, "...I lost a lot of good people."

"Wasn't the *Vindicator* big enough to warrant your Security Officers wearing diffuser bands full time?" Winds asked. "Those simple forearm bands complete a personal field circuit that can't be beaten. You can touch through it, eat through it, everything, but energy fire can't go through it. Diffuses everything."

She ground her teeth together, growling, "You think I don't know that? You think I haven't thought of that every hour of every day since?"

He paused again, taking off his gloves.

"No. I'm a technology kind of guy; explaining as a I go is second nature. I wasn't ridiculing." He flipped a switch on the console. "Ridge, give it some power. See if it jumps the power to your other engines."

"My ship was big enough," she answered his question softly. "We were too big. We never suspected our force would need them. Not on our own decks. By the time I told T'Leah, my Chief of Security, to gear up, not enough of us were able to do so."

The man waited respectfully, not speaking.

She dropped her head, confiding, "I miss her. I miss all of them."

"Okay, here it is," Ridge called back. "Three...two...one..."

Winds and Garriton perked visibly as the regular power surged suddenly, the lights brightening, and the sound of the engines increased.

Drea stormed into the cockpit and dropped into her seat.

"Gideon told me to tell you both something," the woman said.

"What?" Winds asked.

"Hold on," Drea giggled unabashedly.

The woman flipped two switches and shoved a lever forward.

The Raindancer launched forward with enough force to throw Winds and Garriton to the floor. The engines roared then howled further as Drea angled the nose upward in an eighty degree lift.

"Captain Van Pelt," the Science Officer said, "the target starship is on the move!"

The captain of the *Corridor* sat up in his command seat.

"Set an intercept course. Full cruise."

The Unity ship altered its direction instantly. The Helmsman, the pilot, poured on the power, as the bridge crew watched their stations.

"They're rising fast," the Science Officer said.

"Stay on intercept, Mr. Jangg. The-"

"Grekbil," the Weapons Officer interrupted.

"We're closing on them, Captain," the Science Officer said.

"Good. Stay on-"

"Grekbil!" the Weapons Officer, a scarred, bluntly faced Vipon, interrupted again.

"What is it, Mr. Rol?" the captain blurted.

"Weapons range now," the Science Officer said.

"Five fighter craft, Grekbil," the Weapons Officer informed. "Clossing on uss from five pointss of intersscept."

"What?" Captain Van Pelt shouted, looking to the Communications Officer. "Any hails?"

"None, Captain," the Communications Officer said.

"Hail them, Patterson!" he shouted.

"Captain, we're in range to fire," the Science Officer reminded. "I've scanned the ship and pinpointed the Prime Reactor, the wing thrusters, and the shield modulator. All points are ready for Mr. Rol to target."

"Stay on the target," the captain told the helm. "Mr. Rol, stand by."

The Communications Officer looked up to the captain.

"I have the lead fighter."

"On screen!" the irritated leader yelled.

A man appeared on the viewscreen. He wore a white hood and cloak over a white cassock with billowing sleeves.

"Unity captain, my name is David Rule. I'm an Ambassador from the Acolyte Temple for this sector. I'm with four other Acolytes. We protect Messengers, or those who share the Gospel of Jesus Christ, and I greet you in the name of peace and good will. Our Scriptures teach us to do our utmost to live in peace with all those we encounter."

"You have taken a pursuit position of my ship," Van Pelt said. "What peace is it you offer on such course?"

"I see you're pursuing a man who aides Messengers and Acolytes across space," Rule responded. "I'm requesting that you please break off your pursuit of the *Spoken Word*."

"And just why would I give up pursuit of a-"

"For a greater pursuit. The pursuit of peace."

The screen went black then returned to the view of space.

"They are within weaponss range," hissed the Vipon.

"So are we," the Science Officer informed again.

"Scan the fighters!" Captain Van Pelt shouted at Mr. Janng. "Mr. Rol, reroute long range weaponry power to the shielding! I don't want to be sitting vulnerable when they fire!"

A flare of bright light lit the bridge then the ship they had been pursuing jumped to lightspeed in a flash and disappeared.

"The fighters are a mix, Captain," the Science Officer said. "Two Earth fighters, quite old Razor class ships, one Greshan ship, a Lox class, and two Sabb ships, MGP class."

"Never mind that! Do you have a track on that Raindancer?" Captain Van Pelt bellowed.

He brushed at his red beard, his bald spot glistening with sweat.

"Well…no, Captain," Janng admitted. "You told me to scan the-"

"Initiate a scan for jump trails!"

"But, Captain Van Pelt-"

"Do it!" he shouted. "Mr. Rol, are we at maximum defense?"

"Yess, Grekbil."

"Good! Helm, bring us about! Mr. Rol, prepare to engage the fighters!"

The *Corridor* veered about to face the pursuing fighters in the very moment each of those fighters broke into lightspeed and disappeared in a flash.

"What…" the captain muttered, staring at the empty screen.

"They've jumped to lightsspeed, Grekbil," Rol informed.

"I know that!" the captain yelled. "Mr. Janng, to be certain we were tracking them when they jumped! I want a direct-"

Janng swallowed.

"Sir, you had directed me to turn our sensors to searching jump trails…I tried to mention it but-"

The Captain ripped himself from his seat and stormed the Science station.

Throwing Mr. Janng from his chair, Captain Van Pelt began a rushed search for the jump trails. Of course, analyzing lightspeed engine exhalation particles and attempting to map them, for a start, was a difficult thing to do anyway. Then, with all the jump trails in the sector…

"Captain," the Communications Officer muttered. "The lead fighter pilot transmitted a message just before his jump. Audio only."

The captain turned about.

"And? What was it?" he barked.

"Have a blessed journey."

The captain shook with anger.

Gideon Ridge dropped into the pilot's seat. Grundy joined them and chose to watch the cockpit from the back, standing in the door. Winds was told to sit far away from any console and to keep his hands in his pockets, which he did, while Samara Garriton sat in the back.

Kelvan and Kreden returned and the group was all together.

The starlight passed by them in blinding flares and colors, their flight speed daunting. Gideon Ridge pointed at the starstream with a smile.

"Never had a slicker on board," Gideon said. "You helped out a lot, Wastasa, getting us back in the 'stream. We're grateful."

"I'm grateful," he said flatly. "Letting me see this first hand. I came from a very spiritual people but I'm ignorant of such things. I'm fascinated by what lies beyond this life, what the afterlife may be like."

Gideon chuckled, shaking his head.

Samara exploded.

"How dare you laugh at his people? His curiosity?"

Gideon cut her a slicing glance.

"Samara, do you remember being upset by the fact that I shot down all those people in that docking bay?"

"Yes," she responded curtly.

"You're doing it again."

Wastasa Winds chuckled then as Ridge continued.

"It's simple. You just jumped to the conclusion, at lightspeed, I might add, that I was laughing at Wastasa's beliefs or his people or his desire to understand. That wasn't what struck me funny."

"Oh? Feel free to clarify."

"Wastasa was elaborating on how he was fascinated by what the afterlife may be like. I was thinking if the afterlife even resembled wandering around, zombified for eternity, stealing spaceships, I'll just skip dying."

Wastasa Winds and Grundy both chuckled.

The com system buzzed before Garriton replied.

"Gideon, spatial transmission incoming," Kreden interrupted them.

"Open the channel."

"*Spoken Word*, this is David Rule. I've plotted an assist course for our trajectories so that we can accompany you and give you what aide you may need. The *Corridor* is not in pursuit; they were scanning wildly, one thing then another, then failed to follow into lightspeed. Either they were confused or they disliked the idea of facing the six of us."

"Six, David?" Gideon asked.

"Yes. Your ship and five of ours. I brought a band of Acolyte brothers and sisters along with me. My ship and four others. I'll transmit our call signs and digital identifications for you so your systems can automatically recognize us, should anything happen."

"Don't want any friendly fire," Gideon laughed.

"That would be a bad thing," David Rule chuckled over the com.

"Well, welcome to the run," Gideon Ridge said then closed his com.

"The Acolytes, eh?" Wastasa Winds wondered aloud. "I guess your Gospel smuggling is for real."

Gideon checked a sensor display, noting, "That it is."

"I feel bad," the lanky Native American said. "I always figured those were just some heroic rumors, you running around taking a stand for beliefs or your Faith. I thought you were really running contraband substances or weapons to a resistance here and an empire there."

"Most think the same thing," Samara Garriton mumbled.

"I get that a lot," Ridge laughed. "But you don't see me rolling in plat. I'm not in anything for the financial gain. I'm in what I do for God, and for the Peace souls can experience if they can just believe."

Garriton's admiration for him swelled inside her.

Everything about the USAP had tried to eradicate her admiration for individuality, for personal, private standards and sensibilities. Nothing for the individual. Everything for the masses. No standards, unless all could agree on them. No morals, unless they could be aligned with laws by which all could abide. All decided by a faceless entity ruling them.

It did not matter, however. He stirred something in her makeup, in her design, and it made her remember how important personal belief and independent thought really were.

"See that rock solid belief?" Winds asked Garriton. "That's what I want. Something tangible, something life changing. That's why I want to see the dead with my own eyes. I want to experience something... beyond."

"It's not a faith out there," she warned flatly. "It's darkness, thick and evil."

"Then I say let me see that. I just want to see something."

110

"Careful what ya wish for," Kelvan muttered.

The man on the tattered bridge of the Leviathan pulled himself up to his weak legs, his arms hanging from the command seat. Once in the seat, he listened to the silence of cold space and imagined the screams of the lost within the Reaches.

The man twisted to look at a panel nearby. To him, it lit up and displayed a number of jump trails heading for the Reaches and the 'roid shower still running along its edge. Through his eyes, sensors illuminated and readouts scrolled over the screens. Buttons lit and lights flashed, a background pinging ringing in the man's ears. From all of that, he saw a group of ships on the way toward his fleet of scrap.

He concentrated on one single starship…imagining it repowered, moving…

The *Vindicator,* floating derelict in the edge of the 'roid storm, shuddered. Then the Prime Reactor came online.

"Alright, Gideon, I'm detecting an ArcAngel class starship just inside the Reaches," Kelvan's voice rolled. "It's showing signs of power but it's still in enough of the asteroid shower to be masked by rayonnix particles. I'm not sure if-"

"I'm certain," Samara Garriton whispered. "I feel it."

"Well, well," Gideon Ridge said, "the moment of truth."

"Truth," Samara muttered.

"Are any other ships showing on the scopes?" Gideon Ridge asked.

"None show up," Kelvan Hotch answered.

"Not my favorite answer," the man sighed. A glance over his shoulder found Wastasa Winds, the slicker. "Wastasa, you want to do a little more helping?"

The other man nodded, stating, "I'm not going to sabotage my only ride."

"Get your hands out of your pockets and go have a talk with our shielding generator. You might be able to give us a little extra."

"He can't go alone," Samara warned, still not trusting the man.

"He's not," Ridge agreed, waving a hand at the back of the cockpit. "Grundy's going with him."

"Feel the warmth, the love," Winds chuckled.

"One wrong step and you'll feel something," Gideon laughed.

Grundy towered over Winds and leaned down into his face.

CHAPTER FIVE : *Last Glance*

Base Commander Walker Basnight strolled into the council meeting without a single hesitation. He felt he was ready enough for the holomeeting and very little would be surprising him. The truth was that he had some surprises for the council members.

When all the other holographic attendees were projected, they went through standard practices and meeting protocols then someone began the topic.

The only topic.

"We've heard that a ship in a fleet under one of your commodores, under one of your admirals, has seen and opened pursuit of your renegade captain," the Starstalker growled.

"Captain Van Pelt of the *Corridor* made contact and engaged in pursuit," Basnight said.

"Thiss Van Pelt; a good Unity captain?" the Vipon pushed.

"Yes, very loyal, very efficient. Decorated veteran."

"Under what Commodore? What division?" the Toran inquired.

Commander Basnight paused.

"Second Division," he said finally. "Under Commodore Wrigley Zeckinbridge."

Silence hung heavily in the chamber, much like a wet shroud.

"Is this going to be a problem?" the Toran asked.

The Octovoid squarbled loudly, fluidly, the bulbous head glowing white.

"No problem," Basnight declared defensively. "Captain Van Pelt is not as…emotional. A no-nonsense officer."

There was awkward silence. Then there was more questioned concern. It did give way to further discussion, however.

"Under what admiral?" the Chabron asked.

"Admiral Meshach Washington, overseer of our fourth fleet."

Positive comments. Repeated reports of up and coming greatness. Many voiced eventual satisfaction.

"Have you deployed aide to the *Corridor*? I would think that perhaps more ships together would strengthen the spines of our captains against Garriton's rebellion."

"She's not leading a revolt," Basnight snapped.

"Nor should any suggest she is," the Greylik agreed. "She has gone through a lot. A great deal of latitude should be allowed here."

"Please," the Toran pressed. "Have you deployed more help?"

"As a matter of fact, I pulled a ship out of retrofit myself and ordered it to the Reaches to assist. I didn't want to pull a ship with active duties into this, so the newly redesigned *Bloodwind* will be on its way, pending its final inspection."

"Good. Who is your lead on that?" the Starstalker asked directly.

"Captain Joshua Brent. You'll like him; he has only recently been promoted and has not had training under Commodore Zeckinbridge. In fact, they've never even met."

Again, after a positive reception, satisfaction was voiced, and so the council meeting continued. Basnight barely listened. He had been prepped with answers, a first in his time in the big chair.

He was happy with his plan to use the newly outfitted retroship and the new, unannounced captain and he was happy to be doing it without Zeckinbridge's knowledge. Not even Admiral Washington knew to what fleet the ship would be assigned, nor did he know to what division. There was no way the Commodore knew.

He smiled. Between the *Corridor*, the *Bloodwind* and his personal hiring of Cheyenne Winds, he felt he would bring Captain Garriton home alive...and save his own skin.

He touched his earpiece.

"Baron, set a reminder for me. I want to go aboard the *Bloodwind* before they embark."

"I don't understand the orders for communiqué blackout," young Captain Brent said.

He followed close on Commodore Zeckinbridge's heels as she moved from one station to another, to another.

Wrigley Zeckinbridge pulled her soft, fine brown hair back from her face and tucked it behind her ears. She leaned over the helm.

"Are there any fluctuations in the lightspeed, Mr. Retaw?" she asked the Pilot.

The Greylik male, as young as the captain, or younger, cleared his throat. He was one of twenty officers the commodore had hand picked from recent cadets and promoted to take substitute positions on the newly rejuvenated ship. There were approximately another thirty that had helped with the retrofit and had never left the ship, its veterans.

"No, ma'am. All instrumentation indicates a smooth jump."

Zeckinbridge patted the pink hued man on his shoulder.

"Good work."

"Commodore," the captain started again.

"Hold that thought, Captain," Wrigley Zeckinbridge said.

She turned to the Navigator, a woman she had also placed on duty.

Reje Chu, the former Navigator of the *Vindicator*, nodded.

"Course locked, ma'am."

The commodore smiled. She then met the eyes of Communications Officer Niles Respra, who was also formerly of Samara Garriton's command. He nodded quietly. The commodore then found the eyes of Science Officer Wimbel Boatwright. He did not even nod; just his eyes told her he was alert and prepared.

"I don't mean any disrespect," the captain continued. "I simply haven't been briefed-"

Zeckinbridge spun about and put her hands on his broad shoulders.

"That, Captain Brent, is why we have a briefing room."

She wandered away from him with a gesture for him to join her.

Security Officer Mack Penrose, standing at the rear of the bridge by the gravlift, still had his left arm and shoulder in bandages. One eye watched the bridge from under a metal eye patch with a red lens. Diffuser bands coiled around his uninjured forearm and he rested his good hand on his sidearm, determined not be overrun again the way he had been on the *Vindicator*. He would be ready, no matter what.

Through a side door on the bridge, Captain Brent pursued his Commodore. The briefing room was a chamber with a single desk at one end, a sort of captain's planning room. In the center of the room was a massive round table with seats for each bridge officer and visitors. A console lit the wall near the table for animating discussions and research.

The commodore took the captain's seat, the one with the highest back, at the table. Brent was left to choose at random.

"Captain, I realize you don't know me, so let's get this out of the way. I'm not a stickler for rank and I don't have power lust. While we're on this mission, call me Wrigley, unless we're in combat or some official act. Addressing everyone by rank in those moments keeps us alert."

Joshua Brent agreed wholeheartedly, though he was surprised by her gentle attitude. She had seemed harsher when she had taken his bridge.

"I've heard some commodores and admirals are personable. I'm glad to know I'm in your division," he said.

She smiled a warm, embracing smile.

"Good. And I'm glad to have you. So, like I said, in here we can be relaxed. Call me Wrigley and I'll call you Joshua."

"Josh, if you like," he added.

"Josh, good. Now, Josh, you had some questions about your orders, your briefing. I'd like to help if I can, maybe help clear some things up."

"Yes, ma'am. I actually got orders to report to the *Bloodwind*, to start my captain's promotion early because of an emergency situation. Base Commander Basnight personally chose me for it and I'm honored…but he never briefed me. I reported for duty and started what he had given me, the launch prep instructions and so on, and he told me what I'd be doing would be explained just before launch. He never got back to me and I've simply been on deck, waiting."

His brown, buzz cut hair stood at attention just the way he sat. Keen blue eyes watched her for answers nonverbal, unmentioned.

"Clearly," she agreed, satisfied with his words.

The truth was that she had hoped he had been left in the dark until the last moment, just the way he had been, so that she would be free to mold his understanding of everything from the beginning. It was deceptive, even dishonest…but necessary, in her mind.

"Commander Basnight left the last of the briefing up to me, as he knew I would be on board with you, overseeing things."

Captain Joshua Brent eyed her curiously.

"Your mission involves defending and rescuing another captain in our division and our fleet. Her ship was lost out near the Reaches and she went back to see what could be recovered. Unity is afraid that, with the rate of criminals getting into scrap collection, she might encounter trouble. In fact, they sent her incognito in hopes of luring some of the darker scavengers out into the light. We're to bring justice to the area."

Zeckinbridge was counting on Unity's hush orders. Most officers in the Earth Starmada would be unaware of the *Vindicator's* fate. Most would know little of the struggle Samara Garriton faced. The rest would be under strict silence orders.

She was also counting on the false orders she had passed along; the digifile orders, ones she forged, that put her in clear control and also ordered a communications blackout, were invaluable.

Joshua Brent was not dense, however. He was new but he was not dull. The top of his class, he was a keen one.

"I can understand what you're saying," he allowed. "I just can't seem to fit it with standard operating procedures. Running communication blackout is strictly prohibited unless specifically ordered-"

She waved the digifile with the mission orders.

"I understand that, ma'am," he allowed, adding a sigh, "but we also left behind the entire bridge crew, all senior officers previously assigned to the bridge, without even-"

"Josh, are you having a hard time grasping secrecy? I mentioned this was a secret mission, didn't I?" she asked.

"Yes, or course. Multiple times. But, to leave our entire crew-"

She waved the digifile about again.

"I'm new, ma'am. I was never trained to take off out of docking without a prelaunch test, a hail to the spaceport, the bridge crew-"

She dropped the digifile onto the table. He jumped, startled.

"Josh, it's this simple. How many commands have you maintained?"

"Uh, well, ma'am," he stuttered.

"How many starships have you captained?"

"None, ma'am. I mean one. This one."

"And, in your other positions," she started, grabbing a different digifile from two seats away, "let's see, as a cadet, as an Echo Soldier, as a Weapons Officer-"

"I'm raw for command, I get it," he nodded, finally beginning to be rubbed the wrong way. "I was placed here as an emergency captain for a chance to prove myself, clearly not because of my experience. Still, I-"

"Josh, your eye for detail and regulations do you credit. You were a very effective Echo Unit Leader. You were a decorated Security grunt once you were assigned to a ship. You quickly made Security Officer then you were decorated as one of the youngest ever Chief Security Officers. You took a Weapons Officer rank at the same time you made First Officer on board the *Lewistowe*. You're a credit to your uniform. But, Josh, you simply haven't held a lot of command. You have to learn to trust your superiors."

"Oh, I do, ma'am. I wasn't suggesting you were out of order."

"No?"

He stalled completely, his mouth open without any sound.

"You want to know it all. You want to be in on all the calls, all the plans, all the information. Sometimes, though, you just aren't. As frustrating as it is, even when you're a captain, you still have a command structure and it can just sweep you up without explanation. It's the same as if you were a Security Officer being told to watch a door. You guard the door; you aren't always told why."

He sighed again, agreeing with, "I suppose so, ma'am."

"Trust me," she ordered flatly.

"Yes, ma'am."

"Now, our crew is your new mission."

"Ma'am?"

"I want you to move about the ship and boost our crew's morale. Seeing their captain among them will inspire them and also build respect and admiration for you. That's what you'll do until we get to the Reaches. Just remember, they don't need to know all the details of the mission."

"I doubt there's any danger of that," he said and rose from the table.

"Why is that, Josh?"

"Because I barely know anything, Wrigley, and I was just briefed." He folded his arms over his chest. "Permission to go about the crew?"

"Granted."

Oh, yes, she thought to herself. *He is a keen one.*

She leaned back in the big chair. It was a good thing he had not been the one tasked with keeping the Bloodwind Gambit, as Basnight was calling the situation, a secret. If so, she may have never discovered it. She would have been unable to hijack it. No, she was lucky that Basnight's personal attache, Staff Commander Silas Baron, had been in charge of the operation secrecy.

That man's loose lips are certainly going to sink ships, she thought.

The banging in the center engine would not stop. The noise in the port engine had finally ceased but the center was not giving up the pounding rhythm. With each percussive slam, the fuselage shuddered and the mismatched seats in the cobbled cockpit rattled.

"We're going to die."

Pap turned to his brother, Sundar Ridge.

"What?" Sun continued. "We are. We're going to die in some Hunon belly ship-"

"Stop," Sylver growled. "Just cut it out."

Sylver Ridge tightened the straps in his seat. It was a creaking, gray synthetic seat from the cargo bay of a Unity ship long decommissioned. Sun Ridge eyeballed him from the torn, Carda hide seat beside him, one of three in the noisy cockpit. Gill Bardoff sat in the front seat, a salvaged captain's seat from a Starstalker vessel, its carved claws and fangs along the wooden framework still intact. He was the tip of the triangle, the Ridge brothers forming the base behind him.

The Hunon Dinsor Class freighter was one of the last of its kind. It was quite possibly the last one, as Bardoff often bragged. The Hunon people had long abandoned the Dinsor Class and had scrapped most of them for parts.

Bardoff talked about it again, over the roar of the slamming engine.

"You ain't never seen the lightstream 'til you've seen it through the viewports of a Dinsor Class," he shouted back to the brothers.

"Did he say this was a dinosaur class?" Sun asked his brother slyly.

Sylver Ridge ignored him.

"I believe this little lady is the very last of them," Bardoff announced proudly. "Hunon policies ruled them too old and outdated to keep in production then started smashing and stripping the remaining ones. I bought this one and saved her from the pile."

"Who's going to save us from her?" Sun asked under his breath.

Outside the cockpit, the starlight, bright lines and swirls of light blurred by the nearly incomprehensible speed of the craft, flowed by the viewports like glowing liquids. Sylver Ridge knew the old ship was a bit rickety but there was no doubt it was fast.

Sun Ridge did not care. He hated the old bucket.

The fuselage, in honesty, resembled a massive bucket, open mouth up. Three block formations were mounted at the rear, circular rim of the 'bucket'. One was a port engine and engine room, one was a starboard engine and engine room, and the center was a central engine, engine room, corridor nexus to connect all the engine rooms and a three seat cockpit set above that engine room. Then, below the port and starboard engine blocks, a hydraulics room had been built onto each side, with retractable scavenging claws, cutters and the like. They were perfect for dragging trash and treasure into the 'bucket' compartment.

"Had some holes in my cargo bay," Bardoff shouted over the banging rhythm. "Found some of those great big gibseed bins on Pizer Moa they were dismantling. Made a good trade and got enough curved alloys to repair them all. All you got to do out here is keep your eyes and your mind open. Always find what you need. Maybe not everything you want but everything you need."

Sylver smiled and shouted, "That's why your underbelly has 'Gib Plant Seed Processing' painted across that flat green, patched panel."

"Keeps me humble," Gill Bardoff replied loudly. "I like to remember my blessings and where I found them."

Sundar Ridge looked at the panel beside him. He ignored the very first, faint wisps that rose from the circuitry. He had initially thought it a trick of his eyes. It was when the wisps grew slightly and developed that telltale smell of burning wiring that he knew there was a real problem.

"Gill, this thing's on fire!" he shouted, snatching at his seat harness. It was stuck. "Gill! Fire! Get me out of this chair!"

"What? Fire?" Bardoff asked, looking over his shoulder.

Sylver had both hands on his brother's harness, pulling to no avail.

"That ain't no fire," Bardoff chuckled then. He stepped back to the panel, smacked it several times and watched white hot sparks cascade from the underside to the deck plating. Content, he went back to his seat.

To the Ridge brothers' amazement, the smoke stopped. The banging in the central engine suddenly stopped, too. Then the ship surged and its lightspeed doubled in magnitude.

The brothers stared at Bardoff, who grinned back at them over his shoulder.

"That's just how I know the central engine has warmed up. Now you boys get to see speed."

The brothers looked at each other. Sylver began to pray.

"Captain Garriton, I know having a slicker aboard makes you unhappy," Wastasa Winds muttered from his seat. "I know you think of me as a 'bad guy', since I was hired to come get you, but-"

"You're a mercenary, Winds. You're a lackey for the highest bidder, working as a bounty hunter. The fact that you're a slicker is the least of it," Samara Garriton said in a blunt, rash exhale.

"Ouch," he said with a chuckle. "I'm glad we worked that all out."

"She don't play," Kreden noted, eyebrows raised.

"And don't flirt with her," Kelvan added. "Lady has venter skills."

Samara Garriton watched the lightstream flow by the cockpit viewports. How much longer would they be in lightspeed? Where had Gideon Ridge gone with Grundy? How much longer would she be entertaining a slicker? He had finished his task far too quickly. When he came back with Grundy the big Rothidai had left again with Ridge.

She suddenly frowned as her mind wandered. What in the world did slicker even mean?

"Winds, what does your title even mean? Where did 'slicker' come from for a freelance technoid?"

"Unity brats. History don't mean a thing to the Unity Council, does it? They spend so much time trying to change it and spin it they're actively forgetting it. What's the old adage? 'Tell a lie often enough-"

"So, history lessons aside, where does it come from?"

"I know this one," Kelvan rumbled lowly.

"Shut up and let the man drop some knowledge," Kreden said.

"I ain't stoppin' him!" Kelvan snapped.

"Captain," Wastasa Winds said with a deep inhale, "the term was taken from a product used a long, long time ago. Back in the early days of computer cabling on Earth, back when technicians and electricians ran wire through conduit pipes by hand, they used a product called 'slick'. It was a slippery oil, or gel, or watery lubricant that caused wiring to slip and slide easier through the conduits."

She waited, genuinely curious.

"Well, nowadays, beings with technological specialties, technoids, as you called us, took a title from the word. We're the ones who can get into things that can't be opened, or can find information hidden so well it supposedly can't be found, technologically. In the old days they called skills like that 'hacking' and the perpetrators were called 'hackers'. But most of us in this age are more hands on and hardware proficient, so we took a new name. We can slide in and slip out, ease away with what we wanted and be gone. So, like the old gels, we're slickers."

"That's it?" she asked. "Impressive, I suppose."

"Some of them are," Gideon Ridge said, coming back into the cockpit with Grundy. "Wastasa is. We've been running through similar circles for ages. His reputation is galactic."

Ridge sat back in the pilot's seat and Grundy leaned against the wall by the rear entrance.

"No more than yours, Ridge," Winds said. "Nobody moves materials the way you do. The *Spoken Word* may as well be a ghost, according to some sectors. In others…well, it's a vengeful angel."

"People, we're ready to drop from lightspeed," Ridge said, working his controls. He triggered his constant communications lever. "Acolyte squadron, we're going sublight in three." Then he turned back to the cabin. "Wastasa, I know you went back and did a little prep upgrade to the shielding but, if things go sideways…"

"I'll be ready," Winds assured, pulling on his gloves.

One second passed. Two passed. Three.

The lightstream disappeared abruptly and the stars were separate again. Blocking most of them from view was the massive asteroid field near which Samara Garriton had lost her ship, the *Vindicator*.

Drifting, listing to one side, that ship waited for them. Some systems were still active, according to the informative Hotch brothers.

Samara Garriton gasped and rose from her chair.

"When we were making our escape run," she muttered, "and I took a last glance through the rear viewports at her…her systems were dead."

"All of them?" Wastasa Winds asked.

She just nodded.

"Well, somebody turned the porch light back on," Gideon noted.

The Sunbrowser was at full capacity and never closed. The most prominent, sleazy dive on Maximilian Station, it hosted most any and all criminal activity.

Laws, after all, in far too many systems, rarely merited right or wrong. Instead, more were concerned with accepted or not accepted and, even more often, profitable or not profitable. That is how a place of outlaws was often a haven for the moral as well as the immoral. It simply depended on the system in which one was declared a criminal whether the criminal was good or bad.

On Maximilian Station, no outside law held jurisdiction; in the Sunbrowser, everyone was guilty but no one was wanted. And, like outside governments, the station had its own security force and it concerned itself with the good of the station...only.

One of seven Starstalkers, new customers with laps already inhabited by waitstaff and dancers, left the table and headed off to relieve himself. The remaining six ordered more Pagrot to go around the table. There had been a lot of consumption since their arrival and the male and female dancers loved the tips.

A Hunon glanced over his shoulder at the band of wild ones, half morphed into their most felinious form. He swallowed down some of his drink, put it back on the bar then looked to the far back corner of the place.

At a table there, deep in shadow, an Echo Unit of five Unity soldiers from the *Corridor* watched him.

He nodded. One of them nodded.

The Hunon then turned his gaze to the far side of the bar. He met the eyes of a Vipon, nodded and gestured at the Starstalkers with his large head. The Vipon nodded and got up from the bar, adjusted his sidearm holster and dropped the hood from his head. He moved immediately for the Starstalker table.

His approach was casual, relaxed and confident...Vipon.

"Greetingss, 'sstalkerss," he addressed with a hiss, propping on the back of the vacated chair. Sharply slit eyes snapped from one to another, watching.

"We got enough dancers, Slinky," one of the females growled, her eyes challenging.

Her raven black hair fell long about her shoulders. In her semi-morphed form, it had encroached upon her face, covering more of her forehead, the bridge of her nose, and giving her sideburns. When she bit her lip, the Vipon saw her fangs.

"You sseek more than dancsers, if I undersstand correctly," he countered.

"What are you offering?" a big male asked, his form menacing.

His face was furred over completely, masking him with the red hair that was on his head. His fangs protruded from his mouth even with it closed. A Greylik snuggled with him, drinking more Pagrot.

"I'm after a woman, a renegade Unity captain. Sshe's on the run from their Sstarmada and I want her bounty."

"We don't know her, we don't care to know her and we aren't interested in your bounty," a brown haired female said flatly.

"We don't have her and we don't have information on her," a slender, blonde male added. "Whatever you may think you have for us, we don't have anything for you."

The Vipon leaned over toward the table.

"Sshe's traveling with a freighter pilot. A ssmuggler."

"Not shocking," the red male shrugged at him. "Lots of smugglers move sentient cargo."

The Vipon closed his eyes, licked over his lips then snapped his eyes open.

"You made inquiriess about the ssame ssmuggler," he said, nodding. "I thought perhapss we were after the ssame sship. The *Sspoken Word*."

All of the fleshhunters shoved their dancers from their laps to the floor. The black haired female and the red haired male stood.

The dancers made themselves scarce. With that motion, many customers moved away from the area, taking cover, while many got into positions to watch, not wanting to miss anything. The bartender disappeared behind the bar.

The moment was electric. The Vipon would have been sweating had he genetically been able…and had he been anyone else.

"The next words out of your mouth, reptile, could save your unnatural life," the female growled. Her eyes narrowed fiercely. "What do you know of Gideon Ridge? Where is he?"

"Remain calm, 'sstalkerss," the Vipon hissed. "I am not the enemy. In fact, we are default alliess. We are after the ssame sship'ss bountiess."

The male, his snarl a smile, growled, "I don't see any reason to share either ship, occupants or bounties. So…where is Ridge?"

"You are giving me very little insscentive to tell you," the Vipon sneered. "I would think it would benefit uss all, including Wasstassa Windss, to work together."

"What about Winds?" the female hissed. "He owes us money!"

"He gathered uss all to purssue the captain in quesstion. We're all... hunterss...in one form or another."

"Who is all?" the big male asked, looking about. He froze when he looked to the rear of the chamber.

The Echo Unit had deployed, each soldier occupying a tactical position behind cover and aiming weapons. One of them had the absent Starstalker, unconscious, in pulsar cording with a plasma rifle to his head. The area had been evacuated by bystanders and waitresses alike.

The big Starstalker's face caused the others to follow his gaze. Every one of them still sitting jumped to their feet, pulling free their weapons.

The black haired, black eyed female wrenched her side arm free and leveled it on the Vipon. From the bar, however, a brilliant flash of orange light and a deep cough belched from a Hunon particle rifle. The female Starstalker went down onto her back, a gaping hole burned through her chest. The Vipon's Hunon partner braced over the bar, weapon smoking.

The other fleshhunters roared, some pointing weapons at the Echo Unit, some at the Vipon and some at the Hunon. The red haired male, however, called them down. He knew how few of them would survive in that predicament. Seven positions held weapons trained on them and there were only five catamorphs with arms.

He said something in a low mewling only his people understood, his eyes all rage and patient hatred for their Vipon greeter.

"Let'ss sstart again," the Vipon hissed. "My Hunon friend and I work for Wasstassa Windss. We are after the Unity captain your target iss carrying about sspacse. We work with Unity forcsess. That Echo Unit allied itsself to uss. You may do the ssame...or the remainder of your people can be liquidated."

Several of the fleshhunters roared. The big red male put up one hand, causing silence to fall again.

"She was my brother's mate," he growled viciously. "Before we can go forward-"

There was a brief, subdued flare of purple light between the Vipon and the fleshhunters. No one saw any of them move, not until the fleshhunters twitched backward in response. However, the Hunon spun about and jerked backward from the bar. His little form slammed into the floor, wisps of purple vapor rising from his large head.

Similar wisps drifted up from the Vipon's holster.

"You..." the big Starstalker muttered.

The crowd in the establishment went wild with applause. The Vipon had drawn his silenced side arm, aimed it to his left and shot the Hunon, his own partner, in the head. Then he had holstered his weapon.

And he did it all without anyone actually seeing it. His speed was unimaginable...and legendary.

"That's Rala Kess," someone muttered excitedly in the crowd.

"Has to be," another said.

"No one fasster," a female Vipon said.

"I know of your cultural requirementss," the Vipon said to the catamorphs. "You needed the female'ss killer eliminated and the body given to your pack. There he iss. I apologizse for hiss thoughtlesss actionss."

The Starstalker pack stood, mouths agape. The red leader was so shocked that his morphed form faded to near human appearance again.

"I know you," he told the Vipon. "You're...Rala Kess..."

The Echo Unit closed on the group, leaving cover. They let their captive go as the onlookers applauded and cheered, as if all had been a drama enacted just for them. Someone in the crowd called Kess an assassin. Another referred to him as a mercenary, while someone corrected them and called him a bounty hunter. All of it was true. It was also kept quiet; no one wanted the Vipon angry.

"How do we go from here?" Kess asked the red haired Starstalker.

"We will deal with the dead Hunon," he answered. He watched Kess carefully with his green eyes. "As for you and the Unity soldiers, we can work together. You get the Unity woman. We keep Gideon Ridge."

The Vipon looked to the Echo Unit Leader. That man nodded.

"Accsseptible," the Vipon hissed. "In the meantime, we have a plan to capture thesse fugitivess and the ssship. They will undoubtedly land here when they come back out of the Reachess..."

Gideon Ridge glanced at his call sign scopes as he slid his headset over his long hair. He adjusted his audio output swingarm, bringing it close to his mouth.

"Everyone kill your engines. Let's drift for a moment. Set your scans to sweep that ship. David, I'm going to call out your ship names. Answer and make sure I'm right and you can all hear me."

"Agreed," Rule's voice came over the headset and the ship's com.

"Confirm, *Razorhawk*," Gideon began.

"Confirmed," David Rule said.

"Confirm, *Razorwing*."

"Confirmed," said the pilot of the other Razor class Earth fighter, her voice young.

"Confirm, *Tikrek*," Ridge continued.

"Confirmed," the pilot of the Greshan ship, a Lox class spacefighter, answered.

"Confirm, *Gaze*," Gideon Ridge said and motioned Samara Garriton forward.

"Confirmed," the pilot of the first MGP class Sabb fighter transmitted.

Gideon pointed at the listing *Vindicator*, Garriton at his elbow.

"That's her, then?"

She nodded to his question, whispering, "Yes…my *Vindicator*."

Gideon Ridge continued, "Confirm, *Raine*."

"Confirmed," the lady pilot's voice called eagerly.

"Okay, Temple Squadron," Ridge sighed hesitantly. "The good captain tells me the docking bays were destroyed. We aren't going to have a standard boarding location, so I'll have to cut a hatch. Since the rest of you can't dock, stay on alert for us and keep a good watch."

Four replies vocalized 'confirmed' almost immediately and four of the fighters made an approach on the derelict ghost ship. One of the replies was an exception.

"*Word*, this is the *Tikrek*. Our Greshan fighter is capable of making its own door, too. We can accompany you on board."

"Confirmed, *Tikrek*. Awaiting reconnaissance."

Ridge checked all of his available readouts. He queried Kelvan and Kreden Hotch about what could be found with sensors and got a lot of answers, none of which included life signs.

"I'm seeing some power," Gideon said into his headset again, "including that Unity standard Prime Reactor. It looks like some life support is engaged, the emergency bulwark door system was activated and shielding is holding the life support inside, despite the massive hull breaches. However, I see no life signs, I repeat, no life signs. Does anyone else have anything?"

The four fighters circled the starship for a moment.

"That's a negative, *Word*." David Rule's voice was distinctive. "All the same."

"Samara, this is where it gets serious," Ridge said to the cockpit. "I can't find any life signs. I'm sorry. Do you still want to breach it?"

"What did you mean by 'cut a hatch' in it?" Garriton asked. "How do we board?"

"You forget he's a smuggler?" Winds asked. "Man's got tricks for getting in and out."

"I put our belly close to that ship's hull; I deploy magnetic tethers then wind them until we're tight, hull to hull. On our belly, I have a port burner. That's-"

"A piracy tool," she interrupted. "The port opens on our side, then a tube channel extends from there to the other ship's hull and it burns a port into that hull for us to breach. That's illegal in every single system I know unless you have a license to operate a sanctioned emergency craft."

"Exactly," Ridge answered, undaunted. "Pirate, remember?"

"I should have…" Garriton started, rolling her eyes. However, staring at the listing ship, she said, "I want to go aboard. I have to."

"Have to what?" Ridge asked.

"Know."

Gideon Ridge gestured at Winds and said, "Wastasa, it looks like we were clear when we arrived. No need for you to sit here on shield duty. You still want to go aboard with us?"

Winds nodded.

"Okay. Grundy, I want you to pilot. You be ready for anything. You and Drea keep a good watch. The moment something gets questionable, you prep our escape. If we aren't back here when you need to pull away to make a clean run back for Maximilian Station, you leave us. I mean it."

"No, Gideon. I won't abandon-"

"There's no need for all of us to die out here if something goes wrong, you hear me?" Gideon pressed. "Someone has to make it back to tell Pap what happened. Please."

Grundy snorted, stroked one of his horns and growled, "We'll be ready to go when it's time."

"Samara, where do you want to breach?" Gideon asked.

"Central main fuselage just behind the lines that become the nose. That chamber will have access to two levels below. My bridge."

"That precise enough?" Gideon Ridge asked Kelvan Hotch.

"You get Grundy to lock us on and me 'n' Kreden will cut 'n' gut."

"*Tikrek*, we're going in," Ridge said into his headset. "The rest of Temple Squadron, keep your communications on blackout. All generalized hails should be blocked out. Whatever is behind all this uses a corrupting tone pulse to override ship control. Use only short range, direct communiqués with team encryption. Confirmed?"

Again they confirmed.

"Here we go then."

"Yes," Samara Garriton whispered. "Here we go."

Base Commander Walker Basnight trembled where he stood, his hands shaking. His lip twitched. His eyes opened wide in unbelief but his mind was keen. He knew he probably should have seen it coming.

Admiral Meshach Washington stood at attention beside him. Both men stared through the docking bay's shielding, inside the spaceport. The docking bay, registered to a starship called the *Bloodwind*, stood quiet and somber...and empty. It lay open to space.

"Sir?" Admiral Washington said quietly.

"A moment," Basnight warned, never turning to the other man.

Basnight had called the admiral to the bay so he could introduce him to Captain Brent. He had planned to have Washington accompany Brent, give him the benefit of great years of experience. He was going to brief them personally, confidentially, then send them to the Reaches and pick up Captain Samara Garriton.

When Basnight had arrived, he found the bay of their newly refashioned *Bloodwind* empty. Bay codes, records and permissions all listed Wrigley Zeckinbridge as responsible. The good commodore, the very one he had intended to keep at a distance from his secret motives, had absconded with his ship.

Admiral Washington had found him cursing the empty bay.

A war waged inside Basnight. He had believed so long and so strongly in the United Starmada of Allied Planets that he held fierce loyalty to it. Zeckinbridge had been right, however, in that something had to be done to curb their self-appointed omnipotence. They had not always been so tyrannical...but the changes could not be overlooked.

He had taken measures into his own hands, sending his own bounty hunter after the captain most of Unity wanted silenced. Permanently. He had tried to save her. Then, having second thoughts about the wicked woman he had hired, he had planned to send his best admiral out with a green, malleable crew in a newly retrofitted starship.

But the bay was empty. Empty.

"Empty," he muttered.

"Sir?" the admiral asked again.

"Admiral Washington," Basnight finally sighed, "I want you to recall every ship you have in the Second Division of your fleet."

"Base Commander, are you serious? Their patrol routes were already stretched, sir. Between the loss of the *Vindicator*, the Prime Reactor failure in the *Wovenweb* and the retrofit being done to the *Bloodwind,* there were no ships to help with route patrol. We're trying to patrol the major systems we don't even control, looking for Captain Garriton. Every division of every fleet has been pulled thin."

Basnight was literally shaking when he muttered, "Admiral Washington."

"Sir?"

"I want you to recall your entire Second Division."

"But, sir, why-"

"Because they have to go out and catch the other Second Division ship, the *Bloodwind*! They have to go chase down their sister ship! They have to go catch their own commodore, Wrigley Zeckinbridge, who stole a ship to go chase down their sister captain, Samara Garriton! Now call them back!" he erupted wildly, spittle flying from his mouth. "I don't want any other Base Ports getting in on this! Earth can take care of her own! And I want to be able to say my admirals police their own fleets! So, you are going to be in charge and on board a Second Division ship as you bring control back to that division! Is this clear?"

"Yes, sir!" the young admiral snapped to attention, a salute thrown up immediately.

"You'll take the division to Maximilian Station, meet with the *Corridor,* continue the pursuit they began and bring my people and my ship back!"

"Sir?" a voice called behind the two men.

"What?" Basnight roared, spinning around.

"We can't locate Commodore Zeckinbridge and the *Bloodwind* is in full communications blackout," Staff Commander Baron said.

"I know that!" Basnight exploded. "Find them anyway! Now!"

"Commander," Admiral Washington began again.

"Go! Recall the division!" Basnight screamed.

Captain Samara Garriton crept along an empty corridor, Gideon Ridge at her back. She filled the hallway with light from her venter's underscope. The darkness was thick and almost tangible, clinging to them, so it seemed. Garriton had never imagined the ship she had captained so quiet or empty...of course, she had yet to see that it was truly empty. It was unnerving for her but Samara Garriton was nothing if not bold. She swallowed down her nerves and pushed into the darkness.

The goal was to take one of the vertical gangways, the hidden passages that allowed movement inside bulkheads to upper or lower decks, down two levels. That would take them to the bridge.

At the moment, Gideon Ridge was a bit concerned by the emptiness.

Wastasa Winds lit a section, his own floodlight emitting its wide, bluish beam. His left hand dangled by the sidearm on his leg.

"Pay attention to the noises on the ship...if it ever makes any."

He had already shared that the quiet was odd. A ship only recently repowering should have made random sounds intermittently and some steady sounds, as well.

"We need to pay attention to everything," Gideon Ridge reminded. He tapped the face mask on his belt and gestured at theirs. "If life support or environmental controls drop out, we'll have to really hustle to get out of here alive. We can breathe with the rebreathers but it'll be short lived once the ship loses pressure."

Alive. The word haunted Garriton. Had any of her crew stayed alive?

Gideon kept a glance ready for casting over his shoulder. He looked back often. Ahead of him, however, he lit the way with the glow of an open, bracer charged glove.

Behind them walked the pilot of the Greshan starfighter, the Acolyte, Jon Kett. His white cloak and hood almost glowed over the wine red cassock. His arms crossed at his midsection so that he could walk with his hands hidden in the opposite arms' billowy sleeves.

"Don't worry about our rear flank," Jon Kett stated flatly as they rounded a first bend in the long hallway. "I will secure it to my last breath. Hopefully, though, it will not come to that," he chuckled, a grin wide on his face.

Garriton and Winds ignored him, obsessed with the ship and the information hidden within it. Ridge glanced back at him with a grin of his own, however.

"Amen," he said.

Garriton forged ahead with undaunted drive, her lighted scope and her venter trained on the open, black corridor. She cared nothing, or thought nothing, for what had been behind.

Wastasa Winds nervously tapped the handle of the borrowed weapon, a neuropulsar, provided by Dalindrea Ridge. In the other hand, his floodlight bathed the forward and the rear flanks in turns. He made a remark about wanting to see what would be coming...from wherever.

It seemed to the naked eye that the Acolyte had no light but that was because the Acolyte did not have a naked eye. Like most of the Church warriors, he wore eye lenses, invisible to others. They were called spectographic eyelets.

The microtranslation lenses did a number of things but, perhaps most importantly, they altered molecularly according to ambient light. They would shift their makeup to filter light, no matter how bright or dim, for maximum vision.

They took their name from the fact that they transmitted information to a central computer in the Acolytes' gauntlets and translated written languages for the Acolyte, then transmitted it back to the lenses, all almost instantly. Acolytes could look at an unknown language or dialect and immediately it would translate for them before their very eyes.

Garriton shuddered as she rounded a new corner in the corridor. She knew the gangway was in reasonable range, well before a third turn in the hall, but her limited vision of what lay ahead made her shake. Her stomach twisted.

"Careful," she ordered the others, slowing. She turned her face to the rear. "We're almost-"

A long scrubbing, followed by multiple scraping sounds, echoed down the corridor from behind them. She froze in place, stopping the others in stone.

Jon Kett moved first. Before anyone spoke, he pulled his hands from within his loose cassock sleeves. In each hand was a forearm length shaft of bright silver that slid out of his high tech gauntlets.

Wastasa Winds noted the gauntlets and wondered if they had inspired Gideon Ridge to design pulsar bracers for himself but he would not ask about that. Not in that moment. The truth was close at hand; he refocused on the ship.

The noises continued, coming closer, no more quickly and no slower. They sounded frighteningly close and resembled the dragging of a limb on the decking.

"Come on, we're not very far," Samara Garriton decided.

She spun about to lead the way.

Standing before her, glowing in the underscope, an Echo Soldier with *Vindicator* shoulder identification stared with empty eye sockets.

Garriton howled and stepped back, her venter burning the dead man down to the deck.

Four more rounded the corner in a staggering stupor, mouths agape and silent, eyes missing and dark. Gray skinned and somewhat gangly in motion, they resembled scarecrows gone evil.

Gideon Ridge grabbed Garriton and jerked her away from them. He squeezed his hand closed several times and the bracer fired Arclight each time. The neuropulse energies spun the dead about to violently shake and twitch, then drop unforgivingly to the floor, broken.

Garriton vented another one of them multiple times.

"Stop!" Winds shouted, rushing toward the last dead walker. "Talk to us! Tell us where you think you are! What happened to you?"

Gideon snatched him back just as the dead man reached for him.

Samara Garriton shouted at the walker as she burned it down with her venter. There were tears in her eyes.

"You aren't part of my crew!" she shouted at it. "You're dead! You're not here!"

She slipped ahead, rounding a corner. Ridge chased her reflexively, unaware of the new arrivals.

Five more of the undead, two dragging twisted legs and each wearing the ship's uniforms, approached from behind. They groped from the shadows with outstretched, crooked arms.

"In the name of Christ," Jon Kett growled, "back into the shadow with all of you!"

Kett triggered his staves with the thumb pressed, DNA imprint sensors. The staves doubled in length and suddenly arced electricity, white hot, around the entire upper shaft. Then Kett leaped into the fray, staves employed.

Further up the corridor, around the corner, the sounds of energy weapons sang a morbid, fast paced song. Samara Garriton sang along with the chorus, screaming at the walkers while she vented them.

Gideon Ridge blasted them down with a two handed conducting of the violent orchestra, one hand unloading energy on them and the other lighting the hall. There were plenty of targets for both of them; the hall was full.

"Binditrap!" he shouted at Garriton. "I knew it! Smelled like a binditrap from a sector away!"

Watching what was happening unnerved Garriton somewhat. Between the red flashes of her venter, the bluish white flashes of Ridge's bracers and the soft glow of her underscope, the look of the scene was that of a nightmare. The dead, up and moving about, crowding down a hall in flashing colors and white light...

Wastasa Winds watched in awe as the Acolyte kicked a walker in the solar plexus so hard that it slammed back into a bulkhead and sank to the decking. Without touching the floor, Kett bounced from the dead man and spun around to kick another in the face so hard that the jaw came off of the face. The head spun around and the body dropped to the floor. Upon landing, Kett struck one with just one blow of a gravstaff and sent it to the floor. He then jumped forward and whipped the gravstaves in two crisscrossing, x shaped patterns and drove the last two walkers to their backs. The gravstaff energy was stun technology and worked as like Ridge's bracers against the undead.

Those undead bodies still operated by biological, electroimpulse.

Winds pulsed the one Kett had kicked in the solar plexus. It had tried to stand but the motion was nullified. He pulsed the one Kett had kicked in the head, too, just to be safe.

"I got a couple," Winds shrugged.

His light flickered and died.

"Slicker, two, floodlight, zero," Jon Kett laughed lightly.

Winds tossed the casing of the light to the floor with a clatter. Only the gravstaves held by Kett lit the area in a mild, blueish white.

When ten dead walkers, five *Vindicator* bodies and five dead far longer, lay on the decking, smoldering, Samara Garriton fell back against a bulkhead. She gasped for air, her eyes wide.

Gideon lifted her face with one of his hands to look her in the eyes. He flexed the other hand three times and a small, glowing energy shield appeared on his forearm.

"You're okay. Everything's okay," he said.

"They aren't my crew," she spat, struggling for air. "Not them. Not dead. Not like that…"

Winds and Kett rounded the bend and stopped with the two captains.

"We're close," Ridge informed. "Gangway panel. We're almost there."

"Hardly," Winds said. "This was the first floor we entered. We have to go by one more and get onto a second if we're following that deck to the bridge. How many of these do you think we'll face?" he asked, gesturing at the floored, smoking bodies.

Gideon Ridge looked at him sharply.

"I guess you're not as enamored with the dead as you were earlier."

"Well, you know why, so don't be surprised," he snapped.

"What does he mean?" Kett pried.

"Tell you later, if we survive it. If we don't, I'll tell you in Heaven."

"Fair enough," Kett nodded.

"Not my crew…" Garriton mumbled.

"Not anymore," Gideon Ridge muttered.

"Not that it matters," Winds said, "but how do these things kill? They haven't used weapons and they just keep reaching for us!"

"They will use weapons against greater odds," Garriton spat, suddenly coming back to herself, perhaps in the memories she wanted to forget. "They will kill by hand, too. But they prefer to grab and hold...and leech the very life from you..."

Ridge pulled her forward by the shoulders.

"Samara, why do you have to get to the bridge? What is it you have to do? You can see your crew is gone. We could pull back now."

She met his stare, tears pooling in her eyes.

"I have to initiate self-destruct. I can't leave them here…cursed…"

Gideon Ridge nodded slowly, saying, "Okay. But we have to move." He triggered his headset. "Grundy, the undead are really here. Be ready."

"You need me, Gideon?"

"Yeah. I need you to keep those beady eyes of yours wide open. I don't know that we're alone out here."

Then the boarders made for the bridge as one.

Aboard the Leviathan, the one inhabitant gripped the captain's chair arms. Thin fingers tore at the padding. An emaciated face stared at consoles that only displayed for him; without his eyes upon them they remained black. He watched the drifting *Vindicator* on a long range sensor that should not have been able to find it. The rayonnix particles near the vessel should have masked, or at least disguised, the big derelict. Nevertheless, he watched it list in open space.

He also watched a handful of small ships swarm about it.

The captain of the phantom serpentine ship looked to another readout.

Motionless, a squadron consisting of twenty ragtag starfighters from all around the galaxy, in all kinds of shape and ruin, fired to life. Letting the slowest set the pace, they followed a one winged Drennage fighter into an intercept course with the *Vindicator*.

The old Toran fighter class was an antique to say the very least, considering the Toran people no longer produced starships at all. They purchased all of their starships and so on from Unity providers.

"Fly, little broken one…" the maniac muttered. He cackled again, to himself. "Lead these other lost vessels to their destined war…"

The man had no idea his words were silent or that his laughter was mute. Then, when he began to cry, he did not realize he could no longer shed tears from his gray eyes.

David Rule's *Razorhawk* lapped the surrounding area, yet again.

The *Gaze* rode hot on his trail, its Acolyte pilot less than worried.

"I still have nothing to report," Jaka Baddenide transmitted to Rule. "I'm close behind you, though, so when we encounter more of the empty, more of this big nothing, you'll have back up."

"Keep it quiet and alert, Jaka," David Rule ordered.

Following a different orbital lap around the area surrounding the *Vindicator*, the pilot of the *Razorwing* transmitted her own concerns. She banked about on her return course.

"I want to stay close to my father's ship," she reminded the allies.

Paolla Kett's father was Jon Kett, the Acolyte aboard the big ship with the crew of the *Spoken Word.*

"All of us do," David Rule replied. "Don't get distracted."

"I have your flank, *Razorwing*," Taelynn Berreaux, the pilot of the *Raine*, promised. "I doubt we have any need to worry, anyway."

Inside the *Vindicator*, feelings were different.

"I'm worried," Wastasa Winds stated and spun a console about at the captain's chair.

The band had climbed down the gangway two decks, trekked that deck's main corridor then forced the doors on the bridge entry. All had been done without further incident. Inside the bridge they had even found lights working.

"We set this thing to go, how are we ever going to get off in time?" Winds elaborated further. "If we get slowed in a corridor, blockaded by those-"

"Poor creatures..." Samara Garriton breathed lightly. She stared blankly at the viewscreen, one clearly not working. "They were once my crew...my friends..."

"A lot of them were not," Jon Kett said. "A lot are far too decayed to have died recently. Those have different uniforms. Clearly invaders."

Garriton shivered. She remembered the screams of her people as the invaders boarded. T'Leah had been calm, though. She had very calmly decided it was the end.

"I'm in," Wastasa Winds said. He had his gloves on his hands and he had slicked into the captain's console.

Samara Garriton blankly stared into the big, dark screen.

"Samara," Ridge nudged.

She spun to him, wiping her eyes. Then she looked at Winds.

"When my code prompt comes up let me know. I'll confirm the self-destruct with my palm DNA print and my personal code. You have to be the 'other' bridge officer required."

"Not a problem," he said. "I'm already in as T'Leah, your registered First Officer."

Gideon Ridge did not like the blind feeling of being so deep inside the ship with no viewports and no viewscreen. He wondered suddenly what was happening outside.

"Grundy," he said, touching his headset. "Anything?"

His friend transmitted back almost instantly.

"Not yet. But I have a strange feeling."

"Keep that to yourself," Gideon chuckled. "I don't need more worries without facts."

"You know the Rothidai," Grundy said. "Our feelings are as good as facts."

Captain Garriton finished her own input and started Winds on his way to completing things. It was that moment that Jon Kett shouted and threw one of his gravstaves.

The shining staff, arcing electricity as it went, whipped through the air between Winds and Garriton. Both of them, as well as Gideon Ridge, standing to their rear, turned to follow the flying silver staff.

A USAP uniform, followed by others and many that were nondescript, filed through the bridge door and started for the little boarding party. The first one caught the gravstaff right in the forehead and went down writhing.

"Hurry up!" Ridge screamed.

He whipped one neuropulsing bracer to action.

Garriton's venter came to life and the red and blue energies of the weapons cut down the visitors as they came through the door. In a moment, ten corpses were on the floor of the bridge. More were coming into the open passage.

"Gideon," Grundy called over the headset, "we've got company!"

"I know the feeling!"

"I see it but I don't believe it," Grundy muttered, staring at his sensors. "Spearhead formation of small ships, starfighters, of all kinds and origins, coming out of the 'roid field! None of them are in good condition; most read as incapable of supporting life. That makes sense, at least...since I'm reading no active biological indicators aboard them. Phantom fleet, Rule, coming on fast."

"*Spoken Word*, *Tikrek*, hold your positions. We will draw their attention," David Rule transmitted.

Several different voices traded 'confirmed' back and forth.

Grundy was watching his sensors, wondering just how many ships would pour out of the masking asteroid field. Already fifteen had appeared, their glowing schematics mocking him from the screens. The sensors said no life was aboard them...though decomposing biologicals were present.

"*Razorwing*, take *Raine* around to the outside, on the open side of the formation. *Gaze*, stay on me. We'll go out to the fringes of the 'roids. It's time to split hairs."

Several 'confirmed' again.

David Rule flipped his targeting headgear into place. He throttled forward the propulsion levers and soared for the 'roids, his wingman copying his movements. As they did, the approaching formation seemed to veer in the other direction. They seemed to take the bait that the *Razorwing* and *Raine* pilots provided.

"I see changes in their trajectories," Paola Kett transmitted. "*Razorhawk*, they are banking to pursue."

"Stationary telemetry tells the same thing, Temple Squadron," Grundy transmitted.

"Now, *Gaze*!" Rule shouted suddenly.

He veered his deft ship toward the flank of the ragtag formation.

The ragged ships, broken wings and cockpits and smoking engines and all, never saw the motion coming. They were still spilling from the asteroid field in a spearhead formation when the *Razorhawk* and its partner blasted into their flank. Rule destroyed two ships and banked to his right, destroying a third as he went completely through the formation to the other side. The *Gaze* destroyed two ships on his side of the formation, barrel rolled to the left, then destroyed another on the way out of the formation. The pilot, Jaka Baddenide, also left one spinning out of control, smoke and plasma venting from every crevice, until finally it exploded on its own.

Abruptly, Paola Kett whipped the *Razorwing* about and brought Taelynn Berreaux close behind her. The two launched back toward the formation, angling toward the side out of which Rule and Baddenide had come. Where one of them had gone to their right and the other to their left, Kett and Berreaux put their ships into the wedge, 'splitting the hair'. Several of the formerly derelict ships had fallen into the wake of Rule and his wingman to pursue them and all of those, five in total, found the waiting barrels of Temple Squadron weapons. Then Kett and Berreaux ripped from the far side of the formation, much debris scattering across their cockpits.

"Come about again," David Rule transmitted. "Don't lead them back toward the *Vindicator* until our friends are free."

Kett confirmed and banked about, running for the distance into which Rule had flown.

Four fighters were left from the formation but they did not pursue. Instead, they powered down completely and just floated in the scattered remains of its formation.

"I think we scared them back into shadow!" Berreaux said excitedly.

All read their scopes and came about again, bearing down on the remaining four fighters.

"Since when are the dead smart enough to retreat?" Paola Kett argued.

"They're not," Jaka Baddenide said flatly. "*Razorhawk*, I don't like this."

"Nor do I," David Rule growled. "Exterminate the last of them."

"Temple Squadron," Grundy started, flipping a series of switches, "we may have a problem."

Sensors were showing early signs of a much larger body coming through the asteroids.

Back on the bridge of the Unity ship *Vindicator*, things were not any better.

"They don't fire weapons, they don't rush us," Winds said of the dead. "I still don't understand! What can they do to us? How did they kill the crew?"

More than twenty piled in the floor of the bridge with a new band of five scrambling to crawl over the ones in the doorway.

"I told you already! Their touch!" Garriton shouted. She fired the venter again, dropping the first of the newcomers. "I saw it first hand! Their touch drains life!"

Ridge shot down the second two.

"But the life they steal doesn't feed them. They're no more alive than before," Jon Kett said, readying his gravstaff.

"No...and that's the mystery," Winds said and shot one down.

"The dead walk and you find their lack of nourishment mysterious?" Samara asked.

Kett threw his staff and struck the last one, spinning it about and dropping it.

Winds replaced the charge magazine in his 'pulsar.

"I admitted the supernatural ain't my specialty," he said and holstered his piece. "But I know a little somethin' about most of the laws of energy. I gotta figure life energy follows some basic principles and energy never ceases to be, it changes forms. If these psuedo-vampires are sucking life force from the living and they ain't consuming it...well, it's goin' someplace, trust me."

Gideon Ridge ejected a charge pack from his right bracer circuitry and loaded a fresh one.

Kett picked up both of his gravstaves and collapsed them, shoving them back into the metal bracers he wore under his sleeves. Doing so, he knew, recharged them.

Ridge, standing near Samara Garriton, glanced at her venter's energy scale. It was low.

"I'd recharge if I were you," he said.

She smiled sarcastically, saying, "I suppose you would have brought more charge packs if you were me, too. Too bad. I didn't."

The group shared glances with each other.

"We've got to get away from this tomb," Ridge said. "We aren't outfitted to fight half the sector."

The others nodded.

"I'll watch behind us," Kett agreed, "like before. Just give me a second for my staves to complete their recharge."

"A second is about all we have," Gideon said. "When we move, I'll run point. Samara, you follow close."

"I'm with the preacher," Winds said. "We got the back door."

Ridge's headset lit up loudly.

"Gideon, you have to move!" Grundy shouted over the headset. "Incoming battleship!"

Out of the asteroid field emerged a large starship, its shields operational and shoving the asteroids aside like paper. A Ton B'Gru vessel, the approaching starship was a Monarch class battleship, a huge combat cruiser designed for long range missions and heavy combat.

With it flew four small starfighters shaped almost like old Earth jet fighters.

"Temple Squadron, I'm reading that thing as a Ton B'Gru Monarch!" Grundy transmitted. "It's flying in formation with four Drennage fighters!"

The Squadron had already obliterated the remaining fighters that had simply powered down. Each came about again.

"*Razorwing*, take *Gaze* and *Raine* and do a straight run on them," David Rule said coolly. "Full power to your frontal shielding. Evasive patterning but get close and lead them to their left. Then run, moving your shielding to the rear."

"You can't do the swift kick by yourself," Paola Kett snapped.

"Can and will," Rule responded. "Follow your orders."

The swift kick was a five ship ruse. Three would fly close together, magnifying shielding by close proximity. They would often not even activate weapons, using all power for shielding and surviving a close sweep around a hostile target. When the three acting as a target would bank and run, the other two ships, lingering back, would hit the rear of the hostile force.

"The Chamber Cannons on the Monarch are damaged and so is their lightspeed," Grundy informed. "Watch for missiles and don't sit still!"

The trio of shielded fighters ducked in close to the approaching death ships. The Drennage fighters unleashed a volley of wicked green energy bolts, raw and jagged against the black of space. Two were direct hits on the *Razorwing* and three scraped along the *Raine* but their shields held. The events almost exactly repeated themselves in a half breath, the difference being that the *Raine* took all of the hits.

A shower of sparks lit the inside of Taelynn Berreaux's cockpit.

"Shields held," she transmitted immediately. "No worries."

A second later, they were banking away and running, engines roaring. Several blasts rocked them but they had already shifted the shielding to compensate.

The Drennage fighters peeled away from the starship instantly, following the set up. David Rule whipped his *Razorhawk* into an intercept course, charging into the open, expecting them all to follow the trap. And all but the battleship did.

However, that left David Rule on a nose to nose angle with the big starship. It had already loaded its missile bays and locked on to him.

"Rule!" Grundy shouted, watching the scopes.

Five missiles ripped from the fuselage of the Monarch class ship. They spread apart just slightly like fingers, reaching out to grasp the Acolyte's starfighter in a death grip. Rule barely managed to pinpoint each one with his navigation and rolled his little fighter right through the hand of death, missing all its digits. He followed the motion with a strafing run down the starship's body but its shields held.

"Yeah!" Grundy cheered. His celebration faltered, however.

The missiles on the right side of the trajectory, like the others, missed Rule. They were still coming, however, straight for the *Vindicator* and the two docked visitor ships.

Grundy acted on pure instinct. He threw the levers forward for the propulsion on the starboard side, every thruster coming to life. It did not tear away from the *Vindicator*, however, as he had angled the thrust to hold close to the big ship. Instead, it spun the entire vessel, along with Jon Kett's ship and his own, swinging the big derelict to be a shield.

The *Vindicator* took two missile shots into its lower decking. The eruption was cataclysmic for the ship; nearly every deck separated from the fuselage inside. All lower decks were destroyed in the blast as shrapnel the size of starfighters spun into space.

The other missiles flew clear, total misses.

The Drennage fighters hammered the little fighters they pursued. They fired repeatedly, unwilling to let up.

"The moment we shift shields to come about they'll destroy us!" Taelynn Berreaux shouted into her headset.

Jaka Baddenide did not even reply. He grabbed his thruster controls, checked his rear scopes and threw the levers all the way backward. His engines sputtered for a split second then screamed to life again with a full blast of retrothrusters. The enemies bearing down on them from behind had no time to react. Jaka Baddenide's motion sent the *Gaze* rocketing backward, shields at maximum, right into their formation.

Baddenide hit two of the fighters and one detonated immediately. The other spun off, its controls damaged and flight lost. His own ship slammed to one side then another, smacking the young man's head against the cockpit transparency, then spun about completely, the engines dying. The flying lights and shields, down to seven per cent, flickered twice then came back up. The engines did not.

Baddenide wiped blood from his face.

One of the pursuing Drennage fighters whipped about and started toward the stunned *Gaze*.

"You can't have my wingman," David Rule growled.

He dropped from a high angle to blast the stalking Drennage into just so many sparks and dust particles. When he did, he banked about sharply and started back for the starship that still approached the *Vindicator*.

The *Razorwing* took off in a boost of power, the *Raine* staying between their pursuer and the *Razorwing* at a much slower pace. The *Raine* kept her rear shielding active and kept a rear flank angled in the direction of the last Drennage fighter. Off ahead of her, the *Razorwing* flipped about, shields angled to the nose, weapons active. She then made a hard run and hopped the *Raine*, lighting the Drennage fighter with everything she had. The Drennage shields held for a moment but then gave way and it was destroyed.

"*Razorwing*," Rule barked, "tether to the *Gaze*. Pull back to the other side of the *Vindicator*. Be ready to run. *Raine*, you wing for me, now. We're going in on that starship then pull up and head away from everyone. We have to buy some time."

Several confirmed transmissions later, they implemented the plan.

"I'm dead...so to speak," Samara Garriton said.

She pushed up to her knees. Her venter was discharged completely.

Winds and Ridge both fired again, moved forward, and Jon Kett stepped from the gangway. Kett helped Samara Garriton to her feet. It was difficult for any of them to stand with the decking loose and angled after the explosions but they were far enough from the belly of the starship to have survived.

"Not far now," Ridge said. "Samara, pull back. Let Wastasa and me lead."

"What was that, anyway?" Wastasa Winds demanded.

Gideon tapped his headset.

"Grundy said we got a big boy, a battleship. Let's move."

They rushed down the very corridor that led back to the ports they had burned into the hull, almost out, indeed. When they rounded the last bend in the corridor, they thought their worries were behind them.

That is when Samara Garriton gasped and began to cry.

Blocking their path was her former First Officer, the Chabron, T'Leah, as dead as the night is black. She staggered toward them with two other Security Officers.

Samara Garriton covered her mouth with both hands as Ridge and Winds unloaded on her with the neuropulsars. The energy bolts seemed drawn to two metal bands she wore around her forearms, however, bands which absorbed the energy completely.

On they came.

"Diffuser bands!" Winds howled. "They're wearing diffusers!"

Diffuser bands were bands of superconductive metals that formed a resistant field around the wearer, much like an electromagnetic field, that conducted and channeled projected energies into the storage of the bands. They rendered lightweight energy side arms useless.

Gideon Ridge had been in that predicament in times past. He had a solution his father had given him, calling it an early inheritance from an age passed. Out of a hidden holster underneath his coat came an old Earth weapon. He aimed it and squeezed the trigger four times.

The chamber echoed with the explosions of the antique handgun as the light from the barrel cast odd, shadowy glares here and there. Brass shells kicked from the slide and skittered across the deck plates.

One of the Security Officers jerked and fell back, both shoulders and both knees destroyed. The body collapsed in a mass, squirming to stand and still unable.

He fired again, five times, and put down the other Security Officer.

"No!" Garriton shouted and grabbed Gideon Ridge's arm. "Not T'Leah!"

She pulled at him, keeping him from finding aim on her former friend. They yelled back and forth as the Chabron approached them. Winds shouted, too, backing away.

"You won't desecrate her body! You won't splatter her over these walls!" Samara railed.

"You're blowing up the whole ship!" Wastasa Winds howled at her, pulling her away from Gideon Ridge. "Let him go!"

Suddenly, Jon Kett bounded to the front. He struck T'Leah's dead form with his staves, both of them, but her bands absorbed the electrical charge. Only his physical assault did any good.

He followed it with another, not listening to the cries of Samara Garriton that he was hurting her. He folded the corpse's knees with a swift, sweeping leg attack. He jumped onto her and knocked her ceremonial blade from her grasp. Then he started raining staff strikes down upon her, many of which she blocked with mangled arms and rattling diffuser bands.

Samara Garriton tore free of Winds but Ridge caught her up in his arms, urging her to calm down.

Winds jumped forward and grabbed up the Chabron's blade. Kett rolled out of the way when Winds charged, the sword lifted high.

Garriton howled, thrashing against Ridge.

Wastasa Winds buried the blade, point first, straight into and through the prone body of the Chabron. He knew the alloys used by the Chabron for their traditional weapons would be far superior to decking plate and he put all of his strength into the thrust. The long, two handed sword pinned T'Leah's corpse, piercing her torso and punching into the decking.

The dead Chabron reached a trembling hand upward at Samara Garriton as if inviting her to join the ranks of the undead. The former First Officer could not escape the blade, however, and the living were safely out of her reach.

"Monster!" Garriton howled and tore free from Ridge.

Kett caught her that time and the little troop fell back.

The *Razorwing* pulled a tethered *Gaze* just beyond the smoldering *Vindicator* and slowed. Paola Kett watched the scopes and the sensors, waiting.

"Cut me loose," Jaka Baddenide transmitted. "They need you, Paola. You're still in the fight."

"David knows what he's doing, Jaka," she responded.

David Rule led his new partner, the *Raine*, straight for the big Monarch ship. Several missiles blew from the spouts in the head of the starship but none had a lock on the little fighters. They flew wide and did not even cause Rule and his partner to try evasive maneuvers. Instead, they flew right down the port side of the big battleship, strafing the entire way and making the shields shimmer and pulse.

They did no damage, however.

"No effect, *Razorhawk*," Paola Kett transmitted, watching her scopes.

"Come about, *Raine*," Rule said without answering Kett. "We're going again."

"How long can we-" Taelynn Berreaux began.

"Until we don't need to anymore," Rule snapped.

"*Razorhawk*, are you trying to keep all the fun for yourself?" Gideon Ridge transmitted. "I never knew you were selfish; save some of that big antique for the *Spoken Word*!"

Ridge and crew tore away from the *Vindicator* in his Raindancer.

Smiles broke over the faces of the Temple Squadron.

Seconds later, Jon Kett's ship, the *Tikrek*, tore away as well and the derelict was left behind yet again.

Rule led another strafing run down the side of the Monarch ship, no more effective than the one before. Gideon Ridge brought his ship into the mix, hitting from the other side, while more missiles were launched wildly, again to no avail.

"You're welcome to it, Gideon," Rule answered after a moment.

"Escape route is set," Kreden Hotch said from his seat.

"Hold that thought," Ridge said, coming about again.

"Power levels good on every front," Kelvan Hotch said.

"Good to know," Drea Ridge said.

Grundy sat at the Weapons Station, reviewing the more complex sensor systems at that location. Ridge had the pilot's seat again, while Samara Garriton and Wastasa Winds buckled into empty chairs.

"Gideon," Grundy said, staring intently. "You won't believe this."

"Oh, I don't know, try me," Ridge half shouted, whipping the freighter to one side to avoid another missile. "We got undead, empty ships, ships flown by corpses...I'm open to discussion!"

Grundy opened up all of the charged weapons on that run, scattering energies all down the upper spine of the Monarch battleship. Its golden shields shimmered and pulsed again but did not fail.

"That old Monarch is famous," Grundy announced. "Sensors over here are more accurate and precise; that thing's name is coming in clear."

The big ship banked suddenly, taking a new direction. It decided not to pursue the stinging attackers. Instead, it pointed its nose for the sitting ships just beyond them all. It started running down on the *Razorwing* and her disabled tether, the *Gaze*.

"It's altering flight," Rule transmitted. "Paola, make your run, now!"

"She'll never outrun it pulling another fighter; she can't go to light!" Jon Kett interrupted.

Paola Kett slammed her levers to the maximum anyway and jerked Jaka Baddenide into motion. They shot away from the big pursuer but not fast enough. It was already close to firing range.

Rule, Berreaux, Ridge and Jon Kett swept in behind the big vessel, unloading on it. It was to no avail, as the shielding still held.

"That thing is the missing Ton B'Gru exploration vessel that went missing in the Reaches decades ago," Grundy continued inside the ship with Ridge and company. "That's the *Quan Jor*!"

Gideon Ridge's mind spun. The *Quan Jor*. In English, the *Race's Glory*. He knew a lot about that ship; many people did.

One thing he knew, however, was a weakness.

The Ton B'Gru were a self assured people. They were proud of their technology, boastful of its properties and their own advances. All in all, they were much like humankind. They had widely announced their shielding as the best in the cosmos and the near immunity to modern weapons their ships enjoyed.

However, to thinking pirates and smugglers, statements like that often meant something else, if one were to listen correctly. Saying how well it worked against modern tech and how impervious they were to up-to-date piracy was also a subconscious admission that they had forgone older defenses as older weaponry had been outdated. They had the best defense against energy attacks a ship could want; Ridge had always surmised they had ignored most of the defenses against ballistic attacks.

It was a foolish arrogance. The ship itself still carried missiles; it escaped him why they thought no one else would.

Gideon Ridge threw on the heat to his engines. He jumped ahead of the big ghost ship and dropped down to run blockade for the *Razorwing* and the *Gaze*. The rear shields, carrying all the power available, flared with reflecting light.

"Grundy, drop the Baby!" Ridge howled.

Grundy half shrugged, opened an access cover and jerked back a lever as the rest of the crew turned as one to frown at Gideon Ridge.

A screeching resounded through the ship as a belly panel opened and a small, one man escape shuttle lowered.

"Temple Squadron," Gideon transmitted, "I'm about to give a gift to our big bully. Pull away from the Monarch ship!" Ridge then looked at Grundy. "Set Baby's engines on internal overload but don't give her any direction for thrust then cut her loose! Big and nasty won't be able to avoid her!"

Grundy gave a sideways smile and snorted.

"Aye, Captain, you old pirate."

"I resent that," Gideon said and laughed. "I'm not old at all."

Then Baby ejected below and to the rear of the *Spoken Word*.

The corpse driven Monarch achieved target lock on all of the allies.

Rule and Berreaux peeled off to the side while Ridge kept his ship as a barrier behind the tattered ship of Jaka Baddenide.

The escape shuttle fell away, right into the head of the approaching Monarch...and soared right through the shielding that only looked for energy to block. The overloading engines were already smoking when the little pod passed through those shields, hit the nose of the vessel and plowed straight through the hull plating. Then Baby exploded inside the bigger ship's fuselage.

Four missiles launched but their aim was ruined. The bending and twisting of the nose of the Monarch altered any aim it could have achieved. Suddenly, another explosion went off inside the metal skin of the Monarch and the big ship lurched to one side, hull plating ripping from the body like shedding skin. Another explosion followed that one, deeper inside, and a main engine began to vent fuels...and flame.

Suddenly, the *Vindicator* exploded and the shockwave rippled outward so far that it shook the allies. Only the Monarch was damaged by it, however, as the internal explosions had dropped its shields. The shockwave split the fuselage of the *Quan Jor* and ripped what was left of it in two, folding deck after deck like so much tissue.

Cheers went up from Temple Squadron.

"Now," Gideon Ridge transmitted, "let's get back to the station. Unity forces and bounty hunters aren't nearly as dangerous as all this."

CHAPTER SIX : *Frontline*

G ill Bardoff waved the smoke from his face where he leaned into the engine panel. The old man looked at his friends, chuckled lightly, then pointed at the panel.

"Old girl's tired. Got you here in record time, though."

Sundar Ridge cut a sidelong glare at his brother, Sylver.

"Gill, you think that thing can fly back off this way station?"

"What? 'Course she can! She just needs a little rest, boys."

"And a few parts, some paint, an overhaul-"

"Don't start, Sundar," Pap chided. "We gotta find my boy and tell him about the Starstalkers."

"Okay," Sundar allowed. "Let's head down to the club streets."

"Where we going, fellas?" Gill Bardoff asked.

"We're going to find my son," Sylver answered. "Starting at the information brokers. You know, the watering holes."

"I'm a little thirsty, now that you mention it," Gill said.

"You need to fix that...whatever it is," Sylver waved at the smoke.

"You catch up to us," Sundar laughed. "We'll be down by the Sunbrowser."

Gill almost argued but something under the panel sizzled and new sparks scattered. He set about addressing the repairs, minor though he swore they were.

The Ridge brothers walked out of the docking bay and into the main hub of the spaceport level. Several times they nodded as they passed others, while other times they looked right by those who passed. It all depended on the individuals and the impression they gave; it was impolite to notice those who were trying not to be noticed.

Maximilian Station bustled with life and some it was quite seedy. Two reformed smugglers themselves, the brothers would have admitted if asked that it was exciting to be on the chase again. Criminals, refugees, hunters and thieves prowled the station and the Ridge brothers remembered the life well.

It had not been hard to decide where to find Gideon. Almost no one went into the Reaches but those who did stopped at Maximilian Station. Everyone wanted all the supplies they could possibly need and they wanted their ships in the best possible condition before passing into the eerie zone. Gideon would have come that way.

Old Pap limped a little, his right knee a mangled mess since the Blood War. He hitched up loose pants, adjusting his quick draw belt and holster, then shifted the longer weapon he wore with a strap slung over a shoulder.

His brother, Sundar, did not have the limp but he had the belt and holster. He carried a backpack over one shoulder, too, with a thumb tucked under the strap on his chest.

The two traversed the entire span of the spacestation without saying a word. They watched in silence as everyone from the cream of society, there for excitement, to the scum of the cosmos, there for much the same, flowed like a living river from one sordid location to another. One thing they all had in common was a single locale.

No one showed themselves in Maximilian Station without visiting the Sunbrowser.

The brothers broke their silent journey when they reached the famous doors.

Just outside, lying in a pile on the front walk, a dead Hunon, eviscerated and mangled, and a dead Starstalker female awaited sanitation crews of the day.

"Gideon?" Sundar asked, his eyebrows lifting.

"No. The boy don't kill, you know that," Pap said. "Neuropulsars all the way, unless he's fighting 'droids or 'bots or whatever that isn't alive. Then he uses that old Earth gun I got from you years ago."

"And you cheated me to get it, too, Sylver," Sundar declared, nodding as he opened the door. "Dirtiest card game you ever played."

"Don't start that again," Pap warned. "You're a sore loser."

The two entered the establishment, stayed at the door until their eyes adjusted to the dark room, then they went inside and found a nice, tiny table in the very back. Customers from the front to the back watched them and pretended not to, looking but not looking, waiting to be certain they were not there to unload on anyone.

Once the brothers sat down, most went back to their own mindless desires.

Two Echo Soldiers were exceptions. They sauntered over from the bar, both of them carrying their helmets casually tucked under an arm.

"Can we do something for you?" Sundar mewled.

One Echo Soldier opened his mouth to reply but Sylver interrupted.

"If you boys are the entertainment, we ain't interested."

Sundar laughed loudly, as did an approaching waitress and a nearby table of customers. It was difficult to really notice, however, with the volume of the chatter and music.

Before the Echo Soldiers had a chance to say anything, the waitress interrupted.

"What can I get you?" she asked the brothers.

One of the Echo Soldiers, staring at the Ridge brothers, shoved the waitress back and slammed the helmet down on the tabletop.

"Now, you two listen up!" he shouted.

A sudden uproar lifted around the little table. Customers and other waitresses shouted obscenities at the Echoes while the Ridges shouted warnings about manhandling women. The bartender shouted a stern, gritty warning of his own.

The offended waitress, however, flashed bright red all over. She snatched up a low light, table lamp, all metal like much of the décor, and violently crowned the guilty soldier. That man shot downward and slammed his forehead against the table, right beside the helmet, then slumped to the floor.

The other Echo Soldier twisted about toward her, groping for his side arm.

"Hey!" Sundar Ridge exploded, his own side arm suddenly brought to bear.

Eight different customers nearby also leveled weapons on the Echo Soldier. The bartender had snatched up a table leg he kept behind the bar.

It was Sylver who got the man's attention, however, without a word.

Beneath the fairly short weapon usually strapped over his shoulder, the old man levered a cocking mechanism. The sound brought almost everyone to silence. Even the music died.

"Now wait a minute," the man said nervously.

"You recognize this, boy?" Sylver asked. "This is a Lathi Spaceport Agent's weapon. Brutal people, the Laths. Nicknamed this little pup the 'Bay Sweeper' since you could back off a ways and hit everything in a landing bay with it. Energy sweeps wide, son. 'Course, the reason you and me and all the folks in here know of it is 'cause of what it does to a smaller target close up…"

Murmuring spread through the room like wildfire.

"We just need to calm down," the Echo man said urgently. "There's no need-"

The waitress viciously struck the man on the back of his head, too.

He went down hard, across the edge of the table, across Sundar's lap and onto the deck. Both helmets hit the floor and rolled away.

A raucous chorus of laughter rose and the music lifted once again.

The waitress breathed heavily. Her teeth, clenched together very tightly, seemed even brighter white against the stark red of her skin. Her blonde hair had even taken on a pinkish hue when she was angered.

She pounded the lamp back onto the table, its little metal spine crooked and the light broken in its top. She then tossed back her hair and pulled out her digipage. She blew out slowly, much of the red dissipating from her light skin.

"Thank you both for being patient," she said. "What can I get you?"

"We're looking for a friend," Sundar muttered while his brother put away the sweeper.

"We Torans make good friends," the waitress flirted with him.

"I ain't that brave," Sundar said and grinned.

She stiffened as if she might grow angry but her flesh never reddened. She laughed.

"Okay. What kind of friend would you like?"

"We're looking for a particular lady. Name's 'Soru ga Playd'. Have you seen her?" Sundar said slyly.

Truth be told, every humanoid race had a name in their own tongue, used in certain circles, that was code for information. Smugglers, 'hunters and anyone dealing with informants knew the names. Sundar had given the Toran name to the waitress. Most law enforcement would not know it; the code set informants at ease.

"Last I heard, she was out to strike it rich," she said, her lips pouting.

"How rich?" Sylver took over.

"Oh, best I remember she wouldn't be satisfied with less than five hundred Bayles; none of those territorial currencies, just the trade stuff. Bayles, plat, you know."

"For that kind of currency we could just buy the Sunbrowser and sit here ourselves and hear secrets," Sundar barked then softened. He smiled at her again, adding, "No offense."

"She said she wanted to strike it rich, boys," the woman said. "Not just get paid."

"I heard she would be happy with two hundred."

"Someone lied to you," she said, smiling anew at Sylver.

"Even if she knew it was from men who respect women?" Sundar interjected into his brother's negotiation.

"That is the very reason she was only looking for five hundred," she answered, beaming.

"Two hundred and we clean up the guys in the floor."

"What? I haven't even skimmed their things. That's another loss."

"Two hundred and we carry these guys out but you keep whatever you grab from their pockets."

She leaned her head to one side.

"You're sweet. I'll play along. Three hundred."

"Three hundred, whatever loot those boys are holding and you help us drag the Echo Soldiers out the back," Sylver countered again.

Sundar and the woman stared at him.

"What? I'm old. I can use all the help I can get."

She winked and stroked Sylver's beard.

"You're never any older than you feel, babe."

"Uh oh," Sundar said.

"What?" his brother asked.

"If that's true, I'm already dead."

The waitress laughed and winked at him.

Inside the Sunbrowser, in a dark, corner booth, a hooded woman watched the Ridge brothers and the waitress. She tugged the hood, adjusting the cloak on her shoulders.

A Rothidai sat beside her. He snorted and rubbed his biggest horn.

"What's bothering you?" she asked him.

"Nothing," he said, his voice low and gravelly.

"You're a liar."

He snorted again.

"Do me a favor," he began in his grating rumble. "Let it go."

"This is counterproductive," another woman in their booth mumbled.

"How about you come clean!" the first woman hissed.

A bit of her blue, electrically coursing hair spilled from her hood. Her white eyes glowed inside it.

"Easy, Cheyenne!" the Greshan hushed the Ton B'Gru woman.

Cheyenne Winds turned to peer into the Rothidai's small eyes.

"Tell me, Grockforth. What is your problem?"

Grockforth looked around conspiratorially, his large head twice the size of the women's. He pressed large, dangerous fists together on the table.

The Greshan sighed. She ran a smooth hand through her black, feathered hair, her large, round yellow eyes blinking. Her soft, velvet skin, a pale yellow, seemed to pale further as she found herself wondering what the Winds woman would do.

"You know what this is about?" Cheyenne Winds asked the Greshan.

"He doesn't like the idea of hurting old creatures like those-"

"Katril!" Grockforth exploded at the Greshan woman.

"Both of you be quiet!" Winds ordered in her venomous whisper.

The turned and regarded her sharply.

Somewhat contented, Cheyenne Winds said, "Katril, I want you to follow the two old men. Just watch and report. Grockforth, I want you to make that waitress tell you what she told them, since you're too squeamish to deal with old men. Report when you have something."

"Where will you be?" Grockforth asked.

"Meeting with the Echo Unit and those Starstalkers we saw earlier."

"Why?" Katril asked.

"To offer misinformation, dear. I don't want them in the way when those two old men lead us right to Samara Garriton."

"The old men?" the Rothidai and the Greshan said at the same time.

She looked at them in turn with a wicked sneer.

"They're the Ridge brothers. One of them is Gideon Ridge's father. That's what I learned on Sabbor Two, anyway. That, with the witnesses that saw a woman matching Garriton's description, hiring Gideon Ridge, adds up to being a really good lead."

Samara Garriton sipped at a mug Gideon Ridge provided.

Ridge sat back in his seat at the little galley table.

"Feeling a little better?"

"I will as soon as I kill Wastasa Winds."

"No can do. No killing."

"Is that a personal rule?"

"One of many."

"Do you keep a list?"

"Yes, but I can't take credit for making it. It was already listed in the Bible for me when I got it."

She stared at him and he gave her that sideways smirk.

"I had no idea you didn't kill," she admitted, sipping from the mug again. "When you went molten on those Echo Soldiers and on Winds, back in the docking bay, I thought you had killed all those people without a thought. Now, I want to kill Winds myself...for re-killing a friend of mine who was already dead. Funny how things change."

"These are hardly typical situations we're dealing with. And you don't really want to kill him. You're upset, angry. Torn between what was and what is...confused. You're confused. Happens to all of us."

"How do you hold true to rules like 'no killing' in your line of work?"

Gideon chuckled and sipped at his own mug.

"My personal rules are part of my Faith, my deepest beliefs, my fundamental character, Samara. If I did anything less than my best to adhere to it, it would be no more than some vague philosophy, a vapor of an idea blown aside at the first onset of trouble."

"I've met religious people, Gideon Ridge. All kinds, from all sorts of worlds, all kinds of cultures. I want to say this and I hope you take it well. You aren't like any of them. None of them."

"You're not like most Unity captains, either. Normally, a line or two about my Faith sends them looking for their little digifile on acceptable spiritual conversations."

She laughed boisterously and Gideon found it infectious, contagious. She was beautiful when she was laughing…and he realized how often he found himself thinking of her allure. Not just her beauty, either. Her keen intelligence, her courage, her dedication all drew him.

"Fear does bad things to people. Fear of offending others leads us to build more and more walls, hiding who we are instead of sharing who we are. I don't know when I figured that out but it's been haunting me for a while now."

Gideon nodded, saying, "Things weren't always this way."

"I know. My Commodore talks about her father all the time. How he was an ESS Chaplain before Earth joined the Unity Starmada," Garriton reminded him of their earlier conversation.

He was nodding along when the com system buzzed.

"Gideon, you got a holo. It's Uncle Sun," Grundy said over the com.

Ridge stood immediately but turned back to Garriton.

"Oh...Samara?"

"Yes?"

"I'm sorry about your friends, your crew."

She tried to hold her trembling lip still and nodded, eyes down.

Grundy looked back from the viewports with a raised eyebrow ridge when Gideon returned to the nose of the *Word*. Grundy sat in the pilot's seat beside Drea.

"Temple Squadron went to light speed already, Gideon," Kelvan Hotch said.

"All but one of them," Gideon smiled and patted a younger man on his shoulder.

The younger man sat beside Wastasa Winds. They nibbled at a bag of cold frofro berries.

"Thanks again for the lift, Gideon," the young tag along said.

"Don't thank me. Grundy wanted to help you. I told David to leave you and let you row your ship home," he teased the Acolyte, Jaka Baddenide.

"Thanks," Jaka retorted. "That's real love right there."

"Kreden, key in that holo," Grundy said.

"You got it."

There was a holocom on the pilot side of the cockpit, a place left empty that was the size of a full grown man. Colors swirled about like water being drawn into a steep drain then spread out suddenly into an image. It crackled once.

"This thing on?" his Uncle Sundar asked someone then turned to face the holorecorder. "Alright, boy, I hope you get this. Your Pap says he sent a couple already but we never heard back. Anyway, me and your Pap got to Maximilian Station and already had trouble with our voices echoing. The reason we came out, too, is 'cause of those hungry fans you left behind, them we talked about. They're either here or on the way here. This is where everybody comes before going on, they know it and everybody knows it. So, you come back to the station, you be careful; I don't think you been to Church enough lately."

Then the image disappeared.

"Okay, Grundy," Gideon Ridge said. "We don't have to wait now."

"You don't want David's reconnaissance?" Jaka Baddenide asked.

"I just got some of my own," Gideon smiled.

Gideon and his company had stayed at sublight speeds. David Rule put the Temple Squadron, all but the shattered ship of Jaka Baddenide, into light speed to reach the station first. He offered to go in alone and see what might be awaiting them, via the Temple and its own landing and docking locale. Gideon had accepted thankfully.

"We got Echo Soldiers waiting on us," Gideon explained. "The fleshhunters that are after me and Grundy, that band of wild Starstalkers, is probably here, too. If not they will be. Uncle Sun says to land in the Temple landing and come into the station by the Temple itself and to be careful."

Jaka sighed, "I guess you have to cut the *Gaze* loose, then."

Gideon patted the man's shoulder again.

"Sorry, Jaka. This is a freighter. I can't tether and tow into lightspeed. You'll have to get a tugliner to draw it back to the station." He looked up to the staring Grundy. "Drop it off tether and take us to the Temple."

Across an empty star field the little Impulse class starfighter wobbled. Small parts and debris littered its wake. The condition was terrible. Still, it chased after the call, responding to the death tone projected into the ancient moon. A tail of dust and dirt and shattered components lined its path from Draksus toward the unsuspecting spacestation, Maximilian Station.

A tip from the last remaining whole wing vibrated off and drifted back, left behind, left to wander space alone…

…until hit by another of the hundreds of ships lifting from the wreckage of the Draksus dumping grounds.

Draksus was a shattered moon in the orbit of the last Heavenly body before the Reaches, frozen Dor Modo. The moon had, over long centuries, become a dumping ground for waste from around the cosmos. Much of that waste was the remnant share of worn, torn and war-beaten fightercraft and starships. There was no one to complain; Dor Modo had been silent for a millennia.

Races known and unknown, familiar and forgotten, were represented, resurrected to a degree, by the many, many ships lifting from the moon. Their tombs open, their death shrouds slipped away, the crippled starmada lifted into open space and reached a longing, skeletal hand toward Maximilian Station.

Not too far out, a serpentine ship emerged from the Reaches with its own starmada wrapped about itself. The Leviathan writhed in flight, heading right for Maximilian Station, all of its smaller allies with it.

On the bridge, the broken, tormented Captain rolled his eyes back into his head. Dark blood ran from his eyes, his nose and his ears.

"They come…" he said of the Draksus moon's starmada. "They have no sentient forms aboard them…the strain for…for my psioptic power is…immeasurable…"

"Hold their course," the voice rumbled inside his head.

The man began to weep again. How many times had he wept since that night in the Reaches? That night when the voice had spoken the first time…

…and he went about the Leviathan and killed his entire crew…

The man began to laugh, his eyes wide, his pain indescribable.

"Destroy the station, Captain, and any ships that can be must be added. The frontline of the war between life and death, dark and light, must be drawn here."

The man ignited with laughter and began slapping his own face.

Temple Squadron stood in the Temple Landing Bay when the *Spoken Word* touched down onto the shining deck plates. The Kett father and daughter, hoods down, stood arm in arm by David Rule. Taelynn Berreaux wore her hood up but her long hair still blew from its sides in the thrust of landing propulsion. With Berreaux waited another Acolyte, a much taller woman. Her hood was down, her white hair billowing. In her arms rested an extra white cloak.

The *Word* reflected the bay lights about randomly, shining spotlights here and there. Some of them lit the Razor starfighters, the Greshan fighter and the solo Sabb fighter of Temple Squadron with a rainbow of colors. Beyond them rested row upon row of worn, beaten fighters used by the other Acolytes.

Near Berreaux, Sundar and Sylver Ridge waited with weapons in hand. Old Gill Bardoff was behind them, trying to find a distance from his eyes to his digipage where he could actually still read it. He looked up when the landing ramp dropped from the Raindancer.

"Your boy's here now, Sylver. You got time to walk back to my bay with me to get the *Belly Rub*?" Bardoff reminded.

"Will you please stop saying the name of that bucket?" Sundar mourned.

"I'll go with you, Gill. Let's get things started here first, okay? Let Sundar get legs under a plan."

Gill nodded, with, "Sure, sure, Sylver." He winked at Sundar Ridge. "I'm going to will you that fine freighter, Sun, when I die. I can hear the love for it in your voice."

"It ain't love, Gill. That's nausea."

Wastasa Winds disembarked first, Jaka Baddenide at his back. Winds left the frofro berries behind.

The Ridge brothers tightened their grips around their weapons. They knew of Wastasa Winds; they had no idea if he was friend or foe but they were ready either way. Gill Bardoff seemed oblivious, back to reading his digipage.

Grundy tromped down the ramp behind Jaka, eyes keen and alert, hands grasping tightly his halberd. The twin heads on it reflected the bay lights in a prismatic display. Gideon Ridge followed, carrying a small bag with Unity Captain colors spilled over it, bantering back and forth with the Hotch brothers, while his sister, Drea, immediately started to take note of the layout. She always wanted to know the best and fastest way to get out of anywhere she went.

Samara Garriton came last, eyeing her bag in Gideon's grasp, her mind someplace else…the loss, the nightmare, the tragedy, the end…it had become all too real when the crew and the ship detonated.

The Acolyte, Taelynn Berreaux, and the other Acolyte woman with her, met Garriton's arrival specifically.

"Captain, I'm Taelynn," Berreaux began with a smile. She adjusted her wine red garb beneath the cloak. "And this is Kohlene. Kohlene Arria."

"Come with us, Captain," the other woman said.

She, like Paola Kett, wore a scarlet Cassock over white pants and boots. They were the Acolyte vestments of the dedicated scholar.

Though clearly twice the age of the other Acolyte, she was just as beautiful, with flowing, snow white hair and shining blue eyes.

Samara Garriton looked into the eyes of the taller woman and found great compassion in them. Wordlessly, she nodded.

Taelynn found it odd, though she said nothing of it, just how much the two women resembled. Both lovely, both plush women, both with such shining eyes. The Acolyte could have passed for Garriton's mother.

Kohlene Arria took the extra Acolyte cloak and wrapped it about her, flipped the hood into place then led her for the Temple with an arm around her shoulders, Taelynn Berreaux in tow.

Gideon watched her go as he embraced his father. He nodded to himself. It was good to disguise Garriton. A gentle smile pulled at his lips, a relief warming him as he thought of her being safe.

"Boy, you're in a world o' trouble," Pap told him.

"That's nothing new, Sylver," David Rule said, grinning as he embraced the older Ridge.

"Yeah, but I seen that look before. Had it myself more than once," Pap said. "Bet he don't even know it, yet."

"What?" Gideon asked, looking from one to the other. "What look?"

"See? What'd I tell ya? World o' trouble."

Uncle Sun drew close as Pap and David Rule nodded to each other. Gideon Ridge pressed them for an explanation but all he received were chuckles and winks. Sun still kept his eye on Wastasa Winds as he embraced David Rule.

"Pickin' up strays, boy?" Sun asked Gideon.

Gideon followed the older Ridge's stare right to Winds.

"Long story. Relax. He's been a big help."

Jaka rejoined his Acolyte family, hugging most of them.

"Pap, Uncle Sun," Gideon addressed, "That message you sent was great. We would've flown right into the landing bays. I thought, without the *Corridor* on the station showing up on our scans, we'd be all clear."

"Oh, that personnel transport will be back soon enough," Sundar growled. "An Echo Unit is still here. According to a waitress at the Sunbrowser, they left to meet with another Unity vessel further out."

"They'll be back and they'll have a Vanguard class Unity Starship with them," the other Ridge brother added.

"What?" Gideon asked.

"That's the rumor, boy," Pap said lowly. "Echo Unit was telling everybody. Their Captain got a message, a long range communiqué, digital message only. Seems the Vanguard ship was having communications trouble."

"There's more, too," David Rule added as Winds and Grundy reached them. The other Acolytes closed in around them, too.

"Perhaps we should tell them once we are inside," Paola Kett said.

Ridge nodded at her, put his arms around his father and his uncle, the famous Ridge brothers, and the entire group began the stairs of steel that led toward the Temple.

Acolyte Temples were like many Churches dedicated to Christ in the known Cosmos. They supported all the teachings of Jesus Christ and believed in His Divinity without question. Their goal was to present His Message, one of Peace, Hope, Love and Redemption for fallen souls.

The architectural designs varied around space like the designs of independent Churches, too, but Acolyte Temples did keep one thing standard.

Each bore considerable defenses.

The Temple there stood very tall, its entire structure completely independent from the station walls and supports. It was clear why it was built within its own docking and landing station; the Temple reached well high enough to have broken through to another level, had it been in a generally populated area. The base solidly planted itself in a square fortress look, though lovely art displayed itself all around the structure in statues and brightly colored floral arrangements. The multistory base turned into a great, reaching spire after about four floors, and a Cross crowned it at the top. The metals of the outside glimmered, polished to a mirror finish, while the remote turrets on the four upper corners of the square base turned here and there.

The group entered into the base level through automatic, powered double doors, only to face another set of double doors. They stood in a foyer that was walled in polished brass and redressed wood. Beside the doors, on both sides, matching bronze plaques declared the Acolyte Way.

"The ancient Levites of the Old Testament of the Holy Bible were chosen as very special assistants to the Priests, Messengers of their day. They held important duties to the Tabernacles and the people of God. They were selected for this purpose because of their zeal for the glory of God, as explained in the Old Testament Book of Exodus, chapter thirty-two, verse twenty-six. That zeal inspires all of us, the Acolytes, to serve our Father God, His Son, our Savior, Jesus Christ, and Their Holy Spirit with all that we are. It also calls us and empowers us to selflessly serve the body of believers, Messengers of the Faith, Churches, Temples, and all of those in need with nonlethal, merciful but necessary action."

Two Acolytes waited by the plaques and opened the next doors.

The group passed into a Sanctuary with ceilings reaching up for more than two stories. The architecture told a story of great construction and reverence for the building of the past. Red and purple tapestries and carpets paved the metal innards with color and softness. A massive sitting area embraced wall to wall pews upholstered with reds and purples as well. A Cross stood at the front of the Sanctuary where the redressed woods of the pulpit gleamed, where the altar awaited those seeking Truth. Acolytes strolled around the Sanctuary keeping everything pristine.

Rule gestured at the little party to sit in one of the back pews.

"Taelynn and Kohlene should bring Captain Garriton back to us when they have her settled in," David said. "We wanted to disguise her, just in case. I can't foresee anyone invading the Temple but one must prepare for the unforeseen. Once they return and we quickly brief each other, we have rooms waiting for all of you. You should rest. The sleeping quarters are upstairs in the Spire."

A great deal of appreciation was extended to the Acolyte generosity. David Rule, however, dismissed the praise.

"It is the least we can do for those in need."

"I don't think I've ever met Kohlene," Gideon mentioned afterward.

"She's a life long Acolyte. She joined us from a Temple in the Moothalau sector. A true Christian, a loving counselor and a prayer warrior. She is older than I am, too, which is nice. I feel older all the time as our newer recruits get younger and younger."

"She's wearing scholar vestments," Gideon nodded. "The Kett woman is, as well. You've made some great additions to this Temple outpost."

"Well, padre," Sun Ridge said, "we got a lot to cover."

"Let's not wait, then," Gideon said, still admiring the beauty of the Sanctuary. "I'd like to wrap up the briefing and have some prayer time."

"I hear that," Kreden Hotch agreed. "What else will we need?"

"I want a station holo and a holo of this bay," said Dalindrea Ridge.

"Let's see if we can round 'em up," Kelvan Hotch said.

"Captain Brent, I know my orders," Captain Van Pelt said.

The new Captain of the *Bloodwind* and the Captain of the transport, the *Corridor*, spoke over a table in the transport's lone cargo bay. The transport was moored to the much larger Vanguard class vessel with a docking tube providing a junction between the two. The young Captain sat, arms folded, staring at the older, red haired Captain.

Brent had brought two of the *Bloodwind's* Security Officers with him. They stood behind him. The two Security Officers with Van Pelt stood behind him, hands clasped before themselves.

"Admiral Washington gave every ship in the division orders to find and reclaim your ship from Commodore Zeckinbridge. It seems she has made her own orders and has taken off with your Vanguard for a personal search of this sector."

"You expect me to believe this…no, you expect me to hand over my new command? No proof? No questions asked, no information required?" Joshua Brent laughed. "Wrigley Zeckinbridge is one of the most decorated Commodores-"

"Captain Brent, I hereby order you to stand down and relieve yourself of your seat on the *Bloodwind*. I also order you to aide us in removing Commodore Wrigley Zeckinbridge from that ship and putting her in the brig. Is that clear?"

"There is no way I'm going-"

"Captain Van Pelt," an Echo Soldier interjected, running into the cargo hold. "It's the *Bloodwind*…"

"What is-" Van Pelt began.

"What about it?" demanded Brent.

"The ship broke mooring and jumped to light speed," the Echo Soldier said.

"All hands, this is the Captain," Van Pelt shouted into a shoulder transmitter. "Battle stations! Full pursuit of that Vanguard ship! Capture or disable! Any means!"

The balding Captain ran out into the hallway and started for the bridge. Captain Brent gave pursuit.

"Captain Brent, you can stay in the cargo bay!" Van Pelt howled.

"Not a chance!" the young Josh Brent countered. "That's my ship you're after! If anyone brings her in it will be under my watch!"

"Patterson!" Captain Van Pelt shouted at his Communications Officer, once on the bridge. "Get me Admiral Washington! Now!"

"Admiral Washington, the *Corridor* has found the *Bloodwind*. It is locked in pursuit. The young Captain, Joshua Brent, is on board the *Corridor*."

The Admiral pursed his lips and nodded succinctly.

"Meaning Commodore Zeckinbridge is in full control of the *Bloodwind*."

"And she is en route to Maximilian Station."

"Thank you, Mr. Burnett," Admiral Washington said to the Captain who had spoken. "Engage maximum pursuit; I don't care how new it is. Use everything we have, including the quantum fold generators, to get us there fast."

Washington sat in the Captain's Command Seat, leaving the Captain, Wallace Burnett, to stand at the rail that encircled the upper bridge.

The upper bridge was a half level above the main bridge. It was smaller and semicircular where it looked down on the remainder of the command center. Only the Captain's seat, the First Officer's seat, and the Chief Security Officer's seat were atop the half level.

"You heard the Admiral, Mr. Tylle," Captain Burnett said, eyeballing his First Officer.

First Officer Tylle stood from his seat and braced upon the railing.

"Pilot Keer, set a pursuit course for the renegade *Bloodwind*...at full Quantumspeed."

"Aye, sir," the pilot, a Greylik man, said.

"Ready yourself," Admiral Washington muttered to the invisible Commodore Zeckinbridge. "It is time to answer for your actions."

Sylver Ridge told the group the details of all they had missed and all the waitress had confided. He told of the Starstalker hunters, the Echo Soldiers and the meeting between the *Corridor* and a new Unity ship on the way. He told of Wastasa Winds' old friends and how one had killed the other, something the Ridge Brothers had missed in person but had heard about later on.

He also told of the rumors spreading around the station. There were new survivors of encounters with the dead. The phenomena were occurring all over the cosmos...no system was safe.

In turn Gideon Ridge had to pacify Sundar and Sylver as to why Wastasa Winds was with them. He told them it was a long story and that Winds was along for the ride and wanted to see it through to the end.

The truth was that he had never been at odds with Winds; there had never been a time that he had considered the famed slicker and bounty hunter a bad person. Winds was famous for never killing anyone and pursuing only outlaws, though one man's outlaw was another man's freedom fighter. When Winds had awakened after the shootout and had not wanted to be freed, Gideon had seen no problem with it.

"You promised to share something else with us, Gideon," Jon Kett reminded, "when we were still on the death ship."

"Only what you and I and David Rule already know, what all Acolytes know. What all Christians know. We know it from our Faith. The spirits of sentient beings do not linger needlessly and certainly not to pirate technology from the living."

"What do you call all those dead bodies?" Kreden Hotch asked.

"Puppets," Wastasa Winds said. "There was no lingering life in those bodies, no spirits still in the husks. They were empty, hollow...puppets."

"I saw it in the dead eyes," Gideon said. "Nothingness. Flat, lifeless, like in the 'droid revolts. Just like then, these are props, a false face hiding a real enemy. The dead are just like the 'droids were; lifeless, programmed soldiers carrying out an agenda for a mastermind. We're supposed to believe the dead are rising of their own choice, just as we were supposed to believe the 'droids all around the cosmos had revolted. Just like with androids and robots and the way people ascribe personalities to them, knowing full well a machine cannot have a soul. It is the same with these dead. They are not spirits risen from the grave. They are just bodies reanimated, automatons."

"Who...what...who or what could be behind it?" Paola Kett asked in total disgust. She had just returned with Drea Ridge and Kelvan Hotch, holopads in hand. "What force do we credit...or blame...with it?"

"The Psiborn had control over technology with their minds," David Rule said. "Manipulating 'bots and 'droids all over the cosmos was simple for a widespread regime like theirs."

"Right enough. Men and women from all races and species had themselves altered to become the Psiborn, to join this new, voluntary technology race," Jon Kett said.

"But I don't see how they can be responsible for this," Rule added.

"Yeah, for two reasons," Sylver Ridge added. "First off, the Psiborn were all cybernetically enhanced, genetically altered and mechanically merged, to interface with tech in all sorts of ways, even remotely...but they can't move dead bodies."

"And?" Jaka Baddenide asked for the second reason.

"They're all dead," Uncle Sundar spat. "Either dead or in hiding."

"An entire movement of allied beings are gone?" Jaka asked.

David Rule said, "The Android Revolt was a brutal war. Most of those considering themselves Psiborn, those who actually survived, fled the known sectors afterward. They went into the outer reaches of space."

"Those dead bodies we encountered were just shadows," Wastasa Winds said regretfully. "There was no spiritual awakening in them. It was quite the opposite. I have never seen beings more dead."

"They can't fly ships and fire weaponry and repair engines if they cannot think," Jon Kett sighed. "The Psiborn can do those things. What if there were Psiborn who had uncovered something truly dark?"

"You mean pure evil?" Paola Kett gasped.

"Looked like pure evil to me," Drea Ridge said.

"It has to have an origin," David Rule said. "This had to have begun somewhere...sometime."

For the first moment in some time, all voices fell silent. Everyone wrestled with their own thoughts and pondering.

"I may have an answer," Samara Garriton then broke that silence.

She approached from the stairwell, Taelynn Berreaux and Kohlene Arria with her. Garriton had changed clothes, taking on a black Acolyte cassock and pants, uniform of the Acolyte sentinel, as well as the white cloak.

All attention fell to the approaching Unity Captain.

"We had records in Unity Command. Stories. Rumors. Legends. Tales from drifting pilots, navigators, ships and crews. The Reaches... something horrible was birthed in that place...lives in that place...so Unity wanted it investigated...and officially discredited."

"So, Unity Command sent you and the *Vindicator* on a suicide mission? Some kind of first run at whatever was moving in that-"

"No. Not the first run," Garriton interrupted Wastasa Winds.

"What was the first run then?" Berreaux asked beside her.

Garriton gazed off into the Sanctuary, eyes furtive, her lip twitching.

"It was far before my time, before the Android Revolt was over," she sighed. "But Unity Command caught one of the most infamous, one of the most powerful Psiborn...a human named Andreas Riker. His enemies called him-"

"The Psiborg," Sundar Ridge growled.

"Worst of the worst," Sylver spat.

"Wasn't just war with that one," Gill Bardoff said with a pointed, telling finger. "He was demented, cruel! Experimented on little kids, peasants, civilians...man infected whole colonies with biological, technological warfare, trying to force people to go Psiborn."

"Everyone always heard he killed himself the day the last of the Psiborn regime was defeated. A lot of Psiborns who were able fled...but not him. They say he killed himself on the bridge of a monster ship, one he and a bunch of his kind had been building with their minds as well as conventional means," David Rule said. "The ship had more space inside it than most space stations. Made Dreadships look like escape pods."

"He didn't kill himself, did he?" Gideon Ridge asked Samara Garriton, studying her face.

"No. He was captured by the Unity Command forces-"

The older people roared with fury and disbelief.

"And he was exiled," she continued. "They set him out with his massive ship and saw him all the way out to the Reaches. They told him if he wanted to earn a reprieve he had to go into the Reaches and find what...evil...lurked there. The truth is that they never expected him to return...or survive...with all the defenses and weapons on the ship destroyed. They also thought the Reaches would have no technology within it that he would be able to manipulate into repair parts. In short, it was an exile designed to execute him."

"Then why do it?" David Rule asked bluntly. "It makes no sense."

"What did Unity get out of it?" Jaka Baddenide demanded.

"Cybernetic technology," Samara said. "Years of advanced science in a matter of weeks. Riker's private works and designs."

"That ship," David Rule said, "he gave it a name. He was arrogant, delusional. He said the Psiborn were the next step in evolution, in all sentient beings' evolution. And, because they had chosen the step, controlling their own evolution, he declared the Psiborn gods. That was why he named the ship what he did."

"What did he call it?" Drea Ridge asked.

"Leviathan," Kohlene Arria said, her voice a melodious velvet. "No Acolyte or Messenger has ever forgotten the story. The Psiborn named that ship after the symbolism used in the Old Testament. An ancient evil rising from deep waters. A supernatural sea monster or sea serpent. It was part of his disregard for any belief in God, since he had decided the Psiborn were gods."

"You mean the Old Testament of the Christian Bible?" Wastasa Winds asked.

"Yes," Jon Kett said.

"There was more to his mocking, too," David Rule growled, shaking his head. "The Leviathan belief was symbolism in the later days of Biblical writing but in ancient times more than the Hebrew people believed in a massive sea monster. The Greek Hydra and many others were linked to the same traditions.

"There was a belief also that the Earth was a reflection of what happened in the spirit world and in the night skies, or in the stars. Many believed that a deep sea Leviathan was a mirror image to the constellation of Draco, something they saw as a Leviathan in the sky, and they believed that the spiritual, and therefore interstellar, version, Draco, flew about the skies and swallowed the moon or sun temporarily. That is where eclipses came from."

"Delusional," Gill Bardoff said. "Man thought he was some kind of rival force against the Almighty?"

"I didn't know that part," Garriton said.

"What do you know?" Kreden asked. "What was his final fate?"

"They propelled him into the Reaches...Unity's one and only stab at finding out what was in the region...but they never heard from him again. Then he became part of the legends, the rumors. This massive serpent-like ship, snaking within the Reaches and in and out of its borders, occasionally clashing with smaller vessels and destroying them. No weapons would be used, just the crushing impact of collision."

"Part of space travel mythology, just like sailors of olden times seeing sea serpents on any given world with water," Wastasa Winds said with a sigh, "only this was a piece of reality taken right out of the legend and brought to life. He was sent to investigate the rumors and horror stories, only to become part of them."

"You asked if I was the first one sent to investigate the Reaches. I was not. That Psiborg was...and he was one of the reasons I was sent."

"Samara?" Ridge said.m

"Unity received some long range telemetry from a buoy positioned just outside the Reaches. It matched the data transmissions they had taken from that Leviathan a long time ago. Then the buoy was destroyed. After being dragged into the Reaches."

"They believe he's alive, still commanding that ship?" Sundar Ridge asked.

"He'd be older than us," Gill Bardoff laughed. "And two parsecs out of his mind, floating in that wacky zone all this time."

"He could just be dead."

Everyone looked at Jaka Baddenide.

"Think about it. The man died in that place but came across the evil everyone has been talking about. A guy with tech powers and mental powers all of a sudden with supernatural power, raises an army of tech but also of flesh and bone, then tries to launch a war on all life."

Wastasa Winds said, "I don't know what to believe."

"I believe this," Samara said lowly. "We agree it all had to start someplace. I believe it was there. As for how, why and who, I don't think we will ever know with certainty until we go inside."

"We?" Ridge asked.

"Captain, you've done what you came to do. You freed the bodies of your crew and your ship from whatever evil is at work. You made certain you hadn't left any living crew behind. You did your duty...and more."

Gideon agreed with his sister, saying, "You can go back to your life. You can't go back to Unity but you could make a life *someplace*."

"You could all leave this to us," David Rule told Gideon. "You've done enough already. The Acolytes can handle this. Take your family and your friends and leave here."

"We fought this guy in his prime; we'll beat his old man bones, too," Sundar said. "Once Sylver goes with Gill to get his bucket, he can bail if he wants-"

"You ain't sendin' me home to dust my scrap pile," Gill Bardoff said. "I'm in it, neck deep; wouldn't have it no other way. Ain't had to unload on another ship in more years than I care to count. About time this old man shook the fire out of his boots again."

"I don't have a clue what that means," Wastasa Winds muttered, "but I came out here to find out what was behind this. I'm not done."

"I can speak for the crew of the *Word*. We aren't running."

"Well, it sounds like we're all in this together," Rule noted, staring at the resolve in Gideon Ridge's eyes. "We Acolyte pilots need to get our ships prepped. It may take a little while, since we have more than thirty here. In fact, we have more ships than crew. Some will have to be sacrificed, left behind. We'll get that started. Gideon, you and your people should grab a little rest."

"David, about those extra ships," Gideon thought aloud. "Are there any you would like to save, instead of losing? Two or three, more desirable than the others?"

Rule nodded, saying, "I'm sure."

Gideon Ridge looked over at his crew.

"I need some fighter pilot volunteers."

"Yeeeaahhhhhhh," the Hotch twins growled at the same time.

Kreden added, "You got it."

"I'll run one out," Drea Ridge chimed. "But it's got to be fast."

CHAPTER SEVEN : *Onslaught*

M aximilian Station posed before the black curtains of space as if sitting for a portrait. The twinkling starlight, silver studs sewn into the fabric of darkness, glittered over the few places the station did not glow with its own lights. Its metals gleamed, too, in the shining white of frozen Dor Modo.

Though predominantly flat on the very bottom, the spacestation was somewhat spherical in shape. The levels resting atop the foundation rose from the base in a domelike design, each level a bit smaller in circumference than the one below it. The base housed the power plants and generated environmental control, as well as most of the other energy.

The level just above the base foundation was the main docking bay level, which made up the outer ring of that entire level. It was the only level that seemed even remotely defended, large cannon turrets placed at intervals all the way around. The rest of the spacestation looked defenseless.

Though cold metal adrift in the dark of space, Maximilian Station gave a warm welcome to all comers. Lights on the outer surfaces advertised businesses and inns and taverns all over the outpost. Many races and species saw Maximilian Station as a last stop before further travel, a respite from a journey, a haven in a storm.

The starmada swarming toward it saw it as a target, a fatted calf ready to slay.

"Core Operations," said a young docking bay tender. He tapped at the muffed headset rapidly. "Operations, this is Bay Fifty-eight. Can you repeat your last message?" he asked incredulously. "It sounded like you said three hundred and eighty."

"Confirmed, Bay Fifty-eight."

The young human stared without focus at a crate in his landing bay.

"How is that possible? A fleet of that many random ships in a fleet?"

167

"Just get your bay ready, Fifty-eight. We will accommodate as many as we can, first to arrive, first to be served," came a tired response. "You and every other bay tender have the same questions."

"We might be wondering because we don't have that many bays in the first place and a lot already have customers. What about-"

"Those who come when there is no more room will have no room."

"Well, you're Toranish tonight," the bay tender said and chuckled. His face glowed with mischief. "How much longer are you on duty?"

"Operations, out," the female voice countered over the headset.

The young man made a whistling sound as he slid a crate out of the way. He looked out through the force screen walling in his docking pad again. It shimmered with soft yellow energy, holding the atmosphere inside and the vacuum of space outside.

"A lot of customers coming," he mumbled to himself.

The field was a brilliant use for landing ships, for the electromagnetic design allowed solid objects to pass right through it. It merely held air and gases and whatnot in their places. Starships flew straight through the fields, into and out of the atmospheres of stations like that one, without problems.

Some bays held more than one ship, depending on the size of the ship. Others were only big enough to hold one starfighter. Bay fifty-eight was large enough to hold a freighter or, on a good day, a tugliner. Bay Tender Fifty-eight wondered how many of the incoming ships would be his responsibility to receive and tend.

In the distance, he saw bits of movement cross in front of the glow of Dor Modo. Then the dots became like a swarm of something, like bats crossing in front of Earth's moon.

Suddenly, a loud droning sound erupted from his headset. By reflex, he knocked the muffs from his head. From where he stood he could hear the tone blaring from the headset. He rubbed one of his ears.

Across the station, the same mournful sound told of horrors to come. The baleful dirge played through every open technological transmitter.

Core Operations, the offices of the central controlling body of Maximilian Station, shuddered under the loud transmission. All of their operators and attendants were half deafened by the sudden onslaught of sound. They were instantly cut off from maintenance crews and docking port crews and security forces. They were also cut off from the big bosses and their penthouse locales in the upper levels.

Businesses lost local music and entertainment audios as the tone flooded their projection systems as well. Public holocoms lost visuals and the tone sang from their audios. Worst of all, every ship trying to suddenly heard the tone and heard only the tone...

...and their systems began to malfunction.

What is this? the young tender thought. Then, as he picked up the headset, *Is this thing going crazy? Or is the whole system shorting out?*

He slapped it against his leg several times, watching the distant swarm as it filled up his view of Dor Modo. It was a massive cloud of ships.

I hope Core Operations knows how close the station's visitors are.

Core Operations did not. Secured in the center most structure in the station, they only held digital means of seeing outside the station. None of that was working. None of their communications were working. Core Operations was inoperative.

The tender leaned down and slapped the headset against the floor roughly. The tone still blared. He did it twice more, heard a crack in the polymer casing then sighed. The sound was still as loud and as constant.

Nothing can land if communication is this bad, he mused.

He stood upright again and looked up at the energy field.

He never even had time to be shocked or frightened.

A little fighter craft glided through the yellow field as he had seen a thousand ships do a thousand times. His mind was not quick enough to remind him no one had clearance to land, nor was it quick enough to register the oncoming fighter's great age...and its great speed.

The ghost vanguard of a coming storm, a ragged, smoking Seaver class starfighter, hit the young man, his crate and the rear walls of the docking bay. In an instant, everything in the bay was fire and destruction and debris...then two more fighters came in right behind it.

The rear walls and doors gave way and exploded into the inner chambers of the landing area. The force blew patrons and workers and transport 'droids aside like dust in the wind.

At that moment, mismatched ships flew in formation into most of the docking bays that could be seen and targeted from planet-side. The empty, suicide fighters plunged into bays with a hideous agenda, their explosive crashes blowing apart the station from the inside and starting it burning. The entire station shuddered and vibrated violently and systems began to fail.

Around the docking bay level, nicknamed the docking belt, the fields on the space side began to flicker. In seconds of lost integrity, major amounts of atmosphere exhausted themselves through the bays. Ships slid weightlessly across decking plates. Alarms ignited in each, warning of potential failure. And, in many, the fields never came back on. Ships simply drifted into space, as did cargo and crates...and attendants...

In other locales, like businesses and offices and penthouse luxury, lights failed and returned, while some failed, never to return.

On the other side of the station, ships that had made liftoff heard the death call and were betrayed by their own controls. They found themselves turning back to open ports in the station and firing weapons. More than ten ships of varying size and potential unloaded on the defenseless spacestation's docking belt and it shuddered further. Captains all around the belt watched in horror as their own ships added to the destruction around them.

Throughout the station, chaos and horror spoke to the inhabitants with threats and taunts. Madness chimed in as well, driving many to run for the docking bays, working or not...still there or not.

Core Operations issued a mandatory evacuation order, based on their spotty sensor information, though the order would never transmit, even to an interior receiver. Feedback along a central communications relay sparked and ignited all of Core Operations. It went up in a flare of fire and current and plasma discharge.

The screams were lost in the noise of the explosions.

The entire station pitched suddenly to one side, the engine cores operating out of balance and no longer stable, the gravitational maintenance systems bouncing from one extreme to another. On the side with the escaped ships, their dominated controls continuing to send cannon fire into the struggling metals of the station, the gravity amped up tremendously and the ships began to drift back toward destroyed bays.

Almost all of the overtaken ships crashed back into the station helplessly, with the exception of four large vessels wielding considerable armament.

At a distance, one hundred of the three hundred and eighty random ships that had arrived still waited, all trash, derelict ships with no pilots and no crews, looking for any survivors of the station to free themselves. The other two hundred plus flew in suicidal abandon, raining all over the station like hail. They assaulted the station in a way that would never be repaired, a nightmare vengeance wreaked upon the living by the junk dumps from the Draksus moon of Dor Modo. Over viewports and viewscreen windows, across all of the waiting, second wave of abandoned ships, the reflections of flame and explosions flickered.

Still the ships waited.

A brief flash of interstellar light, a crackle of energy, a blur in space. Then the *Bloodwind* appeared.

Materializing from lightspeed as if from another dimension, it was instantly in weapons range of Maximilian Station, though the station looked nothing like it had the last time Commodore Wrigley Zeckinbridge had seen it. She had wanted to be ready no matter what may have been there when they arrived but nothing could have prepared her for a hundred random ships that watched as the station burned.

"What in the-" the Commodore shouted, coming to her feet.

"Commodore!" Science Officer Wimbel Boatwright shouted. "Those ships are empty! No life forms registering at all!"

"Ma'am, should I-"

"Fire!" Zeckinbridge interrupted the gurgle-voiced Octovoid. "Engage those ships!"

"Advance approach Zeta-fourteen," Retaw, the Greylik Pilot, announced.

The ship surged to one side and the nose angled for a direct run on the empty starmada.

"Just fly, Retaw, save the commentary!" Zeckinbridge shouted.

"Weapons lock on-" the Octovoid Weapons Officer started.

"Save it, Gorbler!" Zeckinbridge yelled at the Weapons Officer. "Light 'em up, your discretion!"

Captain Samara Garriton had told her what she had seen and experienced. That was enough for Zeckinbridge. Empty ships, a burning, neutral spacestation...the story told itself, as far as she was concerned. Death was knocking at the door and Commodore Wrigley Zeckinbridge answered with a venter in her grasp.

Four fighters exploded immediately from the frontal assault, their exploding wreckage destroying another two nearby. Almost instantly, shields ignited around each of the junk craft modern enough to hold them. Others simply activated their Gravstar defenses and locked their plating tight. Those so old they did not even have Gravstar adopted evasive maneuvers.

Those with defenses adopted pursuit.

Four large starships, too, ones hijacked from the station by the deafening droning, pulled back from the station and came about to find bearings on the *Bloodwind*.

"Twenty-seven ships in direct pursuit," Boatwright called out. "Two Migroid freighters, heavily armed, one Greylik tugliner and one Toran worker transport, both considerably armed, are now triangulating intercept courses from the other side of the station!"

"Why would they attack a Unity vessel, much less help this nightmare starmada?" Niles Respra exploded.

"They're not," Boatwright said. "The readings suggest they were taken over remotely...and the people aboard each were executed. Life support is out on each one."

Zeckinbridge ground her teeth together.

"Come about, Retaw! Gorbler, roll power to the frontal shielding!"

"Captain, there are so many-" Gorbler countered.

"Gorbler, do what you're told! I didn't get to be a Commodore by accident!" Zeckinbridge howled.

Gorbler's bulbous head changed colors as he unleashed a flurry of noises in his native language. It was rare that an Octovoid bothered to learn the Base language for his division and, though Gorbler had actually done so, he still cursed and prayed in his own.

Again, a flash and a blur in space...then the Unity ship called *Corridor* appeared.

Captain Van Pelt rose from the command seat. Captain Joshua Brent joined him.

"I'd hold off on firing on the *Bloodwind*," Brent said. "My ship is the least of your worries..."

The station pitched to yet another side even as the two captains tried to make sense of what they saw. Without gravitational buffers, everyone and every single thing inside it, if not fastened down, tipped with it, yet again.

Inside the station, turmoil, terror and chaos ran rampant.

Explosions rocked the orbital city's foundations. Supports and bulwarks fell apart without warning, save the occasional precollapse groan and the telltale whine of machinery and metals giving way. Sparks blistered the air and smoke drifted in ghostly, shaded forms as fire broke out.

Like the station needed anything else to waste the air supply.

Corridors imploded, catwalks dropped from their suspension cables and towers. Flooring buckled and some of it rose in a sharp upheaval as the very form of the station gave way.

The man made world was doomed and everyone inside knew that. The screams, the hysteria, the panic all gave it away, not that it was much of a secret. Maximilian Station was burning, giving up the ghost.

The Rothidai pulled the Greshan woman up from the floor and buried his shoulder into the massive, locked bay door.

"Stuck," he grunted, reflexively snorting it in his native tongue.

He backed off, rammed it and backed off again, shaking his head.

"Stop," the Greshan told him. She wiped blood from her forehead, uneasy on her own two feet. "You're going to hurt yourself."

"We will die if we do not open the door," the horned Rothidai said.

He had come with the Greshan to the Acolyte Temple bay before the nightmare began, before the rending of the station. For a few moments, since a corridor had collapsed on them outside the bay in question, the big Rothidai had been digging them free and uncovering the woman.

He had extracted the information his boss, Cheyenne Winds, wanted from the waitress at the Sunbrowser. He hoped no one would find out he had paid for it; his boss would ridicule him as weak. Still, he held no desire to harm women, children and the elderly.

As planned, he had returned to the Winds woman with the information. Likewise, Katril, the Greshan, had done her part and tailed the Ridge brothers to see where they would go. When she found out they were planning to move their ragged ship to the Temple bay, she also returned to Winds with the data.

Satisfied, Winds sent them ahead to the Acolyte Temple, promising to meet them there. She told them she had to send the other hunters in another direction, planning to pretend to help the Echo Soldiers and the Starstalkers with a tip she knew to be false. She was even going to lie to Rala Kess, one of the only beings in the known cosmos she considered dangerous.

Grockforth pushed aside more debris and cursed the woman's name.

"Where is that slicker?" he roared. "For once, she could be useful!"

Katril tried to hold him back from another charge on the bay barrier.

"You can't run down a bay door!" she swore.

Abruptly, the corridor door behind them swished aside only half way with a cascade of sparks. As if conjured by the mention of her name, through it jumped Winds, her technofiber gloves glowing.

"Out of the way, Grockforth," she told the Rothidai with a smirk. "Brutality doesn't win everything. Right, Katril?"

The Greshan blinked heavily.

"She took a hard blow to the head," the big Rothidai said. "It is high time you bothered to-"

The Winds woman moved by them without another word and placed a hand on the access pad for the locked, docking bay door. The glove lit up and the access panel did, too, then a loud hum started deep in the walls. The door shifted slightly with a groan. It shuddered, rattling the wall. Sparks lit up the shadowy corridor where the light was failing.

"Get her ready," Winds told the big Rothidai.

173

The groan gave way to a shriek of metal grinding on metal as the door began to move.

Grockforth looked down into Katril's eyes, steadying her by the shoulder. She nodded, patting him on the arm.

He moved the double ended mace from the strap on his back to his hand. A heavy particle rifle clung to his shoulder from a bandoleer strap.

"When I get this open, I want you to go straight for the Temple! Get me Samara Garriton!" Winds demanded.

The first door receded into the walls completely. The second shifted but stalled, railing against the notion of moving with a shriek of steel.

"How do you even know she's in there?"

The slicker rolled her eyes, irritated by the distraction.

"The old men moved their ship to the Acolyte bay. The waitress told you herself the things they wanted to know and you know why we followed the old men. Gideon Ridge's ship is in there, I would stake your life on it."

"I would say you already have," the Rothidai growled.

The secondary blast door shifted again but only to tease. A cascade of sparks, a shower of hot, burning light dropped over them.

What is holding it? Cheyenne Winds asked herself.

On the other side of that last barrier door, four Acolytes readied themselves. One of them, a woman with black hair under her hood and a wicked scar over her right eye and cheek, rolled back her wine red cassock sleeve. The metallic gauntlet on that forearm beeped when she triggered a small switch on one edge.

"Rule, we have a new problem," she half shouted over a loudly collapsing stand of crates.

The station pitched to the right.

David Rule, Acolyte Ambassador for the Maximilian Station Temple, pulled himself up from the floor of the Temple again.

"What's happening, Candri?" he asked the transmitting woman.

The Ridges and old Gil Bardoff were helping others to their feet, as were the Ketts. Baddenide rubbed a bruised head while Taelynn Berreaux leaned against a toppled column within the Temple. Wastasa Winds and Grundy were madly trying to bypass a jammed passage door.

Candri Prentice grimaced as the blast door shifted another inch. Sparks rained down from the upper slide runners, causing her to duck and sidestep.

She returned to the nearby wall immediately afterward, looking again at the fuzzy, failing security console's display. She lifted the gauntlet, triggered an interface with the console and changed the security encryption for opening the door again.

"A Rothidai, a Ton B'Gru and a Greshan," she muttered into her wrist. "They're coming through. I'm delaying them...but they're coming."

"Impossible!" Rule bellowed, taking the arm of a fellow Acolyte and helping him stand. "They'd need a slicker for that!"

"Not impossible, Rule," Candri said. "I'm watching the door move."

David Rule paused then looked over his shoulder at Wastasa Winds.

"Hold on a second…"

"Make it quick," Candri Prentice said. "If that Rothidai gets inside, stunning him is going to prove a challenge."

Rule had informed the entire Temple that communications, whether in ships or in the spacestation or over small, person transmitters, should be reset. They had to be reset, like they had reset the fighters when facing the dead, for known transmission sources only, just in case the debilitating tone from the Reaches was transmitted as far as the Temple. It was a good thing he had. Communication was important.

David Rule stormed over to Wastasa Winds.

"Can you slick even our best lockouts?" he asked, pointing randomly, gesturing to the outside of the Temple. "Like the main blast doors that lock down our bay?"

"Of course," Winds said. "Just takes a few minutes. Acolyte security is some of the best; it isn't like robbing Unity files from a classified server system. But it can still be done."

"I wish you'd hurry up and do this one," Grundy said, straining against the barrier before them as Winds fought the control panel.

"If anyone else could do it," Rule pressed, "as quickly as you do-"

"Ain't nobody I know of, chief," Winds said, holding his glowing mitt on the panel while keying a line of code into the panel interface beside it. "I mean, unless…"

Rule locked eyes with Winds when the slicker turned to him.

"Cheyenne Winds," Rule said quietly.

At that very moment, Winds said, "My daughter."

"She's as good as you are?" David Rule asked.

"Ought to be. I raised her."

"I think she's outside!" David Rule shouted. She's got help, too!"

"I hope you're wrong, Preacher," Winds spat, mouth twisted into a grimace.

"When she gets inside, are you going to be a problem?" Rule asked.

"No," Winds said gently. "Last I heard…I was a target."

"You're being hunted by your own daughter?" Grundy asked.

"I don't know if she's actively *hunting* me but I've heard-"

"Just work fast," Rule ordered.

Winds spun back to the door.

Rule turned back to the others.

"We've got invaders breaking through the blast doors from the main station," Rule shouted to his crowd. All visitors and all Acolytes inside the Temple had gathered at the frozen door. "I'm about to tell those of us outside the Temple to evacuate. The rest of us will have to follow as soon as we can, so be ready as soon as this door slides open. Get to your ships and get clear of the station. There's nothing more we can do here."

"Except pray, David," Kohlene Arria reminded, her face calm.

There was a peace radiating from her eyes, a compassion glowing on her face that surprised and resonated with those not of the Acolyte order.

The group checked their gear and their garb.

Gideon Ridge pulled his sister and the Hotch twins to one side.

"Stick to the plan. I don't know how many ships we may need but we'll probably need every single one we can get."

"What?" Drea Ridge barked.

"Negative," Kelvan muttered. "No way we're flying out and leaving all of you with invaders in the bay."

"We have to get as many-" Gideon tried.

"You need us, Gideon!" Kreden demanded.

"You're right, Kreden. I do. These Acolytes do. The cosmos does. I don't know what the future brings but I do know your skills." He then looked deeply into his sister's eyes. "All of you. You take those three ships David gave you and you streak out of this place no matter what's outside the bay doors. Whatever happens here, whatever happens to the *Word*, you take to space and do what we all try to do everyday. Represent Christ, rescue the oppressed, share the Love."

They started to resist but he hushed them to listen to David Rule.

Rule spoke into his gauntlet again.

"All Acolytes, this is Ambassador Rule. Temple sensors and station contacts all tell us the station is finished; there is no saving it. The docking belt has failed. The ships remaining are crippled or burning, all but our own in this Temple docking port. I do not know the threat but I know this. If we do not pull out now we may not get another opportunity. There is nothing more we can do for the station but pray, so please find your ships and initiate escape procedures. Copilots, when you are not needed, pray while your pilot flies."

Rule noticed then Kohlene Arria very calmly making her way from the foyer area to the Sanctuary. He gave a quick word to Jon Kett to watch things and he gave chase in a trot.

"Kohlene?" he called as he entered the Sanctuary.

"David," she said from the front. "They'll need you for the exodus. They'll need you all the more before it's all finished, you know that."

He jogged to a stop by the woman.

"All of us need to be ready. The doors are almost open."

"Some of us already are ready," she said with a wry smile, putting a gentle hand on the side of his face. "My moment is not outside the doors. My path doesn't leave this place."

He offered a purely dumbstruck stare.

"We need to seek God in this, David, more than we need to figure out what we can do in our own power. You know this. There is a time for action and a time for diligent, heartfelt prayer. Sometimes, it is time to do both at once. There is action to be taken right here, even as I pray."

"I agree but-"

"For me, it is time to hold the line against evil with prayer...and nothing more than to stand. I have lived a long life and I have run the race and I pray I have run well. Like the Apostle Paul in the Bible, I have come to a place where I feel I can do little more than simply stand. So-"

"You can't give up!"

"-stand I will."

"You can't just stop-"

"The docking shields are failing in the station, David. We have back up shielding, powered from here, but it will need resets. This is the way."

"No," he said, shook his head and adopted a dismissive frown.

She huffed, "I beg your pardon, Ambassador Rule."

"No. Now get to a ship and let's-"

"You know your part, your path. Do you not suppose I would know my own, David?" she asked, her face soft and affectionate but resolute.

"Kohlene, you can't just-"

She sighed and said, "What did the Apostle Paul write in the Book of Philippians? Chapter one, verses twenty and twenty-one?"

He locked his jaw.

"According to my earnest expectation and my hope, that in nothing I shall be ashamed, but that with all boldness, as always, so now also Christ shall be magnified in my body, whether it be by life, or by death. For to me to live is Christ, and to *die is gain,*" she emphasized.

"You don't know that this-"

"Second Timothy, Chapter four, verses six, seven and eight, David Rule," she continued, her voice confident and content.

He locked his jaw as the tears came.

"For I am now ready to be offered, and the time of my departure is at hand. I have fought a good fight, I have finished my course, I have kept the faith: Henceforth there is laid up for me a crown of righteousness, which the Lord, the righteous judge, shall give me..." she trailed.

Rule's voice cracked as he finished, "...at that day: and not to me only, but unto all them also that love his appearing."

She wiped the tears from his cheeks and he embraced her.

"I'm ready, David. I want to go...home. I want to see Him."

"You are such a mighty warrior," he choked. "We all love you."

"And I love you all. Always."

His gauntlet chimed again and he put it up before his face.

"Candri?"

"David, they're coming through but we can hold this point. Just work on getting to your ships. We will slow their-"

"No, Candri, pull back and evacuate. We'll be along afterward." Rule only waited a scarce few seconds as the woman protested loudly. "Candri...pull back now. Right now. It is not a request."

Candri Prentice nodded reluctantly at her allies by the door.

"Don't you wish I was still young enough for that tone to work on me?" Kohlene Arria chuckled.

David Rule stifled a laugh.

"Yes...I do."

"It's time for you to go," the woman said and wiped his tears away one more time. "They need you, David."

Kohlene Arria's eyes were more peaceful and beautiful than he had ever seen them.

"God Bless you," he said, quickly turning away and running for the others.

"And you," she said softly.

Kohlene Arria turned when he was gone. She looked longingly at the beautiful statue of the Savior, the One and Only Son of God. Her face beamed, her smile pure, uninhibited joy. She then moved to the altar and knelt there, though it took a moment to put aging knees all the way down.

"Our Father in Heaven, we need you so very much. For those about to face death come to life, please give them courage and protect them, that we might overcome evil once again. I ask for blessing, Father, bless them and keep them. Shield and protect them. Guide them, please. Make your face shine upon them and be merciful to them. Loving, Father God, lift up your countenance on them. Give them peace. I ask in the name above all names, Jesus Christ, our Lord."

Freighter after fighter after more fighters and more freighters soared out of the docking bay. The individuals on the outside of the heavy barrier door, hearing the ships, worked even harder to get it open. Cheyenne Winds shouted at the access panel, cursing in the Ton B'Gru language and the native language of her adoptive people, too.

Grockforth snorted, spinning the long mace around his hand and stomping.

"Oh, ha ha! Here it goes…" the Winds woman suddenly cackled.

The door finally shifted and slid away with a final cry of friction.

Another jammed door, the one closed tightly on the Temple, did the same thing at nearly the same moment.

A slicker led David Rule, the Ridges and their company out of the Temple, each on their way to a variety of ships. A different slicker led the way into the bay doors for her force, determined to stop them.

The two groups exchanged a brief glance over the considerable distance of the Acolyte Temple bay, everyone freezing in their strides. Inside each of them, it was an eternity in stone; in reality, it was only a nanosecond before everyone was in motion again.

The bay shielding flickered, the Temple backups struggling to hold. It would have been down already if it had been run by the station alone.

"Go, now! Stick to the plan!" Gideon Ridge roared.

Rule ran for his *Razorhawk*. It was very close to the Temple. In seconds he ripped into open space. Other Acolytes did the very same thing, moving for the mismatched fighters and freighters.

Jaka Baddenide doubled up with another Acolyte in need of a copilot in the little fighter, *Carolina*. Paola Kett did the same thing, leaving her own ship behind so that she could copilot for a close Acolyte friend on board a Starstalker Crescent fighter.

Gideon Ridge and his band ran for the *Spoken Word*, though three of them split apart and ran for Acolyte fighter ships. The Ridge brothers and Gill Bardoff veered off for the *Belly Rub*.

Lines flickered in the docking fields, horizontal flares of white and gray. The barrier would not hold forever.

Suddenly, Bardoff pointed and swore. Grockforth was strolling down the middle of the bay, not bothering with cover, as Cheyenne Winds and Katril took up defensive positions behind debris, rubble, a run down cargo mover and the odd supply crates.

The old man, Bardoff, was focused on the big, gray opponent. He never saw a shooter making ready.

Cheyenne Winds leaned over the top of a low rise crate. She had taken the position for sniping at the Samara Garriton entourage but Bardoff made an irresistible target, a silly, lanky old scarecrow in motion. A vicious smile licked across her blue lips as she squeezed one eye closed. She giggled and squeezed the trigger to her Vapor rifle.

Bardoff's torso exploded in a mist of crimson. His body spun about and crashed onto the decking with a limp thud. He barely even cried out when hit.

179

Sylver Ridge jumped to the side, taking cover with his brother behind a large column of metals, ceramics and lighting. His teeth ground together fiercely enough to have bitten through jordainium rivets as his fury boiled.

Gill Bardoff was down and Sylver had seen enough war and conflict to know a Vapor wound when he saw one. Vapor rifles did not just wound. They destroyed. If a target was not armored it was usually fatal.

Sylver roared from his position a guttural, incomprehensible cry of anguish, anger and mourning. Sun spat a slew of harsh expressions in his lowest, deepest voice.

Cheyenne Winds had not bothered to close the bay doors she had opened. To everyone's shock, through them poured three Echo Soldiers, a handful of furry Starstalkers and a Vipon in a long coat. Each ran instantly for cover at random locations, whether behind cargo, behind bay supports, behind control booths or even in low points in the decking.

Gideon Ridge and Samara Garriton found cover while Wastasa Winds and Grundy took respite in another place, at a different angle to the newcomers.

Cheyenne Winds howled with laughter from her place behind her crates. She sat flat, leaning against them with her back. She looked to the side, to the small cargo mover, behind which Katril waited for her orders. She winked at her.

"Complications," she cackled, then thumbed over her shoulder at the Echo Unit and the fleshhunters. "Great diversion, however!"

Grockforth, half way between his own team and the Ridge band, stopped in the open, no cover, and pointed his long mace down the docking bay.

"What is this?" he railed at Cheyenne Winds.

"Attention, Acolyte transport bay," one of the Echo Soldiers announced, his helmet's voice amplification system carrying a great distance. "We seek the criminals Samara Garriton and Gideon Ridge. Once they are in our custody and the criminal starfreighter, the *Spoken Word*, is in our custody, the remainder of you and your ships will be free to go."

Sylver Ridge whipped around the side of the support structure and fired his sweeper without even aiming. He hid again as soon as he did so.

Half of the Unity Soldiers' cover erupted in multiple energy impacts, blasting pieces to every direction.

Cheyenne Winds erupted again with crazed laughter.

"One of those old boondarms has a Bay Sweeper!" she laughed loudly. "This just gained a whole different level of excitement!"

"Fool," the Greshan woman growled. "Is this your doing?"

Winds howled with almost maniacal laughter.

"Come about again!" Captain Van Pelt screamed at his Pilot, a woman named Doranna Wells.

Smoke billowed around several ceiling conduits and two panels in the room had gone black. The *Corridor* had joined the bigger *Bloodwind* in combat with the starmada of lifeless, random ships, only to also find itself in conflict with four starships from the station. The little USAP transport ship trailed smoke and gases from its right engine bank.

"Have we got any communications back?" the Captain howled.

"No, sir," the Communications Officer answered. "We're still being jammed; I'm sure it's the *Bloodwind*."

"What is wrong with that woman?" Van Pelt shouted about Commodore Zeckinbridge.

"We've got a flood of newcomers on short range sensors," Science Officer Janng cried.

"We can't handle anymore hostiles!" Van Pelt shouted.

"Not hostiles," Captain Joshua Brent said, leaning into the accessory panel in the back of the bridge. "Twenty plus random fighters and freighters, all bearing Acolyte signatures!"

Van Pelt sighed, nodded then looked at the Pilot, shouting, "Okay then! Put us on their targets!"

Captain Joshua Brent, exiled Captain of the *Bloodwind*, tapped at his screen. He had rerouted the Weapons Control Station to the accessory location when the official position had erupted in sparks and flame and rendered the Weapons Officer unconscious.

"Captain Van Pelt, shields are down to less than forty per cent," Brent snapped. "Weapons are still at seventy plus, but-"

"Propulsion is failing; the right bank is already burning out!" Janng said. "Sensors say the station is going to explode! Repairs won't be possible!"

Van Pelt waved away their concerns.

"We're a Unity vessel! We'll survive!"

The ship pitched to one side, throwing the Communications Officer to the floor. He hit hard but managed to recover quickly. Several more jerks and snatches against the little ship made Van Pelt turn to Brent.

"Report!"

"Cannon fire from the closest Migroid freighter!" Captain Brent said.

"Evasive maneuvers, Ms. Wells!" Van Pelt yelled. "Brent, blow something up!"

The Unity transport whipped into a formation with several Acolyte ships and made a long, strafing run along a triangular formation of empty starfighters. Several exploded, only a few bearing shielding. The allies came about then and finished the targeted squadron.

The empty fighter force swarmed about open space like metal locusts seeking a harvest to devour. The Unity ships and the newly arriving Acolyte fighters found them surprisingly agile for empty crafts, no crews to guide them. They worked well together, too, giving real trouble to the bigger vessels of Unity command and the Acolyte allies.

Several Acolyte ships had already been destroyed, the *Corridor* was next door to crippled and the *Bloodwind* had its hands full with the hijacked vessels from the station.

The Vanguard ship ripped through a small formation of empty fighters, blowing all of them to debris in a rolling assault with a Migroid freighter and the tugliner still in close pursuit.

The *Bloodwind* jolted several times, back to back, in different directions. The bridge lighting flickered again.

"Retaw! Evasive patterns!" Commodore Zeckinbridge railed.

"Trying, Commodore!" the Pilot answered, shifting a lever all the way forward on the helm. "Hold on!"

The ship whipped about yet again, all on the bridge holding to a station.

"Gorbler, deploy cosmines!" Zeckinbridge shouted. "Anything chasing us too close can have a little surprise!"

"Cosmine deployment hatch is jammed!" the Octovoid shouted, his head a dark purplish hue. "The last cannon hits damaged us through the shielding!"

"Then feed them a Terran missile! We've got to stop those Migroid cannons!"

"Terrans away!" he shouted, slamming one of his eight appendages onto the panel. "I put two missiles into it, Commodore! I'm trying to reload the missile banks but…"

"But what?"

"The banks have jammed now!"

Abruptly, the ship pitched violently and veered into a new course. The bridge lighting flickered and did not come back on. Emergency lighting kicked in and dimly reset the mood of the operations room.

"Left engines offline, rear engines failing," the Pilot said. "Trying to compensate, put more power to them to kick them into action! Give me a minute!"

182

"We don't have one!" Zeckinbridge shouted.

The ship jerked and bumped several times again, back to back, but not heavily.

"Speak, Mr. Gorbler!" Zeckinbridge howled.

"Shields holding!" he shouted. "Terran missiles were a direct hit on the front of the Migroid freighter, went right through the shielding, did massive damage! Still in pursuit. We picked up a formation of those empty ships again, also, strafing us along our starboard flank!"

"The tugliner is charging its graviton beam generator, Commodore, and they're getting close to us!" Science Officer Boatwright informed.

"Retaw, put everything you've got into our good engines!"

"Commodore, it'll put us into a curve; we won't-"

"Then curve us right around the station! Make a run around its back side! Until it explodes, it's the only cover or hiding place we'll have out here!"

"Aye!" Retaw said.

"Mr. Respra," she said to the Communications Officer. "It's time to break communications blackout…start charging the Shofar!"

Ambassador David Rule had just blown apart his fifth empty victim when he saw a fellow Acolyte ship disappear into flame. Four ragged Razor class fighters from a previous production generation swept right through the fiery debris, came about to their hard right and started to chase yet another pair of Acolytes.

"*Raine*, you and your wing rider have a quartet on your back ends!" he transmitted to Taelynn Berreaux and her ally. He was using the secured direct transmission system.

"Confirmed," Berreaux said breathlessly. "*Belle*, flip back. I'll play target."

Taelynn Berreaux cut downward and then hard to her port. Her wing rider pulled up into a roll and followed it all the way over, coming into position behind the four. The four targeted Berreaux, locking on to her signal.

Rule swept downward at a stiff arc and triggered his weapons on the first two ships. One bounced and jerked and shook under his energy fire, the shields shimmering with his assault. The other never even twitched. It erupted into a ball of flame.

The shielded Razor flipped off to its starboard side, falling from formation. Rule rolled his Razor to the side and gave pursuit.

The other two ragged Razor class fighters stayed on Berreaux. She pitched this way and that, rolled to the side and cut up and down but they stayed on her with precision. One fired, followed by the other. The *Raine* jerked and pitched several times, her shields holding.

"Hang on, Taelynn!" the pilot of the *Belle* transmitted.

She triggered the Lath fighter's weapons, a set of plasma turrets on each wingtip. Rolling barrels from each weapon offered up a belch of rapid fire plasma streams. They cut across one of the empty Razors like a plasma cutter in a shipyard, splitting the ship into two pieces and igniting it in a hail of destruction.

She never saw the Migroid freighter closing from her starboard side.

Multiple cannon launches tore the little *Belle* out of existence without a warning and without mercy. The aggressive cannon fire spread also destroyed the last Razor chasing Taelynn Berreaux and detonated right behind Berreaux's *Raine*. Her shields flashed and disappeared, a hatch panel from the engine bank blew free of the little fighter and her propulsion went down instantly. She spun wildly, her engines and her shields down, her control stolen.

The Migroid freighter blew right by her floundering ship and went after another little formation of Acolytes, however. Taelynn Berreaux continued to pray.

Jon Kett's *Tikrek* led a gathering of four fellow Acolyte fighters into a band of ten empty fighters. Kett directed the play while flying in the lead point and the team managed to destroy eight of the ten targets. They peeled back from the last two when a new target presented itself.

The hijacked Toran worker transport had just torn through two Acolyte fighters by ramming them ruthlessly and destroying them but it had done extensive damage to its own nose and fuselage in the maneuver.

"*Ru Bo Tee*, flank *Lifter* on the port side. Prepare to strafe down that thing's side," Jon Kett transmitted. Both of the ship pilots confirmed his direction. "*Redliner*, you and *Saber* chase down behind me and watch my flanks. When I get centered, you two fall off to that thing's starboard side and strafe it all the way down."

"Where are you going, *Tikrek*?" the pilot of the *Redliner* asked.

"I'm Jonah, boys," Kett answered. "I'm going down that thing's throat!"

Four of the empty fightercraft appeared behind the transport and spread out by its sides. The two Acolyte fighters set to strafe the transport's port side split up; one went toward the fighters and only one began the strafing run. One of Kett's support ships broke off as well, streaking forward for the newly arriving fighters, leaving only one to walk Kett to the transport's face.

Kett tried to correct them but, before he could transmit a thing, the engaging Acolyte fighters found open turrets on the transport raining pulse bolts on them incessantly. Though they managed to engage and destroy the empty fighter envoy, the heavy pulse storm from the transport destroyed them.

Kett squeezed his eyes closed as he opened fire on the Toran transport, blasting its nose and the surrounding fuselage to just so much debris. He buried his thrust lever to the back of his panel and flew right into the gaping maw he had created.

The *Saber* stayed true to the plan. It veered off to the starboard side and strafed energy all down the side of the transport, blowing the lightweight, unarmored turrets completely off the ship. What remained of the shielding failed and disappeared, the hull buckling and warping along that ravaged side.

Then, as the *Saber* pulled safely away, Jon Kett's fighter blasted through the transport's hull from the inside. The big ship shuddered violently and ignited into a ball of flame.

Kett did a victory roll as he gave chase for the speeding *Saber*.

Along the run, Kett was joined by a Lath fighter just like the *Saber*. It registered on sensors as the *Dagger*. The three burned through a handful of the enemy fighters then came to focus on the Migroid freighter chasing after Acolyte targets.

"Get ready to make a run on that Migroid freighter," Kett transmitted.

"Indeed," David Rule confirmed, dropping into their formation.

He brought four other Acolyte ships with him.

Kett laughed, "Good to see you, Rule. You want to run the spearhead?"

"Why not?" Rule asked. "I'll call it. Everyone fall in; when we get closer, we can split into ranks."

Rule listened for them to confirm then made straight for the target.

In a different area, three Acolyte fighters formed a very tight, triangular attack pattern. The pilots had worked together often; the uncomfortably close formation was more than comfortable to them.

"I've got point, boys, try to keep up," Drea Ridge transmitted from the lead fighter, a wicked looking, sharply angled Auseptian fighter.

Like the race who designed it, a feathery, insectizoid people, the ship, *Pyramid*, bore four wings. Each wing had its own ion pulse blaster.

"*Pyramid*, don't worry about us. Throw that propulsion to the wall," Kreden Hotch answered. "My *Freedom* won't be left behind."

"This old, blocky Rothidai ship ain't pretty but don't underestimate it," Kelvan Hotch replied. "It moves and responds like it really is a Rothidai, fast, smooth and agile! I might ask Rule if I can trade something for this thing when we're done. I'm falling in love with the *Graystone*, people!"

"Okay, adopt the seventy/thirty and let's vaporize that squadron on our scopes," Drea Ridge directed, bringing them back to focus.

Seventy/thirty was a directive given by a point vessel in a triangular fighter pattern. Being the tip of the spear, so to speak, the point ship would run all shield power to the forefront of the vessel. The two ships on the sides and to the rear would leave a thirty per cent shielding active on the front but a seventy per cent shield concentration in their rear for the good of the group.

"Confirmed," Kreden Hotch called from the *Freedom*, a Riven built fighter with six wings and a rotating plasma cannon in the nose.

"Yeeeaaaahhhhhhhhh," Kelvan Hotch roared.

Then, plan in place, they sliced into a squadron of twenty random fighters flown by the dead.

Back behind the station, the Vanguard vessel *Bloodwind* had opened up on a lot more of the swarming fighters that crowded it. It had wreaked havoc on them, destroying them with cannons and missiles and particle weapons. A badly damaged Migroid freighter still gave chase but consistently fell behind, its systems failing. The Greshan tugliner, however, still gained on them, prepping its graviton beam for grappling them to a stop.

"The weapon is charged!" Officer Boatwright shouted, watching their systems readings.

"Then engage it, Mr. Gorbler!" Commodore Zeckinbridge ordered.

Suddenly, a powerfully loud, majestically tuned horn tone erupted from the Communications System of the *Bloodwind*. The blaring, unbelievably powerful sound rattled every ship with an open channel within its range. The handful of empty fighters, the Migroid freighter still in pursuit and the very close tugliner all vibrated with the resonating note. It drowned out the death call that was transmitting from someplace within the Reaches and the recieving ships instantly dropped power and direction. They were very abruptly not only empty but they were once again powerless.

A cheer went up on the bridge but Zeckinbridge brought them about.

"Don't celebrate, yet," she reminded. "Get us back to the other side of the station; there's a lot left to be done." She closed her eyes then and gave thanks to God. "Just like at the city of Jericho," she said with a smile.

186

The spread out positioning of Starstalkers, Echo Soldiers and the quick draw, Rala Kess, made them a formidable group. Neither the Ridges nor the team with Cheyenne Winds particularly wanted to be first at breaking cover. Grockforth, having no cover already, immediately fell back to the hiding place with his love, Katril.

However, the field in the docking port flickered more and more. No one thought they had much time. Some of the lights in the spaceport had already dimmed while a few had died already.

Sundar readied his weapons, one in each hand, while Sylver jacked the lever on the bottom of his sweeper. A charge shell kicked free and a new one chambered itself. A high pitched whine resounded from the weapon as it charged.

"Wasstassa, what are you doing with thosse people?" the Vipon bounty hunter called from cover. "We came after Garriton in a team!"

"Good point, Rala," Winds shouted from his own cover beside Grundy. "Thing is, we were only a team because Unity Command hired us then asked us to work together. I don't go around killing for currency, you snake, so you stick with your Hunon partner. Where is your little buddy, anyway?"

"The Hunon?" Rala Kess asked calmly. "I killed him…for currencsy…"

"Winds," the Rothidai, Grockforth, rumbled menacingly. "I asked you a question and I want an answer! What is this? You were supposed to send the rest of this scuttle running about after false clues! Did you lie to us, instead? Did you bring these others here?"

"Rala Kess? Unity?" Cheyenne Winds shouted back at Grockforth. "Fleshhunters, an Echo squad and a Vipon assassin come into a docking bay and you ask if I orchestrated it? That's not a double cross! That's the lead in to a bad joke!"

The Vipon spun and darted for new cover, a position he could defend against both directions. He was quick and agile. The Echo Soldiers were slower, as were the fleshhunters, almost every one of them hesitating as they looked for new defensive locations. In the hesitation, some of them moved into the open.

The others in the bay heard the movement. First, they took a peek then they took advantage.

Cheyenne Winds fired that Vapor rifle twice and put down two of the Starstalkers, leaving the others to howl and hiss wildly. Sundar Ridge fired his weapon and blew one of the Starstalkers to the decking, too.

Sylver Ridge fired his Bay Sweeper again, targeting the Echo Soldiers because of their armor. He did not want to kill anyone but he did want to survive.

The blast riddled their cover with damage but also shredded the diffuser bands and armors worn by the soldiers. One of them went down, wounded but alive, so the other two grabbed his arms and they all scurried for new cover.

Sylver levered the gun for a new charge shell.

Samara Garriton triggered her venter four times, putting down one Echo soldier and one Starstalker.

Gideon Ridge leaned out and fired rapidly with both of his neuropulse bracers, putting two of the fleshhunters down and raining stun bolts all around the Vipon's cover.

"Cheyenne Winds," the Vipon shouted, "I can help you! Would you care to work together?"

"I'm not coming out there with Grandpa Bay Sweeper," she snapped.

"You got more problems than that, slicker," Sundar called to her. "You put down a good man tonight and I got something for you."

He locked his jaw, turning a lens on one of his telescopic sights.

"Are you going to let him harm me, Father?" she yelled.

Wastasa Winds tucked himself further down into his cover.

"You got a weapon ready, Grundy?" he asked the Rothidai.

"I left mine on the *Word*, Winds. All I carried was this," he said, holding his halberd.

"Oh, yeah," Winds muttered. "I guess 'cover me' is out, huh?"

"I'm talking to you, Daddy!" Cheyenne Winds bellowed. "You're not still mad about that little misunderstanding on Fenfutti, are you?"

"What happened on the Octovoids' home world?" Grundy asked.

Wastasa Winds grimaced and muttered, "She tried to kill me."

Cheyenne Winds signaled Grockforth.

"Get ready to charge!" she mouthed in an animated silence.

"Charge who?" he growled, looking around the bay.

"Wastasa Winds," she said. "I want him, whether we get our bounty or not!"

"I'm not committing suicide so you can get even with your family," he roared.

Several pulse bolts passed between the cargo mover and the crates, a bolt hitting each of them solidly, too.

Cheyenne gave the Rothidai her coldest look.

"If we don't get on top of this, we don't get out. When this station goes molten, we all die; if you want to push me, feel free! We can see who goes first!"

Grockforth ground his teeth together and snorted.

"I'll charge but I will not run this bay for your father. You pick our most dangerous target. And, Winds," he growled ominously, his burning eyes squinting, "make another threat and I will crush you. I have had it horn high with you."

Winds despised being denied her desires. She could not abide being threatened by the Rothidai. She decided the behemoth had to die.

"Rala Kess, the Vipon. You charge him and put him down."

Grockforth nodded.

Two of the remaining Starstalkers leaped into motion. One fired constantly as they charged the lady Winds and her two compatriots, raining destruction on the little cargo mover and the crates nearby.

Several types of energy passed by them and between them as members of Gideon's crew fired on them but they were unhindered. The other Starstalkers, Rala Kess and the Echo Soldier still standing offered up cover fire.

The Greshan, Katril, crossed her extended arms at the wrist, her venters turned one their sides, and she fired both of them just once. Both Starstalkers ran headlong into her yellow energy bolts and fell to atomized dust in their strides.

The shock of someone using disintegration venters pushed everyone else to pull back to cover and reevaluate things.

Grockforth shot out of cover like a bolt of lightning.

Rothidai men were known all throughout the cosmos for their staggering speed and agility. As large as they were, they often had better reflexes and balance than the lightest of races and their speed was jaw dropping. Grockforth rumbled just ahead of the best aim of his attackers, once they could even rally from cover and fire, allowing him space in front of each volley.

Cheyenne Winds fired her Vapor weapon around the edge of her crate pile then returned to cover. Her blast had torn completely through one of the Starstalkers and killed the other standing close by him.

Two others stepped free of cover to avenge their kin at just the wrong time. On his way toward Rala Kess and his hiding place, Grockforth hit them like a freighter, full on, fast and hard. He had his head down, horns extended. The largest horn passed into and through the first Starstalker and Grockforth lifted his head slightly, pulling the catamorph from his feet. He trampled the second before he could lift his blaster rifle.

The first Starstalker dangled gruesomely from the horns, draped in front of the Rothidai as he charged Rala Kess.

The remainder of the Starstalkers, the last Echo Soldier, and Kess himself launched a full barrage of energy at the charging Rothidai...all pelting the dead catamorph impaled on his horns.

"You have long range!" Katril shouted. "Cover Grockforth!"

Cheyenne Winds simply eyeballed the Greshan woman near her. Katril had already turned away again when Winds twitched.

Sweet revenge on that horned ingrate, she thought.

Winds had killed the woman beside her, her ally and Grockforth's love, with the vapor rifle. Point blank, with no more thought than that.

Gideon Ridge fired from his side of the bay and dropped another Starstalker. Sylver blasted the last Echo Soldier with his sweeper and jacked the lever while Sun Ridge put down the last of the Starstalkers with his particle weapon.

Without warning, Grundy was out and charging across the bay.

That was another thing about the Rothidai males. If two encountered each other in conflict on opposing sides, they had to meet each other in melee combat...it was instinct and tradition.

"Wastasa! Fall back, prep the *Word*!" Gideon Ridge shouted.

Samara Garriton took a shot at Rala Kess, driving him to cover, but the Vipon returned fire as well, urging Gideon and Samara to duck back to safety.

Then Grockforth slammed into Rala Kess and knocked him cleanly off of his feet, through the air and into a support beam. The Vipon's body rang the metals loudly, almost like a bell, before flying off to one side and crashing to the floor. Grockforth stopped the charge and pulled the pulverized catamorph from his horns, looking about for another target. It had not even registered in his mind that the rumble in the deck plating was not the aftershock of his own charge.

Grundy hit Grockforth so hard that the impact echoed throughout the bay. The strike resounded like a clap of thunder and those not in full cover could actually feel the shockwave from their collision. Grockforth came off the deck and flew back a solid seven strides then slammed into the side of the *Belly Rub*.

A wicked, jagged bolt of energy ripped between the two combatants.

Grundy then continued the chase, charging again without hesitation.

Cheyenne Winds cursed wildly. Her well aimed shot at Grockforth had missed miserably when Grundy sent him flying.

Sylver and Sundar broke cover and ran for the two Rothidai, all the while watching the far end of the bay for the homicidal woman.

Suddenly, Grockforth drove Grundy back across the bay in a charge of his own. The two Rothidai bowled over Gideon, Sundar and Sylver Ridge and kept going across the bay. The Ridges were all stunned and, crawling about on hands and knees, tried to stop the spinning in their heads. Samara Garriton ran to them, grabbing at Gideon.

"Get up! Get up before-" she started.

The docking fields vanished before she could finish. Before.

For a gut wrenching, heart rending moment, atmosphere gushed from the open portal in such a vacuum that all of those standing fell to the decking, just as disoriented as Gideon Ridge. Winds of rage ripped through the bay and sucked a lot from the open maw and into the cold of space. A couple of small fighters even shifted and the prone bodies on the floor slid for space as if sliding downhill on ice.

Then, in a miracle, the backups kicked in one last time and the barrier shimmered, crackled and came back online. Everything stilled.

Everything and everyone except Cheyenne Winds. Standing by the downed Ridges and lady Garriton, she leveled her Vapor weapon and burst with laughter.

Samara snapped her head up and saw the woman covering her.

"You wanna win?" the slicker howled. "Take chances! I didn't grab on for life in that little storm! I let it suck me all the way over here!"

Samara Garriton tensed, considering whipping up the venter.

"Garriton, let's go," Winds laughed. "I mean, it's been fun, but I want my currency. As soon as I get you back to Unity Command, I get a lot of plat and a lot of favors, too."

"This place is done," Garriton said as more lights went out. She dropped the venter as Winds closed on the prone forms of the Ridges. "We won't make it out. The only ship belongs to the Ridges and Wastasa Winds is prepping it for them. I'm pretty sure he won't let us on board."

Cheyenne Winds gestured over her shoulder at the old freighter, the *Belly Rub*.

"I have to admit, that one is tacky," Winds said, "but I think a slicker can get it to fly. Once I pull out the dent my partner put in it-"

"It's spoken for," a low voice said nearby.

Cheyenne Winds spun around to find the speaker but he found her first. Sundar Ridge hit her as hard as he could in the mouth with the butt of his broken rifle.

The huntress staggered backward, dropping her Vapor rifle, but never lost her footing. The towering woman's blue lips ran gray with the blood of her people and marred the tanned complexion of her pretty face. She swept back her blue, shimmering hair from her white eyes that glowed with an undeniable, murderous fury.

Garriton scurried away for her venter.

Grundy had been trading massive blows with Grockforth. It was a tiring war to wage but they had the endurance to do it. The battle pitched first one way then the other, each landing mighty strikes that would have killed other races or crushed stone and bent metals. Both had the upper hand at one time or another and the two finally locked into a grapple, stalemated in their strength.

Meanwhile, Gideon Ridge got back to his feet. On the floor remained Sylver Ridge, his father, but he was stirring as Sundar Ridge tossed the broken weapon aside.

"Cheyenne Winds, you move, you die," Samara warned, glowering at the mercenary, her venter leveled with genuine intent.

"She's lucky big boy broke my popper when he ran over us. I'd have blasted her a viewport in her torso," Uncle Sun growled.

"Do you really believe-" Winds spat but gasped an interruption.

Without a warning, the station did what it had been threatening. It finally died completely. Someplace deep within the power banks, a rolling hum came to a stop for the last time. The violent shudders of a failing machine quieted, the vibrations stilled...and peace found the station at last.

All the lighting failed altogether.

Gideon, helping old Pap stand, barely had time to shout.

"Get to the *Word*!"

Then the Temple backups fell silent forever. The force field holding in the atmosphere disappeared. The atmosphere evacuated itself through the open bay anew and throughout the chamber things both living and dead lifted from the decking.

Cheyenne Winds had left open the blast doors leading deeper into the station. The vacuum could suck a lot of air from a bay and do so rapidly but the Temple area was pulling air from the open doors nearly as fast as it lost it to space. The windy storm was far better than an empty vacuum. At least they could all breathe.

The ships shifted again, their metal feet screaming as they slid across the plating. The combatants, those still alive, clung desperately to heavy objects and bay supports, calling out to each other, shouting threats. The end seemed unavoidable, however, even if it had been delayed.

The two Rothidai returned then, walking side by side, clearly on a mission. Keen, diminutive purple eyes, the typical shade of their people, saw through the darkness as clearly as if it were daylight. The gargantuan warriors, their gray skin bruised and cut by the blows they had rained upon each other, had apparently forged an alliance, a truce. It was exemplified perfectly when Grockforth slipped on a loose plate in the deck. Grundy caught his arm, steadied him then onward they marched.

When they reached the others, the giants split apart with a last nod at each other. They unstrapped their family weapons, the double headed mace and the double headed halberd, clanked them together then parted.

Grundy then grabbed Pap and Sundar in one arm and Gideon and Samara Garriton in the other. He carried them all as if they were no more than laundry.

At Sundar Ridge's shouted orders, he stomped to Gill Bardoff, dead on the floor. The old man's corpse would have been long gone into space if his clothing had not snagged a loose, metal decking plate. Grundy grabbed up the corpse and tromped for the *Spoken Word*.

Finding it powered and ready, aimed for an escape liftoff at any moment, he gratefully carried them all aboard.

The slicker, Cheyenne Winds, railed at Grockforth above the din. She dangled in the torrent from a steel support column. Grockforth would have aided his allies, too, just like Grundy. He had intentions of doing just that. Honor demanded it. But, in the debris and bodies blowing around him, a form he could not mistake blew into his arms. Katril, his beloved Greshan, flew right to him.

Horror struck him harder than anything Grundy, the Ridges or the Echo Unit could have done. When he saw the vapor rifle wound straight through her and the death in her large eyes...the giant warrior felt eviscerated.

Horror. Desperation. Despair. Then the rage. Rothidai rage.

Like Grundy, his mass was great enough to keep him anchored to the floor and his strength was great enough to resist the storm and still carry allies. In his bloodrage, he decided he had no allies. He had no friends. He had only enemies, chief of whom was Cheyenne Winds.

The Rothidai snorted, roaring in utter abandon. Then he charged the woman. In the exhale of a dying station and the impending vacuum, Grockforth slammed into the place where his target held fast to a beam. Her wiggling body had been whipping in the winds like a banner but, when the storming Grockforth made landfall, the metal supports wrenched free of the decking. Decking plates ripped up and flew away. The Rothidai plowed through them and barreled beyond, crashing through the remaining ships still tethered. After that damage, most of the bay finished coming apart and the remnants flew into space.

Wastasa Winds and Grundy flew Ridge's freighter out of the bay with a flash of thrust, barely evading the final collapse of the Temple Bay, and they were gone.

There was no looking back for Wastasa Winds, though tears did roll over his cheeks. His daughter, his child, too violent and too dangerous to rescue, was lost to him like the spacestation dissolving on their sensors. Already he was asking himself what else he could have done.

Grundy wondered whether his fellow Rothidai would survive. They were enemies but it was their way. Honor. Compassion. Depth.

Their thoughts were derailed, however, when they noted the carnage outside the station. They saw the wreckage of the war against the dead and doubted their own eyes, calling for the others to come and see.

All were too distracted to notice when two final ships tore from the inferno, trailing bits of flame and debris...

David Rule looked to his right and his left as they made an approach.

"This is *Razorhawk*," he called as they initiated final targeting on the Migroid freighter. "The seven of us are going in hot. *Tikrek*, feint a dead on attack and then run down the port side for the tail section. *Carolina*, using the starboard side, you do the same. Once at the ship's tail section, light it up. Do your best to kill those engines."

Jon Kett confirmed the plan and ran a hand through his red hair.

Jaka Baddenide, flying as a copilot and gunner to a young lady Acolyte, gave confirmation for the *Carolina*.

"*Saber*, you and *GoldArc* do as much damage as you can to the weapons arrays. Scan, target, destroy."

Paola Kett offered confirmation as copilot for the *GoldArc*. It was a catamorph Crescent fighter piloted by her close family friend, Candri Prentice.

The Lath fighter, the *Saber*, delivered confirmation, too.

"*Dagger*, *Spania*, keep an eye on the missile bays. I don't want a single one to make it to launch."

The *Spania*, a ragged old freighter, transmitted a confirmation by way of a lot of static.

The other Lath fighter agreed as well.

"*WildCard*, stay loose and float around, being wherever and whatever you need to be," David Rule ordered. "I'm going to do my best to keep that thing's attention and play bait."

"Not a problem, *Razorhawk*," the last pilot said. "I can handle it; I am the *WildCard*, after all."

"Don't get crazy, Rabeau," Rule warned the pilot. "Now...engage!"

Their aggressive run began in a sharp dive. The squadron fanned out into a sweep format, dropping toward the starship with a vengeance in mind.

Not far away, however, the last of the ragtag junk fighters from the moon graveyard formed into a cohesive unit as well. Their destination... the Acolyte squadron.

"*Razorhawk*, I'm seeing a twenty plus junker gathering on my scopes," the pilot of the *Dagger* transmitted. "That's not all, either. I'm seeing spatial disturbances in two places; we're going to have company coming out of lightspeed."

"Never mind that," Rule ordered. "Everyone remain on target."

"You ignore your smaller playmates," old Sundar Ridge transmitted. "We got somethin' for 'em."

The old man sat at the weapons console in the *Spoken Word*.

Rule praised God. The Ridges had made it out of the station.

Then the station itself blew apart in a majestic blast of sparks and flame and spinning shrapnel. The energy wave pulsing out from it spiraled in blues and greens and lit the dark of space, flickered in the reflections on everyone's shielding then dissipated.

With that, Maximilian Station became a forgotten location, a place only reachable in memory.

The Acolytes fell upon the enemy freighter with swift decision. The first sweep of the assault was met with cannon fire but the Acolytes were far too quick. They rained the attack like a thunder cloud dropping a storm as they slid across the enemy hull, almost touching it. Off the rear they glided then came about quickly.

The *Tikrek* and the *Carolina* began their rage against the engine exhausts of the big Migroid freighter. Their rear approach was all weapons and fury.

The *GoldArc* and the *Saber* ripped down both sides of the big freighter with lightning speed and destruction. They focused on weapons ports and power banks, tearing entire sections asunder with their weaponry.

The old freighter, the *Spania*, led the run on the missile bays, though there seemed to be little offering of missile offense from the big Migroid enemy. The *Dagger* pilot felt obliged to comment even as the enemy was filling his space with return cannon fire.

"This thing's not arming missiles, *Razorhawk*," he transmitted.

"Stay on task," Rule ordered again.

"I'm just looking at my readings and-"

"Pay attention to the run!" the Acolyte Ambassador ordered sharply.

It was too late, however.

The *Dagger* buckled in the center fuselage and the wings folded forward just before the little starfighter became a burning husk in the openness of space.

David Rule locked his jaw tightly against the emotion. He evaded yet another barrage of focused fire from the nose of the Migroid ship, sweeping hard to port and leading it into yet another direction. His team continued raining on the big starship while he continued leading it around by the nose.

Gideon Ridge took the pilot seat. Beside him, his father dropped into the copilot's spot. Grundy moved back to the engineering console. Gideon threw another thruster into his attack run and glanced at Wastasa Winds.

"Go over there with Uncle Sun," he directed. "Turn our shielding up as high as it'll go, Winds, and then some. Grundy, keep our systems leveled out and don't let us overheat or burn out. If it starts that way, tell Winds and shut us down."

Grundy snorted sharply.

Winds palmed the defensive systems with his gloves and remarked, "You got it, Ridge."

"Uncle Sun, keep the shields rotating, setting and resetting, heaviest deployment angling with approaching fire."

"You ready for full out war, boy?" old Pap asked. "Can you youngsters keep up?"

"Yessir," Gideon replied. "Learned from the best."

"Indeed, boy, indeed," Pap chuckled.

"Anything I can do, Gideon?" Samara Garriton asked, strapped into one of the seats with no console.

"Pray, Samara," he said.

Pray? He gives that to me? How long has it been? What do I say?

Gideon Ridge looked over his shoulder at her stymied face.

"Just talk to Him, Samara. A child to a Father, it's that easy."

The freighter set its run for a strafing style, aiming low on the coming squadron of empty junk fighters. Gideon and Sylver Ridge hoped they would stay in formation until recognizing an attack and, by that time, the *Spoken Word* would get a full run on them.

Winds was all too aware of what Gideon Ridge was planning. He and Ridge had both watched Earth football once or twice and Winds recognized the approach. Ridge was going to be an offensive defender, a heavy blocker.

Shields well above maximum, Ridge intended to bowl through the little squadron and physically destroy as many as possible by ramming through them. The shielding, if it held and Sundar Ridge could keep it fluid enough, would hopefully still be near maximum when the fighters turned about to fire on them. The *Spoken Word* would survive the return volley.

"Hold on!" Pap shouted to the cockpit.

"Pray!" Gideon added as a rain of energy washed over them.

The fighters fired on them but Ridge buried the throttles. The Raindancer freighter blasted through the fighter formation in an arcing pathway. Target shields buzzed and failed at each impact. Metal tore and ripped apart, engine banks and energy stores erupting in bright colors and flame.

Inside the cockpit, Gideon and his crew watched as they flew straight through other ships, outside them in one moment, watching their insides erupt the next then passing on to a new victim. Every ship they hit jerked and pounded them but the shields, though flickering wildly, held.

The intense attack rendered fighter after fighter torn and ruined, no more than so much debris and shrapnel left in the furious wake. When the Ridges had passed the little fleet entirely, most of it was destroyed and burning. As they came about, they began a second run on the fighters that could still move...

The Ridges ended the fighters in half a run and started back for David Rule's group.

David Rule's Razor class jumped and bumped under the cannon fire of the Migroid freighter, each shot getting closer to the Acolyte bait ship. The little fighter's shields flickered heavily, sometimes dropping completely for a few seconds.

Suddenly, after filling in here and there as an assault craft, the *WildCard* veered onto course with Rule, actually positioning itself slightly above and behind Rule. Just as it did so, a direct hit from heavy cannon fire battered it and slammed it from side to side but its fresh shields held well. The Mustang class Earth fighter leveled off despite the attack.

"Your shields are toast, Rule," Rabeau Loist transmitted. "I'll run blockade for you. You put that little Razor in the distance and let us finish this."

"Already...done!" shouted Alexi Carver, pilot of the *Saber*.

He buried his fighter into the nose of the Migroid freighter from a sidelong approach. Carver was spinning his ship in a roll as he did it, his shielding set to maximum, his rapid Lath weapons firing constantly. He chewed the nose off the freighter and soared safely through to the other side.

Eruptions started down the long Migroid fuselage.

A cheer went up from the Acolyte squadron, rallying again as others joined the gathering. Seven other Acolyte fighters also drew close from their last engagement some distance away, allied with the Unity transport, the *Corridor*, in formation with them. They eased to a drift to come aside Rule's Acolyte squadron.

The Ridges floated into the little gathering even as one last ship joined them and slowed to a stall. The limping Vanguard ship, the *Bloodwind*, eased up to their little group.

Abruptly, appearing out of nothingness and a flash of starlight, a band of fighter ships dropped from lightspeed and began an approach from the direction of Dor Modo. Just a small expanse away, a second flash revealed another group of ships, all fighters, as well, except for one. The other ship was a fighter carrier vessel.

Grundy, staring at his scopes, spoke inside the cockpit and transmitted it, too. The transmission, as had been arranged by the band, was encrypted and directed communication.

"Gideon, Acolytes, allies," he began lowly. "That fighter carrier is a Starstalker class."

"Yeah, big boy, we all see it," Jaka Baddenide transmitted. "We see their five loose fighters, too."

"The other band of fighters, the ten band," David Rule said, "is made up of Hunon Interceptors."

The fighter bands drifted to a stop, still at a distance.

"I read life signs in all of those ships…living life signs," Grundy informed.

"I hope this isn't going to be a fight," Alexi Carver transmitted.

CHAPTER EIGHT : *True Unity*

M aximilian Station was a memory. Its bones and its guts drifted with the skeletal remains of literally hundreds of ships. A war had erupted between the living and the dead. A lot of life was lost. A lot of destruction floated as proof. Shrapnel, debris and wreckage remained as the last testament to a station and many ships, full of life, having met ships full of mystery and the unknown in battle.

Awaiting the new arrivals in transmitter silence, the survivors drifted in a unified formation. They were an odd spatial militia but they were together, unified in an attempt to survive the unbelievable, the unimaginable.

Waiting, sitting calmly, even as the survivors brought shields online, the newcomers in the distance remained transmitter silent.

"Commodore," Boatwright muttered on the bridge of the Vanguard class *Bloodwind*. "We're looking at ten Hunon Interceptor fighters. They're wickedly deadly. Out there near them is a Starstalker starfighter carrier with five of their Crescent fighters flying vanguard. There's no transmission from them so far…"

"Mr. Respra," the Commodore growled. "Prepare communications. We're going to have to share information and plans at some point."

On the *Spoken Word*, Sundar Ridge triggered their directed communications and he spoke.

"Those Hunons ain't here to scavenge this mess. Those are Interceptor fighters. The Hunon Interceptor class is the baddest bully they have unless you move up to a battle cruiser."

"The Starstalker fighters are Crescent class; they aren't pushovers, either," Samara Garriton transmitted from her own *Spoken Word* headset. "That fighter carrier is a ShatterRealm class; identifying transponders are identifying it as the *Ferali 5*. It's lightweight but it's not weak."

"We have to try to communicate," David Rule said flatly.

"They think so, too, Rule," Grundy transmitted. He glanced at Gideon as he pointed to a flurry of green notification lights along his console. "I don't know about everyone else but we're getting hails from the new squadrons."

"We haven't even spoken with the Unity ships," Jon Kett offered.

"Then maybe it's time for that, too," Samara Garriton said from Gideon's ship.

On the Unity transport ship, the *Corridor*, the Communications Officer looked at the Captain.

"Patterson?" Captain Van Pelt answered his unspoken question.

"We're getting a blanket hail for all of the ships in range, Captain. It's a directed, controlled communiqué...but it's a simple encryption model. Anyone accustomed to communications could decrypt and receive it...anyone alive..." he finished, his eyebrow raised.

"Do it, Patterson. Let's hear what all of these people have to say."

On the *Bloodwind*, the Commodore gave the same order.

"Attention, ships in the Dor Modros system," Rule transmitted. "This is David Rule, Acolyte Ambassador for the Acolyte Temple in the Dor Modros system. This is an invitation to engage your holosystems for this transmission so that we can see each other as we get to know each other. There is an enemy in this sector...pure evil."

"Agreed," answered Captain Van Pelt and the nearby Captain Brent.

"Gladly," Commodore Wrigley Zeckinbridge answered.

"Indeed," Samara Garriton replied with the nearby Gideon Ridge.

"Let's get it over with," Sundar Ridge snapped. "Hail the two fighter squadrons who were late to the party."

Then newcomer transmissions were relayed.

They immediately earned responses.

"Agreed, Ambassador Rule. I will project in my entire force's stead," a Starstalker female responded. "We are glad you fared well. There seems to have been a serious battle here."

"I concur. And I will attend and answer for my people," a Hunon Pilot answered.

David Rule breathed deeply and smiled.

"Thank you both. It is good to meet you."

Gideon quietly prayed thanksgiving to God.

The man screamed. The strain, reaching across the cosmos to animate so many machines, pulled at his very being. His mind struggled to hold his atoms together, to hold his flesh and bone together…to hold his sanity.

He often wondered if it had failed to hold to the sanity.

That voice, the driving force in his beleaguered subconscious, pushed him, prodded him to do more. To give more. To reach farther. He felt sometimes as though he was not even in his body anymore; the pain told him stories of separation while his conscious thoughts drifted, scattered like forgotten leaves on the wind.

Sometimes, he could remember his name, though it had been so long since anyone called it. How long had it been? How long had he been alone, his crew on the Leviathan long dead? How long had it been since he had watched them kill each other…

Andreas Riker. His name was Andreas Riker, he told himself. And, had his gray face not been so stiff with pain, he would have smiled.

But that voice corrected him.

Only the Psiborg remained.

The man screamed…but only in his mind.

Gideon Ridge and Samara Garriton sat in the galley. Holocommunications were rerouted there for receiving and projecting so the two could sit at the table and see and hear their allies while being seen and heard.

In the room was Commodore Zeckinbridge's image, transmitted from her private counsel room. As others spoke with and interacted with her, they would appear to her in that room aboard her Vanguard ship. The same went for Captain Van Pelt of the USAP transport ship and his private chamber, though the visiting Captain Josh Brent would join him in that room, live and in person.

The Acolytes were represented by David Rule and he could be seen as a sitting image in the other ships but in his fighter he could only receive transmitted images much smaller than life size. All those speaking with him would be shown on a HUD projected onto his fighter's view screen.

The heads up display method was used by the lead Hunon Pilot, too.

The female Starstalker had a presentation room aboard her vessel and sat in it like the Unity leadership and projected that same way.

David Rule started the meeting with a simple prayer of Thanksgiving. Some did not feel the need to participate and he was more than kind to their undue irritation. He quickly pointed out that they did not have to pray but he was going to. It was not a matter of infringing on their right not to pray, for he was more than happy to leave them out of it; if they contested his right to pray, however, it was about them infringing on his rights.

When he was finished, he asked who would like to begin.

"I will," Samara Garriton said.

"I object to this," Captain Van Pelt declared immediately. "She is a wanted-"

"Stifle that, Captain," Commodore Zeckinbridge snapped. "I'm the ranking senior officer in this sector and I say let her speak."

"You're not going to be ranking anything when Unity Command gets out here-"

"Excuse us, loud human," the Starstalker woman interrupted. "You hang on to what little command structure you have here. There may not be a United Starmada of Allied Planets by the time you get reinforcements."

Van Pelt, Garriton, Brent and Zeckinbridge all gasped a single word.

"What?"

"You know less about your precious Unity Command than we. Let the Garriton woman speak. We will give you what we know when it is our time. This woman is the survivor to the *Vindicator* incident; we need to hear what she has to say."

"Her other crew survivors are on board with me," Zeckinbridge announced. "We couldn't leave you alone, Samara. We're with you."

"Thank you...all," Samara said.

"How is my ship, by the way, Commodore?" Joshua Brent asked.

Zeckinbridge never skipped a beat.

"Holding her own. Must be the veteran crew and leadership."

Rule suggested that Samara share all that had occurred to her. She did so, leaving out no detail, sharing even her return run to the starship to free any who might be left trapped on the *Vindicator*...her rebellion against the Command.

No one contested her claim. They drifted in a field of battle where tons of ships had been at war without living crews. Her story was far stronger in that setting than it had been at Earth Base Command.

That was the cue for the Acolyte leader, Rule, to share that his people and he had experienced it first hand with Garriton on that return to the ArcAngel class starship. There could be no debate. The dead walked and fought and searched...for something.

Then the Hunon representative agreed with Rule.

"I have seen it first hand, also," the diminutive male assured. "I am Security Commander Wahll, deployment leader of the Hunon vessel *Firebringer*. I was tasked with the safety of a deployment team as we went aboard a derelict space station."

"Scavenging," Sundar Ridge muttered, garnering a warning glare from Gideon Ridge.

"We prefer to call it...reclamation." The Hunon cleared his throat and continued, saying, "The dead were all over that station. I and another Security Commander tried to save the scientific crews but two of us were just so much of an afterthought. Our entire deployment team was massacred and I lost my fellow defender also. I would have been destroyed with them, with that space station, with my deployment team, if I had not found an escape pod still operational. My ship torpedoed the station to free itself from a droning tone that nearly took over its controls. The ship luckily found my jettisoned pod and brought me back aboard."

Van Pelt was clearly irritated by the story but Captain Brent hushed him, demanding they act with an open mind. Once the two Unity captains finished their bickering, the Hunon continued.

"Our legends have long told that evil has always risen from the Reaches. If the undead rise against the living, we knew the source would be within the Reaches."

"Fairy tales and sailor stories!" Van Pelt shouted. "The early explorers of Earth thought the Earth was flat and that sailors could run off the world! They believed in sea monsters and giant squids-"

"And the Leviathan," the Starstalker speaker interrupted. "Yet, the Starstalkers hold the same suspicion about the Reaches...and we also believe in the Leviathan within them."

Everyone was silent for a long, chilling moment.

"I am Captain Prentia, former Captain of the Starstalker *Ferali 4*, StarWarp carrier class...until it was debilitated and destroyed by a horde of the undead. I and one other fighter pilot were the only to escape and I was even shot down over our world system's burial moon, Blou, where the conflict occurred."

Those hologathered sat in rapt attention, aside from Van Pelt. At least he kept his silence.

"We were in that location because a Chabron ship, a Dreadship called the *Scythe*, had crossed into our region at the moon. We were in talks with that ship, trying to determine its intent, when both of us were attacked. We fought together...and lost."

"The Chabron are fellow Unity members," Captain Van Pelt snapped. "Why were you investigating their actions?"

"Our burial regions are sacred!" growled the Starstalker. "Your cries of Unity fall on deaf ears, human. More and more 'unity' means nothing for the individual or the individual race, stepping on them time and again for some appeasement to a larger group. We tire of being stepped upon. Indeed, after my encounter, the Starstalker Council has been considering leaving Unity Command. Too long have all of our races worn the muzzle and the bonds of 'unity' rule."

Murmurs lifted from several attendants.

"They are not alone," Zeckinbridge admitted. "We hear stirrings from the Chabron, too."

"That is treasonous!" Van Pelt shouted. "We have made oaths and committed aide and resources to each other! If any were to leave us it would throw the Command into chaos-"

"This is not the time, nor is it the place!" Zeckinbridge shouted.

Silence ruled, if only for a brief time.

David Rule broke its reign first, returning to the discussion of the Reaches. It seemed each race had suspicions of what lurked inside the region. A decision had to be made on just what to do about that.

He shared all that had been discussed about the man known as Psiborg. He shared the concerns of his actions and identity as well as his people's ability to control technology. Then he discussed how there could be no doubt anymore about the possibility of the undead.

"This starmada of the undead," Van Pelt started again. "What are we looking at? I can scarcely imagine these things...but I was indeed here for this battle. How many ships with dead bodies are moving against us?"

Joshua Brent chimed in with, "My first question, tactically, would be this: why were the undead not in all of these ships? We see a lot of debris that is purely technological, no bio remains, at all. Is this a different conflict altogether?"

"Not at all, kid," Sylver Ridge said. "Back in the Android Rebellion, it was a common ruse to animate some derelict machinery or whatever to distract from a bigger maneuver. That's what this was. The trash moon, Draksus, is close by and lots of different peoples have been using it to ditch old ships for generations. It was convenient and distracting but the real war is still coming on. Trust us."

"We have to bring Unity Command into this," Captain Arn Van Pelt growled. "This will take a fleet to stop. We need to get them on board."

"They won't come," Captain Josh Brent sighed.

"I think I know better whether or not they will," Van Pelt snapped.

"Captain Brent is right," Commodore Zeckinbridge said. "This ship I am in, his command, all of that was pushed through prep so that they could get Samara back before she could make waves. Unity Command is not going to respond to this in any way that suggests Samara was right and they were wrong."

"They hired bounty hunters to come after her," Gideon Ridge added.

"We still have to try," Van Pelt said, far less sure of himself.

Captain Prentia took the lead again.

"I think there may be a better way to get aide. A more direct way."

"What is better than getting Unity Command?" Van Pelt asked.

"Going to the races themselves. As free races, not as Unity subjects. Going to all races, ones that are and ones that are not part of Unity."

Van Pelt scoffed at the idea, saying, "Too long. It'll take too long."

"Either way," Captain Brent bypassed, "how big is this death fleet?"

"This starmada of bones stands to be one of the largest ever seen," David Rule warned. "Think of how long beings have been dying in space with their technology. All the accumulated bodies and starships that have passed. It would be immense and that is probably an understatement."

"Immense I can understand," Captain Van Pelt allowed. "But how can a fleet that big be in more than one place at a time? I mean, travel time between the Starstalker moons, the asteroid belts where the *Vindicator* was lost and the Hunon encounter location are considerable. How is it possible?"

"We think there may be an answer inside those Reaches," David Rule nodded. "We are wondering what's in them and if it's possible that there may be a fold in space there, or a wormhole, or something else like that."

"Then we need to act quickly. We could move out to one of Unity Command's relay stations, patch into long range communications then contact every life bearing world in the cosmos," the young Captain Brent said. "They could send aide immediately, those who will."

"No," Gideon Ridge countered. "The communiqué assault this fleet uses could corrupt any long range transmissions if the fleet encounters it, receives it. The only safe communication systems are directed transmissions, between short range locations, with encryption safeguards set up for sentient recognition protocols. Like the way we're communicating in this limited range now."

"Then how can we warn the races? Get help?" asked Van Pelt.

"We'll send emissaries," David Rule answered calmly. "The Acolytes and Messengers have always been taking the warning against coming evil to every race. This will be no different."

There was little debate; though there were opponents and proponents to the plan, no one had a better idea.

"In the meantime, the remainder of our gathering will watch this route. If a major force emerges from the Reaches here, we will be all there is to slow it until a larger resistance can arrive," David Rule stated flatly.

"Suicide," Joshua Brent sighed.

"No, the dangerous assignment will be the small infiltration unit we send into the Reaches to quell the evil at the source," Captain Prentia presumed. Her presumptions were correct. "If that is the thought process at work here."

"It is," Samara Garriton noted. "I don't see another way."

With little more talk, the decision was adopted unanimously.

"Look," Gideon Ridge said with a smile, "real unity."

Eight of the Hunon Interceptors fled the area. They had their assigned destinations and time was incredibly important. Eighteen of the twenty available Starstalker Crescent fighters followed them, only to break off and head for different locations, and they left two fighters and the mother carrier behind. The mother carrier, the *Ferali 5*, was to host a gathering of allies in person.

In the meantime, more than twenty Acolyte fighters and freighters left the sector, too. David Rule kept a specific handful of ships and allies with him, renamed them the official Temple Squadron for the sector, and sent the rest to follow the same mission the Hunon and Starstalker fighters were following.

Warn worlds. Warn races. Warn systems and spacestations.

With them flew the *Freedom*, the *Graystone* and Dalindrea Ridge in the *Pyramid*. Neither Kelvan nor Kreden Hotch were pleased; they preferred to stay and fight. They understood the importance of the message, though, and resigned themselves to the greater mission good. Drea Ridge took the news better than Gideon expected. That is, until he learned what sector she had been given.

She was to warn the outposts along the Forroweld Web. That area of space was the one in which her husband had gone missing. Gideon and his father both knew Drea would be looking hopefully for some sign of the expedition ship *Rogan* and her husband, against all odds. It had been two years since the vessel had simply vanished but her hope had not.

Rule and seven other Acolyte ships docked on the Starstalker carrier. So did the two Hunon fighters, the *Spoken Word* and a small shuttle from each of the USAP ships. The meeting was to be in person but not all were attending. The leaders of the representative allies would attend; the rest would check over their ships and beg repairs and refuels from the Starstalkers.

"I don't think they make parts for these anymore," a Starstalker technician choked over his own humor. "Just because we towed you in doesn't mean we can work miracles."

The Acolyte pilot and owner of the *Raine*, Taelynn Berreaux, spat a giggle of her own. She picked up one of the blistered diverter coils and tossed it at the tech.

The technician grinned, his catamorph teeth showing.

The moments like that one between the races, as they worked together, hoped together, prayed together and even played together, showed true gentleness and acceptance of each other. Gideon Ridge wondered if Unity Command ever questioned where they went wrong.

"What's with the long face, brother?" a Starstalker woman called.

Gideon and Samara were staring across the massive docking facility that overlooked the individual bays.

"Just thinking-" Gideon started. He abruptly stopped, however, and shouted, "Lorrayanka!"

The brunette Starstalker, just as tall as Ridge, rushed toward him from her security detail. Her team was there to accompany the delegates to a chamber to meet Captain Prentia.

Gideon embraced the woman warmly and they squeezed each other.

"Brother?" Captain Samara Garriton questioned.

"It's a long story," the catamorph said with a wink and a smile. "If we can get all these nightmares wrapped up maybe we can all sit around and tell some good stories."

She and her security team told the group to stay close then led them for the gravlifts. In a few short moments, all were sitting down in a dining chamber with Captain Prentia.

David Rule brought two fellow Acolytes to the table, Jon and Paola Kett. They sat at the far end of the rectangular table, opposite Captain Prentia, her Chief of Security, Lorrayanka, and the Hunon representative, Commander Wahll.

On one side of the table, the Ridge brothers, Gideon Ridge, Samara Garriton and Commodore Wrigley Zeckinbridge sat. Captain Van Pelt and his Security Chief, Taylor Patrick, as well as Captain Joshua Brent and a Starstalker security guard lined the opposite side of the table alongside a Ton B'Gru no one knew and no one recognized.

Introductions were passed about, bound with smiles too forced to be genuine. Only Captain Prentia did not stare at the Ton B'Gru, nor did she do the opposite, as many did, stealing glances then looking away when he returned a gaze.

The Starstalker Captain instead reminded everyone why they were there, asking for ideas, opinions, and suggestions.

"Wait for Unity Command. Let them apply the fleets to this situation," Van Pelt said.

Several eyes rolled and murmurs came to life.

"We've moved beyond that," Commodore Zeckinbridge said flatly. "If you have anything new to add, feel free. If not, keep that to yourself."

The male Ton B'Gru chuckled, his shining white eyes glowing.

"You have something to contribute, Falmarr?" Captain Prentia asked the Ton B'Gru.

He nodded, the white light about his eyes glowing further against his dark skin. Electric charges pulsed through his long, blue hair.

"Waste no more time talking about the Unity Starmada and their Command Council. They have avoided the Reaches like the Corrin Flu for their entire existence."

Captain Brent and Captain Van Pelt offered up arguments immediately. They were shouted down by Commodore Zeckinbridge and torpedoed by the harsh, personal truths experienced by Samara Garriton.

"You got a better idea?" Captain Van Pelt demanded of Falmarr.

Falmarr lifted his right hand which was gloved in technofiber. A three dimensional orb of bluish white light swirled in his grasp. He pitched it up into the air, caught it then threw it to the center of the table. Above the table, hovering, the pulsing orb popped and expanded into a swirling, detailed star chart. The device had everyone's attention, all looking for familiar points, when he spoke.

"I am Falmarr, of the Marr house of Ton B'Gru. My grandfather was Bramarr; some of you, those who know the history of our cosmos, know now what you see before you."

"I do not fit that category, obviously," Van Pelt spat.

Several others echoed.

"That's 'cause you ain't old enough to," Sylver Ridge said.

"Pap," Gideon sighed.

"And ain't none of 'em educated," Sundar Ridge said.

"None of you know?" the man with the white eyes asked.

"The Acolytes know," David Rule said. "Our Temples hold a great vault of knowledge."

"Our people know, too," Captain Prentia said.

The Starstalker heads nodded.

"No offense, Falmarr, but can we pull this back to a point? We have work to do."

He shrugged at Zeckinbridge.

"I suppose. It just means that I have to supply you-"

"I'll give the history," Sylver Ridge interrupted, "save you the trouble. Ton B'Gru live a long time, so their generations stretch out a bit, like their speeches and conversations."

Several people chuckled before Sylver continued.

"His grandpa, Bramarr, is the one from so long ago who's responsible for sending their Monarch ship, the infamous *Quan Jor*, into the Reaches. The expedition was supposed to map it," The old man said and leaned forward, tapping a marking on the image between all of them. "Right there. Ton B'Gru call sign for the *Monarch.*"

"There are no star charts for the Reaches," Joshua Brent said flatly.

"Captain Brent, I believe, if you will be patient, you are about to learn differently," Paola Kett said gently, a twinkle of sarcasm dancing in her deep blue eyes.

Brent locked eyes with her. The Acolyte was undeniably lovely but there was more about her, he could feel it inside himself. He found he could scarcely look away.

Captain Prentia gestured at the imagery.

"The fate of that Monarch vessel is well known, whether your histories are up to date or not. It was lost in the Reaches on its expedition and never heard from again. All hands missing, all transmissions lost, all transponder and beacon signals vanished. Well...until now, that is."

Very briefly, the Acolytes and the Ridge crew were urged to share with the others how the *Quan Jor* had come out of the grave and attacked them when they had sought out the *Vindicator*. They also mentioned they had destroyed it.

"What does all this have to do with-"

"Captain Van Pelt," Falmarr interrupted, "there were apparently failsafe measures taken by the late Captain of the Monarch vessel. There were prerecorded actions set should the ship ever power up again, should it ever reach open space again, where open transmissions could be made. When that ship, powered by whatever evil is in the Reaches, made its attack run on these people, it transmitted a data file back to our home world. It came to our centralized government but also to our family's personal research and development organizations. The late Captain had set the ship to do so."

"The star charts?" Joshua Brent gasped, looking at the three dimensional glow anew.

"And a history of points visited by the *Quan Jor*, listed with routes taken and the areas where certain things began to happen to the technology on board. Also listed are points where the crew began to be... disturbed."

He folded his hands together on the table before continuing.

"The Captain was wise enough to have logistics systems monitor the way their mental states degraded. The descent into madness was fully documented by the ship's computer systems. The records are all intact, so we finally have maps of locations, as well as warning points to avoid as we go to the major port of question."

"Star charts..." Van Pelt gasped.

"A road map with all the detours and failed bridges already noted on it," Sundar Ridge said. "From the Reaches. Who would've thought?"

"My grandfather," the Ton B'Gru said.

"You came because of this?" Jon Kett, Paola's father, asked. "How could you get this far out, this quickly? Your world is quite a long-"

"Our people did not take Captain Garriton's claims lightly. We know of the darkness surrounding the Reaches. When the *Vindicator* was lost and the story began to be whispered here and there, my government sent me out here immediately. I was not far from the Starstalker sector when Captain Prentia's carrier was taken. I went to them immediately. Captain Prentia and I started our way out here, gathering intelligence and allies," he said with a nod to the Hunon, "and my home world sent me the transmissions, encoded, when the old Monarch launched them. I was already here when I got these."

"We needed your arrival when we were fighting that drone starmada," Jon Kett said honestly. "We could've saved a lot more people in the station."

"You need us now even more," the Security Chief of the carrier said.

"What are we up against?" Gideon Ridge asked of Lorrayanka.

Falmarr made some gestures with his gloved hand. Several areas in the charts opened further, growing, coming closer. In those areas were dot after dot after countless dots of light.

"Are those..." Captain Joshua Brent breathed.

"...energy signatures?" Paola Kett completed.

Captain Van Pelt's Chief of Security gasped, "No way."

"Oh, I'm afraid they're exactly right," Falmarr said. "It is a starmada the size of which has never been seen."

"Impossible!" Van Pelt howled.

"There are thousands of ships!" Chief Taylor Patrick shouted in agreement with his Captain.

"Tens of thousands," Captain Prentia corrected.

"How?" Jon Kett breathed. "It looks like every ship that's ever been lost, from every race, has been gathered..."

The Ton B'Gru snapped his fingers. List upon list upon list began to roll over the hovering display. The lists were of starship wrecking and dumping grounds, as well as famed battlegrounds.

"Information coming in tells us that all of these places seem to have lost their derelict and damaged spaceships, even their destroyed scraps. No one saw them go but they're gone. It seems they're gathering into a central starmada of mass proportions inside the Reaches."

Captain Prentia nodded at Falmarr.

"Thank you, Falmarr."

He changed the holoprojection back to the star charts.

"They're coming straight for us," Lorrayanka said.

"It seems like two forces at work. One controls technology. The other manipulates the dead," David Rule said with a sigh.

"We have something new that may help," Lorrayanka informed with a gleam in her catlike, soft amber eyes. "The charts have given us a likely source location."

"Is that the major point of question you mentioned?" Commodore Zeckinbridge asked.

"The deepest landing point charted in the Reaches. It seems to be a dead, stone world but it isn't. It's an asteroid, a very big asteroid. No life signs indicated. However, a facility seems to have erected itself. It's a shipbuilding facility…and the 'roid has an atmosphere."

"Repairs," Paola Kett and Captain Joshua Brent said at once.

They looked at each other instantly. Kett allowed a tiny smirk to tug at the corner of her full lips.

"The transmitted charts named the asteroid with random coding. While it is nondescript, it serves the purpose. ABC-Zeta Lan. But the charts name the actual facilities with more panache. They're named the Stone Tombs," Falmarr added.

"Repairs. For the ships of the dead," Commander Lorrayanka muttered.

"We can't turn aside a starmada that size," Van Pelt argued, going right back to the issue closest to his ship. "With every fleet from every world, I don't know that it could be done! We would have to gather them all here to fight as one! If this bone starmada sweeps over one system at a time, nothing will stop it!"

"That is what our emissaries are going to share, Captain Van Pelt," Captain Prentia said.

"But it will never happen in time! Not before it gets to us!"

"No…it won't." Lorrayanka pointed to the rock in the chart. "That's why we must discover the source of this force and destroy it. Captain Prentia has tasked our navigation officers with plotting a course for a raiding team, through the Reaches, safely, to that asteroid. A small force will storm it. Our goal is to destroy what fuels the evil."

"And the ships you're asking to come here?" Zeckinbridge asked.

"They will gather and make a stand here, trying to hold this force still and stop its rush into our cosmos. In enough time, they will inevitably be overrun. But the small team we send to the rock in the Reaches will be the real maneuver, the real hope."

"If they fail?" Sun Ridge asked.

"Pray they don't," his nephew, Gideon, answered.

"Any volunteers?" Captain Prentia asked.

The docking bays within the *Ferali 5* bustled with activity. Technicians and pilots and crews hustled from one place to another with repair equipment, supplies and fuel cells. They prepped the last two Hunon fighters, the two Starstalker fighters, the ship belonging to the Ridges and the Temple Squadron ships of the Acolytes. They had no idea which ones would wait there and which ones would be used to run the Reaches but it mattered not. All needed repairs and refueling, no matter the mission.

Aide crews were sent via small shuttles to the two USAP vessels, the Transport class and the Vanguard class. The Transport class, the *Corridor*, needed serious repair but there was time. All the pilots and command crews involved were told to rest and sleep as much as they could.

Fresh minds were needed as surely as fresh fuel.

Gideon Ridge knew he was no exception but his mind would not stop turning. He sat alone, once all the others had seemed to have gone to sleep, in an observation chamber. It overlooked the launch tubes for fighters, transparent walls acting as an open view outside the ship and into the passages used by fighters and by technicians in the bays.

One of his most prized possessions, an authentic paper copy of the Bible, bound in leather, sat on one leg. He closed tired eyes, thinking of which passages to read.

"You need to be asleep."

The young Ridge snapped his eyes open to see Wastasa Winds.

"May I?" the considerably older Native American asked, gesturing to a seat near him.

Gideon nodded with a quick point and an arched eyebrow.

Winds sat and leaned back, staring up at the high tech ceiling.

"Got a reason you're up?"

Ridge smiled.

"I'm all grown up, Winds. I make my own bedtime."

"Everyone else is asleep."

"Obviously, that's not true."

Winds chuckled in his low tone.

"Nothing gets by you, Gideon."

Gideon Ridge smiled in a tired, worn way that mirrored weariness.

"Seriously. Everyone was saying you got picked to head up the suicide mission into the Reaches. Shouldn't you be resting?"

"Thanks for the confidence," Ridge said. "But no. I can't sleep. I tried. Something's just not…right. It's like I know something's off but I can't tell what it is. Something that's going to happen."

"Gideon, you're about to go into the Reaches. Anyone would be feeling off."

Ridge shook his head then decided to drop it. It was too hard to explain. It was more than the Reaches.

"Your daughter," Ridge said finally, changing the subject. "I'm sorry about what happened on the station."

"Grundy says his Rothidai kin was supposed to load them up on a ship and try to get out like we did. At the last, he turned on her. That means, somewhere along the way, she betrayed him like she does everyone. Either way, I'm sure she got out. She always does. She stole, killed or lied her way out."

"That face doesn't look sure. Why you can't sleep?"

Winds sighed, "There's just so much a man can carry in his life, Gideon. Leaving my own kid to die in a spacestation is a little too heavy to bear and I sure can't sleep through it." He wiped a tear, cleared his throat and waved it away. "But you're worried enough-"

"I don't worry, Winds. I pray. Tell me about your girl."

"What?"

"Tell me. The whole thing, not a passing digicard; I want the whole database."

Winds leaned his head back and he drew a deep breath. Staring at that highly technological ceiling full of wiring boxes and conduit, he locked his jaw for a moment. Finally, he spoke.

"Me and my wife adopted her. Her parents were traders, some big time movers with her people, back on their world. They got into some questionable deals on Earth and bolted, them and their whole organization. But they left their kid. She was staying with the workforce childcare option. Apparently, they didn't have the time or the desire to go get her before escaping."

His pause gave Gideon a chance to shake his head and grunt.

"That's what we said," Winds said. "There just ain't words."

"No, there aren't."

"So, we adopted her. Loved her. Took care of her. Taught her. She was okay, to be honest, until my wife died. It messed with Cheyenne...It messed with her really bad. I don't think her mind was ever right again."

"Death of a loved one can wreak havoc on us," Gideon said.

"Well, she was a natural for my line of work, being a slicker, with her physiology and predisposition to energy and electricity. She took to it very well. I contracted out my skills to law enforcement agencies and organized peacekeepers of one kind or another. She did, too, until she moved out. Then..."

"Then...Cheyenne Winds."

"Yeah. I should have stopped her long before that. I knew she was messed up. But who wants to admit that about their kid? Who wants to wrestle with that kind of truth? No, I think denial was way easier."

"You're a typical father, Wastasa. You were trying to deal with the situation but hold onto your hope. You love your daughter," Ridge eased.

"You sure? I think I left her for dead tonight. That's not love."

"Tell me the rest of it."

"She went off the rails. I'd been known to pull bounties for legal agencies; my skills always made that a bit easier. She got into bad bounties, Gideon. Bounties on file but assassinations in truth. And she pulled them from anybody, anywhere. She had no more moral compass at all. I heard she was getting a reputation for killing partners when they became less useful. It was all going down a black hole and I mean at lightspeed."

"I heard the same things," Gideon said.

"Eventually Rala Kess worked with her once or twice. We crossed paths during a time they were apart, both of us looking for her. Him for a job, me for a chance at helping her. We agreed to travel together for a while. Long story short, we found her running a scam on a little, low tech planet, allowing the population to live if they would pay her enough."

Gideon Ridge waited patiently.

"I had to try to stop her, Gideon. It was the only right thing to do. I tried to stop her like a father, though, not a man, not a warrior, not an official. Like a dad."

"What happened?"

"While I was being a dad she vented me. Rala Kess saved my life, pulled me to cover, held the crazy girl at bay until she gave up and retreated."

"That was way out of character for Rala Kess," Ridge muttered.

"Yeah...turned out he was too wanted to go back into Unity jurisdictions. He wanted to work with me so I could get him under the radar here and there. As it turned out, he made a decent partner for me, agreeing not to kill and whatnot, until he decided he didn't need me anymore on this little excursion."

"When did you get that memo?" Ridge asked.

"When he let you draw on me in that landing bay and put me down. You're fast, Gideon, one of the fastest I've ever seen. But you're no Rala Kess, not even close. He could've stopped you, he was that good. But he had an agenda. Who knows? Maybe he had already run into Cheyenne and made an agreement. I'll probably never know. I just know my little girl was leaving messages for me all over the cosmos that I was on a short list of dead men. And she was coming to fix that."

"Wow."

"Yeah."

"So, you want it straight?"

"Yeah."

"Ready?"

"Yeah."

"Here it is: you're sitting here with me because you can't sleep. You're crying, trying to hold yourself together, to keep yourself sane after everything. You're ready to put yourself on the hypothetical chopping block because of everything you didn't or couldn't do... because you love her, Wastasa. You love her."

"But Gideon-"

"No, it's my turn. You had your turn," Ridge said, holding up a pausing finger. "The father in you is in trauma. He can't accept the loss of his little girl. But the truth is harsh and a lot clearer. The thing is, I don't think you want to see that clear truth because it's harder to swallow."

Wastasa Winds locked his jaw against the welling emotion.

"You lost that little girl a long time ago. I don't know what sins of the past you wrestle with but a lot of things happen outside our control. You can't control that your wife passed away and you can't control how it impacted Cheyenne. You couldn't control her desire to kill you or her attempts to do just that. You couldn't control her trying it again in that spacestation and you couldn't make her get on the ship with us or call a truce with us until we could all get off the station. You did the very best you could for all the people who were there, Wastasa, including your daughter. She made her choices. Those choices are out of your control."

"I just don't feel like I did enough..."

"That tells me you care and that tells me that, more than likely, you did everything you could."

He stared sidelong at the smuggler.

"You think so?"

"I do. I know you would've waited for your daughter if there had been any chance she'd come with us. You knew better. You're second guessing yourself because you care so much. So stop."

"I hope you're right."

"He usually is," a woman's purring voice interrupted.

Winds and Ridge looked up to see Lorrayanka strolling for them, extra side arm belts hanging from both shoulders. She was an absolutely beautiful catamorph but the weapon belts drew the most attention from both men.

"Those for us?" Winds asked.

"The others said you lost your gear on the station," Lorrayanka answered. "I figured, since the two of you are refusing to sleep, you may want to try on the replacement equipment Captain Prentia authorized for you."

"Unless you have a Bay Sweeper, my dad isn't going to find much relief from replacements," Gideon Ridge muttered.

"Well, sweepers are illegal in most systems," Lorrayanka answered. Then she giggled, fangs visible. "Captain Prentia was happy to get that old violation off her ship. I have no idea where that thing came from but I know who was an awfully happy old Ridge to get it."

"Wow," Gideon commented and laughed. "You actually had one."

"Good thing your father carries all those charge shells; that sweeper had been in the weapons hold for who knows how long. I couldn't find a single shell for it."

"Personally, I don't need anything. I didn't lose any weaponry. I wear mine," Gideon reminded and held up an arm. He tapped the bracer. "You can give what you brought me to Wastasa."

Wastasa Winds rose from his seat, took both low draw belts and hung one over each shoulder.

"Gladly. I'll take two," he said. "And, with that, I'm going to try sleeping again. Thanks, Lorrayanka, for the juicers. And thank you, Gideon."

"Rest easy, Wastasa."

"By the way, how did such a young guy get so wise?"

Ridge held up his Bible.

"I don't depend on my own wisdom, Wastasa. I read and listen then follow the leading of Jesus Christ. He guides me and often gives me words...when I don't have any for myself."

"Right again," Lorrayanka added.

Wastasa Winds examined the Starstalker anew.

"You're a Christian, Lorrayanka? You're not even human."

"I've never found the wisdom in anything else in the cosmos that I have in the Bible. Once Gideon shared the Gospels with me and I began to trust, I couldn't read enough."

"But you're from a different world, a different-"

"Winds, the Bible speaks of taking the Faith to the ends of the Earth," the woman said.

Winds was confused and said, "And?"

"After the Earth was so badly ravaged by humans, time and war, the far reaches of the planet, the ends of it, so to speak, were the colonies established by Earth on other planets. Where they settled on new planets, they encountered yet more Gentiles...all of us, waiting to hear the Gospel," the Starstalker informed.

"Someday, Gideon, I want to know about your Faith. All about it. I need solid answers and you're the only person I've ever met who was sure he had any...and could present them in a way that convinced anyone else."

"No time like now," Gideon smiled.

"I need to sleep, Ridge. After the battle, okay?" he asked.

"You sure you have time?" Gideon called after him. "Coming to God needs to happen before death, Wastasa."

Winds did not respond, nor did he slow.

"I hope he's listening," Gideon Ridge lamented.

"It took me time to trust," she reminded him.

"I suppose."

"I'm glad I listened when I did, though," the Starstalker told Ridge.

"Me, too. Facing what we're facing, everyone needs to take an inventory of their beliefs. No one is ever promised tomorrow."

There was a long silence between them before either spoke again.

"How is Drea?" she asked after a time.

Ridge found her eyes and saw the genuine understanding there.

"Resolute. Determined. Single-minded." He then added with a huff, "Stubborn and broken at the same time."

"I have been there," she said honestly.

"I remember."

"My brother was a good soul," she continued, "and losing him, the way we did, never any closure...it carries a terrible weight."

"Dandru was one of the most brilliant minds I've ever met. Drea says that was one of the first things about him that drew her."

"She liked his wild side, too, his primal side," Lorrayanka laughed. "They were so good together."

Gideon Ridge reached out and took her hand.

"I just wish I knew what to do to make her as good on her own."

"We need to pray, Gideon. It is all we can do."

"Yes. Then we need to pray for the fight," Gideon Ridge nodded.

"Amen."

CHAPTER NINE : *Fear No Evil*

T he oldest Ridge jerked the lever down on his sweeper and left the lower tubing open. Beneath the barrel, he pressed shell charge after shell charge into the loading chamber.

"I wonder if that man knows that weapon is illegal," Captain Van Pelt, Captain of the *Corridor*, muttered to those close enough to hear. "If we were in Unity space-"

"We're not, you wouldn't and that old man would smear you across the bay," Commodore Wrigley Zeckinbridge snapped, her jaw clenched tightly. "Be quiet."

Captain Prentia had just arrived on the overlook platform in one of the bays. Below, shuttles from both Unity starships sat close to the Acolyte fighters, docked and ready. Prentia was a gorgeous vision of Starstalker loveliness, her ceremonial silver armor shining against her soft skin and her blonde mane. A thick, red cloak hung about her.

The security team following her about was also in ceremonial armor, mostly blued. They knew and admired Prentia, though she had only inherited the *Ferali 5* command after the fall of the *Ferali 4*. An ailing, aging Captain had stepped down in deference to her experience.

"I trust you all slept well enough to rescue the cosmos," she said loudly, "though I doubt any of you slept any better than I. Death knocks at the door today; some of us will answer bravely, surviving the conflict to come. Others will not survive and the living will be left to sing songs to their honor. Whether you die or you live on to sing, this day we are brothers and sisters. USAP officers, Acolytes, Starstalkers and Hunons, Humans, Rothidai...no matter our blood, our race, our place in the universe...today we are family. We are the family of the living and our enemy is death itself."

"Makes you proud, don't it? Just being here," Sundar Ridge muttered to his brother.

"Well, yeah, I s'pose it does."

"This dead seeks the living," she furthered. "It hunts living beings. If there are not more of us in number waiting here, the starmada may veer into a pursuit of our small raiding party. The force here must lure them away from the Reaches for the very good of the raiding group. Then we are here to hinder the starmada, should the party fail. We have sent warning to the races; we will stall and slow the starmada here while that message does its work in the other systems. Any questions?"

"Are we sure the breakdown of crews is still the best?" Samara Garriton asked, eyeballing Captain Gideon Ridge.

"We're on the launch decks. Let's not start all this again," Commodore Zeckinbridge said. "We spent more time than we should have. It has finally been decided. If we stay with our plan, I think we'll find it's the best one."

Garriton took a deep breath and looked up.

Acolyte Paola Kett glanced at Captain Brent and he met her eyes.

"Is your force ready?" David Rule asked Captain Van Pelt.

"Yes. My Chief Security Officer, Taylor Patrick, is going to accompany the raiders. You asked for a veteran security officer. He's my best. The rest of us will push the *Corridor* to new glory."

"Welcome aboard," Ridge waved.

Patrick nodded at Gideon Ridge with, "Thank you, Captain."

"All of you, say your farewells. Time is not our ally in this. Once everyone takes their places, our Raiders will leave the sector and go at the Reaches from another direction; we hope the moving starmada will stay on course...for us."

"That is some hope to have," Lorrayanka laughed lightly.

Others shared a smile, too, but Gideon saw no such levity on the face of Samara Garriton. Her beautiful countenance seemed overshadowed by her disdain at her place in the day.

Apart they moved, marching toward their ships as if to war. Indeed, it was to war, and there was no person there who did not know it. They would leave as allies and those who regrouped would do so with a new bond between them.

Those who did not regroup would be dead, their adventure over, their lives forfeit, having shown love for others in the greatest possible way.

"Fighter pilots, meet me by the launch tubes," David Rule called loudly. "We need to establish and remind each other of our call signs. Breaking into smaller squadrons may be a good plan, also."

The Unity Officers broke for their shuttles while the fighter pilots followed Rule. The Ridge family took the Raiders for their ships, though Gideon Ridge threw looks over his shoulder for Samara Garriton.

Rule reached his Razor class fighter, his white cloak and cassock billowing about him in the hum and localized rush created by prepping engines.

"I have a list of those in fighters for our run. Echo your call sign when I call it to verify and identify, please." David Rule pointed to himself with his thumb. "I'm *Razorhawk*."

Confirmed, several answered.

"Hunon Interceptor, *Jokra*."

The Hunon Commander, Wahll, saluted in the way of his people and repeated the name.

"Hunon Interceptor, *Stuto*."

Wahll's companion Hunon nodded, saluted then repeated the name.

"Starstalker Crescent fighter, *Ristar*."

A Starstalker pilot, a huge male with a majestic, red mane, saluted as his people did and answered with the name in return. His voice was already deep and gravelly, the pilot ready for battle.

"Starstalker Crescent fighter, *Moonscar*."

"Here, Rule," Captain Prentia said flatly, strolling up at the last minute.

Rule almost questioned her presence but she spoke first.

"*Moonscar*, ready," she mewled, her eyes giving no room to question. She was leaving her carrier to fly a fighter herself.

"Temple Squadron, Lath fighter, *Saber*," Rule continued.

"*Saber*," answered Alexi Carver, a tall, sturdy man in Acolyte clothing.

"Temple Squadron, Lox fighter, *Tikrek*."

Jon Kett answered with the name.

"Temple Squadron, Rundoon fighter, *Carolina*."

Ziva Lieve answered with the name of the ship, reminding Rule that she would be solo in the fighter. Jaka Baddenide had been serving as a munitions operator on the heavily armed craft but she felt she could handle it alone. Baddenide had been assigned to the Raiders.

"Temple Squadron, Chabron mini-freighter, *Spania*."

The pilot and copilot both saluted and answered.

"Temple Squadron, MGP fighter, *Raine*."

Taelynn Berreaux threw back her white hood and answered. Then she looked over her shoulder and threw a wave at the Starstalker technician watching from the repair stations.

"They got her running again; I may as well go with you."

Several chuckles passed around.

"Temple Squadron, Mustang fighter, *WildCard*," Rule continued.

Rabeau Loist, a diminutive man, elfish in nature, answered.

"Indeed, sir, I am the *WildCard*."

"Good. That's the squadron as a whole."

"What's good about that?" asked Taelynn Berreaux with a wry grin.

"Relax, Taelynn," Alexi Carver chuckled. "You got me. I figure we got this, solid as Jordanium."

"Super alloys aside," Rule warned, "Pay attention. We'll be in three formations. Captain Prentia, if you would be so kind, I'd like you to be a formation leader. Please lead our Hunon allies and your Starstalker ally."

The pilots involved acknowledged his decision.

"The *WildCard* will stay with me and both of us will move all over, no formation to hold. We will be wildcards, for lack of a better term, and our actions will hopefully be hard to predict. Jon Kett, pilot of the *Tikrek*, will lead the rest of you in formation."

The others agreed.

"Good. Now go. And may the Grace of God Almighty shield and protect you."

They broke into runs for their fighters with the exception of Jon Kett. He looked for the raiding freighters and the crowd standing with them.

His daughter, Paola Kett, waved to him from the shadow of the freighter she would board. She blew him a kiss.

The raiding plan had included not just the *Spoken Word* but an additional, battered cargo unit from the Starstalker carrier. It had a name, of course, but old Sundar had balked at it immediately. He had grabbed a canister of bay marker paint and sprayed *Belly Rub* on both sides of the cockpit. In response to the stares, he just nodded.

"For Gil Bardoff. He would've liked it."

"You sure you want to do this run? On this ship?" Captain Josh Brent asked the Kett daughter.

"I'm an Acolyte, Captain. I don't fear death. I know where I'm going when life ends. I would think you would be more concerned, since you aren't going into battle at the command of your starship."

Brent shrugged, offering, "I don't know what to think. I was taken from the *Lewistowe*, a ship I loved and a crew I loved and a Captain I trusted, and thrown into a command seat on the *Bloodwind*. Then things went really crazy. My career is probably over, so I figured I would just bow out of the ship thing and serve where I'm best."

"You're best work is raiding the Reaches?" she asked with a grin.

"No, I've just been in security and Echo Forces and Weapons Officer positions...I feel more at home with a venter on my side and armor over my face. In the USAP we called it 'anonymous justice' gear."

"My experience has seen a lot of anonymous in Echo Soldiers but justice has been thin," Sundar Ridge said.

"Maybe I can be the exception," Brent told Sundar.

Candri Prentice and Jaka Baddenide, two more Acolytes, joined the little group at the loading ramp. Jaka wore the white cloak and black cassock, pants and boots, vestments of the sentinel. Candri Prentice wore the white cloak, too, but over wine red.

"Let's get aboard and get gone," Sylver Ridge said flatly. "If my boy beats us to the Reaches, I'll never hear the end of it."

At the *Spoken Word*, Gideon Ridge watched his half of the Raiders move up his loading ramp. His friend, Grundy, led Security Chief Taylor Patrick, who was decked out in full Echo armor.

Last to walk the ramp was Commodore Wrigley Zeckinbridge. She had adorned herself in Echo armor as well. At the top of the ramp, she turned back and saluted Samara Garriton, her most trusted Captain, who stood sour faced, finally having come to stand with Gideon Ridge.

"I don't like it!" Samara Garriton snapped at Ridge. "It isn't what I signed on to do."

"Samara, you signed on to find out the fate of your ship and your crew. We did that."

"I want to see it through, Gideon! I don't want another command! I want to raid with the rest of you, follow it to the last!"

She had her hands on shapely hips, her Starstalker replacement venter slung low on her right.

Gideon Ridge eased close to her.

"It isn't another command. It's your old one. You came out here for the good of the *Vindicator* crew members you left behind. Now, the crew members that remain have come out here for you. You're a natural for this command. They're here for you; you'll never forgive yourself if anyone else commands the *Bloodwind* and the rest of your crew is lost."

She snapped her head to the side and looked back at the starship shuttles. Staring away, she spoke.

"It isn't…it's not just…" she floundered.

Gideon reached out to her gently and cupped her face on one side.

Big, blue-green eyes looked back to him, fluttering.

"This isn't the end," he said softly. "We'll see each other again."

"You can't know that!" she snapped, turning her face from him. "There's no way-"

He turned her face back. He leaned in and kissed her softly.

"You know the Faith," he said flatly. "You have to believe. Even if death claims us, this is not the end, Samara. You know it."

She stood to her toes and kissed him again. Deeply. Intensely.

"I want your peace with things, Gideon," she said afterward.

He slipped his Bible from inside his jacket and put it in her hands.

"The map to the greatest peace you could ever know. There's a page in the back that lays it all out. The rest is a journey you follow as you go."

"When we get back-"

"Don't wait," he said. "Read at least that page while you wait."

"Gideon-"

"Read it."

"Okay."

"I mean it."

"Ridge, I will," she promised.

"Good," he said and turned away. He strolled up the ramp.

"You just walk off like that?" she gasped. "I mean, after the kiss, the exchange we've had, you just spin and walk off, not even looking back-"

"I'm coming back, Garriton," he said, pausing just a moment. "But, if I don't go now, I don't know if I'll be able to."

With that, he was gone, his memory a phantom still on the ramp. Samara Garriton would not step back from his ghost until the ramp itself left her behind.

She stepped back a few more paces as the engines intensified.

"You better come back," she growled at him quietly.

It seemed to be a much longer walk than it truly measured as Samara Garriton retreated for the *Bloodwind* shuttle. When she reached it, Captain Van Pelt was standing by the shuttle for the *Corridor*.

"Captain," he greeted.

"Captain," she responded.

"The Commodore may have left you with the new command but I want you to understand how this is going to-"

"Let me save you some breath," she sniped. "This command is made up of a bridge crew that has been working with me for a long time. When it comes to starship engagement, we've logged more time together than you've been in the chair. You take your direction from me, not the other way around. Be a good Unity soldier and just board up."

He tried to respond but she abandoned him for her little jump ship.

"Yes, ma'am," he said sarcastically to her closing load door.

The shuttles soon followed the freighters out of the launch tubes and headed for their starships. The two freighters broke off in two different directions, heading for deeper space in opposite flight paths. They would raid the Reaches from two distant points, attempting to avoid the bone starmada on approach.

The two Unity vessels waited patiently for their captains.

"This is Commander Lorrayanka," the Starstalker ship transmitted directly. "I will be in command of the *Ferali 5* in Captain Prentia's absence. I wish you all blessings and providence from Almighty God. We will do our best to aid you in this dark time and I nod in deference to you, Captain Garriton, for you have more command experience than I. Any direction you have, feel free to share."

Captain Garriton answered for herself from the docking transport.

"Thank you, Commander. We just need to work together; keep an open com channel between us. Each of us."

Both of the other commanding officers acknowledged her.

"God be with us," Samara Garriton whispered.

The gravlift stopped Captain Samara Garriton at bridge level and she stepped out of the thick light. She waited in front of the bridge door, holding it closed with a palm on the interface, gathering herself. Deep breaths and slow exhales tempered the nerves roiling within her and she let the doors open a few moments later.

"Captain on the bridge!" shouted Chief Security Officer Penrose.

"Mack, it's good to see you," she told Penrose with a big smile.

"Welcome back, Captain!" several others offered almost at once.

Garriton moved around the bridge, feeling her confidence build. She went to the nearby science station and squeezed the shoulder of the man there saluting her.

"Wimbel, how are you?" she asked Science Officer Boatwright.

"Better now, ma'am. Ready to defend the sector."

"How are you?" she asked the Communications Officer at his station. She was moving with great comfort, even something of a sense of zeal. She took his hand.

"I am well, Captain," Niles Respra answered. "We've missed you."

"And I have missed all of you," she answered. Then she trotted down the three steps to the helm station and squeezed the shoulder of her Navigator. "Reje Chu, you are a sight for sore eyes."

"Hardly, ma'am," the young lady answered, tears running her cheeks. "You are."

The Greylik Pilot stood to his feet and saluted her.

"Welcome aboard, Captain."

"Thank you. And you are?" she queried.

"Pilot Retaw, ma'am. And just let me say that I am sorry your former Pilot did not survive your last battle on the *Vindicator* but I am honored to sit in for her now."

Tears welled in Garriton's eyes.

"Thank you, Mr. Retaw. I will miss Pilot Vissk but you are not sitting in for her. This is your station, your ship. Be proud of it."

"Yes, ma'am."

Gorbler, the Octovoid Weapons Officer, stood and saluted as well.

"And you are?" she asked him, staring at him with fascination.

"Gorbler, ma'am, your Weapons Officer."

His fluidic voice gurgled his English but he was surprisingly clear. Few of the Fenfutticnessoks, or natives of the Fenfutti home world, bothered to learn other languages since theirs was so difficult in itself. When they had joined Unity Command most races had been unwilling to bother learning it. They had even renamed the people Octovoid for their bulbous heads, changing colors and eight appendages so that they did not have to mangle the translations of their native name.

"I've never met another from your world working a bridge assignment," she smiled. "It's good to have you here."

Gorbler's huge smile belied the smallness of his face and tiny eyes.

"Thank you, ma'am. I was born to break the norm."

Garriton laughed lightly, saying, "Then it's definitely good to have you here. Hopefully we can beat the odds we face together, as a crew."

A unanimous rally of hopeful words and feelings echoed in the bridge space.

"All right, then, let's get to work. Mr. Respra, do we have that open com to our fellow starships?"

"Yes, ma'am. All of the individual fighters have joined as well."

"Good. Let them know we are ready and able to meet this threat."

He grinned with, "Yes, ma'am."

Commander Lorrayanka, the Starstalker leader on board the *Ferali 5*, looked around her bridge just after Samara Garriton's message. She stopped her gaze on Wastasa Winds.

"Mr. Winds, are you ready?"

"Yes, and you can just call me Winds." He slipped on his slicker gloves. "You just need to know I could burn out every circuit, receptor and logistics relay in your system. It's worth a shot but-"

"Proceed. We'll take the chance."

"Okay. If you can spare a body, send someone to lead me to your sensor banks."

With that, a Security Officer was dispatched with Wastasa Winds for another deck.

"Commander," a nearby helm operator said, "how did we end up with him? He's a notorious mercenary and slicker. I don't feel comfortable with him walking around-"

"You don't have to feel comfortable. Just do your job. Captain Prentia said she wanted him here. She wanted us to have more advanced options and a slicker can bring out the best in technology. And sometimes, just sometimes, a little trust can bring out the best in someone who straddles the fence from time to time."

Multiple decks below the bridge, the tall, black haired security woman watched Winds closely. The two entered a room through a double blast door and paused, Winds drinking it all in.

"You have impressive sensor banks," he muttered, somewhat awed. "It's surprising that your Captain wanted me to boost these and not your shielding or your weapons. I could even probably adjust your hull integrity with-"

"Mr. Winds, I don't have any input in that. I'm just supposed to bring you down here and give you any aid I can in bolstering sensors."

He grinned, muttering, "Get to work. Gotcha."

She smiled coolly then said, "Let me know what I can do."

He moved to the biggest display in the chamber and threw the two main levers on each side of it. He then grabbed the contacts below the levers, spread out his fingers on each hand and touched the display with his hand spans.

The display came to life and began running code across the normally simple viewscreen.

"Come on machine," Winds growled lowly.

He closed his eyes, concentrating, using his will to rearrange the coding, multiplying it. Neurologically, he was linked to the sensor grid through his slicker gloves while he commanded it to go above and beyond its listed abilities.

Suddenly, both of his eyes popped wide open. His nearness to the screen gave a reflection of his face in the display that the Security Officer could see from her direction. He was afraid. Coding, reflected on the curve of the man's eyes in the light of the screen, faded and took with it the reflection. The screen suddenly became a picture...

...a picture of death.

"Open a com to your Commander!" he demanded suddenly, sliding his hands around the display and the central interface.

"What is it?"

"Do it!" Winds yelled.

227

The Officer pressed a wall com and held it down.

"Commander Lorrayanka, this is-"

"Get your shields up! Now! And tell the others! The starmada is here, it's right here!" Winds screamed. "They're masked! Warn the other ships!"

Lorrayanka howled at her bridge crew.

"Shields, now! Maximum levels! Hail the others, tell them the starmada is here and using a masking field!"

"Commander, Winds has the sensors rebooting...I see it..." her Science Officer muttered.

"Spit it out!" the Commander yelled.

"The source of the mask...it's the Leviathan..."

"Evasive maneuvers!" Lorrayanka railed on her helm crew.

"There's a disruption forming close to us! It's the biggest Unity ship signature I've ever seen, a quantum drive signature, and it's about to emerge from quantum jumpspeed!" the Science Officer howled.

"Ma'am, Winds has hijacked the Communications array with his link into the sensor banks," Lorrayanka's Communications Officer shouted. "He's sharing what we can now see with our allies and with that newcomer ship, the Unity *Longreach*!"

"Good! As long as he encoded it safely, someone has to educate them!"

Lorrayanka threw off her one shouldered cloak and flipped a switch on the command seat, her fangs extended and her hair lengthening before she could even speak.

"All hands!" she roared. "This battle has begun!"

CHAPTER TEN : *Engagement*

O n the supercarrier, the Grim Reaper class, *Longreach*, Admiral Meshach Washington leaped to the observation rail at the height of the bridge. The Captain was beside him and the First Officer joined them. All three gave a split second of personal denial with mouths agape after the Communications Officer relayed the situation.

Then all three spoke.

"Shields!" the First Officer yelled at the Defensive Weapons Station.

"Evasive maneuvers!" the Captain shouted at the Helm.

"Fire on that monster!" Admiral Washington demanded of the Offensive Weapons Station, meaning the monstrosity in the center of the fleet of death.

Already the thunder of exploding charges and energies against the stiff shielding of the *Longreach* rolled deafeningly throughout the ship. The supercarrier gave back, however, its wide array of assault munitions raining on the Leviathan and its nearby allies.

Only the Leviathan withstood the opening volley from the Grim Reaper class Unity ship. More than twenty nearby fighters and freighters, occupied by the dead, rejoined death once more, obliterated by the sweep.

The USAP supercarrier, albeit impressive, had come into the zone too hot. Evasive maneuvers were not quite enough; its trajectory took it right toward the nose of the serpentine death ship at too great a speed. It could not make the necessary responses and the Leviathan did not even try. The crash was imminent.

"Brace yourselves!" Pilot Keer howled.

The scream of rending metals and the static discharge of shielding colliding with shielding sang the song of destruction. Left to dance were the biggest Unity ship in production and the largest ship on record. The Grim Reaper class supercarrier managed to veer just enough to avoid the head on impact but it still dragged its belly down the upper spine of the snake ship with catastrophic results.

The serpent ship snapped to a halt, several sections compressing and collapsing in upon themselves, while the upper fuselage tore from the side ribbing in a length equal to the size of the Unity ship. If it had needed an atmosphere, it would have been dead in space, for all life support would have been compromised.

The dead do not need life support, however.

The *Longreach*, on the other hand, lost a lot of life support, a lot of the underside of its fuselage and deeper compartments. Fire broke out and sparks flew even as the shielding tried valiantly to reboot its processes.

The two ships ground to a halt, the Unity ship pierced and held in place by the Leviathan's upper spine and plating. The death ship had taken on the supercarrier, minute in size comparison, to wear like a necktie.

Neckties can often choke the life from a wearer, of course.

"Captain!" the Science Officer cried. "We've got hull breaches on decks fifteen through forty-five and we lost ten cargo chambers altogether! Shields are rebooting but we have system failures all over the ship!"

"Shields at sixty-nine per cent and climbing again," a Weapons Officer shouted.

"Fire everything you have from the belly of this carrier! And charge the Might!" roared the Admiral.

"But we need the power for our shields-" Captain Wallace Burnett countered.

The Admiral shoved the Captain away from the overlook rail.

"Do it!"

The supercarrier jerked and bounced with hail after hail of fighter fire coming from the reacting starmada. The shields on a supercarrier could last a lifetime against such small gauge bursts, however, and Admiral Washington ordered the crew to reserve power, not to return fire. They were attracting attention, he told them; let the other ships hit the smaller enemies which were totally unaware of their pending doom.

Surprisingly, the big serpentine ship seemed to falter and stall. Lights and beacon flares flashed and faded intermittently.

"Hold still a few more moments," Washington growled. "If I get that quantum cannon charged, you're back to being history."

The Vanguard class *Bloodwind* ripped by the two entangled ships, raining destruction upon the smaller vessels about them.

"Fire!" Captain Samara Garriton shouted again.

The Captain was trying to be heard above the barrage of attacks gifted them by the dead. In the background boomed the pounding drums of impact on their dwindling shields.

Multiple *Bloodwind* weapons unloaded on the starmada of bones, ripping enemy fighters and freighters to shreds by the handful. The spatial charges alone on the impressive Vanguard class ship offered death like a buffet meal; open to all, seconds and thirds invited. With the particle cannons and open chambered plasma turrets, the starship handed out destruction with a wanton flare.

Pilot Retaw leaned close to his display, squinting at the faded images. The ship was doling out so much energy that the readouts and displays had gone to conserve status. He moved like lightning never the less, changing course over and over and over again. More often than not, he could keep better control and tactical reaction in the big Vanguard than the smaller, more agile enemies could and that was keeping the USAP vessel alive.

Gorbler was no slouch, his eight appendages working overtime, constantly stealing power here and shunting power there to keep the shielding and the hull plate reinforcement fresh. He was also the *hands* in *handing out punishment* to the roaming dead.

"Pull us back a little again!" Garriton howled, the latest impact almost throwing her from her chair. "As soon as you do, turn on them and rush them! Mr. Gorbler, keep the onslaught heavy!"

"Captain, weapons energies are down to-"

"No bad news, Gorbler!" Garriton warned. "This will be a long fight, so you need to save some of your fractions and ratios for later!"

The crew noticed the relatively small *Corridor* streak by on the viewscreen, its turrets alive with energy. Seven more enemy fighters exploded into dust and fire.

"Good aim!" Captain Van Pelt cried on his bridge. "Keep it up!"

The Weapons Officer said nothing in response. Instead, targeting more enemies was the only offered reply.

"Wells, take us down the big boy's back!" Van Pelt shouted his order to the Pilot. Then he called on the other officer again. "Let it hold whatever you have, Rol!"

"Coming about!" Pilot Doranna Wells called back, holding to her station as the little transport bounced about in assault fire.

"Sshields at fifty-nine perscent!" Rol shouted then flipped open a glass cover. The Vipon Officer palmed the panel beneath it. "Ready to unload chargess, Grekbil!"

"Wells?" Van Pelt asked.

231

"Right...now!" the Pilot answered, turning the transport to move along the spine.

"Chargess away!" Rol cried.

The first three of the drop charges carried on the transport passed right through the shielding of the Leviathan, igniting the snaking fuselage in raw energy and destruction. After that, the *Corridor* dropped another twelve charges against glimmering shields, unable to pass cleanly through them but pounding them nevertheless. Then the transport peeled away, taking the fight to another squadron of long dead fighters.

The *Ferali 5* was doing the same thing.

Commander Lorrayanka slammed her fist against her seat.

"Recalibrate shields, now!"

She leaned away from a wide spray of coolant emitted from overloaded carriers above her. Two more bursts opened on the bridge and bathed two back up stations in noxious gases.

"On it," her Weapons Officer promised.

"We see they can give, *Ferali*!" she shouted at her crew. "Find out how well they can take!"

Her ship had been swarmed by three squadrons of ten fighters at once. They had destroyed several ships but their shields had taken a pure pummeling.

The Weapons Officer blistered the open space with raw plasma from their cannons and dropped another four fighters.

"Fires on decks two and seven, Commander," the Science Officer informed. "We're having power loss on the starboard propulsion units as well as the sensor banks."

"Reroute!" Commander Lorrayanka yelled. She then spun her chair to the Weapons Officer. "Enough trading blows! Net those bugs!"

"Yes, ma'am!" the Weapons Officer answered.

He quickly drew a line across the screen of his console with his finger then tapped the display in the center of the line. Outside the vessel, launched from two evenly spaced propelling stations on the hull, a glowing, yellow energy web spun into space. It expanded exponentially as it flew, energy arcing between its strands, until it impacted with eleven of the swarming fighters, each caught going in some different direction.

Each of the ships fluctuated in power levels on touch, electricity like lightning shooting from one ship to another, from one strand of the net to another, until all of them erupted in blinding explosions.

A rallying cry of celebration swam the bridge.

The carrier jerked sharply to one side.

The Science Officer said, "Captain! Winds transmitted a diagnostic report to my station! It's a breakdown of the combat, the statistics of-"

The carrier took another blow that dropped the bridge lighting for a second and pitched the ship to the other side. Luckily, the lights returned.

"Quickly!" Lorrayanka ordered him.

"His sensor work shows that the fighters respond efficiently at combat speeds!"

She rolled her eyes then snapped, "That we knew! The impacts of their attacks gave it away!"

"Ma'am, he predicts that, at just a tiny margin above standard combat speeds, the fighters would be almost useless!"

It hit her suddenly just what he meant.

"Well, don't just sit there!" she howled with a grin. "Helm, throw on the speed!" She looked to the Weapons Officer again. "Route any excess power to our shields, Xerstou, and don't fire too conservatively! Light these bugs up!"

Wastasa Winds had realized, by study of the readouts and display captures, that the death ships were very efficient warmongers at standard combat speeds, which were the speeds that most ships used when engaged in spatial combat. Above a certain speed, standard targeting equipment lost efficiency. Maneuverability suffered, too, and shielding took a beating when too many ships were in the vicinity. Therefore, most ships fought at a given speed for their size and technology.

Winds had discovered that by adding a bit more speed and sacrificing optimum efficiency in targeting and handling, they could engage the enemy with virtually no resistance. Whatever was controlling the technology carrying the dead was limited after all; above speeds considered standard for optimum combat engagement, their action and reaction times would be far slower and less accurate.

Winds had then hijacked the communications and sent the information to the allies.

"Well, that's good news!" Samara Garriton shouted on the *Bloodwind*. "Retaw, amp up the speed! Gorbler, up our shielding! We're going to do a little bumping; I'd like to survive it!"

On the *Corridor*, Captain Van Pelt had taken the news seriously and put it to good use.

"Wells! Up our speeds!"

She agreed just as David Rule swept by on their viewscreen so quickly they did not even recognize his speeding Razor fighter. He was wearing a tail of fifteen fighters in pursuit.

Rule flew erratically. The mass of enemies close behind him flooded the space about him with energy fire but his speed was detrimental to their targeting. It seemed at any given moment he was a scarce second ahead of all they did.

Captain Prentia swept downward toward his enemies. She flipped a handful of override switches and opened fire on the dead, her weapons chattering at fully automatic function. Seven of the fighters jerked and spun then exploded before the others broke pursuit.

"You're clear, *Razorhawk*," the Starstalker said.

"My thanks, *Moonscar*. Where is your group? You're flying solo."

Captain Prentia howled with laughter.

"At these speeds, flying in formation could be deadly. We are safer zipping about at random, doing our best not to plow into our enemies."

She veered off then and set aim on another group of death fighters.

The others had come to the same conclusions. Most had broken out of formation, flying for one band of the dead or another, only to turn immediately for a different group, then another.

Most of the dead could not follow the allies with targeting, much less give viable pursuit.

The allies of life quickly lost count of their successes. The ships, fighters and freighters they had destroyed tallied too quickly in number to track. It was in the hundreds, most would have agreed, which sounded hopeful...until the remembrance of the starmada size came to mind. The starmada of bones was thousands of ships strong. Despite the fact that they were arriving in waves, time would wear on the defenders and so would overwhelming odds.

Added to the fact that the opposing big ships, like the Dreadship classes and the carriers, had not even begun to reach the conflict, the situation was all too sobering.

With another thousand allies, they could not hold that point in space. The battle that would shape life in the cosmos would be fought someplace in the Reaches.

Admiral Meshach Washington stood on the bridge of the *Longreach* and tried to think around what he believed to be inevitable. He would eventually see all of the allies aflame.

"Pilot Keer!" he cried while the Captain and the First Officer shouted orders to the defensive and offensive Weapons Officers. "Can you get us dislodged from this monster?"

"No, sir! Engines are still not responding with enough power to pull away!"

The Admiral grabbed First Officer Tylle by the shoulder and turned him about.

"Deploy every member of this crew who can fly a Scorpion!"

"But, Admiral-"

"Officer Tylle, we have a hundred fighters in our bays! We need to deploy them; this isn't going well!"

Captain Burnett stepped between them.

"We'll be struggling to keep this ship operational under the lack of manpower!"

"We're not operational now!" Admiral Washington exploded. He ground his teeth together and leaned close to the Captain. "Unless we get more help, we will die here anyway. We may as well put all the players on the board and hope it buys us a little time. If we don't, when our allies have been overrun, we will be destroyed right here, impaled and unable to maneuver! Deploy all the fighters and that's an order!"

The Captain bowed up at Washington, about to argue further. Behind him, Officer Tylle engaged the com system and spoke.

"Emergency deployment! All pilots, report to launch! Scorpions away! I repeat, all Scorpions away!"

Several of the bridge crew turned and looked at the Admiral and the First Officer.

The call of all Scorpions to launch is the first in a series of commands that comes down when a supercarrier is in terrible danger. All over the ship, the sound of every launching bay powering up echoed in the corridors.

The Captain slammed his hand onto the rail.

"I will not let you cripple my crew! I'll call a full retreat first, Admiral-"

Washington snapped his fingers at the nearby Security Officers.

"Take him," Admiral Washington said of the Captain. "He is relieved of duty."

There was a brief tussle but, in the end, the Captain was gone from the bridge.

Over the next few moments, the First Officer and the Admiral stood in silence. The next few after that, they were handling questions from tactical and from the struggling helm. They even advised the Navigator on a course to plot, should engines come back online. Eventually they noted the passing of their Scorpion fighter craft on their viewscreen.

"Captain Burnett just wanted to keep his ship together," Tylle finally said.

"I know. But, as a Unity commander, he should have thought of the greater good. That's who we are."

The First Officer raised his eyebrows.

"It's who we used to be," the Admiral corrected in a mutter.

Tylle smiled wryly and queried, "By the way, did I just get promoted?"

Washington returned a sarcastic grin with, "Ask again when we make it home."

Amidst the thunder of raining attacks on the *Longreach*'s shielding, the sound of cheers rose from the lower bridge. They had been holding their breath, hoping they would live until the Might was charged. As one of the Weapons Officers turned and shouted, the quantum energy cannon known as the Might was live.

"Indeed!" Washington yelled. "Then show this snake ship some Might! Fire at will!"

The entire Unity ship shuddered. Deck plate upon deck rail rattled loudly, while the roar of power build up vibrated every surface. The bridge lights faded then died altogether, followed after by all the rest of the lighting on every deck and in every chamber.

The engines died completely. The shields crackled and buzzed then dropped.

Every member of the bridge crew held their breath tightly.

Then came the eruption.

From the belly of the ship, through a portal larger than any of the landing bays, golden white light sprayed free like water from a whale's spout. Only, with the quantum energies, the discharge came with the roar of a lion and a propulsion all its own. The blast threw the *Longreach* free of the *Leviathan* and the Unity ship careened away from the battle, all systems and power dead, adrift and out of control.

That was the least of the Unity problems. Unknown and unrealized by the crew of the big Grim Reaper, their ship had taken far too much damage to safely emit that much quantum energy. Systems had not just overloaded throughout the vessel. They exploded. They blew decks apart and chambers apart. They ignited fires everywhere and stole all semblance of power and balance. Systems gave up all over the vessel and sprayed energy in all sorts of directions...

...then all was black.

The quantum blast did something far worse to the *Leviathan*. Massive energies tore through it and severed the ship into three parts, none of them left in great shape. It also continued beyond it and annihilated some hundred or more of the newly arriving starmada forces.

The lights went out all over the big enemy ship then they went out in all of the smaller enemy ships as well. Power systems in all of the death ships stalled and died.

The bone starmada drifted to a standstill, dead in space.

"Captain, enemy forces are depowered completely," Science Officer Boatwright said on the bridge of the *Bloodwind*.

"Open our channel," Captain Garriton said to Communications Officer Respra.

"Channel open," he said in his Jamaican accent.

"Allies, this is Captain Garriton. Our enemies have lost power. This is not the time to pull back; form on the *Bloodwind*. Let's take this fight right to the heart of the dearly departed."

"Are you mad?" the Captain of the *Corridor* stabbed over the com. "Fly deep into their formation? So that when they repower they can devour us?"

"Stay if you want," she responded. "Those who will, follow us. No power means no shields. As we fly into the starmada we'll carve a swath of pure carnage into their ranks."

Voice after voice acknowledged her plan.

Captain Van Pelt of the *Corridor* rose from his seat on the bridge.

"Ms. Wells," he said to his Pilot, "move us to a defendable position near the Admiral and the *Longreach*." Then he added, "I know their power is reading null but keep trying to hail them, Mr. Patterson. They'll need us if that big monster ship comes back to life."

"Captain Van Pelt," Doranna Wells stalled, her beauty masked in her concern, "should we break away from the fight? The *Ferali 5* as well as the *Bloodwind* may need us to flank-"

"Take us to the Admiral's ship," the Captain growled.

She acknowledged his order and engaged the engines.

Andreas Riker wept openly, unabashedly, though his face did not show it. It was happening inside his twisted mind. His wide open eyes, always fixed that way, rolled back in his head under the strain.

"Power the starmada, Psiborg," the voice ordered darkly.

"I can't!" he screamed in his head. If he had been using his physical voice his throat would have bled. "The pain! The feedback! The effort is too great, too brutal!"

"You do not know pain...not yet."

The grayed man forced his eyes to focus. He saw from the inside of the bridge through massive openings in bulkheads and hull plates the twinkling stars...and the firelight flickering from each and every starmada ship destroyed by the new assault of the defenders. They were carving a path away from the *Leviathan*, cutting deep into the ranks of the dead, and heading for the Reaches.

"I have to stop...I can't concentrate..." he mused.

"Then you can never go home," the voice threatened. "You will wander the Reaches with the ghosts of your crew and their voices..."

"No!" he screamed. "No, you promised!"

In his mind the lunatic cries of his dead crew began flooding his memories.

"No!" the man cried.

"Power that starmada. Move the boneships, Psiborg, or here you will stay forever."

"I need time!" he mourned. "I need rest!"

"There is no time, no rest. Already, they are navigating the Reaches."

"What? No! They have just begun to start through the starmada formations!"

"They are not alone, Psiborg, and they approach. Invaders. A small team. They have a star chart. They managed lightspeed. They will not pass through the natural barriers. They will not be hampered. They will not be mad when they arrive; they will come with clear minds full of justice and vengeance."

Riker screamed anew. Then he went silent, even in his mind.

He struggled to imagine the power levels on the starmada crafts, struggled to will them to come back to life.

Deep in the starmada, a Reaper class Unity ship trembled…and a bridge light ignited.

Sundar Ridge flipped a series of switches over his seat and nodded at his brother.

"Ridge brothers to passengers," he said over the interior com system. "We're making our approach on the rock at lightspeed. We'll give you word when we drop to sublight; be ready to hold onto something. We won't be going in easy."

Sundar killed the com.

In the deep of their hold, three Acolytes and a Unity Captain waited on pins and needles. The moment was approaching when their actions just might alter the course of history in the cosmos…for better or for worse.

Jaka Baddenide knelt upon his knees. His hood was down and his closely cut blonde hair looked almost as white as the hood. He held his hands palm to palm, his forefingers pressed against his lips and the fine hair of his mustache and beard.

He prayed fervently and Candri Prentice was doing the same.

Her dark hair fell about her face, masking her somewhat.

Captain Josh Brent watched them curiously from his seat beside Paola Kett.

"Shouldn't you be praying?" he asked her.

She chuckled and asked him, "Shouldn't you?"

He drew a sudden breath but said nothing.

"I pray often each day. Besides that, I know my faith and my God and my destination; it would seem to me that someone confused over those things needs to pray more."

He shook his head and offered, "I never said I was confused."

She leaned her head to one side.

"Then you have faith?"

"I was taught as a child."

"You need to know what you believe, Joshua, not what you have been told to believe and told not to believe. Your faith has to be a part of you, the main foundation of who you are, or it's not a faith at all. It's a theory, a disjointed idea of a possibility."

"I know. My great grandfather told me often."

"Then you're ready? Ready to face death? To face your Maker?"

"What? No, not really. I mean, who is?"

She looked at the other Acolytes then looked back to him and smiled.

He nodded, commenting, "Okay, yeah. You and I are different, that's all. Faith works for you. But consider all the souls in the cosmos who don't have a faith. Consider all those who have other faiths before you even think about the ones who don't know about faith, or those who know about faith and don't believe. That works for them. Can you really say you're better than they are?"

"And now the 'better than' argument is thrown into play," she giggled. "Would you also like to put down the 'my own truth' gauntlet?"

He shrugged with, "Might as well."

She shook her head, still smiling.

"First off, I'm not better than anyone. My faith tells me that all sentient beings are the same; we're fallible, faulty and prone to selfish desires. It tells me no one is better than another, because we all need the same help. Then it tells me that God loves us and loved us enough to send His Son, Jesus Christ, to die and pay for all those sins and failures we have. That way, we could be clean and grow close to Him.

"As for the 'my own truth' syndrome, that is a movement designed to make any lifestyle acceptable in the face of morality and civilization. Someone says what you are doing is wrong. You say it is not, according to your own truth. To get around responsibilities, obligations, morals, self control and all forms of 'right and wrong', people began a long time ago to work around 'right and wrong'. The first way to do that was to attack accepted truth, so that there could be no decision on 'right and wrong'. If there is no accepted truth, but only a shifting truth from one being to another, then how could there be a standard set of morals or 'rights and wrongs'?"

"So you believe your faith should control-"

"No, I don't," she said somewhat sharply. "I believe the teachings of Christ. He taught that we needed to be an example and share His Gospel; He never once suggested taking over worlds or enslaving others, forcing the Gospel on them. His disciples taught that as well, reminding us that Jesus wanted us to do our very best to live at peace with all and respect all. This conversation has been an example of what I believe; I haven't sought to control you, only to share with you. At any time you could have told me to stop sharing with you and I would have."

"Well, I read the Bible on databases back in my childhood," he said somewhat arrogantly. "I know in the Old Testament it was fine to kill people of other faiths and destroy people who did not believe-"

"And you could bring that up if I were adhering to the literal letter of the Old Testament, Joshua," she chuckled. "But I'm Christian, a New Acolyte. We follow the entire Bible, yes, but adhering to the teachings of Christ in the New Testament above all else. Many things in the Old Testament were for the area in question or the peoples in question or the time in question. Jesus Christ came and changed the way followers of God were to interact and behave. Never, not a single time mind you, in the New Testament did Jesus tell anyone to harm anyone else. He always taught peace, forgiveness, mercy and freedom. We are all free to be just as bad or uninformed or whatever we want to be, but He loves us, wants better for us and has provided better for us."

Joshua Brent waited a moment, digesting. He seemed torn, uncertain of how to proceed. He looked into her clear blue eyes then offered a wry grin.

"I'm probably torpedoing any chance of getting to know you after this is all over."

She shook her head.

"Not at all. I love to get to know people, to share and learn."

"Well, I meant a little more. You know, like a personal interest," he said, deepening his voice. He let his eyes close just slightly. "You're not like any other woman I've ever met. I can see us spending a lot of time together, sharing, opening ourselves to each other…"

She met his eyes directly as he seemed to lean in toward her. It stopped him cold.

"What?"

"Do you find me attractive?" she asked flatly.

Mischief lay behind her eyes.

"Well, yeah, isn't it obvious?" he snapped, a bit irritated.

"I find you quite alluring," she admitted, her smile growing.

He let himself smile a bit.

"Good to know…"

"You should also know that is the last thing I factor into a relationship."

He sighed.

"Can we talk about something else? Like dying on the little rock out here?"

Gideon Ridge glanced at Grundy. The big guy had been uncharacteristically quiet during the run.

"What's wrong, Grundy? We've been on more dangerous runs than this one."

Wrigley Zeckinbridge was in a seat near the back of the cockpit.

"Name one," she said.

Gideon gave her a look over his shoulder.

The Security Chief from the *Corridor* sat with the Commodore, both in their armors, and he glanced at her to decipher Ridge's look.

"He hates it when I butt in," she said with a smirk. "That's why I do it."

"How do you know the Captain?" the handsome young Officer asked bluntly. "You seem like close friends."

"She's more like a sister," Gideon Ridge said from the front. "An annoying sister."

Grundy snorted, blowing his his horn hairs.

"Imagine; having two Dreas. But...do not tell her I said that."

Gideon Ridge laughed.

"He was very close to my father when he was teaching. Gideon was one of his star pupils," Zeckinbridge said and smiled. "He loves me."

Ridge began to cough into his hand.

Grundy chuckled, the sound a low rumbling of his deep voice and short snorts of air.

Patrick shook his head.

"So, what's the deal?" Gideon asked Grundy again.

Grundy hummed for a moment.

"Grockforth," he said finally.

"The Rothidai in service to Cheyenne Winds?" Gideon Ridge asked.

"It was a sad reminder to me what many of my people have done to survive. There is no honor in working with her, no integrity. With her, he is a criminal, a pawn...a disgrace. I was so ashamed to see one of us so used, so enslaved by evil. Yet, when given a chance to do something good, he jumped at it. There was good in him...and now I wonder if he made it off the station."

"Deep thoughts, my friend," Gideon informed him. "Is there more?"

"Yes. I'm really hungry."

Ridge smiled and said, "You and me both, partner."

A relay began to hum then a light ignited over the center console.

"Okay, people," Ridge said, "hold on. We're about to drop from lightspeed and I'm going in hot; be ready."

"Good to know," Wrigley Zeckinbridge said and cinched herself tighter into her seat restraints.

"Asteroid ABC-Zeta Lan on rapid approach, Gideon," the Rothidai rumbled. "Engaging holographic display for visual."

"The Stone Tombs. One massive facility. Are there above surface landing fairways?" Gideon Ridge asked.

"I am plotting a landing plan for the closest one near the entrance to the interior caves and caverns."

Taylor Patrick leaned forward, trying to peek at the holomaps.

"Good. Anything on long range sensors within the Reaches?" Gideon Ridge asked his big partner.

"Not a lot," Grundy answered Ridge. "There is a disturbance close by that 'roid, though. Another ship is about to exit lightspeed there."

Gideon frowned then moved three levers back with his left hand.

"We have to beat my Pap and Uncle Sun to the 'roid," Gideon stated. "If we don't I'll never hear the end of it. In the meantime, get ready to drop from lightspeed," Gideon ordered. "And...three, two, one..."

He and Grundy both shut down lightspeed instantly, no gradual shift attempted. The fluid light of the blurred gases and colorful dusts of the Reaches suddenly turned into clear, separate visual presences outside the cockpit.

The *Spoken Word* shimmered as it appeared out of nothingness and flew right into the projected atmosphere around the asteroid.

From another angle, the same could be said of the dirty, dented, renamed *Belly Rub*. It flew straight into the atmosphere around the Stone Tombs, lights from landing areas rolling over its viewscreens.

The two freighters barely pulled to the side to avoid a collision. Both were safe, however, and immediately started searching for landing protocols.

"We're here," Gideon said. "Grundy, light this place up."

Captain Van Pelt watched from the bridge of the little transport ship as their recovery lights spilled across the hull of the battered and powerless *Longreach*. Parts of it floated nearby the main mass; the supercarrier was missing whole decks and wingstations.

One hundred Scorpion class fighters had exited the massive ship just moments before the quantum blast. They had created a formation about the carrier, waiting to defend it.

"Hail those fighters," Van Pelt ordered Patterson. "Let them know to hold their position. Admiral Washington will not be left defenseless while we are here."

"Captain," the Science Officer countered, "shouldn't they launch a run on those death ship ranks? Before they repower-"

Van Pelt spun on him.

"And leave Admiral Washington adrift and powerless? Is that your idea, Mr. Janng?"

"No, sir, but-"

"Patterson, transmit my order. I am a ranking starship Captain; should any of the fighters disagree with my orders, remind them that they are bound to my order until one of their commanders on the supercarrier gives them further orders…whether Mr. Janng likes it or not."

"Acknowledged," Patterson said darkly.

The non-Unity starfighters had been sweeping about and destroying the drifting death ships at will. Once they fell in with Captain Garriton and Commander Lorrayanka, forming one considerable mass of allies, the two starships and the fighter formation cut into the ranks of the dead like a machete, chopping chunks out as they moved toward the heart of the enemy.

"*WildCard*," David Rule called, his weapons flaring wildly, "fly close with the good Captain Prentia and her *Moonscar*. Keep an eye on her squadron. I'll close in on the *Tikrek*. Keep moving but make sure to destroy as much as you can of the enemy starmada."

"*Razorhawk*, I'll do it but the least you could do is make it a challenge for me," Rabeau Loist transmitted, laughing as he rolled over and flew through debris and dust left behind in the wake of his blasts. "Shooting derelict ships isn't exactly a test of my skill."

"Take the blessings you are given," Captain Prentia commented.

Her Crescent gutted one of the derelict Corvette class ships.

"And keep your eyes wide open," Alexi Carver said, running the weapons of his *Saber* at full capacity. "If you don't, Rabeau, a guy like you or me? With the skills we have? We'll fall asleep on this run."

"Drop that talk, *Saber*," the squadron leader and pilot of the *Tikrek*, Jon Kett, ordered. "Flashy flying isn't all that keeps you alive out here. Without God's provision, none of us will make it back."

His quick fighter unleashed its heaviest weapons, two reserve quadracite missiles. An entire section of fighters went up in fire and debris and caused two more small squadrons of them to explode as well.

The Acolyte Pilot of the *Spania*, the old style Chabron craft, launched a series of missiles as well. Ship after ship of the dead exploded.

"You have to admit, *Razorhawk*," she transmitted, "this is child's play. To be honest, I even killed my shields. I'm routing the power to my weapons systems. May as well-"

"Get your shields back up," David Rule ordered sharply.

"What? Why? We can-"

"Now!" Rule ordered again.

Even then, he could see a flare of light in the distance.

"Look out!" Commander Lorrayanka howled suddenly from the *Ferali 5* starship.

"Incoming!" Jon Kett transmitted from his fighter, the *Tikrek*.

"We're reading a surge of raw, scattered energy-"

"No!" Captain Samara Garriton railed from her bridge on the *Bloodwind*. Her Science Officer was hushed by her cry. "Shields to maximum, now!" she shouted.

Suddenly, space was ignited by a falling rain of white and silver energy particles. It dropped from a downward arc originating deep within the starmada, shining brightly as it cascaded down onto all of them.

The ships of the dead all around the allies flared and glowed with contact and shimmered then exploded. The allies watched their shielding do the same thing, shining, shimmering then popping with a concussive discharge of energy. The ships arced power from one to another and to the debris in open space. Readings went wild, power fluctuated, shields faltered and more systems threatened to go down completely.

An exception was the *Spania*. It erupted like a volcano upon contact, no shields active to absorb any of the discharge.

"Evasive maneuvers!" Lorrayanka shouted aboard her carrier.

"Shields are still down!" her Weapons Officer shouted.

"Get them back up!" she screamed then hissed as her Starstalker teeth grew and her fingernails grew to claws.

The cascading weapon had unnerved quite a few allies.

"What was that?" the *Saber* transmitted.

"It was a Starlight Cascade!" David Rule transmitted. "Pull back!"

All of the allied ships scattered and fell back immediately, their shields still flickering and their systems cutting in and out, fighting for stability. All but the ship under Captain Samara Garriton, the *Bloodwind*.

"Do we fall back, Captain?" Pilot Retaw pushed, their bridge silent.

"Shields are still down," Gorbler reminded strongly.

"Starboard engines are experiencing-" Science Officer Boatwright began.

"Give me all the speed you can in sublight," Garriton ordered suddenly. "Reje, take us to the ship that fired that cascade."

The Pilot opened her mouth to speak but, seeing the look on Garriton's face, she stilled.

"Now," Garriton said.

"Yes, ma'am."

Garriton wandered away from her seat and toward the viewscreen. She moved to the center of the bridge and propped her hands on her pronounced hips.

"Now, we end it, Bordin Mo, for the last time," she growled.

The bridge crew looked at her.

"That's right, everyone. I know that ship. The *Judgment*. And our old Captain, Bordin Mo. He always led off with the Starlight Cascade, knowing full well it left the ship power deficient, even if he was already low on power...let's go show him why I always advised against it."

Reje Chu fired all the engines and caused the ship to leap into motion. The crew leaned into the thrust and stiffly watched the derelict ships pass by their screen. The big Reaper class battleship loomed ahead of them, power dead again and adrift.

The other allies had fallen back to a safer position but communication chatter revolved around Samara Garriton's move. Many of them called for Captain Garriton to bring her starship back but she shared a bit of information that changed their minds. The dead Captain Bordin Mo liked to start off with the Starlight Cascade, knowing it would leave his energy levels depleted. He also loved to wait for a large contingent of relief ships to arrive and release another cascade on them with his emergency power.

"He won't use it on one ship," Captain Garriton transmitted. "We'll take care of him ourselves while he waits for the rest of you to get close enough to bombard."

The others agreed, though they felt helpless, staying behind to do nothing.

That was before the transmission from Captain Van Pelt of the *Corridor*.

"All ships! This is the *Corridor*! The *Leviathan* is repowering and the admiral's supercarrier is still dead in space!"

It was true; lights flickered and ignited on the full length of the serpent, in all the sections, even those no longer connected to the main section. Here and there, like an answer or an echo, lights flickered in random fighters and freighters through the body of the starmada, though most did not stay on.

"Scorpion fighters, launch an attack now! We must debilitate the main ship once and for all!" Van Pelt ordered in his transmission.

Commander Lorrayanka ordered her ship to hold their position; she would not so lightly abandon Captain Samara Garriton and her appointment with the Reaper ship, the *Judgment*. The moment Garriton transmitted the go ahead, she would bring her carrier to her aid. In the meantime, she gave the order to target and destroy smaller ships all around them while their power was still out and her blistering attack began.

"All *Stingers*, this is *Sting Leader*," a new voice transmitted. "Strike squadrons, follow your *Spearheads* in formation and fall in with the *Corridor*; lay siege to that big enemy ship! Hold squadrons, form on your *Spearheads* and set up a defense pattern; defend the *Longreach*!"

Fifty Scorpion class fighters, separated into squadrons of five, allied with the USAP Transport under Captain Arn Van Pelt. Transmission chatter began as the leader of each little squadron, the *Spearhead*, called out a frequency change then offered directions.

The other fifty fighters, grouped in squadrons of ten, fell back to fly orbits around the *Longreach*, adrift and black.

"Take this big ship to the academy!" Van Pelt shouted as his own transport led the run.

He ordered the first volley of with a gleam in his eye.

David Rule and the Acolyte forces returned to lay waste to the bone starmada formations near the *Leviathan*. Should the big ship awaken, the Scorpion fighters and the USAP transport starship would be too busy to fend off the countless fighters drifting in close to the enemy leader. No, Rule and the other Acolytes would carve them back and make room for escape.

Captain Prentia and her little squadron of fighters fell close to Commander Lorrayanka and the carrier. They aided her in the pulverization of countless small vessels in the vicinity while waiting to see the outcome of Samara Garriton's bold run on the Reaper ship.

"Hold steady! Buffer our shield projectors!" Garriton yelled.

Pilot Retaw leaned the Vanguard class ship to port as they swept by the big Reaper. The *Judgment* offered no follow up of the Starlight Cascade and the crew was impressed; Garriton clenched her jaw in recognition. Bordin Mo would hold it in check, waiting for more responders. He would want to use it on multiple ships, just as she said.

"Captain?" Gorbler questioned as they passed completely by and she gave no fire order.

"Patience," she snapped through clenched teeth. "Mr. Retaw, bring us about."

Just then a loud explosion railed against the hull of the Vanguard ship and the power flickered. The ship jostled and shifted to one side under the impact and red lights lit up across the bridge stations. An alarm began to sing a funeral dirge on the Captain's own monitor by her chair.

"Report! Boatwright, report!" she demanded, falling back to her seat.

The Science Officer's station was singing as well.

"That wasn't an energy attack at all, Captain!" he said loudly. "That was a ballistic attack, a physical torpedo casing armed with old world explosives! The casing walked right through our shifting shield matrix and dumped that damage right on the hull!"

"Gorbler, I need a trajectory! Who launched it?"

"On it Captain!"

"Boatwright, have all hands abandon deck twenty! Gorbler, intensify shields in that hull breach! Reinforce hull integrity everywhere with the Gravstar generators!"

"Shall I pull back until-" the Pilot started.

"Retaw, put us on a dead end course with that Reaper!" she howled. "Gorbler, give the old man a taste of Terran missiles!"

"Two away; reloading!"

Ahead of them, drifting in a seemingly helpless list to one side, the ravaged *Judgment* waited. Bits of it, entire decks in some points, were missing. Launch bays for Scorpion fighters were devastated; no fighters could come or go from the battleship anymore. Six engine chambers remained of ten originally equipped. Fire and detonation had mangled the hull in many locations and even on one side of the bridge; when they got close enough, Captain Samara Garriton knew from memory they would be able to look right into the open maw of a torn and battered bridge deck.

She locked her jaw. Would Bordin Mo be standing there, looking out?

The first Terran missile slammed into the side belly of the Reaper. The second chased it in, hitting only three valsics above it. The plume of green and yellow radiation billowed wildly then the old Reaper class exploded exponentially in its lower extremities. All of the launch bays blew to dust, as did all the remaining cargo holds. Hammer cannon batteries went up in flame and a flash of discharged energy and two more engine compartments blew themselves to nothingness, obliterated completely from the physical world. It looked like the *Judgment* had digested a honotron device and then detonated it.

In flares of energy and fire, the Reaper flipped over backward and began to roll away in space. It collected quite a few depowered fighters in its wake, destroying them completely.

"Mr. Retaw, bring us about again. Mr. Gorbler, gift the enemy with more of the same."

Retaw banked the Vanguard to starboard on its pass while Gorbler was triggering hull cannons as they went, cleaning out more of the drifting starmada. He had been doing that as they made passes.

In a small, empty spot in the starmada, the cannon blast struck shielding on a ship that was not there. The blast split against the shielding in a colorful prism of shimmering energies.

The ship was cloaked, the starlight at its outline distorted.

"I have a trajectory on that ballistic attack, Captain," Boatwright had just begun.

"I do, too!" Gorbler shouted. "Rayonnix particles trail all the way back to a ship we had not seen until now! It definitely has power reserves; it's running a cloaking device!"

"We *all* see it, now! Stop writing an essay on it! Put a full spread on that ship!" Samara Garriton shouted. "Missiles, cannons, stick someone out on the hull with a venter! Destroy that ship!" she growled.

Retaw had just altered course to put their nose toward the invisible target when the Science Officer shouted.

"Brace for impact!" Boatwright yelled, no time for details.

The seemingly beaten Reaper class, the *Judgment*, erupted with a secondary Starlight Cascade. Garriton had known it would come and it would take the old ship's last reserves of power. What she had not anticipated, however, was that the cascade would be modulated into a concentric pulse wave of incredible magnitude…

…and aimed directly at them.

A full spread of attacks had just been launched by the *Bloodwind* on the hidden starship, pummeling it beyond its defenses. It appeared and exploded catastrophically under the firepower.

Then the silvery light of the Starlight weapon hit the Vanguard.

"Ready yourselves!" Captain Garriton shrieked.

The engines went out instantly. The ship spun out of control, tearing through a great number of smaller starmada fighters. The shields dropped immediately with a loud pop and a discharge of energy that ignited a great number of bone starmada vessels with explosions.

Several decks on the Vanguard *Bloodwind* caved in as the ship plowed through more starmada drifters, hull integrity lost on deck after deck. Power went black almost right away but flickered several times. Emergency reserves kicked in quickly. The magnetic clamping and locking of deck passage after passage echoed through the ship, resounding like the heavy knocks at the door when death comes calling. It let the crew know that there were more breaches in the hull than anyone cared to count.

It also let them know that, unless power could be restored, reserves would eventually fail and the magnetic locks and emergency atmosphere shielding would fail.

When the *Bloodwind* finally stopped, pieces of fighters and freighters still jutting from its body, electrical energy arced everywhere from it. Fire broke out on several decks, eating up valuable oxygen, and alarms screeched instead of singing. The bridge lights flickered again, casting morbid shadows over the prone bodies of the bridge crew. All of them were piled on the decking, shaken from their seats like dolls.

Samara Garriton forced her eyes to open in the shadowy flickering. Without hesitation she forced her way up to a knee near her command seat.

What was that? she demanded of herself. *That old Reaper never had that weapon! A focused Starlight Cascade blast? Since when?*

Then she remembered the Psiborn. An entire 'race' of supercharged slickers...that made perfect sense, much to her ire. In her mind, she had been facing Bordin Mo. In reality, she faced something worse, something that could simply use him and his knowledge, then do so much more.

On the *Ferali 5*, murmurs and gasps blanketed the bridge.

"Garriton!" the Starstalker Commander screamed. She then ordered her Pilot to action. "Go! Now!"

Captain Prentia shouted the same order to her fighter squadron.

"The Reaper's cascades are done! Destroy as much as you can on your approach then start sweeping the area! We will leave the Reaper for Commander Lorrayanka!"

"Save me a piece," Samara Garriton transmitted, her voice full of pain. She wiped blood from her hairline, adding, "This isn't over."

CHAPTER ELEVEN : *Raiders*

T he *Belly Rub* clattered down on its landing gear, grating along the metal platform upon which it tried to land. Thrust adjusted, the Ridge brothers tried again to set down, finding the attempt far more successful. The freighter still slid a bit on the smooth face of the landing pad before settling down.

"What's the problem, Sun? You land on ice?" Sylver chuckled.

"It's the *Belly*. Thrusters are pulsing. Makes me wonder if the Starstalkers have cleaned these scopes and injectors lately."

"Oh, sure," his brother chuckled again. "And you ain't just so old that your hands shake on the stick."

"One thing I don't have is-" Sundar started, finger pointed.

"Pap, Uncle Sun," Gideon Ridge transmitted, interrupting them.

Outside the cockpit screens, Gideon's ship settled down beside them, facing the opposite direction. His lower fuselage cannons swept here and there but found no targets.

"Yeah, boy?" Sundar answered.

"Looks like we have two different sets of cavern structures and passages to infiltrate. Do you have a preference?"

The old men shrugged at each other then Sylver pressed his transmitter switch.

"Why don't we take the set our ship is facing. The other set is behind us; you take them, you're facing that way."

"A scientific solution," Wrigley Zeckinbridge noted behind Gideon.

The young Ridge offered her a smirk then touched his headset.

"Fine. In case we did not arrive unnoticed-"

"Boy, I was teaching tactics at the ESS Command Academy before you could ride your hovercycle. You trust ol' Uncle Sun. We'll hold back, watch the fort so to speak, cover ya'll. You take your team and move in."

"Confirmed. We'll keep transmission headsets active. *Word* raiders, out."

"Confirmed, son," Sylver Ridge answered. "Be careful. *Belly* raiders out."

"That sounds disgusting," Sundar griped, moving for the exit to the cockpit. "*Belly* raiders…like we're some stomach virus…Hey, raiders!" he howled down the corridor into the cargo areas. "Get primed! We'll be second team up but we need to be ready!"

Movement and preparations began that mimicked the work on the Raindancer freighter. The crew from that Raindancer had to move more quickly, however, as they were going first.

The young Ridge reflexively checked his lower back for the secret weapon and holster he kept there. Finding it, he palmed all the extra magazines of ammunition he had for it inside a coat pocket. Then he nodded to no one other than himself and moved to his loading ramp.

Grundy waited there for him, his family weapon strapped on his broad back. He already had the readings displayed on the environmental analysis monitors by the ramp; he had run scans of the strange atmosphere offered by the asteroid after landing.

"I cannot understand why the dead maintain an atmosphere."

"Me neither, big man. Just make sure everybody keeps a rebreather with them, just in case," Gideon Ridge said.

Grundy snorted and placed a large weapon on the floor at the ramp.

"You looking for serious resistance?" Ridge asked, tapping Grundy's weapon with his toe.

Grundy hefted the big Rayne Launcher and propped it onto his shoulder.

"Well, if we don't need it and I take it, I'm just a little overly prepared. If we need it, as strong as it is, and don't have it…now that would be disastrous."

"I can't really find a flaw in that," Gideon said.

Rayne Launchers were canister shaped cylinders about the size of a common trash can. They were carried on the shoulder by heavy assault 'bots in the days of the uprising. A very effective weapon design, the Raynes fired heavy charges in rocket form, energy form, or ballistic pellet form, from eight separate barrels inside it that rotated for use. The weapon was strong enough to penetrate many forms of shielding, from old fashioned body armor to systems as strong as individual fighter shields.

Wrigley Zeckinbridge had just dropped the face shield on her Echo armor into position when she joined them. Chief Security Officer Taylor Patrick stood close by her. Both of them were checking the power levels on their venters and their long arms, both particle rifles.

"What's out there?" the Commodore asked. "Can we breathe?"

"Yes. If there is any problem, it is with your lungs," Grundy said.

"Sobering thoughts," Patrick mumbled.

"We're ready, Ridge," the Commodore said.

Gideon palmed the access panel.

"Heads up. We're in a real dead zone, if you'll forgive the pun. We have no help and no reinforcements coming in. We're it."

They deployed, marching down the ramp and looking in all directions.

The landing area both freighters had used stretched out significantly between two hills. The face of each hill had blast doors closed over cavern openings. Stretching out the length of a Reaper class battleship, the landing zone still made up a very small percentage of the surface of the asteroid. More than twenty times the size of the landing steel was the mountainous, jagged rock of the asteroid surface, uninviting and impassable. Some carved pathways to other points were visible but they led to observation towers and environmental control compounds, not to the stations within the rock. Only the two blast doors held interest for any of the raiders.

The young Ridge led his raiders for the door they faced.

"What are we looking for again?" Officer Patrick asked lowly.

"The source of whatever is raising derelict technology to flight," Zeckinbridge said.

"And raising undead armies to fly in them," Grundy reminded.

"Take everything nice and slow," the young Ridge cautioned. "We don't know-"

From a distant watchtower, the whirring of a spinning machine echoed across the landing space. Abruptly, golden energy fire ripped from the tower and began to eat up the steel platform all around them.

"Down!" Gideon Ridge cried.

As he jumped for the decking, he shoved Wrigley Zeckinbridge to the decking with him. Grundy, amazingly quick, pushed Patrick aside and dropped to cover for himself.

"Freeze still!" Grundy roared.

Everyone did so as he slowly fitted the Rayne's eyelet over one eye. He flipped open a switch cover on the weapon then pulled the actual trigger and let fly three rockets.

One was shot down almost immediately by the rapid fire, multi-barrel, rail mounted long arm. The ionic particle chain blaster, developed by the Migroid people, could easily cut a starship in half in seconds. It had no trouble then following and shooting down the other rockets.

The watchtower exploded in a dazzling spectacle of light, fire and sparks, however. Two plasma disruptor weapons then fired from the *Belly Rub* again and destroyed two other towers.

They fell in a mass of debris, dust and fire, the danger gone.

"You alright, boy?" Sundar asked over the young Ridge's headset.

"Automated defense weapons locked onto anything moving faster than the dead!" Sylver Ridge said.

"All good here," Gideon Ridge said, touching the headset with a hand. "And thanks. That cover was right on time."

"So, change of plan," Sundar Ridge said. "I'm staying behind to watch our birds. The *Belly* guns might need to cover ya'll on the way out, too."

"Confirmed."

"We have to get out of this open space," Officer Taylor Patrick said, his security perspective kicking into gear.

"Agreed. But we don't know how many more automated systems may be here, so stay calm, stay reserved," Ridge said, nodding.

The small group finished their journey to the craggy mound holding the big blast door. Gideon Ridge and his big companion set about trying to crosswire the controls while the two Unity armors kept a paranoid vigil over the landing area.

They were watching when the other raiders scurried from the loading ramp of Sundar Ridge's renamed Starstalker freighter. He waited in the cockpit while the other five raiders deployed for the far blast door and entry point to the undersurface base.

Calmly they moved, quickly but not in a mad rush, lively but not in an all out run. Sylver Ridge set the pace and he was only moving so fast at his age. Behind him followed the Acolytes, Paola Kett, Jaka Baddenide and Candri Prentice. The Unity Captain, Josh Brent, brought up the back end of the movement in his armor.

"I was Security," Joshua Brent noted with a shrug as the old Ridge gave him the nod and pointed at the blast door.

The young Captain went to the panel and began dismantling it, his first step in bypassing it. The armor he had donned did have a few tools in the belt.

Paola Kett pulled her hands from her billowing sleeves. She slipped metal staves from the gauntlets on her forearms, squeezed her fingertips into the handles and made the staves extend somewhat. They arced brightly with electricity, casting a blue hue over her white cloak.

Candri Prentice gripped the energy coils that fed directly from her gauntlets. The coils pulsed with a vibrant crimson glow of pure energy. Her gloves were insulators and manipulators at the same time, allowing her to wield the bright energies like whips, energies that could extend for more than fifteen feet. Her white cloak glowed in a pink haze.

Jaka Baddenide held two staves at first like Paola Kett. Once he extended his, however, they did not charge. He screwed them together, forging a metal staff of considerable length then squeezed the grips. A green arc of electricity leaped about on the shaft then, casting that vivid hue over his cloak.

Joshua Brent, having no luck with the security console, looked at the pacing old Ridge.

"You got ten seconds and I'm knocking it down with this sweeper."

The young Captain shrugged, saying, "Be my guest."

Sylver jacked the lever on the sweeper and listened to the hum.

Joshua Brent scurried for cover.

At the other door, Grundy fussed at the panel in his native tongue, while his friend, Gideon, shouted at it. The wiring had just shocked them for the fifth time.

Grundy said something even grittier, more guttural.

"Watch your language," Gideon Ridge warned.

"What makes you think you even know what I said?" Grundy snapped.

"I don't. I can't speak your world's language. But tones are universal and I didn't need a translator for that one," he said flatly.

"Good thing you do not read thoughts," Grundy growled.

Abruptly, a loud discharge echoed from the other blast door. The young Ridge's team looked over to see that blast door give way and slide open in the distance, smoke rising from old Sylver Ridge's long arm sweeper.

"Your Pap is in," Uncle Sun transmitted to the young Ridge.

"So we noticed-"

The young Ridge's door swept aside suddenly as well. The controls beside the door flashed and went out in a cascade of sparks.

"Uh, Uncle Sun, we're in, too. Door controls must be linked here; one opens they both open."

"Good luck, boy," Sundar Ridge offered.

"Who wants the point?" the young Ridge asked his team.

"That's me," snorted Grundy as he hefted the Rayne into his grasp.

Chaos reared an ugly head in the black of the starship bridge. Voices cried in pain and in concern and in anger. Some cried in silence; those were the voices of the dead.

"Is anybody left alive in here?" Admiral Washington screamed. "I asked for a casualty count! Somebody get me the damage report!"

Most could not hear him. He pushed his way about with a hand held floodlight he found at the security station, though not much was left of the bridge layout. Large chunks of the ceiling blocked passage and crushed stations. The decking of the floor had buckled and tossed aside seats and panels. Wiring draped like waiting snakes, their fiery breath just the arcing power that was the last of the reserve the giant ship held. Flares of light blinked on and off, just long enough to toy with the eye and cause illusions.

Bridge Officers lay here and there, some wounded, some trying to restore power, some trying to restore order. Some were dead, torn and broken like discarded 'droid molds.

"Admiral!" a younger man shouted, pushing his way through a Navigation station.

The Admiral reached out his free hand to grab the First Officer's lapel. In motion, he realized he could only manage a weak grasp with that arm. A glance at his own shoulder revealed blood and the torn uniform. He latched onto the younger man weakly.

"What do we know? Status report!"

First Officer Tylle wiped the blood off his own forehead and pushed it from his eye.

"All Security Officers on the bridge were killed, sir," he said immediately.

"I saw them," the older man answered.

"Pilot Keer is alive, sir. He's aiding Science Officers Borgua and K'Writ with the injured. One of the Science Officers is dead; all the Navigators were killed. One of our Communications Officers was killed; both others are gravely wounded. All of our Weapons Officers were killed save Officer Breach. He's been trying to get his systems back online."

"Without power?"

"He's…intense."

"He's your new First Officer," the big Admiral said flatly.

"Sir?"

"Face it, Tylle. You're the Captain, now. You need a First Officer for your crew."

"Yes, sir."

"We need to get power back. Get your Science Officers on the job."

Tylle shook his head, his brow furrowed.

"Admiral, there's-"

"If we can't reroute it they'll have to take the manual gangways and go find a way to get it done. They'll have to find a way, make a way!"

"Admiral, all due respect, but you can't be serious! This ship is finished! We'll be lucky to keep our injured alive until help comes!"

The Admiral put the light right in Tylle's eyes.

"Tylle, we get power back or we die. Help isn't coming."

Tylle's lip quivered.

"Dismissed...Captain," the Admiral muttered.

Tylle shuffled off for the other living bridge members.

The digital screen setups were destroyed but the viewports were open and clear. Through them, despite the spider webbed cracks, Washington could see the conflict outside.

His Scorpion fleet engaged fully the enemy vessel, fighting alongside the transport under Captain Van Pelt's leadership. Even in the few seconds he watched, he knew things did not look good. The enemy ship took great damage but it continued to repower. It also seemed to repair and rebuild, sucking debris and energy from the conflict into damaged flanks and absorbing it.

"Impossible..." Washington muttered.

"That's not possible," David Rule transmitted to the other fighters.

Not only was the big ship repowering and rebuilding but the littler ships about it were coming back to life as well. In fact, all across the system, the ships of the dead seemed to reignite with power all at once. Suddenly, the bone starmada was very, very dangerous again.

"*Razorhawk*, advise," the pilot of the *Saber* requested instantly.

"*WildCard*, stay with the *Moonscar* and her squadron, as planned," David Rule answered while he fired on yet another newly powering fighter. It erupted into dust. "The rest of you form on the *Tikrek*. *Saber*, you and I will fly on his left rear. *Raine*, *Carolina*, you have his right."

The Acolytes gave response and fell into formation.

David Rule altered his frequency slightly to reach a wider audience, still without chancing transmission exchanges with the starmada.

"Scorpion fighters, press your speed," he explained. "Trade accuracy and efficiency for added speed. It will tax the dead beyond their abilities."

He received several responses, most unbelieving, until Captain Van Pelt interjected his orders. Obey the suggestion, he was ordering. It will keep you alive longer, he promised.

"I see a mass of starmada fighters," Jon Kett transmitted from the *Tikrek*. "Let's carve a path there."

"I'm running shield overload," David Rule informed. "*Saber*, you run weapons hot."

The *Carolina* volunteered to amp up their shields and left the *Raine* to jump up her weapons on the other side of Jon Kett, the point ship and the center of the flight pattern.

It was a common tactic. One flank of a triangular ship formation would have one ship, usually in the front, overfeed their shielding and let the shielding expand away from the ship, helping to shield others. The more secure partner, in back, would heat up their offensive systems and prepare to deal monstrous damage.

Then they were engaged.

The Acolytes stabbed into the enemy formation like the tip of a dagger. The little squadron twisted the blade, so to speak, as they drove it in, the squadron turning and repositioning within the flesh of the enemy formation. Weapons raged and ripped through the death ships and the retaliating dead struggled to respond. Their enemy was inside them; they turned to react and crashed into each other and fired on each other. They suffered from the hands of the Acolytes and from their own inadequacy.

Several of the Acolytes transmitted celebrations.

Insanity, one of the Scorpion fighter pilots thought. Insanity...

The *Corridor* flew by him, firing like mad on the giant enemy. Most of his other Strike Squadron members were in motion, as well, but he had disengaged his engines. It seemed pointless to him, impossible. Insane. What was the point, he wondered. He refused to press beyond optimum engagement speeds, too; if he could not hit his targets, what good was fighting?

He would never be answered. The newly found power of the *Leviathan* reached out from a cannon bank and wiped him from the physical plane.

He was not alone. Some seven fighters had already succumbed to the firepower coming back to life before them. They were piloted by those refusing to fly at pressed speeds. Van Pelt's transport had taken some solid hits as well but his shields were holding. At his advanced speed, the blows were glancing at best. Things still looked ominous, however.

Things were looking bleak on other fronts as well.

"Scopes say all ships are back to power," warned the Starstalker fighter, the *Ristar*.

It flew close by the *Moonscar* of Captain Prentia. The two of them had just blasted through several fighters on the way for the *Judgment*, acting as support for the Starstalker carrier vessel, the *Ferali 5*.

"Stay on task," Captain Prentia ordered in response. "Fighters with me, burn down whatever small vessels you can; when Lorrayanka brings the carrier against that Reaper battleship she does not need to be distracted by smaller enemies."

Prentia blasted her way through several small fighters, firing with a 'quantity over quality' style of targeting. Every time a ship of the undead fired on her she was already gone and the blast hit another of the dead. She had several close calls, energy grazing over her shielding, but nothing seriously damaged any of her systems.

The *Ristar* had the same experience. The Starstalker pilot engaged a trio flying in formation, sweeping downward at them. All three fired on him, the jagged bolts of raw power slipping over his hull haplessly, as he twisted in flight and rolled toward them. He destroyed the two flanking fighters and passed the middle one unharmed. He strafed along another group, destroying several in the other mass, before turning about to reengage the third of his previous targets. It was stardust in seconds and the *Ristar* was back to war.

The Hunon Interceptors brought a nightmare to the dead. The two fighters soared in and out of enemy formation, flanking the two Crescent fighters. Even when they were not firing, the Interceptors were so fast and agile that the enemy could not get a lock on them to fire at all; when the undead managed to fire, it was random and went wide, ripping into one of their own. When the Interceptors actually fired, their deadly particle accelerator rails opened up wide beams of utter destruction on multiple ships at once.

"I want one of those," Rabeau Loist laughed in transmission. "*Stuto, Jokra*, I have your rear defense."

The pilot of the *WildCard* swept along behind them, watching them wreak havoc, targeting those ships that attempted to turn about on them. He tore through more than his fair share of the dead, too. He was the *WildCard*, after all.

On the *Ferali 5*, Commander Lorrayanka and her crew cut a swath of carnage until it reached engagement range with the Reaper class *Judgment*. Their speed made them difficult to target despite their size. The undead fighter craft in their way that they could not target at that speed they simply plowed under.

"Shields holding," Weapons Officer Xerstou reported as two more rammed fighters exploded in their wake. "We have a lock on the Reaper, too. Shall I fire?"

"Give that ship a full array," Lorrayanka ordered, her fangs bared. "Let it hold one of everything this Starstalker vessel has!"

"Weapons away!" Xerstou shouted and palmed a very particular panel.

The Commander roared her approval, fangs long.

Energy banks from all over the ship came to life, dumping massive power out at the big battleship. Missiles blasted from the launch tubes in plumes of fury while the netting cannons charged.

What happened on the screens of the *Ferali 5* made knots of her crew's stomachs.

The full array of their weaponry pelted shielding between themselves and the Reaper target. Three ships, fully cloaked, suddenly appeared as weapon after weapon from the Starstalker vessel impacted their shielding. All three of the rather large, heavily armed ships took damage; cloaking kept shields at a lower efficiency than maximum. None of them exploded, however, and all began charging weapons.

The only good news was that the cloaking systems had dropped and their shielding was badly debilitated; the Starstalker leader hoped they were severely damaged and would not come back up.

"Evasive maneuvers!" Lorrayanka yelled. She flipped a switch on her chair as her Pilot banked the big ship to port. "Winds, I thought you were still on our sensors!"

"Nope," he transmitted back from someplace in the ship. "I'm on your shielding! You think you've been ramming ships and keeping full shields just because of Starstalker ship quality? That's been me!"

She slammed a hand onto her arm rest, ground her teeth then hit the switch again roaring, "Understood! Stay on them! I think we're about to see just how much you can give them!"

The Starstalker ship veered away and started back for safer positioning with the three new ships in pursuit.

Samara Garriton had been watching from the viewports aboard her disabled ship. She had stirred the battered and stunned bridge crew of the *Bloodwind;* it was time for them to act once again, to move with the flickering of emergency power coming to life.

"Give me something!" Garriton shouted.

"We have thrusters, that's all," Retaw shouted over the crackling of shorting console panels.

"Weapons are offline," Gorbler added, holding the bruise on his big head. "Shields are rebooting; we might have as much as thirty percent when they ignite."

"Hull integrity is seventy percent, at best, around the weapons banks and engine compartments. It's less in connective corridors. Highest is around the bridge. Eighty-four percent, at most, during fluctuation. Energy levels are so low that-"

"Enough!" she interrupted Boatwright. "I've heard enough. We've got to get back in this. The longer we sit here the more new enemies arrive and the more that arrive the less chance any of us have of holding this starmada at bay. And I don't have to remind some of you what it will be like if we're boarded."

"We have Navigation," Reje Chu offered meekly.

"And full communication," Respra told her, holding his earpiece.

"Great, we can shout at the undead and scare them off," Garriton said sarcastically. Then she paused, one eyebrow raised, her head turned toward the Communications Officer.

"Captain?" Respra said.

"Stand by," she said, a smile tugging at her pretty lips. "We may just have to raise our voice."

"Shall I charge the Shofar?"

"Indeed," Captain Samara Garriton said, wiping a stream of blood running down her cheekbone. "Indeed."

Sylver Ridge limped a little when he walked. It was not a detrimental impairment. It was more of a characteristic, a bit more color tossed onto the canvas of a long life. His right foot, just scarcely skewed to the outside, moved well and did not drag. It was visible, however, that the right leg or ankle had taken quite a bit of damage in the past. The one thing it did do was help him set the pace.

No one wanted to be in front of him, either, while he held the sweeper.

"Nice of them to leave the lights on," Captain Joshua Brent muttered.

"We're expected," old man Ridge said flatly.

"Don't just count on the worst," Brent countered. "We have no way of knowing that."

"The dead don't need lights, Captain," Jaka Baddenide frowned.

The hair lifted on Brent's neck.

"Wonderful."

The corridor wound downward. Smooth walls of alloyed metals curved as elegantly as carved and polished wood. Lights, built into the walls and covered by protective screens, glowed in a soft, gray ambiance. One section would have a flat floor then, after a curve, the floor would become steps winding downward. After that another flat section would be waiting…and on the journey went.

No doors lined the walls. No windows offered a change in the view. Each new level looked and felt the same as the last. The monotony, of course, was not lost on the invaders. After a time, it began to bubble up.

"Do we even know where this goes?" Josh Brent asked.

"You want to go back? Help yourself," Sylver Ridge quipped. "I can't take you back by the hand, boy, but nobody's making you come along."

"It just seems so endless," Candri Prentice said, pulling back her hood.

"Can't be much further," Jaka Baddenide said flatly. He pointed to the next curve. "Markings on the wall. We haven't seen any of those."

"Can anybody read them?" Josh Brent asked.

The group slowed when it neared that far curve and found a blast door beside the writing. Brent looked about for an answer to his query.

Paola Kett pulled away her billowing sleeves. Her armbands in view, she tapped a code on the back of one.

"You got it, Paola?" Jaka pressed.

"Yes, Jaka."

A gentle glow in the eyelet lenses she wore lit her lovely face.

"It's Migroid," she muttered, reading. "Extremely old...it's not an active dialect. It's a marking for a ship bulkhead...the engine room."

A clack of metal on metal echoed down the corridor and the stairs behind them.

Brent spun, his weapon leveled and ready. Baddenide and Prentice did the same. Paola started to turn but Sylver Ridge held her in place.

"Can you open that door?" he asked her pointedly.

"Yes...maybe...I mean..." she stuttered.

"Do it, girl." He levered the old sweeper. "We'll watch the hall."

Paola Kett began punching codes into her armband and walking toward the blast door.

Old Ridge stepped around the corner into which the others were simply peeking.

"Get back here!" Brent ordered through clenched teeth.

"Show yourselves!" the old man howled, banging his hand on the corridor wall.

Then they came.

Captain Samara Garriton clenched her teeth as her emergency power flickered.

"Captain, I don't think...wait a second..." the Pilot began, fighting his arcing console for control.

"Retaw, I don't want to hear anything else we can't do," she warned. "You move us back into the mix, into the middle of our enemies, with whatever you have. Even if it sets fire to the bridge, move us!"

The *Bloodwind* groaned as the engines strained and the thrust fought at full power to get any real speed. The magnify options on the viewscreen failed and readouts died; all that was left was the physical viewport. Emergency lighting failed and all was dark on the bridge save the light from the station consoles.

"We're wide open," Retaw said with Chu nodding. "We have some thrust but it's unfocused, pushing to a bunch of random directions."

"But we're charged," Respra added, nodding at the Captain.

"Hail the *Ferali 5*, Mr. Respra," she ordered. "You tell them to kill their power at a split second before you ignite the Shofar. You tell the other fighters in range. Then, when we reach a point to do the most confusion, you let it roar. Let it roar, Mr. Respra."

"Yes, ma'am, confirmed."

David Rule's squadron moved quickly, scorching across space with a plume of destruction in their wake. The enemies were massing, however, moving in on them, focusing more on them. The living were a challenge and a severe threat. The challenge was being answered.

"They're coming in from everywhere!" Alexi Carver transmitted from the *Saber*.

"Stop crying, *Saber*. You're the one who said you needed a better challenge," a melodious voice chimed.

"Why do you only remember my great lines when it doesn't suit me?" Carver asked.

"*Saber*, *Raine*, drop the chatter," David Rule barked. "Carver, you I can understand. Taelynn, you know better."

"Taelynn Berreaux, dropping the chatter," she giggled as she blasted a ragged enemy fighter.

"Another pass and we'll pull back to the *Bloodwind*," Rule announced. "Captain Van Pelt, Scorpion fighters, I would suggest you do, as well."

"We won't abandon the *Longreach*!" Van Pelt hailed, even as his ship took another heavy blow to its shields. "Scorpion fighters, stay on target!"

"We can lead the enemies away from the *Longreach*," Rule countered. "Be wise, Captain, as well as bold."

"Stay on the *Longreach*!" Van Pelt ordered the Scorpions.

Captain Prentia, piloting the *Moonscar*, pulled up from a dive run on a small enemy group. She left four ships just floating debris, two others damaged. The *Ristar* destroyed the other two and the Starstalker Pilot let out a transmitted roar. He rolled his ship triumphantly, celebrating yet another win.

"Graylocke, watch your-" Prentia transmitted.

From her kinsman's blind side, a very old Vipon fighter swept into line with him and fired. Venomous green energy arced wickedly from the pointed ship nose and struck him squarely. His shields fell almost instantly and the energy blasted him from space.

"No!" Prentia howled, whipping the *Moonscar* to her port side.

Rabeau Loist fell on the Vipon with all his weapons firing, however, and eradicated it before she could complete her vengeful arc. The *WildCard* then destroyed four more of the Vipon death squadron, leaving them a matter of atoms adrift.

Captain Prentia lined up with the last one and burned it to ash.

"*Moonscar*," Loist transmitted, "we should fall back to the *Bloodwind*. *Razorhawk* informs of a plan-"

"I heard the plan!" she bellowed. After a moment, she added, "Thank you, *WildCard*, thank you. I will fall back. *Ferali 5*, I recommend you pull back to the *Bloodwind* again, too. There is a plan in place."

Commander Lorrayanka nearly fell from her Captain's seat as a new impact dropped the shields completely. A flicker later, they rekindled.

"Acknowledged, *Moonscar*, as soon as we evade our friends!" she howled.

Another blast shook the big carrier and the lights threatened to go off. Venting gases sprayed from conduits in the rear of the bridge as two consoles arced electricity to the decking.

"Wastasa Winds!" she shouted, holding her transmission switch.

"I'm on it," Winds came back. "Why do you think we've lived this long? Can't you find a Pilot who can outmaneuver at least one attack?"

"Sensors and scopes down!" she shouted at her Science Officer. "Give the power over to shields!" She then flipped another communiqué control. "Engineering, give me all the power you can to the engines and to Pilot control! Pilot Argor," she shouted back at her bridge Officer, "evasive maneuvers constantly! One behind another! Gradually take us back for the *Bloodwind*!"

A chorus of confirmation came back to her.

"Xerstou!" Lorrayanka shouted angrily. "Target those ships! Fire at will!"

"Confirmed!" the Weapons Officer said.

And on the battle went.

Ships of the living, allied together, moved in formations and protected each other on their way to the *Bloodwind*. All along the way they rained fire and fury upon the dead.

CHAPTER TWELVE : *Doors*

T he raiders led by the Rothidai, Grundy, took a direct line downward into the rock. Long, sloping deck plates angled downward like a smooth, placid metal river. Then, from time to time, curves would lead to a stairway, steep and utilitarian, that took them to yet more sloping, smooth plates. Grundy walked faithfully on point, that big canister on his right shoulder, looking to the young Gideon like a trash can held horizontally.

"Looks like he's carrying a trash can, doesn't it?" he muttered lowly.

Zeckinbridge, nearby, shook her head.

"Only to you, Gideon."

The stone walls were interspersed with metal supports and bulkheads and long term ignition lighting. It was the kind of self sustaining lighting that kicked on in starships when their systems failed. Ignited from within with a mild radiation, they would glow indefinitely. The halls, marred with the burns and pock marks of energy fire, seemed to go on forever, as well.

"How deep does this go?" Taylor Patrick asked.

"No way to know," Ridge said. "Scans wouldn't penetrate the composition of the 'roid very well."

Grundy tromped further down the next sloping plates, gesturing for the others to remain behind. They stayed at the bend in the hall while he advanced alone. Ahead of him was a massive, double blast door, cracked open where they should have met together in closing. A body lay in the gap, arms still locked in a death grip on the doors to each side, resisting the closing as it crushed from it the life it once had. It was still, lifeless and silent but it spoke a warning to the troop.

Do not come any further, it whispered. *Death waits.*

"Grundy?" Ridge pressed his big friend.

"A stone vampire," Grundy growled and crouched beside the corpse.

"A what?" Zeckinbridge asked quickly.

"Vampire?" Patrick demanded, gripping his weapon with both hands. "You mean like the old Earth-"

"No, I do not. It is what we called this people," Grundy said back to the others. He motioned them forward. "The people of Migross."

The unit tightened until all were looking at the dead Migroid before them. Like the others of his people, he had been gray and black rock, his skin as dense and tough as stone. Though his eye sockets were emptied over time and decay, they had once been white, shining above a skeletal nasal cavity. Most odd remained the blatantly missing mouth, another trademark of the Migroid race. They absorbed life energy for food through the only soft areas of their bodies, the palms of their hands.

For those interested, it was of great note that palm to palm touching with a Migroid was considered highly intimate and was only allowed among betrothed individuals.

Taylor Patrick shivered as a chill ran over him.

"Migross," he said nastily. "I hated that world. Black sand and black granite world, very cold, with gray waters…that brutal cold, all day and all night wind-" Patrick started again.

"As cold as the vampires themselves," Grundy muttered lowly.

"Grundy," Gideon Ridge cautioned. "Remember what we talked about where vengeance and prejudice are concerned."

Grundy nodded hesitantly, conceding, "Yes, I know…but some feelings are harder to overcome than others. I am still a work in progress, Gideon."

The Rothidai had once waged bloody war with the Migroids for more than a generation. That is when the Rothidai had initiated the term stone vampire. The Migroid way of 'eating', absorbing the life force and energy from any living thing, plant, animal or sentient, was also a formidable weapon to use in combat. The Rothidai had seen a lot of it firsthand on the battlefields of Migross and those on their own home world of Corrin. It was doubly disgusting to the Rothidai that the Migroid's most intimate touching, palm to palm with their own kind, was also their way of feeding...and killing...other races and beings.

"I take it the stone gentleman is dead," Wrigley Zeckinbridge said, turning her gaze to the gap in the doors. "I wonder what lies beyond these doors."

"That closing blast gate would have cut even my dense physical structure in twain. Imagine him running from something beyond the doors, falling here after his allies set the doors to close then being clamped here in excruciating pain until death…who knows how much later."

"It's hard," Patrick said. "To imagine, that is."

Grundy turned his head to Gideon Ridge and said, "I feel compassion for him for that fact, Gideon. I think that may be progress."

"Hate can't offer compassion. That's definitely something else working in you, big guy."

The Commodore ventured close to the gap in the doors.

"I wonder…"

A slam of dense bodies crashing against the metal barriers resounded in the corridor. Arms reached through the gap in random grasping, the bodies on the far side fighting each other for a chance to get through the hole. Wrigley Zeckinbridge did not even have time to react; a vise of a hand latched onto her chest plate at the collar band and jerked her forward for the gap. She screamed.

Then she was flying backward, her chest plate gone. It dangled from the hand of a Migroid reaching through the gap. It had no white light in its eyes.

The Commodore sailed several feet down the hall and onto her back. Grundy had reflexively snatched Wrigley free and tossed her away.

Then he swept his big family weapon off his shoulder. He drove it downward across the reaching hands. The metal of his weapon sparked over the rough, stone skins of the undead clamoring to get through the gap.

Many other metals would have been useless against that hide. The Rothidai alloys that were folded into family weapons, however, staggered the imagination. They could rend and cut other metals as easily as they could Meekin webs...and the appendages of the Migroid undead.

"Fall back!" Ridge ordered loudly, backing away himself as he pulled Zeckinbridge to her feet. "Grundy, fall back!"

Taylor Patrick triggered his face shield into place. Fully armored, he knelt by the last curve and leveled his weapon.

"Back up!" he told the others. "I'll hold the hall!"

Grundy charged back to where the young man waited.

"Not alone, you won't," he growled, angling his Rayne for targeting.

Over half of the Unity Scorpion fighters, defenders and assault teams were a matter of memory and dust. More and more of the dead starmada rose from distant graves, appearing from the colored gases of the Reaches, only to wage war on the living.

Perhaps most horrific realization among the living was that each of their own, having fallen in battle, if not entirely destroyed, would reawaken as an animated enemy.

The main enemy ship itself regenerated at a rapid rate, reaching out with energy and taking matter and power from nearby enemies and allies, dissolving them and devouring them then adding them to its own mass.

One of those long reaching bands of energy barely missed Captain Van Pelt's ship, the *Corridor*, as it swept by in another strafing attack run.

"This is Captain Van Pelt!" the man shouted as his Communications Officer opened the channel. "We can't hold off this whole starmada for the Admiral's ship! Starstalkers, *Bloodwind*, all you Acolytes, we need help now! Form on my ship and let's take this leader thing out!"

The *Corridor* glided over a section of the giant *Leviathan*, unloading with all of its available weapons. The ship's shielding was too weak to block out the damage, so the attack was very effective. However, as soon as the Unity Transport ship had passed by it, the ship began to rebuild itself again, draining mass and energy from yet more allies and enemies.

"It's restoring again!" Van Pelt howled. "Form on us, now!"

"Fire!" Commander Lorrayanka yelled at her Weapons Officer, ignoring the communications chatter. She had been doing so for several minutes as they engaged the trio of enemies exchanging attacks with them. More enemies were closing, too.

One of the three large enemies engaging the *Ferali 5* twisted in its center under the attack. The panels buckled and the hull distorted...then the ship exploded into nothingness. The two remaining ships returned fire.

The *Ferali 5* jostled violently again then bumped and shuddered several more times. Sparks showered the bridge and a backup console exploded, spraying glass.

"Shield generators are failing!"

Lorrayanka ignored her Science Officer and flipped her console switch again.

The ship jolted as soon as she spoke and the lights dimmed.

"Wastasa! Pull what you can out of those shields! They're failing!"

"Then I'm shutting them down!" he transmitted.

"What?" she shouted. "Say again, Winds!"

"I've got to drop them to do a quick reroute of power and reboot them to full power!"

"It better be really quick!" she ordered.

"Commander-"

"Fly like you've never flown before, Argor!" she ordered the Pilot.

Again they shook under heavy assault and the lights died for a moment then returned to life. Argor rolled the big carrier to its starboard and pressed for more speed then tipped to port and sped up again.

The two pursuers fired one after the other, time and again.

"We cannot stay beyond them forever!"

"Time!" Lorrayanka answered. "We just need a little time!"

Abruptly, across their screens, the Acolytes flew with weapons at full spread. Their starships peppered the pursuing enemy ships with energy and then swept away, only to return and do the same thing again. The *Moonscar* was with them, Captain Prentia's ship. The band was luring the enemy ships away from the big carrier.

"*Tikrek*, take the Temple Squadron and pull that Rundoon battleship off the *Ferali 5*. *WildCard* and I will join the *Moonscar* and the Hunon Interceptors and we'll pull the Rothidai freighter away," David Rule transmitted.

Multiple voices acknowledged the transmission.

"Come to us," Captain Samara Garriton transmitted. "We're ready."

"What about the Admiral's ship? What about the *Longreach*?" Captain Van Pelt demanded urgently in a follow up transmission. "He needs us all!"

It was a good question, after all. The Scorpion fighters had devastated their area's enemies but they in turn had been thinned greatly. Less than thirty of their ships remained, with more enemies arriving. Plus, the *Leviathan* was charging weapons after its long slumber. The dragon was awakening.

On the USAP supercarrier, the *Longreach*, Science Officer Borgua called out at the top of his lungs.

"We have reserve power!" he yelled then stumbled over an overturned console station on the twisted, burning bridge.

Washington panned his floodlight in the man's direction despite the flickering of dim emergency lighting coming to life. The pale gray of the glow looked ghostly.

Former First Officer Tylle, newly made Captain, charged one of the crackling terminals. He keyed the controls madly, trying to access something in desperation.

"Borgua, K'Writ, get me shields! Now!" he called.

"Belay that order!" Admiral Washington challenged. The two Science Officers and Captain Tylle spun to look at him as he elaborated. "Gentlemen, this ship is a Grim Reaper class! We're a supercarrier! I will not allow one of the flagships of our planetary alliance to sit adrift and shield itself in this battle! Get me one more charge for the Might! Let our quantum cannon burn that snake into oblivion!"

269

The hum of power sang softly behind the crackle of sparks and shorting consoles. Hisses whispered as gases sprayed intermittently from broken conduits. Gentle buzzing and static argued here and there as displays frazzled and systems tried a reboot.

Ominous clanging resounded deep in the farthest points of the supercarrier as the dead docked with them.

In all of it, the living bridge occupants were silent for a long, decisive moment…then came the howl of pride and approval.

"Might! Might!" they chanted while Admiral Meshach Washington's chest swelled.

Slowly, the energy built upon itself.

Across the arena of war, the Rundoon battleship was close behind Temple Squadron.

A blast bumped all too close to the *Tikrek*, Temple Squadron's leader, and the readouts in his cockpit blinked out for a second. The Rundoon ship was firing repeatedly, raining all about the fighter group with spatial charges, direct energies and with missiles too close for comfort. The pilot of the *Tikrek* veered to one side again.

"It's overly fond of me!" Jon Kett transmitted, his shields barely deflecting another blast.

"Not just you, *Tikrek*! That spread fire is all over me!" the *Saber* answered.

The *Saber* peeled off course and shot into another small clump of enemy ships. Not only did it take him to some cover but it was most rewarding to see enemy fighters being blown to pieces by the Rundoon. The big battleship still followed, plowing through more of its own death ships in pursuit.

"*Carolina*, *Raine*, get that thing's attention!" Kett ordered from the *Tikrek*.

Both ships acknowledged and fell into a pattern approach. Tragedy shattered the plan, however. A band of the dead swept in to cut them off.

"*Carolina*!" Taelynn Berreaux tried to warn from the *Raine*.

She was too late. Even as she rolled and evaded the barrage of fire power poured out at them, the *Carolina* took too many direct hits. The shields failed before the pilot even realized it and the ship was gone into scrap and a plume of flame.

Berreaux swept her ship about and razed across the bow of the Rundoon battleship then turned and ran. The enemy fighter group laid into pursuit as the Rundoon ship started a turn to come about and chase her, as well.

"I'm on the fighter squadron," Jon Kett called from his *Tikrek*. "*Saber*, get that battleship off her tail!"

"Allow me!" Commander Lorrayanka roared from the open channel of the *Ferali 5*, her voice feral. Then the Commander pointed at the viewscreen for her bridge staff. "Fire everything!"

Out of nowhere it seemed the Starstalker carrier appeared, weapons alive. The Rundoon tipped and jerked and stalled as blasts pummeled the shields until they failed utterly. On the onslaught rained until the battleship itself began to buckle then to break apart. A moment later, it went up spectacularly in fire and pieces.

"Now," Commander Lorrayanka growled lowly, "eat those dead fighters!"

The *Ferali 5* fell into pursuit of the fighters plaguing the *Saber* and the *Raine*.

No Starstalker ship was available to aid David Rule and his battalion, however. One of the Hunon fighters, the *Stuto*, sadly erupted in flame and spun out of control, taking with it two fighters of the dead. The Hunon Security Officer, Commander Wahll, swore vengeance in his native language from the seat of the *Jokra*. All the while, the Rothidai freighter chased them.

"Everyone divide!" David Rule ordered from the *Razorhawk*.

"Fly into enemy battalions! The dead ships cannot aim well! They cause great destruction, more to their own in close quarters!" Captain Prentia added.

The *Jokra* and the *Razorhawk* swept into the fleet of the dead nearest them, weapons blazing a path through it. The chasing freighter lobbed attack after attack and wasted ships of the dead left and right, unable to hit David Rule and Commander Wahll, and unable to stop itself from trying.

David Rule punched in a command on his right panel and a projected display lit a small part of his cockpit screen. The lights counted the number of ships emerging from the Reaches yet again…and that number was staggering.

Rule veered off for the distant *Leviathan*.

The Rothidai freighter kept on him. Rule evaded it well despite, the freighter's use of spatial charges. The charges laid waste to the fighters of the dead trying to engage Rule.

Captain Prentia settled in behind the freighter. She hammered the big ship's aft shields to the point that they began to shift color.

Commander Wahll wreaked havoc on enemy fighters as he also pursued the big freighter. He kept the individual fighters off Captain Prentia as well as he held their attention away from David Rule.

"*Razorhawk*," Prentia transmitted, "you're moving away from our rendezvous point. Circle around and let us pull back to the group."

"Negative, *Moonscar*," Rule answered. "You pull back with the others; I'm flying straight for the serpentine monster and I'm dragging this freighter with me. Nothing in space wants to be battered by Rothidai spatial charges, not even that thing."

"Insane," Prentia accused.

"Do not do it, Ambassador Rule. It is too dangerous," Wahll transmitted from the *Jokra*.

"Oh, I don't know," Rabeau Loist transmitted from the *WildCard*. He brought the little fighter alongside Rule and started a vicious razing of the enemies in their way. "Sounds pretty stable to me. Then again…" he chuckled, trailing off as he sometimes did, "…I am the *WildCard*."

"Captain Prentia, Commander Wahll, pull back to the rendezvous. We'll do this and be right behind you," Rule transmitted.

For Wahll and Prentia, there was no argument left to make. They came about, facing a torrent of oncoming fighters, and began the long flight back. Shields at maximum on their fore panels, weapons alive, they began to carve a swath back to the others.

A blast shook the *WildCard* and the shields shimmered. A warning light flashed in the cockpit while a buzzer sounded intermittently. Then a stray energy bolt from a sweeping Greylik fighter, piloted by the undead, popped against the very hull plating of the *WildCard*. A panel buckled and exploded from the engine compartment in a shower of sparks.

"*Razorhawk*, I'm still with you, but just so you know…"

David Rule breathed heavily in transmission and spoke.

"Rabeau, you need to pull back to the others. You'll never make-"

A spatial charge erupted all too close to the two Acolyte fighter pilots. Rule's ship jolted to port, the hull complaining, but the shields held and the integrity of the ship remained intact. Loist felt the blast quite differently, his ship flipping twice to starboard, his controls shuddering as if he had no control at all. Inside the cockpit, alarms rang out anew even as several panel switches sparked and gave off light smoke.

From one engine compartment, the raw energy fuel, no longer contained, glowed brightly in space. Rabeau Loist managed to pull back into line with Rule but the console readouts threatened a dangerous future.

Loist fired on a newly targeted enemy and only one set of cannons lit up. As the enemy erupted into oblivion, Loist triggered his communications again.

"*Razorhawk*, I'm control shaky, shield dead, and weapons have gone down to fifty percent. I have a trailing fuel cell and the hull is straining-"

"*WildCard*, fall back. Rendezvous with the others. It's an order."

"We both know I won't make it there, David," Loist said calmly.

"Rabeau, go back," Rule's voice came, more concerned than strict.

"You fly back for the others, David. Let me do this."

All about them enemy ships were torn asunder by the charges from the freighter, missing them constantly. Debris bounced from Rule's shields constantly and racked loudly against the other man's hull. Each time it caused him to tense and wonder if it would be the piece that ripped his ship open to space.

"I'll drag this freighter to its end," Loist said. "Let me do that. For all of you. For Christ, my Savior. I don't want to just blow up at random when the systems have done all they can do; I want it to be in the midst of a feat to be proud of. No man has a greater love than this…"

"…than to give his life for his friends," Rule answered. "The Gospel of John, Chapter Fifteen, Verse Three. Amen, my brother. Amen."

Rabeau Loist watched Rule's Razor class fighter sweep back. He saluted his brother.

"Don't worry, David. I know where my soul is going and I'll see you in Heaven someday. And, for right now, who knows? I might even come out of this alive. I am the *WildCard*, after all."

"Indeed, you are," Rule answered. "Indeed."

Rule buried his nose into the oncoming dead, weapons raging.

Another buzzer sounded in the *WildCard* and Loist turned it off like the others. Several more near misses rocked him, not to count the better than ten burned grazes across his hull from close calls with oncoming fighters. Still, he brought both the *WildCard* and the unnamed Rothidai freighter very close to the serpentine gargantuan, the *Leviathan*. Near the big enemy ship was the drifting *Longreach*.

"You have Might at the ready!" Tylle shouted to the Admiral on the *Longreach* bridge.

"Then use it, Mr. Tylle! And if this be your last act as Captain of the Unity supercarrier *Longreach*, then you be proud! When you fire this weapon, you end that massive snake ship where it is! This could be where we turn the tide of this battle, where whatever this is learns…wait, what is that…"

From the bowels of the serpentine starship, channeling all along its hull and through its shields, a mass of raw, multiphasic energy lit the big enemy ship like a beacon. For a moment the ship radiated brilliantly. Then all of the charging energy flooded from the nose ports of the ship in a massive wave.

The tsunami of multiphasic, multicolored light sprayed forth in a cloud of raw power. At twice the size of the Unity supercarrier, the wave radiated with a life of its own…bringing death all on its own.

Captain Van Pelt, in the *Corridor*, never managed a final order.

The last band of Scorpion fighters attempted to move but could not, the eruption from the big serpentine ship far too fast and too vast.

The *Longreach*, proverbial finger on the trigger of their Might weapon, sitting on the precipice of an expected victory against a far larger foe, disappeared in the flood. The crew was too slow, its leader too fond of speeches. Before the Might was unleashed, devastation arrived and the supercarrier was fundamentally, atomically undone. Vapor, dust, a trail of colored atoms adrift, the big *Longreach* was no more.

The wave obliterated them all, transport to fighter to supercarrier. They were wiped from existence, nothing but vapors, memories.

Rabeau Loist and his *WildCard* had just ducked under a squadron of the dead and breezed by the *Longreach*, planning to come about and take the firing freighter to the snake ship. However, the wave of raw power washed the Rothidai freighter away, too.

The *WildCard* disappeared from all scanners and scopes as well.

Countless fighters, piloted by the dead, were caught in the wave and obliterated. There were not even parts to scavenge for the *Leviathan*, nothing to suck in to adopt into itself.

Among the living, a long, hard breath was held, no words offered, no response to the event emitted. Scanners do not lie, however. The energy emission had been off their scales. The only positive side of it was that the big ship had fallen still and dark, drained, at least for a time. It drifted motionless and more lifeless than ever.

On the other battlefront, the allies had gathered back with Captain Samara Garriton and her *Bloodwind*. Drifting in close to each other, all of them had killed their power to avoid their communications systems carrying the coming sound wave through their circuitry.

"Do it now," Samara Garriton growled at Officer Respra. "You give these dead a wake up call."

The man nodded resolutely and palmed his control panel.

Suddenly, the *Bloodwind* unleashed a sonic wave, a powerfully loud, majestic horn tone, for all of space around itself. The railing sound raided every ship with an open communications channel within its range. Ships shook and jolted as the call flowed through the communications first then through all the systems in each vessel.

It drowned out the death call that was transmitting from the source in the Reaches, overcoming the control. It left ships from the Reaches all the way to the far side of what had once been Maximilian Station powerless, motionless...once again dead.

In a virtual sea of death ships, all floating adrift and lifeless, the allied starships kicked their power back on. Inside each there was a bit of relief and celebration. For a moment, there would be a respite from the onslaught. Perhaps, they considered, their team of invaders would find the source and destroy it before power could be restored to the drones.

"This isn't over," David Rule transmitted a reminder. "My scopes say there are better than ten thousand ships still on the way…and they are not fighters. They are freighters, battleships, corvettes…a real starmada. Whatever energy blast the *Leviathan* just emitted left it drained completely, it and the ships around it. However, we have no idea of when they will come back to life. They were not victims of the *Bloodwind* weapon."

"What should we do?" Commander Wahll asked.

"Those who can should destroy as many enemy ships as possible, working your way outward from here. Those who cannot should remain here and wait for repairs," Captain Prentia said.

"Captain Prentia is right. Work your repairs as quickly as possible," Commander Lorrayanka transmitted. "Our bays are open to help you."

"And pray," Rule added. "Pray."

An army of the dead, led by empty eyed Migroids, spilled from the gap in the blast doors in random, staggered numbers. They looked much like draining drops of water falling from a colander, a few here and there, some together with others, some alone.

Taylor Patrick squeezed off several beams of particle energy, burning multiple corpses into pieces. He raged at them, shouting his warning and his disgust. The former Echo Soldier and active Security Officer knocked them down quickly, eyes squinted. He ground his teeth together as he raged against the coming horde.

Grundy fired once and ignited a crowd that had penetrated the barrier. The remaining Migroids were vaporized in the blast. Again Grundy fired that big canister weapon and the two blast doors buckled and shifted, their groan of bending metals a death groan. He fired again and the doors blasted backward and soared down the corridor, knocking down countless enemies in the darkness that lay beyond.

Gideon Ridge stepped around the corner with his weapons blazing. Shot after shot put down the rushing dead. His face was set, determined and unexpectedly calm.

Commodore Zeckinbridge also joined the fray, her weapon hot. Body after body fell victim to her barrage.

On they came, nevertheless.

Stiff legged and disjointed, storming the turn in the hall where the living had taken position, the dead advanced. One after another they fell, too, parts missing, lives missing, motion missing. Often, when Grundy unloaded with the Rayne Launcher, the team had a brief respite as enemies had to catch up with the gap in their numbers.

Gideon tapped the communication device about his ear.

"Hard to hear you, Uncle Sun!" he shouted. "We're kinda busy!"

"Patching your com to your Pap's, boy," Sundar replied.

"Pap?" Gideon asked.

A very loud burst of raw energy crackled at first, then a voice.

"Son, your uncle's boostin' transmission juice with ship relays," Sylver Ridge said. "We're up against a Migroid hull's blast doors, been fighting Migroid dead…I think we're about at the bottom of all this."

Again the old man triggered the sweeper.

"Us too!" Gideon shouted.

The sweeper went off again loudly.

"Gideon, remember, transmissions are weak this deep in this 'roid."

The old man heard his son reply, told him he loved him then killed his transmission. He levered that sweeper again, kicking the charge shell from the chamber, and saw an empty feeder tube.

"Cover me!" he shouted at Joshua Brent.

He shoved a handful of charges into the tube.

Brent upped his firing, fanning his targeting about the corridor to drop the closest of the dead as they got near.

Without the fear of the old man's wide spray from the sweeper, Candri Prentice and Jaka Baddenide rushed out into the corridor, face to face with the dead.

Candri whipped an arm out and one of those arcing, crimson coils of raw, manipulated energy lashed out and tangled three undead assailants. The dead Greylik, Rundoon and Vipon corpses jerked and jolted as the energy feed shocked them, overwhelmed them and dropped them to the decking.

Jaka Baddenide leaped closer to his targets, swinging his staff around in a fan like spin. The glowing green hue blurred in the air as he swept the long weapon around elegantly. It arced with the energy pulse each time he struck a body, sending it to the decking. Then Jaka would back away and roll it about in a defensive kata, presenting the spinning staff as an impenetrable shield. Again and again he dropped the staggering undead, their mouths open with nothing to say, their eyes empty with no vision left in them.

Brent felled another handful of bodies then looked back over his shoulder.

276

"Get the door open!" he howled at Paola Kett.

The Migroid door suddenly shot to one side with a hiss, fully open in a heartbeat. Paola could not step back quickly enough to avoid the charge of the undead. Instead, she rolled to one side like a cat, coming up with her glowing staves in her grasp. A handful of the corpses chased her to the side, reaching, grasping, while the main flood of bodies rushed old Ridge and the young Joshua Brent.

Paola Kett struck one solidly, the arc of power shaking her enemy to the floor. She stepped back, dodging reaching arms, then kicked the legs out from under that body. She turned and put two more onto the decking with a wild set of swipes from her staves then had to strike the one she had only toppled to render it unconscious. She struck it across the head with both staves.

The old man simply triggered his newly loaded sweeper. Kett was far enough to one side to be spared. So, he blasted the mass of undead from the doorway into dust and smoke.

Brent spun to look behind himself again, to see what was happening. Paola Kett ran his way then jumped completely over him where he crouched. The old man levered the sweeper and fired again, putting down a new mass of enemies, then levered it yet again. Brent turned his weapon to the open maw of the passageway and triggered it time and again, dropping the dead who spilled through between the old man's shots.

Kett chased the action into the former corridor where her fellow Acolytes fought. She soared through the air into a clump of the dead, landing in a cat like crouch, her staves flipping about like arcing electricity. She dropped a handful of enemies even as Candri Prentice and Jaka Baddenide did the same.

Prentice's energy whips and Baddenide's arcing staff seemed indomitable, inescapable. The mass of oncoming undead never slowed, however, as they had no mind of their own, anyway. Success was not measured in their empty eyes. They simply did what they did…the outcome was not even in the equation.

Joshua Brent's weapon gave a buzzing warning. He tossed it aside and pulled two handheld blasters from his belt. Both of them fired at once then one after another, raining more terror down on the horde.

Again Ridge blasted the opening with his Bay Sweeper. The big, sliding blast door fell back into the far chamber, the damage incurred by the blasts too much to endure. The massive metal door crushed quite a few of the dead.

Just after that, the flow slowed. The undead thinned greatly. Then they just stopped.

"Paola!" Joshua yelled at the young woman. "This way!"

Kett looked up to see nothing but a massive hall of oncoming death from her way, so she decided to pull back. She shouted at the other two fighters to fall back as well.

"Into the corridor!" she ordered them.

They agreed and the trio ran for the open chamber.

Thunder sounded down the hall behind them, coming closer with each boom.

They charged into a darkened hall, enemies rallying behind them, the unknown before them. In that, they were not unlike Gideon's team.

Gideon Ridge and the Rothidai, Grundy, led the way beyond their set of blast barriers. The Rayne Launcher was carving a definitive path, Gideon's pulsars taking down stragglers. Patrick and Zeckinbridge brought up their rear, watching behind them, dropping the odd pursuer as it came.

Down a long, dark corridor they went, just like the other team of invaders, closing on a central location and the secret of the dead…the undead…and perhaps the Reaches.

Captain Samara Garriton sat in her command seat, Gideon's Bible in her hands.

Adrift in a sea of unpowered, inanimate starship fighters, the Unity Vanguard ship, the *Bloodwind,* cradled a crew harried by repair demands. Station after station helped organize repair teams as they struggled valiantly to put their ship together again in hopes that it would survive another round of battle with the dead.

"The Gold and Orange repair details are all on the engine issues," Science Officer Wimbel Boatwright continued. He had been updating the bridge, the Captain especially, ever since the Shofar had shut down the enemy ships. "Purple detail has taken the shielding matter and has had reasonable success. I would recommend that-"

Captain Garriton waved away his suggestion.

"Fine, fine," she allowed, knowing Boatwright was good with manpower applications. "Handle this, will you, Wimbel? You just let me know when we have enough of anything…to do…anything."

"Confirmed," he said. "We do have enough power in reserve for another round with the Shofar."

"Hold on to that. We may yet need it."

She eased her finger over the Scriptures where Gideon Ridge had placed a bookmark. He had underlined several verses but one leaped out for her. She was reading in the New Testament Gospel of Matthew, Chapter Twenty-eight, verse Twenty.

"...and lo, I am with you always, *even* to the end of the age," she whispered aloud the letters in red.

"Amen," someone whispered on the bridge.

She could not tell which Officer had said it. Samara looked upward. It would be the end of the age indeed if God did not help them. Yet, despite all the years she had poured into every single thing other than faith, in that most crucial time, at that most distant corner of the cosmos, she honestly did not feel alone. Something was stirring inside her.

She began to read again.

Near the *Bloodwind* drifted all of the allied vessels in need of repair. Each one had deployed crews as best as possible to set things right. Fighters in bad shape had been taken into docking bays again on the *Ferali 5* and the *Bloodwind* to be fixed as much as possible. Then each had deployed yet again to get a jump on the dead.

The sonic attack employed by the *Bloodwind*, called the Shofar, overwhelmed enemy systems and broke any transmissions received from other sources, just like whatever was initiated from within the Reaches. The dead could receive no instruction, no control, and fell silent, still... once again dead. And, while dead, they made wonderful targets.

David Rule, Acolyte Ambassador, had just flown his *Razorhawk* through another squadron of the sitting targets when he radioed the *Ferali 5*.

"Commander Lorrayanka," the carrier's Communications Officer perked on the bridge, "Ambassador Rule has destroyed another ten of the dead. He is transmitting to us."

"Reengage limited Communications relays," she allowed. "Let's not start throwing on every light again, however. We need to reserve power."

"Go ahead, Ambassador Rule," the Officer said.

"Lorrayanka, I've had an inspiration."

"Do tell, David."

"We both know how poorly the enemy works. How slow, how mechanically, how basically the ships navigate, fire and counter. Enemy control is crippled even in this freedom of open space."

She nodded though he could not see her. She could hear his weapons discharging time and again behind his voice.

"We do," she said aloud.

"What if conditions were even worse?"

"How do you propose to make it worse?" she asked.

"I was thinking of luring them into the atmosphere of Dor Modo."

Silence. Stunned faces. Not even enough breath to gasp.

"I take it you like the idea," he chuckled.

"Rule, if we go down into that atmosphere-"

"We'll have an even higher advantage."

"-we'll be flying blind."

"It'll help even the odds, too."

"We'll have to slow down our speed."

"Our speed to targeting ratios can level out, increasing accuracy."

"Losing a ship in that ice is a cold way to die!" she finished.

"It's colder in space."

Silence. Blank stares.

"Am I the only one you've tried this on?" she asked.

"So far. What do you think?"

"I don't know. Just how well do you fly blind?"

Grundy snorted and rubbed the hair around his main horn.

Gideon Ridge patted his big friend's back.

"Open that door, Grundy."

"Just getting out my pass code," the Rothidai said with a low, rolling chuckle.

He tossed aside the Rayne Launcher and approached the large, ship sized barrier before them, some three bay lengths away. The invaders had battled their way to the latest, biggest barrier and had paused. More than one of them wondered how many hours they had traveled.

Deep inside the rock that was Zeta Lan, at the climax of yet another amazingly deep, intricate set of drilled and plated tunnels, the other invasion members waited at a new barrier of their own. They, too, had fought to the bottom of their twists and turns.

One of the Acolyte women, Paola Kett, read the markings.

"What about it?" Captain Joshua Brent asked her.

"Terribly old. Very early Greylik technology, language. Looks like another cargo bay door from a really old starship." Her eyes were even more lovely in the radiating light of her eyelets. "And before you ask, no, I can't open it. It has manual locks and seals operated by wheels and levers from the other side-"

Sylver Ridge's Bay Sweeper went off multiple times.

Each time, the blast barrier rang like a bell but held, inspiring Joshua Brent to join in, blasting away at the door.

"You'll melt your weapons before that door goes!" Paola Kett shouted at them.

Behind the group, Candri Prentice swept her energy whips outward and struck a walking corpse. A handful of pursuers had finally caught up to them, staggering toward them with slow but determined manners.

Jaka Baddenide leaped into a trio of the looming dead. He landed in a crouch and whipped the staff about, taking the legs out from under two of them. He drove the staff into the midsection of the third corpse, knocking it backward. Then a quick flip of his hands spun the staff about yet again and struck both downed enemies in the head.

He looked up to see the third nearly on him again but a crimson whip arced about it, shocked it to the deck plating and left it motionless.

Jaka glanced over his shoulder at Candri Prentice.

"Thanks. I owe you."

She laughed and said, "That's around four hundred you owe me."

"So, who's counting?" he asked and gestured down the passageway. "Looks like that's all of them for now."

The shooting waned then stopped altogether.

The blast barrier had taken on a distinct glow but showed no signs of breaking down.

"Any ideas?" Brent asked the group.

Abruptly, the barrier shifted and started to move to one side.

The Acolytes readied their weapons and split apart, taking up positions at varying points. Joshua Brent leaped back and crouched, his weapons leveled.

Sylver Ridge just jacked the lever on the sweeper and stood his ground.

A second later, the young Gideon Ridge peeked around the side of the door.

"Well, Pap, come on in. We did all the work and opened the door for you."

The young Ridge and his team stepped through the doorway.

"Actually, I opened the door," Grundy said with a snort and a sideways smile.

"No one else could budge the manual locks." Zeckinbridge nodded at the big Rothidai. "Grundy turned the wheels and popped the latches like popping knuckles."

"Speaking of which," Grundy said, "who was over here torching the door? The lockout wheels and gears on our side got as hot as a supernova."

Pap and Joshua Brent shared an uncomfortable glance at each other. Grundy thumbed back at the door, glowing hot on that side.

"I don't know what you were doing over here but you would've never made it through that kind of blast barrier."

Paola Kett huffed, saying, "If only someone would have told them."

Captain Joshua Brent rolled his eyes as old Pap chuckled.

CHAPTER THIRTEEN : *Dead Walking*

T he invasion group slowly entered the newly opened chamber.

Silence came with them. For a long moment, only the sound of their collective breathing could be heard. Finally, young Captain Brent exhaled generously.

"So…it's the undead repair shop of the cosmos. Cuts down on manpower costs, I guess."

The inner chamber was cavernous. It spread out like a disease, eating away at the core of the asteroid and filling it with its own purpose. The echoing chamber inhabited a massive space bigger than the landing areas in most of the smaller spaceports he had seen. It would have been possible to park the *Bloodwind* inside the cave with room to spare. All across the opening waited relics of past wars and conflicts, long decommissioned or half destroyed starfighters, ready to be taken by crews of the undead into battle.

The plethora of automated machines in the chamber worked to make the repairs so that would be possible. The undead corpses milling about in the deeper center of the chamber seemed to wait upon that very thing…or something else darker of intent.

"They didn't even react to us," Gideon Ridge said. He pointed to the corpses in the distance. "It's the strangest thing. They don't seem to even know we've breached the doors."

"How did you breach the doors? From your side, that is." Sylver Ridge asked.

"Grundy again," Gideon smiled.

Grundy rubbed the front of his main horn, straightening the fine hair there. With his other hand he shook the Rayne Launcher then dropped it to the floor with a crash of metal.

"It is empty of rockets and energy now," the Rothidai lamented. "But it got us through."

"We plowed through our tunnel's blast door, into here, and heard the noise your band was making on this one."

"Just about had it, too," Captain Brent lied.

"How have your pulsars held out?" Pap asked his boy. "Do your stuns still work on the dead?"

"They work on the same principle as their weapons," Gideon said of the Acolytes.

"Neuro energies for stunning the neurological system of living forms," Paola Kett said.

"Even the dead have to have neurological pulses to actuate physical, biological bodies," Candri Prentice added in explanation. "Even if those pulses are being cast into dead bodies from some other force."

Jaka Baddenide chuckled.

"Works on everything," he said. "Drops mechanized things, too, overwhelming the electrical systems."

"Which is why the pulsar array from the *Spoken Word* works on ships," old Pap finished. "I knew that part; good to know the rest. So how did you find us?"

"'Besides your noise? We started wandering the periphery of the chamber and found your door. It's approximately forty-five degrees, around the circumference of this room, off our entrance. We didn't know it led to the tunnels you had taken; we were going to get it open so we had more than one exit option," Wrigley Zeckinbridge noted, propping her hands on her slender hips.

"Not a bad plan," the old man agreed. "What now?"

"We stick to the plan," Gideon answered. "We sent Chief Patrick up some of the scaffolding just inside the entry. It reaches really high and has several small panels and so on for cover. He's going to keep a hawk's eye on the room from above. We need a volunteer to work their way back to him," he pointed along the wall.

"I can," said Candri Prentice as she pulled her hood over her head.

"You'll be his back up. Don't let anyone scale your platform. Keep him free to put sights on targets from your perch."

She nodded, threw a glance to Paola Kett, nodded again, then left them.

"He's going to need more long ranger to back him," Zeckinbridge added.

"That's where you come in, Captain," Gideon told Joshua Brent. "Work your way around to the other side wall and head upstairs. Do the same thing, using a long arm to put things down at a distance."

"Mine went dry and I was out of magazines. I tossed it and I don't have-"

Zeckinbridge unstrapped a long arm from her shoulder and tossed it at the young man.

"He'll need a partner, too, watching his back so he can concentrate on long range work."

The Commodore looked to the Acolytes.

Paola Kett pulled her staves from her sleeves.

"My pleasure."

"How about me, Gideon?" Zeckinbridge asked.

She swept the Palimar 9 from her shoulder as Gideon Ridge pointed straight up. The group looked that way and saw that the ceiling ran with crossed catwalks more like an intricate web than walkways.

"Remember the elevator we passed? I think that's where it goes."

She shrugged, saying, "Not a problem. If I have to, I'll climb."

"I hope not," Jaka Baddenide said honestly. He tapped his staff on the decking. "I hate climbing at heights."

"And he's your backup," Gideon Ridge nodded.

The two of them moved away quickly.

"That leaves you, me and Grundy, Pap. You two ready?"

Grundy snorted.

The older Ridge nodded with, "Let's wrap this up. I'm hungry."

"Me too," Grundy agreed emphatically.

"You know, that makes three of us."

The lights were back on.

Lights. Activity. Power. Motion.

The bone starmada no longer drifted motionlessly, lifelessly. Again it moved, snaking in from open space, taking formation once again, plotting conquest…as if alive. Enemy of life, alive again…stalking the icy atmosphere of Dor Modo.

The allies of life had pulled back from the bone starmada. At its reawakening, the living turned to the idea David Rule had posed. They retreated to the frozen atmosphere of Dor Modo, the planet closest to the Reaches and the debris field that had once been Maximilian Station. All too revived, the *Leviathan* starship had dropped into the atmosphere as well, prodding the starmada of bones into active, unrelenting pursuit of the gallant, ridiculously outnumbered allies.

"I need more power, Winds!" Commander Lorrayanka roared over her com. "I need weapons back!"

The *Ferali 5* jolted roughly yet again, a recurring theme for the living allies. The starmada of the dead gave pursuit and assault.

"You've got what I can give!" he called back. "I'm stealing from all sorts of systems trying to keep your shields up!"

"You heard him!" she then yelled at the bridge crew. "Evasive maneuvers! Deploy retractable foils! Use this atmospheric flying to our advantage!"

"If we cannot get weapons online-" her Weapons Officer started.

"We will have to become he weapon!" Lorrayanka roared.

"Commander?" two of the bridge crew said at the same time.

"We outfly them and we run over them!" she cried. "Shields are holding! Ram every enemy you come to! Run them down!"

"Commander, we have hull breaches on five, ten and-"

"Seal them! Use reserve power if you have to!" she shouted at her Science Officer. "Right now, shields are our only weapons and I intend to use them!"

"At our power levels-"

"Just do it! Find a way! Seal us up!" she interrupted.

"But life support could drop below-"

"We'll open a window, Officer! Do as I say!"

The following blast shook the ship to its bowels but it held together.

"Scopes show a lot of fighters focusing on the *Ferali 5*, Captain Prentia," Commander Wahll transmitted from his Hunon Interceptor, the *Jokra*. "Shall we assist?"

Captain Prentia, of the *Ferali 5* herself, adjusted her fighter controls.

"*Moonscar* to the *Jokra*," she transmitted back. "That is a negative. Stay on target. My Sub-Commander, Lorrayanka, will do the *Ferali 5* proud!"

Captain Prentia had ordered her little squadron to fly into the face of the giant enemy.

The *Moonscar*, the *Jokra*, and the *Saber*, an Acolyte on loan to her, swept into and through many smaller enemies, carving them to pieces, en route to the massive enemy ship. They were not willing to turn back, nor would they turn aside.

"*Tikrek*, I'm showing more than five thousand ships and I don't mean just light starfighters! They're scattered all through the upper atmosphere…in pursuit!"

Jon Kett, at the helm of his *Tikrek*, whispered a prayer. He fired his weapons array and downed four fighters in his path. Then he hit his com switch.

"*Raine*, we don't have to remind God how big our problem is. We just have to remind the problem how big our God is."

"Amen," David Rule transmitted. The others could hear his weapons crying havoc in the background. "Amen, Jon. Taelynn, don't be afraid. If this be our last flight and our last fight, let us remember how we pass on. We leave a plane we valiantly defend for a far better plane already won for us."

"I know, *Razorhawk*," she answered, her weapons howling. "The number is just…staggering."

"Forget it," Jon Kett replied with a chuckle. "Imagine how embarrassing it will be for the forces of evil if even one of us survives with the odds stacked against us like this."

"Get ready," David Rule said. His ship jostled about him, his readouts flickering, and he returned fire. "When *Moonscar* gets in that thing's face, I want us ready to pull its attention sharply away from her."

The group fell transmission silent again.

On the bridge of the *Bloodwind*, the interior silence was broken by Science Officer Boatwright. The ship had been mauling the bone starmada fleet when encountered and it seemed the enemy had assigned new pursuit ships.

"Captain," he started slowly, lowly.

"That formation," she told Officer Gorbler, pointing at the digital displays projected over the natural viewscreen. "Burn it."

Gorbler unleashed a full array of heavy firepower, destroying a squadron of more than fifteen enemy fighters. He and many others of the bridge crew gave smiles and nods to each other, enjoying the repairs their crew had been able to make during the downtime. The *Bloodwind* was formidable yet again.

"Captain," Boatwright said in a much louder tone.

"What is it, Mr. Boatwright? Spit it out."

"We are being actively targeted on long range sensors by a pursuit spearhead," he announced. "Three starships of considerable size and firepower, flying in a three point fighter formation…they have weapons locked on and seem to be biding their time."

"Of course they are," she said. "They can't guarantee sensor locks from very far away in this atmosphere." She pointed to another point on the screen. "Those right there. Dust them, Gorbler."

"Captain," the Science Officer pressed, "we should be ready when they get close."

Samara Garriton glanced over her shoulder at the man. She could see the concern in his eyes.

"What's back there, Mr. Boatwright?" she asked directly.

"Two Chabron Dreadships," he sighed.

"Ouch," Garriton said lowly.

287

"They're flying formation on a Reaper class…"

The entire bridge crew held their breath together.

"…the *Judgment*. It's the *Judgment*, Captain."

Garriton leaped to her feet and stormed his station.

"Impossible," she muttered. "It was in so many pieces…"

"Readings show new parts and partitions in that ship," Boatwright said, pointing to the station displays. "It looks like it's actively rebuilding itself in downtime."

She slammed a fist onto his console and stormed back to her chair.

"It ends here. Come about, Mr. Retaw!" She dropped into the seat. "I don't care if it does rebuild itself and steal parts from its allies like that big serpent ship! It ends here!"

"Captain-" Retaw began.

Her fierce glare scorched him to silence.

He then found his voice once again and spoke loudly, "Yes, Captain. Coming about."

Respra opened the audio channel for the bridge to hear.

"Captain, transmission."

David Rule's voice, deep and rolling, filled the bridge.

"This is *Razorhawk*. Our Acolyte fighters, along with Captain Prentia and Commander Wahll, are going to engage the *Leviathan*. We hope to be too small and too fast to be targets and, in that, we will keep it busy so it will not target either of you, the *Bloodwind* or the *Ferali 5*."

"Ouch," Gorbler muttered.

"Be advised, however," Rule continued, "We have thousands upon thousands of enemy vessels already within this atmosphere, many of them large ships, no longer just the quick starfighters of the starmada. I pray for each and every one of us and I transmit this now. Do not lose hope. Whatever drives this evil, it does not seem to have use of sensors within this atmosphere. They are limited in reach and targeting. We are blessed. No matter what happens, God will make a way. This evil will not prevail, no matter the numbers. Those of you who pray, do so now; our team within the Reaches needs it. That is where the deciding battle will be waged."

"Amen," Commander Lorrayanka transmitted.

"Amen," Samara Garriton answered. Then she looked at her Science Officer. "Calculate the best way to assault the two Dreadships to maximize damage to particular systems. Coordinate with Mr. Gorbler and put their weapons out of commission. I want them flying about uselessly while we settle up with Bordin Mo and his *Judgment*. Clear?"

"Confirmed," both Officers echoed.

"Then take us down Bordin Mo's long dead throat!" Garriton said.

The cold chamber taunted the living, the raiders, with mystery. Walls, some made of clear composites and some hewn from the very stone and ores of the asteroid, mazed about with confusing intricacy. It was clear right away that Gideon's idea of putting people in high places was genius. In the midst of the aimless staggering of the dead and highly technical marvels running themselves, the bird's eye view was a navigational boon.

"The corridor you're on dead ends…if you'll forgive the expression, folks…into a band of walking nightmares," transmitted Taylor Patrick.

Candri Prentice, standing watch at the hatch to their nest position, shot him a look.

"That is just pure *pun*ishment," transmitted Wrigley Zeckinbridge from her position in the high catwalks.

"Thanks, Patrick," Gideon answered then pointed to another corridor and led his Pap and Grundy that way. "Even if your jokes are sour."

They traversed the crooked paths toward the center of the chamber, beyond the building and rebuilding locations all across the massive room. It was difficult to make progress when they constantly stopped and turned to avoid the walking corpses.

"What do you think we will find?" Grundy asked Gideon.

"I'll tell you," Pap interrupted soberly. "Crazy old Andreas Riker. Or what's left of him. He was a lot of machine a long time ago. Who knows what he is now?"

"Psiborg," Grundy uttered.

"With a darker something, too…something evil. Pure evil. No Psiborn could manipulate the dead. This is…different," Gideon warned.

"Commodore, the pathways on my side are blocked off. They're almost out of advancement room. How do things look from your angle?" Josh Brent asked by com.

Taylor Patrick answered first.

"Closed off on my side, too, Commodore. You have to find a way for them."

Gideon and his team stopped still, glancing about at the machinery that was strewn around. Each made certain their weapons were ready for about the twentieth time.

Wrigley Zeckinbridge trotted over the narrow catwalks with Jaka the Acolyte in close pursuit. She moved with swift efficiency, surefooted and light of motion. She and Jaka neared the center of the upper walks before stopping.

"Okay. I can steer you toward the center using the telescopic sights on the Palimar but you ought to know the center of this place is another closed room of some kind. It looks like a bunker…"

Abruptly the dead began to notice things. Sound, sight.

The raiders.

Dead walkers sought out the ladders and scaffolding to the nests the team was using. Some scaled the beginnings of the catwalks, working toward the heights, while others began to converge on Gideon's location. The groans began…

…and a handful of bodies walked onto the passage with Gideon Ridge and his team.

"What alerted them? The mention of the last chamber?"

"I don't know, Grundy," Gideon said. "We need to-"

"Light 'em up," Pap ordered and fired that sweeper.

Open air charges exploded on both sides of the starship, shaking it as if with a huge fist. Then another exploded just below it and the turbulence threatened to kick out the inertial dampeners.

The *Bloodwind* did not shy away, however. Her captain would never allow that.

"Engage them! Give another volley!" she bellowed. "Evasive maneuvers, Rallson Pell rolls, anything, but get us closer and fire!"

Gorbler and Retaw barked acknowledgment as another explosion shook their hull.

The *Bloodwind* blistered the air with firepower as it rolled to starboard. The three combatant crafts loomed closer every moment, their attacks closer as well, but Captain Samara Garriton's ship danced gracefully clear and wreaked its own brand of havoc.

The huge spaceships had exchanged attacks and advances for retreats several times. Garriton's ship had taken damage on several passes but the majority of the casualty was held by the Reaper class *Judgment* and its two wing ships.

The Chabron Dreadships were intimidating but neither had working shields and one was venting gases and smoke. Its weapons systems were destroyed, targeted early on by the impressive Octovoid at the Weapons Station.

The other ignited in a flash of flame and a plume of green energy and began dropping for the planet's surface. The second run on it had found the weapons banks hard to hit but the engine core was relatively in the open for picking.

Across her bridge, Garriton watched her crew burst into cheers and laughter.

"That's right! Take them down!" she shouted. "Come about!"

Far away, in a section of air all to itself, the giant serpentine destroyer, *Leviathan*, obliterated more of the ships of the dead than their living enemies could. It flew dreadfully near to other derelict ships, drained their power, then assimilated the physical parts as well with magnetic self-reconstruction. Fighter after freighter after battleship it swallowed and on it flew, coming for the living.

Captain Prentia growled deeply in her throat.

"Final approach," she transmitted from her ship, the *Moonscar*.

"*Saber* on your port wing, flying aft," Alexi Carver transmitted. "I'm ready."

"The Hunon *Jokra* on your starboard wing, flying aft," Wahll called. "Ready."

"*Tikrek*, *Raine*, and *Razorhawk* are far above you, flying extremely wide," David Rule replied. "Ready."

"Shields routed to our forefront, all you have," the Starstalker Captain ordered. "Increase speed. We will strafe down the starboard side of its nose and bridge and make a run down its spine."

"Acknowledged, Captain," several voices transmitted at once.

"Engage run in three...two...one...now!" she howled, diving with her ship.

Like suspected, the giant ship was slow. The three ship assault team flew right through its attacks, even its thickest barrages of energy fire. They streaked downward, leveling off at its bridge level, then opened up with all they had as they strafed along its side. It had yet to reactivate shielding and the run opened up a gash the size of a freighter all along their planned run. When they cut for the spine they opened up its hull.

Then they veered away.

"Route power to your aft shield generators!" Prentia roared. "Get some distance!"

Predictably, the massive monster turned to pursue them, fire trailing from its long, wicked wound. Forward cannons opened up immediately but no solid hits were attained.

"Now!" Rule transmitted.

The Acolyte trio swept downward at the rear quarter of the snake. All three ships opened up on the monster ship, punching holes and tearing bits of the fuselage from its frame. They slid close, doing as much damage as possible, then swept away again, angling to retreat.

The big ship came about quickly for its size.

"Again!" Captain Prentia called out and led another run.

While they played the serpentine spacecraft like a Khendra ball, bouncing it between them, Prentia's First Officer still commanded the *Ferali 5*.

Commander Lorrayanka gnashed her teeth as several more impacts shook the big ship.

"Commander!" the Science Officer started for the third time.

"I do not want to hear it!" she howled. "Unless you are about to say we miraculously have weapons back online, keep it to yourself!"

Three more impacts, two explosions. Outside, the shields flickered.

"Commander!" he shouted, despite his given order.

Lorrayanka yelled something at him that was drowned out by the successive impacts that wracked the ship, its shields and its hull.

Then the flight became somewhat quiet.

"We've...reached a clearing..." her Pilot said, awestruck. "No enemy vessels nearby..."

A cheer rose all around the bridge. In response, Lorrayanka leaped to her feet and began pointing and commanding.

"Deploy every crewman we have for repairs! I want shields and weapons back online and I want it so quickly my head spins! Jettison every bit of cargo, stores and equipment we do not need immediately and drop to emergency internal power only! Reroute power from long range sensors, lightspeed engines, long term life support and anything else we do not need to fly in this atmosphere! Use it to bolster hull integrity and shield regeneration! We have a break; let us use it wisely!"

Bridge crew members shared the commands with different departments as the Commander dropped back into her seat. She flopped her head and her long hair back over the command seat and stared at the ceiling and its flickering lights.

The Pilot turned his seat back to her.

"You broke the record, Commander."

She would not raise her head but answered, "What record is that?"

Pilot Argor chuckled, his fangs showing.

"Most ships ever rammed and disabled or destroyed by a StarWarp class Starfighter carrier ship. The *Ferali 5* is going down in Starstalker history, Commander."

"See? Now that is news worth reporting."

Weapons Officer Xerstou spun his chair about, smiling in admiration.

"How did you know the shields would hold? How did you calculate it that quickly?"

She lifted her head finally and said, "Faith."

"One hundred and seventy-eight fighters or freighters sent smoldering, falling out of the sky, by running through them," Argor said, shaking his head. "Definitely the record."

"Commander," the Science Officer spoke again, "for the record, shields were at one third of *one percent* after that last ram...barely enough to hold."

"Seems more than enough to me," she answered. "We're all alive, aren't we?"

"Commander," the Communications Officer interrupted sharply. "Incoming direct transmission from a fighter on approach. It came upward from the planet's surface."

"We have held open channels for all our allies," she said.

"This starfighter has not previously transmitted."

"What starfighter?"

The man hesitated. Then, "It is an Acolyte fighter, Commander. It is a Razor class. The designation is *Razorwing*."

"Filter it, restrict it and divorce your reception from our internal systems," Lorrayanka ordered. "Then find out who it is."

A short moment or two passed. Then the Officer lifted his headset.

"The fighter Pilot admits stealing the fighter from the Acolyte Temple bay," he said incredulously. "However, he claims loyalty to us...in the face of the undead threat. The Pilot is a Rothidai. Grockforth."

"Cheyenne Winds!" Wastasa Winds shouted as he stormed the bridge. "My daughter! Does he know anything about my daughter?"

The Starstalker Commander nodded at her Communications Officer and his station.

"Go on, Winds. Go and ask him."

The Ridges ran for the center of the chamber, the big Rothidai charging with them. Weapons surgically sliced through all enemies and put them back to death on the rock and metal flooring, bodies clanging in the fall. The dead were taking more damage before falling, resisting the reclaiming grave.

"They sound like metal hitting the floor," Gideon noted as they blasted their way through the masses.

"Tougher, now, too."

Grundy nodded at the oldest Ridge's words.

"These are not just dead. They are Psiborn dead."

"These dead are cybernetic," Gideon transmitted to the teams in the ceiling. "They take more to put down. Be careful."

The shooters in the teams acknowledged what the Acolyte fighters quickly discovered. Fighting the new undead as they reached the hatches was more challenging. The shooters often had to turn their weapons from blasting ground level threats to aiding their own defenders. Still they were triumphant. Nothing took the nests from them. And it was good that they held their posts. The shooters kept an almost constant rain of fire in action to slow the closing rings of the undead.

In time, the Ridges reached the central room Wrigley Zeckinbridge was telling them awaited. Grundy was last to turn the final corner, his sidearm spent. He dropped it.

The moans of the dead rose. Scuffing resounded along corridors behind them.

Before them, a massive cargo door blocked their path. The control panel flashed several colors over several buttons at random intervals. No pattern seemed to be in use.

"I don't think the sweeper can budge that blast barrier," the old father said.

"I know my neuropulsars won't," Gideon sighed.

Grundy pulled his big family weapon from his back strap.

"Perhaps I can open it."

Neither of the Ridges thought the well meaning Rothidai could pry open a blast door of that magnitude. It was evident in their eyes.

Grundy snorted, blowing the little hairs about his horn.

He strolled to the point where the barrier locked against the thick wall, the wall on which the console glimmered. The big warrior felt along the edge of the wall where it met the door.

"Grundy," both men said.

"You doubt I can move it," the Rothidai growled. "Care to wager?"

Neither man responded.

The Rothidai felt along the seam of the door and wall a little bit longer, seemed to find a favorable spot, nodded then patted the location. He backed away, lifted the halberd, then struck out brutally.

His blow completely destroyed the access panel console, grounding all the electrical power together with the metal head. Arcing power discharged into the wall and door, smoking on the weapon as it heated it. Then the power faded and the lights about the panel faded with it.

The magnetic seal hummed loudly then failed and the door clicked.

Grundy raised an eyebrow and smirked back at the men. Then he pushed the door back.

"You cheated," Gideon complained, hands upturned questioningly.

The weapons in the rafters fired furiously. The dead rushed to further action and the previously oblivious, worker corpses began a march on the central chamber. It was all too clear that the chamber was off limits to the living...punishable by death.

"We can't just leave the others out here," Gideon said flatly, looking upward. "The undead walkers are moving with new zeal. If we go inside here and close them out, this whole chamber will turn and pour onto them-"

"This was the plan, Gideon," Grundy said. "If we falter now, it will all be for nothing; if we do not succeed, no one will live at all."

"The big boy's right," Pap Ridge nodded. "You know I named you after the Bible hero, Gideon. From the Old Testament. He was unsure of himself and everything he was supposed to do. Then, when the odds were at their worst, he found that it don't matter, as long as we have God. We have God, son. Now let's do what has to be done."

Gideon Ridge looked into his father's eyes. The truth glistened in them.

Grundy forced the door open enough to slip inside. The three did so and then closed the door behind them.

Taylor Patrick, Joshua Brent and Wrigley Zeckinbridge all watched them close the door through their telescopic sights and immediately turned the heavy weapons back to the dead climbing up the ladders to their nests.

Paola Kett, Jaka Baddenide and Candri Prentice defended the perches as best they could, fighting hand to hand with the undead. All had backed away from the hatches as the dead had massed and overpowered them, forcing the hatches open, but they fought on, holding them back. They were very relieved when the shooters turned their attention to helping them turn back the death tide.

Wrigley Zeckinbridge transmitted to the two Unity Soldiers.

"Work your way to the far end of your perches," she ordered, her weapon firing in the background. "When you do, make the jump from them to the central scaffolding and climb up to the ceiling rafters! Work your way down to us and we will hold this one position as a unit!"

Patrick acknowledged and began to move, while Brent did the same, only with more trepidation. Their Acolyte partners were even quicker to move and more agile about it as well. All began making their jumps, the shooters first, covered by the Acolytes, followed by the Acolytes, covered by the shooters. Then they all ran for Zeckinbridge's location.

In the atmosphere of the ice planet, time was running out like sand slipping through the tightest held fingers. Inevitable. Unavoidable. Inescapable.

All around the battle zones, sensor banks squawked with bad news. There were more ships flooding the frozen atmosphere. A lot more ships.

Tens of thousands of ships, despite the fact that they were the numbers already expected, made a daunting approach. Morale took a terrible blow.

"Captain! The number is staggering! We have to pull out! The time to abandon this conflict is now!" Officer Boatwright shouted aboard the *Bloodwind*.

He was nearly drowned out by the explosions pummeling the shields.

"As you were!" Captain Samara Garriton howled back at him. She braced herself in her seat. "Return fire! Evasive maneuvers! Get around behind that thing!"

On their screens loomed the *Judgment*. Smoke trailed from many damaged panels on the Reaper class monster but it was still in the fight, raining attacks on the Captain and her crew.

Even as Gorbler assailed the big enemy again and Retaw dodged another assault, Boatwright called out to the Captain again.

"Captain, every ally ship in this atmosphere will be destroyed in seconds once the full wave hits! We have taunted death as long as-"

"Enough!" Garriton yelled. Then she yelled at the screens, pointing. "There, Gorbler!"

Gorbler launched the last missile of the *Bloodwind* at the area the Captain had indicated. The bent and smoking outer hull covering the *Judgment*'s weapons hold was a tempting target, indeed.

Almost as if it sensed her intentions, however, the big Reaper veered to one side and let the missile ignite against a lower cargo hold. The maneuver put the big enemy on a course to run face to face with the newly turning *Bloodwind* and its Captain.

Oddly, Garriton smiled from her seat. She seemed pleased at the enemy's new direction.

"Now, Mr. Gorbler, give that ship our best," she chuckled and pressed herself back into her seat.

In her mind, Garriton pictured Bordin Mo, long dead Captain of the Reaper ship, sitting in his command chair, as well. She stared venomously at the bridge on the screen, knowing his hollow, deathly white eyes would be staring back from his end.

The bridge of the *Judgment* was badly damaged, one side wide open to the elements, the remaining side showering the fuselage with sparks and smoke. Its shields were down; it had been angling that bridge away from battle on purpose.

Samara Garriton was not easily beaten, however. She knew which way the ship would move to protect the smoldering weapons banks and she knew where to put her ship to meet that protected bridge…one step ahead of the dead.

"Fire!" she howled.

In her mind, she could see the face of Bordin Mo. If the dead could look surprised…

Gorbler unleashed a barrage of remaining weapon energies into the open bridge.

The ship shuddered, faltered then began to blow apart deck by deck.

Retaw did his best to pull the *Bloodwind* out of the fury of the exploding Reaper but he could not avoid all of it. Flame, debris, energy discharges and smoke wrapped about the victorious *Bloodwind*, while turbulence and wracking forces shook the ship. Retaw was shouting even as the bridge crew shouted their success.

"Engines failing!" he called suddenly.

The ship began to sink in the atmosphere. Alarms went off throughout the bridge.

As the *Bloodwind* started downward, the *Ferali 5* was on its way back into the fray. It had earned a respite, having rammed its way to success and escape earlier in the fight, but they had dodged the engagement afterward to enact much needed repairs. With the *Razorwing* fighter flying escort, the Starstalker carrier had made enough repairs to rejoin the impossible mission.

"We cannot survive against such odds," Commander Lorrayanka's Science Officer said flatly. "Tens of thousands, Commander…the engagement is impossible."

Wastasa Winds sat on the bridge, monitoring engineering scopes.

"Winds, what is your word on this?" the Commander asked.

Wastasa Winds did not answer. He was busy but that was not why he had not heard. His mind and his heart lingered in the past, in Maximilian Station. He pondered his daughter's fate, afraid to ask the newly arrived Rothidai for details.

"Winds!" the Commander snapped.

"We already knew it was impossible," he answered glumly, distantly. "We're not in this to survive; we're in this to slow the expansion of the bone starmada. The good news is that your engines are nearing a hundred percent again. So, if you do decide it's time to cut and run, looks like we'll have the juice to do it."

Lorrayanka held her breath for a long moment, running her tongue along her fangs.

"Commander," the Science Officer pressed.

"Pilot," she growled, ignoring the other man. "Put us on an intercept course with that serpentine monster ship. We've got at least one last run in us before we turn for escape, wouldn't you say, Mr. Winds?"

Wastasa Winds smiled sadly.

"At least one more."

The Commander nodded, echoing, "One more."

Winds moved to the Communications Officer. He gestured at the headset.

"Put me through to the *Razorwing*," he said.

A moment later, the Officer handed him the headset.

"Rothidai, this is Wastasa Winds."

"This is Grockforth," the Rothidai returned. His voice was dark, somber. "I regret your loss of your daughter...though I cannot lie. I do not regret leaving her. She betrayed me and killed my only love and-"

"I know her nature, Rothidai, well enough already. You didn't kill her in vengeance when you had the chance; I can't fault you in not saving her, either."

"Still, I can offer you a bit of hope," the Rothidai answered.

"Oh? What is that?" Winds asked.

"I have chosen to resist the evil with all of you and I have chosen your ship to aide. It is done. The loyalty with which I tried to honor your daughter I will give to you. I am with you until whatever end comes."

Winds handed the headset back to the Communications Officer.

"Poor guy. That kind of loyalty, tied up with Cheyenne, brought to this place..." Winds muttered.

"We're closing on the *Leviathan*, Commander Lorrayanka," the Pilot informed.

Lorrayanka turned to the Communications Officer and commented, "Let the ally fighters know our trajectory. We don't need to get in their way."

Swarming about the big enemy ship were the ally fighters, attacking in two teams to lure it one way and then another.

"Seventeen fighters en route to intercept," the *Tikrek* transmitted. Jon Kett banked to one side as the big serpent ship fired at him, missing once again. "Like that thing needs help."

The *Razorhawk* and the *Raine* swept alongside him.

Captain Prentia unloaded on the snake ship, as did her wing mates. She watched it carefully to be certain it turned about to come for them then she rolled over and began a retreat. The *Moonscar*, the *Saber* and the *Jokra* flew away desperately, dodging a blistering array of weapons fire.

"Rule, you and your two flyers disengage so you can greet the fighter squadron you've detected on the way," Captain Prentia transmitted. "We will lead the *Leviathan* away from you and away from that squadron coming to aide it!"

Rule acknowledged the plan and took up a new route. Jon Kett and Taelynn Berreaux fell into line with him. The three accelerated and flew headlong toward the coming squadron.

"Shields to the front! Weapons at full spread!" Rule ordered when they got close.

The three of them cut through the seventeen band like a dagger through weak flesh. The blood of the squadron, flame and debris and raw energy discharges, spilled wildly where they carved their paths. As they exited through the rear of the formation, eleven fighters had been destroyed and the three had only taken damage to their shields.

The six remaining fighters banked hard and came about at the same time Rule, Kett and Berreaux did so.

Abruptly, spatial charges ignited in the air all about the fighters, both sets. Four of the death fighters were destroyed instantly. Rule's *Razorhawk* and Kett's *Tikrek* were battered and shaken and knocked off course, their shields knocked out completely. Berreaux's *Raine* lost its shielding and was knocked off course, too, but in a totally different direction than her allies. The last two death fighters of the squadron fell in behind the *Raine*, while an unexpected, ragged freighter fell into pursuit of the *Razorhawk* and the *Tikrek*, firing more charges at them left and right.

"Split!" Rule shouted in transmission, jerking his controls to one side.

Kett banked to the other direction, wondering which of them the freighter would follow.

"I'm having trouble shaking them!" Taelynn Berreaux transmitted, the two fighters hot on her tail foils. "I can't raise shields!"

All around her their energy fire sizzled in the air, some blasts so close they burned her fuselage's paint into a blackened smear.

"Hold on," Rule urged, banking again.

He brought the *Razorhawk* about and settled in behind the freighter that had moved into position behind Kett and his *Tikrek*. Immediately he lit the freighter with a full spectrum of his offenses, cutting it to shreds.

The freighter stalled, shook then fell from the sky like a stone.

The *Raine* shook as it took one blast to a wingtip then took another hit to the undercarriage, where the landing gear stowed itself in flight. The little ship whipped to one side, beginning to shake violently in the absence of one wingtip.

"I'm losing control!" Taelynn Berreaux cried.

Out of nowhere, a Mustang class Earth fighter ripped into range of the *Raine* and her pursuers. It fired into the two death ships, the one rapid autocannon blowing the ships into pieces. Then the Mustang class fighter angled downward and moved into a parallel flight with the *Raine*.

"Relax, Taelynn, I got you," a familiar voice transmitted. "Hold steady."

Rule and Kett were close behind the little Earth ship and Taelynn Berreaux.

The Mustang class fighter was scarred and burned over two thirds of its exterior with some small panels buckled and some missing, exposing wire and circuitry. The idea it could fly astonished the others. It launched four cables with magnetic anchors and locked them on the fuselage of the *Raine*.

The Pilot of the Mustang shouted his success in transmitted glee.

"Rabeau?" David Rule transmitted in utter shock.

"Loist?" Jon Kett called in echo.

"You two sound like you've seen a ghost," Rabeau Loist answered. "You guys know I'm the *WildCard*."

Loist pulled up sharply, hauling against the other ship, leveling both ships against the pulling gravity.

"We thought you were dead!" Kett shouted.

"No way I'd miss the last fight," Rabeau laughed. "That wave of energy from the big ship really did almost kill me. Burned my ship, shorted a lot of things out. I was dead in space for a while, no com, no engines, no weapons, all systems down."

"What happened then?" Taelynn Berreaux asked.

"Systems just kicked back on. I don't understand it…but hey, I'm here. God has a reason for the miracle and I'm blessed. I don't have to know the why."

"Amen," Rule said, his heart swelling with love for God and His grace. "But you aren't here for the last battle."

"Why?" Rabeau asked.

"You're going to pull Taelynn out of the atmosphere, since she can't do it with a damaged wing. Then the two of you are going to start out for Earth."

"David-"

"My order stands," Rule interrupted. "Someone has to survive this. Now go."

There was more resistance but it was quelled. For David Rule, Rabeau Loist had been given a miracle and an extension of his life and would be sent home. He would not ask the young man to die there again.

Rule and Kett then turned to find Captain Prentia and her fighters again, all of whom were running from the *Leviathan*.

Old Uncle Sun waited nervously on the lowered ramp of the *Belly Rub*. He squinted his eyes at the generated lights here and there, below the natural light given off by the swirling, colorful, nebula gasses above.

ABC-Zeta Lan, lifeless rock in the morbid Reaches, hosted the subterranean Stone Tombs. Structures and facilities, tunnels and tombs, the catacombs wore the ominous name appropriately. They were carved from the rock belly of the asteroid itself and they were full of the dead.

The artificial atmosphere was produced by the patchwork, cobbled technology inside the rock and on the surface. Infested with the dead or no, that meant the locale had once been active for the living.

The dead do not need an atmosphere.

That thought haunted Sun Ridge the most. At some time, the living had planned to make use of the facilities in the rock. Where were they, who were they and what…or who…had happened to them? He wondered why something, or someone, held the atmosphere active so long after any living being had been there.

"I feel like Goldilocks and, any minute now, the three bruins are gonna come home," he said grimly.

He checked the rebreather mask at his belt then checked his holstered venter. He pulled the chamber slide back on his longarm, checked the power pack and slung it over his shoulder again.

"Hurry up, people," he growled. "I don't wanna be here when Momma, Papa and Baby get home."

He saw his breath in the cool, generated atmosphere. It wafted to his right, caught in a false breeze, the illusion of real weather.

To the right of Sundar and his ship sat the *Spoken Word*. His vision drawn there by the apparition of his own breath, Sundar Ridge stared at the flashy freighter for a long moment. Something about the rear, starboard landing gear held his gaze.

He smiled a sideways, rueful grin.

"I guess I am gettin' old, after all," he called. "I should've sensed you there a long time ago."

A form stepped from hiding and the cover of the ship.

CHAPTER FOURTEEN : *The Invitation*

O ver the icy planet, the *Bloodwind* dropped in altitude quickly.

"Engines still not responding!" yelled Pilot Retaw as he keyed sequence after sequence.

"Navigation has gone black!" Reje Chu echoed.

"Shields are down completely! Weapons systems are flickering," Gorbler said.

"It's a system wide computer failure; we're losing one bank of controls at the time," Boatwright pointed out to the Captain. "Soon we'll be a flying hunk of metal, flying downward only!"

"Deploy all repair teams immediately!" Samara Garriton ordered the Communications Officer. "Engineering takes precedence!"

"We'll need our shields-" Gorbler started darkly.

"I want to fly first!" Garriton shouted.

Outside, the cloudy cold of Dor Modo rushed by them quickly. The nose and the bridge started turning downward toward the ultimate stop each hoped would not be reached.

Samara Garriton closed her eyes and took up the Bible again.

The map to the greatest peace you could ever know. There's a page in the back that lays it all out. The rest is a journey you follow as you go, Gideon had told her.

When we get back - she had started.

Don't wait, he had said. *Read at least that page while you wait.*

She glanced at the loose page in the back, something Gideon had put inside to keep, to remember. It was a note and a simple prayer.

The note said that God was faithful to His Word and would never go back on it. It also said that He promised to never turn anyone away if they came to Him for forgiveness and eternal life and they genuinely meant it. She remembered from her youth that going to Heaven was called having the soul, the spirit, *saved*. She also remembered that God wanted that for all so that they could live in paradise with Him after death. The bottom line was that the Creator of all things, Almighty God, loved each and every one of His creations and hoped they would come home.

A line in the note was underlined; _Salvation is simple_

Then the prayer.

Almighty Father God, please forgive me. I know I have done wrong and fallen short of what I should have been. I don't understand everything but I want to learn. Please teach me. From this time on, please save me and take me to be your own. Lead me and show me the way. Please keep me, forever. Lord Jesus, please be my Savior and come into my heart and live through me. In Jesus' name I pray.

"Amen," she said aloud in her seat, having prayed the prayer.

Engaged with the enemy, Alexi Carver yanked his _Saber_ out of the line of fire again. Giant death ship aside, he was in a good mood.

"Good to see you, Rule!" he transmitted. "It's about time, too. I thought I was going to get all the credit for destroying that thing!"

David Rule and Jon Kett had just arrived in time to blast and distract the behemoth so fervently in pursuit of the other fighter.

It was still long from the destruction Carver optimistically predicted.

Captain Prentia swept her fighter into another dive and unloaded on the giant serpent. The _Jokra_, flying partner to her _Moonscar_, slid in close and wreaked considerable damage along the upper ridge of the ship.

"Again!" the Starstalker Captain ordered, banking and coming about.

Commander Wahll followed closely, loyal and intense.

The _Tikrek_ and the _Razorhawk_ struck the massive enemy from another angle, pulling it in that direction. They turned to flee, giving the _Saber_ an open shot at the side of the bridge. Carver flew into position and let off three missiles, his last, then banked away.

The _Leviathan_ death ship jolted from one end to the other as the projectile explosives blew three quarters of the bridge into oblivion. Several other compartments erupted in billowing flame and the long starship shuddered in flight. It then seemed to stall. Lights all along the body dimmed.

"What did I tell you?" howled Alexi Carver. "I love being right!"

"It's not down, yet," Jon Kett answered.

Just as he said it, the enemy ship blasted an onslaught of energy at the _Razorhawk_ and the _Tikrek_. Both ships' shielding lit up brightly but their energy levels did not drop.

"Rule…"

"I saw it, Jon," David Rule transmitted. "That thing's power levels are very weak! I believe now is the time!"

With that, the other fighters acknowledged and all redirected for an attack run on the giant serpent. Before they could get another run under way, however, another starship entered the arena.

"Fire!" Commander Lorrayanka roared from her bridge.

The *Ferali 5* appeared from the cold cloudbanks, seventy-five percent of its weapons blazing. Close by, the stolen *Razorwing*, under the command of Grockforth, added its firepower to the fray.

The serpentine enemy jerked and twisted. Its metals screamed, its innards burned. Pieces began to fall from the sky to the cold entombment they would find on the planet below.

A roar of success, a scream of victory, went up from the living in their scattered ships.

A roar of dismay, a scream of anguish, went up into the ceiling of the central room. Even the echo was bloodcurdling.

"What was that?" demanded Grundy, his double ended halberd in his hands. He crouched, ready to charge. In warning, he snorted, blowing the little hairs on his horn.

"Easy," the younger Ridge calmed. He made a fist of each hand, charging the neuropulsar bracers. "Pap?"

The older Ridge looked over his shoulder at the other two. He stood out in front of them with the sweeper.

"That's the raw, mechanical cry of the Psiborn. Voice amplification. I'm betting it's the Psiborg himself, Riker. Sounds mighty unhappy."

The trio pressed beyond several rows of parts and equipment on shelves taller than any of them. The room was poorly lit compared to the rest of the building and shadows crept around every corner and every aisle. A long few moments passed as they wound their way to the central point of the chamber, the metal rafters and ceiling invisible in the dimness.

All the while, the voice that had cried out so hollowly whined and wept in the distance.

They exited the shelving maze and sidled alongside each other, finally facing the center of the round room. What they saw was not only surprising but disgusting.

In the center of the circular room waited a highly technical reproduction of the bridge of the *Leviathan*. There were no walls, of course, but there was an elevated platform with the Captain's command seat in the middle of it all, with a replication of each system's post and console used by the bridge Officers. At each position, awaiting orders at each post, a dead Psiborn body occupied the seat allocated to them...

...and each one was wired into the consoles like another piece of technology. Most of them were more technology than flesh, so tied to the systems that they had become the systems themselves. The only one that seemed alive at all was the Captain, the man called the Psiborg.

Andreas Riker.

Rebellion leader. Insurrection upstart. Wartime general.

Restrained, wired up, captive...all but a zombie himself. His gray skin looked like death already; his white eyes belied his last remnants of life. The tear running down his emaciated cheek gave testament to the last of his emotions.

He whimpered.

"You..." his voice gurgled, his mouth unmoving. The voice was strained and broken though it carried over the com system in the room.

"He..." Grundy rumbled brokenly.

"He's part of this system. He's less flesh than ever," said the older Ridge, blanched by the nightmarish vision.

Gideon stepped a bit beyond the other two.

"Andreas Riker?" he asked firmly.

"Was... Now..." the mechanical voice crackled.

Veins stretched against the leathery gray flesh in Riker's neck. White eyes, bulging, ran tears.

A glance around the mock bridge showed a terrible fact. All the once living Psiborn, taken over and absorbed by the consoles and systems, had fully died. No life at all glimmered from the technorganisms. No fleshly life and no mechanical life. The lights were out at each station. The power was down. No one was left other than Riker.

Grundy and the Ridges had no idea that the assault on the real bridge of the *Leviathan*, in the ice cold air of Dor Modo, had expended what was left of the bridge crew's lives.

All except for Riker. Captain. Captive. A piece of the technology.

"You're done, Riker. It's over. The others..."

"They're dead, Psiborg," Pap interrupted his boy. "Not like there's much left of you. But they're gone completely. It's done."

The corpse with the wires and the glowing eyes shifted his gaze to the older man. His mouth twitched, his throat tensed. Instead of crying, however, the audio in the room let go of a maniacal laughter that chilled the raiders. Riker's mouth twitched with his laugh.

Grundy looked at Gideon. Gideon looked back at him. Look out, they told each other.

"Never. Never finished. Never free. Never loosed from the machines. Never dead!" the Psiborg howled in a shrill audio transmission. His eyes flashed.

Tearing free of the console wiring, the dead bridge Officers rose to their feet, fully undead, their technological sides fully expired. In their grasp were the bridge crew weapons they had once held at their stations on the ship.

The door behind the raiders swept open again, as well, the dead outside stumbling into the chamber.

"Pap, the door! Grundy, the right!" Gideon howled.

Above the chamber, in the dark of the metal rafters and ceiling, a small hatch slid to one side.

Gideon Ridge opened up the pulsar bands on the left side of the stumbling crew. The stuns that had previously worked so well faltered; the dead seemed stronger in the chamber. Several returned fire and a blast tore into Gideon Ridge at his lower right side, sending him to the floor.

The sweeper still made dust and memories of the dead, however, and Pap put the weapon to devastating purpose. He blasted group after group that poured into the rearward door.

Grundy charged with his halberd and struck one Officer's body, snapping it into pieces. He hit the following one with the same results then began to work his way across the right side of the bridge. Several blasts struck him, however, slowing him, yet he fought on.

Suddenly, a whizzing sound of friction sang from the rafters. Down thin cords, supplied by their gauntlets in tight, mechanized coils, the Acolytes dropped at a controlled rate from the high, distant ceiling.

Candri Prentice was the first to hit her feet, her whip charged and flying. Paola Kett was second, her staves lit and striking. Jaka Baddenide hit last and he ignored the room's Officers. He ran to the aide of Pap Ridge whom he found reloading, about to be overrun.

The Bridge Officers leveled weaponry on the newcomers but never got off a shot.

One blast barked from the rafters. Then another. And another. Zeckinbridge, Brent and Patrick rained energy shots down into the encroaching dead from the open hatch.

Pap had reloaded by then and Jaka Baddenide had to leap out of the way. Pap cleared the doorway again, jacked the empty cartridge free and chambered another.

Grundy reached Kett and Prentice with Gideon Ridge under an arm, all the remaining bridge Officers in pieces or downed by the Acolyte weapons. The team turned to view the doorway. Pap already had it clear.

Grundy turned back toward the Captain...the captive.

"It ends now!" Grundy roared in warning.

Burned spots on his torso and one leg still smoldered in the halflight but he seemed oblivious. It took more than burns from sidearm blasters to drop a Rothidai, or even get through their hide, for that matter.

A dimness veiled the light in Riker's eyes as the glow diminished. His body quaked then the flat eyes were only, for lack of a better term, human.

"Run..." he begged over the transmitter com.

The raiders looked at each other, uncertain of the moment.

"Let me down. I wanna be on my feet for this," Gideon said to his friend.

He braced an arm against his side wound but squeezed both hands and lit both bracers.

A pop and a crackle sounded, followed by a fluid ignition of black flame. It came to life directly in front of the command seat, the air itself suddenly burning with blackness. Taking a shape a lot like a doorway to some unmentionable place, the black fire swirled and fed upon itself for a long moment...then a shape walked out of the burning dark.

Andreas Riker, or what was left of him, began to cry.

The raiders prepped in fighting stances.

The fire lessened, burning more on the figure and dying out in the background.

"What..." Grundy started.

The figure was taller than the Rothidai.

Pap raised his sweeper.

"Don't matter what. Same methods of stopping it."

The figure, a blur hiding within the dark fire, cleared as if coming into focus through a hazy lens. The flame popped and sizzled and coursed over the ominous form but lessened. As it waned, it began to take a particularly discernible shape and design.

Paola Kett, studious and scholarly Acolyte, named it for the others.

"It is a Fallen," she growled, her lip snarling. "From the early beginnings of time..."

The shape stomped forward, hidden completely in armor pieces forged of black flame. It fluidly flickered like flame but held the iron look of armor in ebony casting. From helmet, with spikes, to stomping boots, a flaming suit of armor with spikes here and there tromped forward another few steps.

"A what?" Grundy pressed, swinging his halberd about.

Jaka Baddenide yipped with laughter. He strode to the front of the raiders, clacking his arcing staff on the floor.

"An evil spirit, big man. A foul death dealer," Jaka chuckled.

Grundy looked to Gideon, who stood close to Candri Prentice.

"A demon, my large friend," Candri gave Grundy the answer.

"One of the original fallen angels," Jaka grinned and looked about.

"What's so funny?" Grundy demanded.

"I've been whipping evil's butt a long time," Jaka said. "Feeding the oppressed, helping the downtrodden, reaching out to the lost. But this is the first time I've had the chance to do it literally, in the flesh!"

A wretched, grating howl, low and vibrating in the floor plates, ripped the air. The stink of death filled the area. Then black fire exploded out of the creature's form and flooded the chamber. Lost within a searing wave of black flame were all the raiders.

The chamber filled with the fire as the Psiborg screamed.

Around the globe of Dor Modo, the ragtag ships of the dead plummeted to the planet's surface. Some of the living thought it was the defeat of the big serpentine ship that had dropped the power to the rest of the bone starmada. Others thought the raiders had accomplished their goal already. Though no one knew the truth, that the raiders were temporarily distracting the source of the evil, it mattered not to the defenders. Depowered ships in the atmosphere of Dor Modo dropped like stones. The fleets still outside the biting atmosphere and winds of the planet simply stalled in space and floated, dead to the defenders.

In truth, they were stalled but not ended.

Blowing into parts and pieces as it fell, however, was the *Leviathan*. It would be lost again, Dor Modo claiming it in icy finality. The dragon would not rise again.

Captain Garriton was praying to Jesus Christ that would not be her fate and that of her crew. She clutched the Holy Bible Gideon had given her and squeezed her eyes closed as the bridge crew called out the failing systems and the lack of power.

What could she do? The ship was finished. They were falling for what might be the last time. Would they all die on Dor Modo? Her chest ached and her breath froze inside her. No, she told herself. No. There was an answer. A way out.

She prayed all the more that Jesus Christ would reveal it to her. If there was a miracle to be had, she knew it would come from Him. She had heard that in her youth. It was from God that all true blessings flow.

She considered Gideon Ridge a blessing in himself. She had been blessed to have met him. She had been blessed to have spent time with him. She opened his Bible again and read another passage as the ship continued to fall.

"Captain!" someone urged but she was not listening.

Another echoed the sentiment.

The Captain silently prayed, answering no one.

The other ships realized the *Bloodwind*'s predicament. Each had turned and plotted a course for the falling starship. Enemy ships fell all about them, streaking for the surface of the planet, and each of the living allies desperately wanted to stop Samara Garriton and her crew from sharing that fate.

The last thing any of them expected was a sudden recovery of power by the seemingly defeated starmada of bones. Nevertheless, all across the atmosphere, all around the orbit of the planet and all over surrounding space, enemy ships powered up one more time. Lights came on, engines whined, weapons charged.

A falling Chabron freighter, armed to the teeth, lit up just after dropping right by the living. It turned in the rapid descent, unable to get its engines to engage but managing to angle itself to face the living. It released every torpedo it carried as it disappeared into the mists.

Fifteen Warrant Strikers plumed exhaust en route to the Acolytes and their allied companions, ripping the air and the cold of Dor Modo like slicing through cream; a zig here, a zag there, always straightening up.

Warnings blared in each cockpit of the living, their sensors screaming at them to take evasive action.

Other death ships began pursuit as well, not to mention the rallying of forces from outside the atmosphere.

Our edge is over. The sheer number will finally take its toll. I can handle this part, though, Alexi Carver thought.

He rolled his ship about to face the coming strike, armed everything he had left and threw open his throttle.

"*Saber*, come about!" David Rule demanded. "Everyone else, split!"

Two Tresslan fighter ships, occupied by the dead and trailing parts, swept into the path of the oncoming Warrant Strikers while attempting to pursue those still alive. Both of them were utterly obliterated by two of the projectiles. The same happened with a Ton B'Gru starfighter, a Migroid freighter and a rickety old earth transport.

"Five down already," Carver sang from his fighter. "Here we go!"

"Alexi, no!" Rule shouted.

On board the *Ferali 5*, there were other concerns.

"Commander, we are in range!" the Pilot said to Lorrayanka.

"Engage!" she roared, her fangs showing.

Her crew had pursued the dropping *Bloodwind* straight down into the deeper atmosphere. They were visually blind in the mist and icy winds but Lorrayanka would never let up.

Her Weapons Officer engaged their graviton beam by instrumentation guidance. Immediately the ship snatched about and seemed to drop faster. They had gone fishing in the dark and caught an awfully big fish.

"Reverse! Full reverse, now!" Lorrayanka howled, strapping herself into her station.

"These engines were not meant to carry two ships, at length, in an atmosphere, Commander! Holding the gravitational pull of two-"

"Unless you have a solution, do not present me a problem!" she warned her on-bridge Engineer. "Full reverse and hold until we start to rise! Or, at least, until we stop dropping!"

The power systems raged and the ship bucked and shimmied violently. Several pressure lines blew apart on the bridge overhead; the Commander wondered how many would be blowing apart all over the ship. Process fluids and steam sprayed across the bridge.

"Winds!" she howled.

Wastasa Winds ran from one console to the next, clearly frazzled.

"You got one of me, woman! Yellin' doesn't speed me up, either!"

Lorrayanka clenched her teeth.

Captain Samara Garriton and her crew climbed up from the floors of the *Bloodwind*. They had not come to a stop, of course, but a jolt had greatly slowed them, throwing at least the whole bridge crew from their seats.

"Graviton beam," Respra told his Captain with a hesitant smile. "The Starstalker carrier is transmitting; they have us in a graviton beam."

"We haven't stopped," Science Officer Boatwright said darkly. "Their engines won't be able to hold us both off the surface. We were already dropping at such a great rate…"

"Momentum," Retaw whispered.

Momentum, in flight…

At that moment, the Captain had a flash of the Scripture she had read. It had been the Book of Isaiah, Chapter Forty, Verse Thirty-one.

"But those who wait on the Lord Shall renew *their* strength; They shall mount up with wings like eagles…" she whispered aloud.

Her eyes sparkled and she thanked Jesus Christ for the answer.

"We need wings!" she shouted at the crew.

Several of them jumped, startled.

"Boatwright, can you manipulate our graviton beam?" she pressed.

"Yes, it's pretty versatile," he answered. "But, with all the systems failing, I don't even know if I can get it online, much less do much-"

"Mr. Respra, do we still have Communications?" she interrupted.

The Jamaican Officer tilted his head and chuckled warily.

"I don't want to brag, Captain, but I'm the one system you've had the whole time."

"You're going to make one more transmission and shut it down," she said.

"What?" he protested.

"Mr. Boatwright, when he signs off and shuts his station down, I want all that power relayed to the graviton beam!" she proceeded, not listening to any protest.

"I don't know if-"

"It's not a question, Boatwright!" she barked. Then she looked back to Respra. "Tell the *Ferali 5* to cut us loose, fly out level with us, recapture us, then pour on all the speed they can! Horizontally! Horizontal to the ground!"

"We'll still drag them down-" Boatwright started.

"They won't have to stop us! You're going to spread out our graviton beam, disperse its energy patterns and reverse the polarity! It won't pull toward us, it'll push against us! And make it just as wide as you can, Boatwright!"

"To catch as much as wind as possible!" Pilot Retaw shouted, his face beaming. He was nodding emphatically. "Wings! She wants you to make wings, Boatwright!"

Science Officer Boatwright had no time for agreement, nor did he have it for disagreement. Garriton immediately spun back to Respra and told him to make the transmission, which meant Boatwright had to jump into modifying the graviton beam systems without any conversation.

"Commander Lorrayanka," the Communications Officer started over on the *Ferali 5*, "Captain Garriton says she has an idea."

He then relayed the plan.

Commander Lorrayanka agreed, though she was somewhat afraid it would lose the *Bloodwind*, which she said aloud to her bridge.

"Commander, it isn't any worse than where you are now," Wastasa Winds said, joining Boatwright at his station. "If you keep on like you are, you're going to burn out your own engines and then we'll all fall."

Lorrayanka ground her teeth together and sliced the padding of her chair with her claws.

"Do it!" she roared.

Meanwhile, Alexi Carver held his energy weapons at the maximum spread on his flight toward the Warrant Strikers. Two then two more then three more after those were struck and destroyed in the air. Carver swept his nimble *Saber* in and out of the Strikers as if they were floating still.

Three remained and soared by him. He was unable to stop them all.

"Heads up, people," he transmitted. "I knew they couldn't get me but three managed to get by me. Keep your eyes open and dodge those last three."

He was already banking to come about when Rule corrected him.

"It's not us they're after," he said. "Not anymore! You engaged them! They have an artificial intelligence! They hunt anything that takes down even one of them in flight! I tried to warn you, to get you to just let them miss us all...now you have to run from them, Alexi!"

Carver's sensor warnings became very loud. He turned about just in time to see on his screens three approaching signals. When he broke off to one side, his stabilizers whined. He turned so sharply that three warning buzzers involving fluids and coolants lit his display. Two of the Strikers ripped by him, streaking through his exhaust plume, while one whisked by him, just barely missing his nose.

This should be interesting, he sighed inside his head.

"No worries," Carver transmitted with a chuckle. "I got this-"

"Alexi!" Jon Kett howled.

Carver went up with his ship in a furious rage of flame and smoke. The first redirected missile had returned and blistered him on contact.

Multiple allies wailed at his fall.

David Rule called them down, however, telling them to focus.

Commander Wahll, within his Hunon *Jokra* Interceptor, vied for the squadron's focus.

"Allies, look at the skies!" he transmitted in his heavy accent.

The squadron had been pursuing their two starships. From time to time, they blasted death ships from the air, defending their two bigger, busy starships. Other times they flew into a group of approaching ships of the dead and led them away. The *Bloodwind* and the *Ferali 5* had too much to manage already; they did not want, nor did they need, attackers.

However, as Wahll cried out to them, each looked up to the skyline and fell silent. They would not be able to protect the ships much longer.

They were facing the arrival of the starmada of bones...in force.

Across the skyline, as far as the sensor banks could read, ships filed into the atmosphere in a swarm. They came on like a massive cloud, the kind of black cloud created by volcanic disasters, covering half of a world at the time.

"There's nothing more we can do," Rule told the rest. "Turn, flee this place. There's no way we can turn aside the flood of the starmada. All of you go. I will fly after the starships to see if there is anything I can do."

They tried to argue it but Rule shouted them down. Eventually, they turned their ships for space and slammed their throttles to the backstop.

All fled, except Captain Prentia and her *Moonscar*.

"I will help you aide the *Bloodwind*," she transmitted. She swept alongside Rule. "After all, my own ship is with her. I will see the *Ferali 5* to her end."

"Prentia, please," he started.

"Rule, I can no more leave now than you can."

Rule almost argued but his words would have fallen on deaf ears.

In the distance, the two allied starships had changed their angles. The Starstalker ship had begun pulling their ally horizontal to the ground. That ally, Captain Garriton's ship, had managed to shape wings from the force projectors in the graviton beam assembly. Their nose had risen until their ship was level to the ground, too, no longer falling. Slowly, they even began to rise.

On the bridge of the *Ferali 5*, only two people spoke.

"I cannot believe it," Officer Xerstou muttered lowly.

Lorrayanka grinned over long fangs.

"It is working!" she roared.

There was shock on the bridge of the *Bloodwind*, too.

"It's working," Boatwright sighed. "Captain, it's working. I thought you were crazed but...you've saved your ship...and us."

"Wrong," she chimed happily, a wide and beautiful smile creasing her face. She lifted that Bible. "Jesus Christ did this. I was told to do this. I was given the inspiration! I had no clue..." Her eyes rolled tears downward over her face. "Praise God. Don't praise me, Boatwright. Praise God."

"Amen," said Reje Chu.

Retaw turned his seat around to the Captain.

"My systems are still down, Captain, but I have confirmed it by the manual gyroscopic display in my station; we have leveled off, apparently 'flying' behind the Starstalker ship. They are gradually applying more thrust and angling slowly upward, too. They're going to pull us out of the atmosphere and right into space if their engines can hold out."

Garriton leaned back in her seat. A deep breath later, she laughed softly.

"Take us home, Commander," she said to Lorrayanka, though the Commander could not hear it.

"Commander Lorrayanka," Xerstou called once again, "we will not be able to engage the enemy any more if you intend to be caretaker to the *Bloodwind*."

"Agreed," she said.

"The planet's skies are already black with death," he continued. "I recommend transferring all available power to the shields and expanding them to at least a deflecting level for their ship."

"Do it," Lorrayanka growled. "I hate to leave a battle but we cannot do much else. There are too many. If we would rescue our allies, we must flee. So...shields. Gradual increase in thrust. Take us away from here," she told the Pilot, "while we can still fly."

"I'll head back to your generator deck and see what more I can squeeze out of the shielding generators," Winds said with a wink at the Commander. "Might even sweet talk your engines. They need it."

"Transmission," the Communications Officer started. "It comes from the *Razorwing*."

"Open channel," Lorrayanka said.

"Starstalkers," the voice of Grockforth echoed over the bridge. "I am reading your intention. Shielding, no weapons. Towing that other ship. Moving for space."

"Yeah, the best we can, anyway, Rothidai," Wastasa Winds said.

"I am going to stay close to you. This *Razorwing* will be your weapons if anything gets too close."

"I don't know exactly what to say," the Commander said. "Thank you. You have been a most loyal ally."

"We have a lot of enemies between us and home, whatever home awaits. Do not thank me. Not yet; not until we are clear."

David Rule had earlier sent the *WildCard* to space, towing the *Raine*. The *Tikrek* and the *Jokra* had followed them when ordered to do so. The *Razorhawk* and the *Moonscar* rejoined the two starship carriers, one pulling the other, and their escort starfighter, the *Razorwing*. Together, reluctantly, they turned for open space and the stars.

"We are your escort," Rule called to the larger ships. "No matter what happens, keep on task. Get free of this place. We will hold the dead at bay."

The Starstalker vessel confirmed understanding, though the Commander did not like it. Running from a fight rubbed the mane on the back of her neck the wrong way.

"*Razorwing*, I will-" Rule had just begun when Captain Prentia howled an interruption.

"On your port side!" the *Moonscar* transmitted as Prentia yanked her controls about, energy spraying from her weapons systems.

An enemy ship appeared out of nothingness, streaking right between her ship and the *Razorhawk*'s port flanks, while another shot directly over them both. Her assault blasts chased after the latter, struck the tailshaft and the open exhaust port and destroyed it completely.

"Where did they come from?" shouted Rule.

The Ambassador opened his rapid fire weaponry and struck another ship down one side of its fuselage. It jerked and twisted and fell for the surface, crippled.

The enemies had simply appeared. They had not registered at all on scopes and they were sensor invisible, as well, until they simply popped into reach.

Prentia roared, her fur thick and her fangs long. Her blood was hot with the war. She banked about almost instantly, blasting a pair of fighters into steam and dust.

David Rule did the same thing, chasing the mindless assassins.

"Beware!" the Rothidai yelled, rolling into a spiral between the two veteran fighters.

The *Razorwing* unleashed a brutal, merciless onslaught of energy weaponry as he spun in his swirling flight path. Five undead fighters had flown out of the mists, appearing from nowhere, and had targeted the group. All five of them erupted under the attack of the Rothidai.

Rule fired his weapons again just as Prentia did, as well. More fighters exploded and disappeared back into nothingness.

"Success, Rule," Captain Prentia transmitted, relaxing a bit.

"And our thanks to you, *Razorwing*," Rule told Grockforth. "But the mystery remains; how did they just appear here, undetectable to systems and even to our own eyes?"

"Indeed," Prentia started. "I would have never-"

Abruptly, a massive starship materialized out of the mists and appeared on the fighters' sensor displays. Before Prentia could finish her thought, Rule and Grockforth were screaming for her to turn aside.

She never heard them. The *Moonscar* slammed into the starboard wing structure, an insect flying into a turbine blade. Her shields collapsed instantly and her ship folded like so much foil wadded in a child's hand.

The fire and explosion took the remains to oblivion.

Rule opened up all of his weapon banks and razed the bow of the big, Psiborn ghost ship. It shimmered and began to disappear again, cloaking device reengaging on the big fighter carrier.

"Rothidai, your part here is done! God Bless you!" Rule howled. "Now run! Take to space! I will lead this ghost away!"

The *Razorhawk* banked hard and ripped away. The Psiborn stalker gave chase; Grockforth watched the pattern of mists swirl in the air as the invisible hunter moved away.

Seconds away from ignoring the order, the Rothidai jolted in his seat and pitched to one side. An energy blast rattled his ship.

Over him flew two more fighters from the Psiborn carrier ship, a parting gift left behind. They continued beyond Grockforth, however, sights set on the struggling *Ferali 5* and the *Bloodwind*.

The Rothidai threw his throttle bar to the wall. In seconds he was on top of the two fighters. He unloaded on one of the fighters and tore it cleanly out of existence, barrel rolling to one side to avoid the scrap it left in his path. Then he fell in behind the other one and readied his assault, steadying his little fighter. His hand squeezed the trigger.

Nothing happened.

Dumbstruck, Grockforth squeezed the trigger mechanism again. Again, nothing happened. His readout indicated a power failure.

The Psiborn fighter reached weapons range and targeted the *Bloodwind*. Grockforth watched on his instrumentation as the enemy fighter armed four missiles. Again, he triggered his weapons.

Again, his readout indicated a power failure.

Nevertheless, his vow remained. He would aid the Starstalker efforts and their allies...even if it required his death. The Rothidai flipped open a cover and palmed the panel below it. Suddenly, power surged anew through the engine matrix and propelled the *Razorwing* forward at nearly twice his speed.

The use of reserve power for a fighter's sudden thrust of speed was not available on all light vessels. On the ones capable of it, it was called enacting the Afterglow Cells.

Grockforth had no weapons left but he had shields. Hoping they might hold, he let the Afterglow Cells shoot him like an arrow right through the fighter he pursued. The *Razorwing* tore it to shreds and ignited all four of its missiles before they could launch. They exploded in close proximity to the Rothidai and his little ship, throwing it into a massive spin. He fought for control of the *Razorwing*, streaking in a downward spiral for the frozen planet below him.

Smoke billowed from his port side as he finally fought the downward spin to level off. He attained level flight again but the damage was apparently very critical. Damage reports scrolled over his screens in long type. Shields were completely down. Percentages scrolled. One bank of engines was out. A depressing re-ignition time rolled by. Weapons systems had fused. Odds flashed one after another over his screens describing the likelihood he would ever get them back up and running. Hull integrity was at fourteen percent. It would be a stretch to get the little fighter to break the planet's gravitational pull without compromising the fuselage and life support.

No shields. No weapons. Half engines. Ravaged hull. Still, as he watched the two ally ships lifting away, he nodded and smiled to himself.

"Make your run, my friends," he transmitted. Then even his communication array sparked and failed.

He took great comfort from the view of the escaping allies as his engines fizzled out finally and died. They stalled and the *Razorwing* began to fall.

Though the *Ferali 5* called out to him time and again, he could not receive it. Away he fell into mist, ice and into a legend of whom songs would be composed, songs about honor and loyalty.

Far across the frozen skies, the *Razorhawk* had narrowly escaped a similar end. David Rule's ship was painted with burns and buckled plates and the front cockpit screen was spiderwebbed. The Psiborn carrier had been too much for one fighter but, just before delivering a final barrage, it had turned and started up out of the atmosphere. Rule's scopes told him the other ships in the death fleet were doing likewise.

"They retreat back to space." David nodded to himself, whispering, "Thank you, Jesus."

He continued to track the fleet and their course but did not like what he saw on the other side of them. The bone starmada, gathered in force, waited for something. It was more than immense. It was galactic.

Rule dropped power to his weapons and several other systems, trying to eke out enough energy to bolster his shields and his engines. Then he pointed his nose for space.

It was a short time between breaking the atmosphere and rejoining all the ships that had fled the planet. They had all gathered close to each other, waiting...

...waiting to see what the thousands and thousands of derelict, dead flown starships of the bone starmada would do. They made a barrier, a wall, in space and waited. On what, none of them knew.

The sensors in the *Razorhawk* had shown the oncoming storm clearly enough. Nothing was like seeing with the eye, however.

He liked the view less in person.

Rule joined the tiny squadron of allies where it faced a wall of dead.

The *Ferali 5*, the *Bloodwind* and the *Razorhawk* drifted, close together. The *WildCard*, the *Raine* and the *Tikrek* floated in a three point formation. The *Jokra* waited alone. The weight of all the ships and pilots they had lost settled onto their shoulders.

A chorus of welcome embraced Rule, but he could not help responding by asking the question all considered giving life.

"Why are the dead all facing the other way?"

"I think they fear us," the Hunon, Commander Wahll, offered in jest.

"They should," Samara Garriton replied, her communications repaired. "The *Bloodwind* still flies and, while she does, she fights!"

Several of the allied ships offered up a rallying cry, too.

One by one, group by group, squadron by squadron, the engines and weapons of the bone starmada began to warm and charge for battle.

"You think they heard you?" Respra asked Garriton on their bridge.

"Wait," one of the other allies called. "I'm reading something…"

"Me, too," another said. "I think it's a-"

"Lightspeed distortion?" another called excitedly.

Without warning, a break in space occurred on the other side of the starmada wall. It was not just one break, either. One was answered by another and another and multiple more. All along the battlefront made by the undead ships, space pulled itself apart, energy arcing from one point of distortion to another. Light flared here and there and the swirl of great power appeared.

Then they appeared. The races of the living.

Ship after ship, carrier after carrier, fighter after fighter. Hundreds of them. Some wore the USAP markings. Others wore independent world colors. Others still wore no alliance markings at all. Battalion after squadron after single battleship broke from lightspeed, materializing in the arena to face the starmada of bones, their weapons at the ready. Countless fighters, as far as the sensors could read, peppered space with light...and hope.

Without hesitation, they immediately unleashed the entire array of their weaponry, the battle engaged before they were even in the field of combat. Ships reaching well over five hundred strong, not to even begin counting fighter ships, unloaded on the bone starmada.

The destruction was massive.

Of course, the bone starmada was awakened and the war began, volleys launched from and received by each side.

"Are there enough to stop it?" someone transmitted.

"No," Rule answered flatly. "But there are enough to hold it for just a while longer...hopefully just long enough."

"If you want to survive, make for the other side of the dead!" Captain Samara Garriton transmitted. "We're behind enemy lines; no matter how the battle goes, we have no allied forces over here!"

Her ship still had no directional power. Only when the *Ferali 5* surged ahead did Garriton's ship move; they were still being towed. Under their own steam or towed by a friend, however, all the allies made for the other side, trying to survive as they passed through the expanse.

Sundar Ridge smiled that rueful, sarcastic, half grin his nephew had inherited so honestly. He traipsed to the bottom of his landing ramp.

"Come on out, Sparky," he grumbled, peeking around the landing formation. "I mean, I should've known. Nobody gets rid of a pest like you so easy. Like cockroaches, you slickers. Just won't die."

"You," the newcomer groaned. "The old man, Sundar Ridge."

"Right the first time," Sundar Ridge hissed.

His weapon lay across his arms like an old world shotgun would have across the arms of a frontier town's defending sheriff.

"The old man who gave me this," she snarled.

Cheyenne Winds pointed to her own face and the abrasion left by Sun's rifle strike, from the last time they had met. Her slicker gloves glowed with a blue current much like her own biocharge, glowing in her hair.

"What's wrong, Winds?" Ridge barked. "Miss me? Get lonely, all by yourself, floatin' in space?"

"No, I just came to correct a mistake," she almost purred.

"Yeah? Do tell."

"I shot the wrong raggedy, broken down scarecrow of a man on that station," she taunted.

Sun Ridge's smirk shrank and faded completely. One eyebrow arched sharply, the opposite eye squinting.

"That's a true statement if I ever heard one," he growled. "Problem is, how do ya fix somethin' like that?"

"You go kill the one you should have."

She pressed her left fingers between her right, tightening the right slicker glove, then tightened the left glove using her right fingers.

"Seems to me that doesn't work all the way around."

She took her turn at being coy.

"Oh? Do tell," she said and shrugged.

Arcing blue energy linked her thumbs and forefingers.

"No matter what you do, Sparky, you can't bring Gill Bardoff back."

She cackled like a lunatic, gesturing about herself wildly.

"Do you really believe I came all this way for you, old man? Do you think you would be worth half the trouble I had tracking the *Spoken Word* into the Reaches? Do you actually think I would trade one set of bones for another? Old man, you aren't even a flicker in the flame!"

She started toward him only to stop again immediately.

He had leveled his rifle at her.

"How did you track us, Winds? I mean, you should enjoy this conversation. I don't see many in your future. Take your time."

"I have to thank Rala Kess, first," she said with a false smile.

"So, you're here with that reptile," he surmised, inconspicuously glancing here and there from the corners of his eyes. "May as well get the merc out here, now."

"Rala Kess was in no condition to come with me, not that he would have been bold enough, anyway. I am afraid the Reaches are not for everyone. Besides, he was broken up pretty badly by my Rothidai and that's saying a lot. Vipon bones don't break easily, all that gristle and the joints and-"

"Get on with it," Sundar Ridge said.

"All of you flew away and I scrambled for a ship," she said simply. "I happened across the one Rala Kess had landed on after Grockforth knocked him into orbit. He was begging me to take him to safety, I asked what it was worth and he said the most beautiful words I had heard..."

Sun Ridge glanced about again and eased back up onto the ramp.

"Like?"

"He said he had a masked transponder, a signal transmitter-"

"I know what they are, Sunshine," Sun said.

She giggled and cracked an arc of energy from her glove into the air.

"He said he had placed one right in the *Word* while they were inside it. When my father slicked into the loading bay Rala Kess was with him but they agreed Kess and the Hunon would pull back. They followed Wastasa's lead and only he stayed aboard...he and the transponder Rala Kess placed, of course. True to form, Rala Kess kept that secret to himself. Just in case. Then I came along and he promised to give me the coding and the frequencies of the transponder."

"Nice story. Too bad there's no way a handheld transponder could-"

She giggled, stroking her slicker gloves.

"I just adjusted the communications system in the fighter we stole-"

"There's no way such a short range-" Uncle Sun started again.

"-then dropped Rala Kess into an escape pod and I let the slicker daddy made of me do the work."

Her eyes were murderous. Rage peered from within their light.

"All the way here..." Sun Ridge muttered.

"All the way here. Of course, even I can't work miracles. I had to keep the fighter in reasonable range. Not that hard to do, all things taken into account," she mused aloud, stepping to her left, toward the ship.

"I suppose not, since you made it here," he said, sounding bored.

"I slipped into the debris fields here and there and killed the power whenever possible until the *Word* shot into the Reaches. I gave distant pursuit, hiding in the densest of the nebula formations, using a program of my own that tracks and semi-autopilots...all in all, I'm good, Ridge. Very, very good."

321

"Well, even if nobody else is ever proud of you, Princess, you sound proud enough of yourself for everybody."

She shrugged, adding, "I am what I am. I even landed far enough beyond the ridges back there to be just so much more static on your sensors. Then I started walking. Sorry I'm late to the party. It was nice of you to wait for me. Now, where's daddy?"

"You made a real effort, Cheyenne," he said with a nod, "comin' all this way...just to get shut down. Figured I ought to at least greet you since Wastasa couldn't be here to do it."

"Where's my father, old man?" she demanded suddenly.

"Out of reach," he said.

"Poor old Ridge," she muttered venomously. "Didn't Wastasa ever tell you not to let a slicker get to close to...your ship?" she shouted and suddenly lunged forward.

Her glowing hands reached for the underside of the *Belly Rub*.

Sundar Ridge fired into her agile form with extreme prejudice. He hit her five times from the time she jumped and the time she reached the *Rub*. She twisted and spun about in the air, shrieking, but still reached the underside of the ship with the glowing slicker gloves.

A brightly colored energy discharged from her hands. Electrically it arced down the underbelly of the ship, the landing gear and the metal loading ramp.

Sun Ridge jumped about wildly, caught in the arcing power.

He grabbed at his left arm which simply would not stop twitching and aching as if impaled. He tried to take a deep breath but could not. Then he stumbled, clutching at his arm, first, until grabbing his chest on the way to the decking.

He toppled over onto his back and stared at the underbelly.

"Tick tock, old Sun," he whispered to himself.

He clutched his chest at his heart and closed his eyes.

The new battle began without a precursory warning, an arrogant transmission or a volley of warning blasts over someone's bow...it just exploded into action, much like the spatial charges launched into the mix. One moment, silent brooding came from the massive bone starmada. The next moment, the dead were moving faster than ever and all the ships inhabited by the living found themselves fighting for survival.

The Starstalker carrier, Samara Garriton's Unity ship in tow, propelled across the gap between the warring forces like a blur. To be caught would be destruction and the Starstalker Commander, Lorrayanka, was having none of it.

Samara Garriton had her Communications Officer issuing a widespread, encoded communiqué to the races of the living continuously, informing them of the restrictions on communication. The dead have a weapon, they were shouting at the newcomers. Protect yourselves from the death song.

Unity Reapers engaged the dead. The ships of the dead rattled the defenses of the gathered independent fleets. Independents rallied to the challenge, only to see Unity ships aflame in the midst of it all. Death… offspring of the dead, carried like a disease.

And it was spreading.

The veterans, those who still had weapons online, tried to fight but they did so from the fringes. Most of the ships in the engagement were far larger and more powerful on both sides. The ragtag survivors fought from sneak attacks and hit-and-run vantage points, doing their best to survive what could be the last battle…or just the last battle for them.

Their ships razed and fried, with missing hull plates and flickering shields, David Rule and his *Razorhawk* led Jon Kett and his *Tikrek*, along with Commander Wahll and his Hunon Interceptor, the *Jokra*, into guerrilla raids against the enemy fleet.

Still alive but out of commission, ordered to make for safer space, flew Rabeau Loist and his *WildCard*, towing Taelynn Berreaux in her *Raine*. They will survive to tell the story, David Rule thought quietly even as he fired on another enemy. They will carry on for all of us, no matter what happens.

Still the battle raged. Across the engagement, ships on both sides exploded and burned. The dead were destroyed as some of the living became the dead. The cycle was hideous that way…

"…and it was all a part of a plan," a grating, churning, rumble of a voice thundered in the interior chamber. "The dead make more dead and an army grows."

Pure evil radiated from the black figure, body parts shaped like armor and trickling black, liquid flame from every joint. The spikes all over it steamed in the air and smoke rose from it. The masked face bore only glowing yellow eyes as features and they burned with hatred for the living. The hate was much stronger after the black flames had hurt no one, to the demon's disbelief.

Afterward, for whatever reason, the creature had been making a speech about the evil from the ancient times but it was not worth noting. The creature was full of lies like all evil had always been.

"Evil, shut up," growled Grundy. "Enough of you."

"The voice," Andreas Psiborg Riker tried to say, his face twitching, sending his voice by transmission in the room's audio amplification. His grayed eyes widened as his throat tightened. "That voice in the chaos…"

"All it can do is be a voice," Paola Kett said flatly. "It had no idea it would face a band of beings inhabited by the Spirit of God. The dark fires of the shadow have no power over any of us."

"Acolyte…" the creature growled lowly.

Floor panels vibrated in the rumbling.

"That's why it's biding time, making speeches," Jaka Baddenide sneered.

"Silence!" it bellowed and the room quaked.

Candri Prentice laughed.

"It knew from the moment the fire didn't hurt any of us. Any supernatural power it might still possess is worthless, powerless-"

"Stop it!" the thing bellowed again.

"-against sentient beings with Christ in their lives, their hearts," Gideon Ridge said. "It is powerless against Jesus," he smiled. "Powerless against those who belong to Christ."

"I do not require any Blackfire, any of the flame of death, to destroy ants like you!" it roared wildly. "I can crush-"

"You are nothing more than a whisperer, an influencer!" Paola Kett shouted. "You are no warrior demon, just as I suspect you weren't a warrior Angel! You are a Fallen but your only remaining power is in suggestion! Those who will not listen to you, those strong enough to ignore you and those who have Christ are immune to your 'power'…if it can be called such."

An open fist lifted high materialized a sword of black flame just as a shield of it materialized on the opposite forearm.

"I was once an Angel! My physiology is still superior to any!"

Grundy snorted and huffed angrily, "We'll see."

Riker moaned, "Why didn't you run…any of you…why?"

The demon roared in a gurgling howl. Into the door to the outer chambers flooded a horde of the dead, rudimentary hand weapons taken up from loose equipment and tools.

Pap Ridge spun about and blasted a whole wave of the corpse army.

Still in the rafters, the Unity soldiers showered the oncoming mass with precise bolts of energy that dropped them in their tracks.

Candri Prentice ignited her whips and began to crack them around the demon when Grundy charged it, Jaka Baddenide right beside him.

Gideon Ridge saw the bigger picture, realizing Paola Kett saw it also. She broke into a run up the bridge section of the chamber for Andreas Riker with Gideon Ridge not far behind.

Grundy drove himself into the demon, his horn piercing the unreal shield and the thing's arm. The crash slammed the creature back into the closest wall and the shield arm flew wide. The shield flipped end over end into the air, fading from the material dimension until it was entirely gone, disappearing into thin air.

Enraged, the howling, corporeal spirit charged back at Grundy. It took a handful of steps only, however. One of the whips of Candri Prentice lashed about its legs and tangled them together and down the big creature went.

Jaka Baddenide flipped through the air and came down in reach of it. His arcing staff drove mercilessly down into the creature's head with the sound of thunder. The wild arc of electricity from the staff, running over the head and shoulders of the creature, grounded into the floor plates.

It raged to its feet and shook its head wildly. A split was visible in the black, fiery helmet while one of the yellow eyes split and blackened. That one eye glowed all the more.

It charged Baddenide, sword lifted in approach. Jaka bounded away from it, fast and deft in his evasion. The one swipe the creature did try met with futility as Candri Prentice lashed the thing's wrist and stopped the sword arm still. Wild electricity arced down the arm and into the whole form.

The thing tried to pull away but Grundy slammed into it anew. Instead of striking head first he swept into the creature with a brutal swipe of his halberd. Candri Prentice let go as the thing flew backward into a wall of observational equipment, destroying the gear completely.

"How dare you-" it raged, pulling itself up.

Jaka Baddenide was on it again, however. His staff struck the thing's knees, wobbling the legs, then struck the sword hand, the throat and the head once more in a flurry of swirling attacks.

Again it went down.

Paola Kett had run directly to the area where Andreas Riker had been nearly consumed by the nearby interfaces. She had begun unplugging part of the wiring that tied Riker to the consoles and stations about him.

"I can't get this one," Kett said to Gideon Ridge as he ran up behind her.

Her gauntlet projected a hologram of an analytical wiring diagram which she reviewed between unplugging wires from the man.

"Stop! What are you doing?" Riker asked in his alarmed daze.

"We're freeing you, Riker," Ridge answered, grasping the coil Kett had been pulling.

"Whether you like it or not," the young Acolyte muttered.

"You cannot...do not...I cannot...must...not..." Riker muttered.

Gideon Ridge pulled free one of the main interface coils. It tore roughly from the man's neck and a putrid, pungent, greenish brown fluid sprayed from the interface jack.

For the first time since the raiders' arrival, Riker's face moved more than a twitch. His mouth twisted into a grimace. The gray eyes even fluttered.

"No...you must not...the crew...they will die..."

"They've been dead," Kett corrected, taking Riker's head, his face, into her hands.

Ridge grabbed onto another coil, one that lanced into the man's right temple and braced his other hand on the side of the man's head. Paola Kett burrowed into Riker's dead eyes with her own bright blue orbs.

"Your crew has been dead a very long time. Only your machines were keeping them in a form of stasis, keeping their bodies from decaying, but their lives were gone long ago."

Riker exclaimed in pain when Ridge pulled free the temple cable.

"Not true..." his raspy, strained voice insisted. His words did not transmit over the audio systems in the room. "They were alive...until your people...killed..."

"No, Andreas," Kett corrected gently.

"Your ships...killed them..." he insisted again. "Destroying the... Leviathan...destroyed them...the voice told me..."

Gideon Ridge tore free a major cable and Riker convulsed. Then Andreas Riker screamed.

The evil in the room had just shoved Grundy away. Riker's scream spun the dark thing around. It started for Riker but those engaging it in combat were far from finished.

Prentice lashed its legs together again, stopping it cold. It reached downward to grab at the energy whip and the other whip wrapped about its groping hand and pulled it back to one side.

The black creature roared and raised the flame sword for a strike down on the whip. Jaka struck it a solid jab with the end of the staff in the small of its back, right in the spine. The thing arched its back and Baddenide struck again, his flurry of spinning staff attacks bludgeoning the creature's head, knees and sword hand.

The sword flipped from its grip, fading from existence.

"Back, you tiny-" it railed angrily but Grundy cut it off.

The massive halberd came crashing down on the thing's helmet and a shower of fiery coals exploded from it. The helmet was no more, a cloud of black dust smoking from the head in its stead. The creature folded at the knees and went to the ground.

Andreas Riker blinked rapidly for a moment then focused on Paola's beautiful eyes.

"They…were dead…all this time…"

"Right," Kett answered. "You've been tricked, Riker. By an evil spirit, a whisperer. It got you to do things. Things you are still doing. Do you understand?"

"I can…remember…I remember it all, now…"

Gideon Ridge saw a rush from his peripheral vision. His hand reacted and the old world projectile weapon, the gun gifted him by his family, leaped to level. It popped five times and two undead attackers jumped and jerked and went to the floor.

Paola Kett had not even seen him draw the weapon. She stared at him, surprised.

"Riker, you were tricked by an ancient evil into doing a terrible thing," Gideon said.

"I was lost in the Reaches. I was exiled," Riker said dreamily.

"Yes," Kett agreed, pulling more wiring free.

"The crew lost…lost their minds. They began to do things. I began to do things…I watched them kill each other…I killed the last of them…" Tears broke from his grayed eyes. "What did we do to each other? To the cosmos? A voice said to do it and the crew would live. They would operate the Leviathan from a remote place. Forever. Never die. Now look at them. Look at me!" the emaciated, skeletal man screamed.

The demon stood. A humanoid head remained where the black helmet had been. Charcoal skin and yellow eyes replaced the black, fiery armor but it looked every bit as tough. Words grated from a clenched mouth and stiff jaw. Black hair ran from the scalp to the back of its neck and down into the armor just like it linked over the jaw to form a razor thin beard.

"You feel wrath now!"

Suddenly it lunged and hit Grundy with a resonating attack. The hit echoed in the chamber as Grundy flew back into a mass of communications relays and tore them all to the floor.

Jaka attacked, his staff a blur. The thing deflected the blows with an agility that was surprising. Jaka pressed the advantage, however, pushing the thing back toward the open door of the room.

In a flash, Grundy was back, the halberd whipping around them.

Candri popped her whips across the thing's bare head and spun it off balance again. It staggered into the mass of pressing dead, cursing the living party.

Old man Ridge popped another shell into the chamber of his sweeper. Candri heard it clearly and leaped backward. Jaka and Grundy did, as well. The language spoken by a levered sweeper was universal and a lot more definite than empty curses.

The creature stiffened visibly. Its eyes popped wide, the glow less intimidating and more alarmed than they expected.

It knew that sound, too.

The plume of widespread energies exploded from the barrel of the sweeper. The machine array caught in the wave was obliterated utterly. The last bits of the blast door that had survived the previous blasts were lost in the bright flash that was their end. The dead, rushing as best they could into the chamber, disappeared in a flood of raw, disintegrating energies, ceasing to exist just as quickly as they had come through the breach. Another trench was burned in the floor plating and the rock of the structure and part of the walls where the blast door had been was gone.

All that remained was the shadow creature.

It was wounded, however, no doubt could be found. The black, fiery armor glowed with red, spiderwebbed cracks everywhere. One arm of armor and one leg, on opposite sides, were missing. The coarse, thick black hair had been burned away completely. It was on one knee, braced on one arm, shaking, howling.

"You fight an…immortal!" it then roared, struggling to stand.

"I say we test that theory," Sylver chuckled, popping another shell into the sweeper.

"Kill me," muttered Riker as he began to weep bitterly. "Stop what has been started with my people…stop the war on the living…kill me and the machines will fail. The dead will fail, too, and return to the grave. The voice said it needed my mind and my will, the sheer force of mind, I use to manipulate machines. It is using my will to manipulate the dead…"

Paola forced his face back toward hers when his head jerked backward and he grimaced with pain. He began to scream.

Gideon Ridge looked over his shoulder at the demon. It was standing, the black armor reforming on its vile body. Blackened coals of flame forged into armor again, appearing from nothing.

"It's giving the pain to Riker and trying to remake itself," Gideon Ridge said to Kett.

"Listen to me!" Kett shouted. "Listen! Whatever you are experiencing is in your mind! It's not real!"

"That's the problem!" Riker howled then fell still. His eyes flared a dim yellow. "Whatever is in this one's mind is real enough!" the demon's voice blurted. "To stop him you have to kill him! Are you ready to do that?"

Riker's form and the demon form laughed with the same voice.

Pap Ridge spun around and shouted at Paola Kett and his offspring.

"Finish unpluggin' him!"

Gideon saw the demon rushing him. Pap had his back turned; the demon wanted to destroy the sweeper.

Gideon reacted by sheer instinct and took off for his father, his fists balled tightly in the bracer's gloves. They charged quickly to blue but kept building, lighting into stark white.

The demon ran headlong toward the old man, flaming weapon rekindled.

Then Grundy was there. Right in the thing's face, Grundy gave that charge and drove his horn into it. His halberd came down like a freighter on the creature's weapon arm and the forearm plates shattered into a thousand fiery coals. The arm itself bent, too, not at a joint. The creature roared in pain and fell aside, totally missing Pap Ridge, the sword dissipating once again.

Grundy bellowed with pain himself and pulled away from the creature. He fell back clumsily, whipping his head about. His horn had been burned off half way down and he grabbed at it with both hands, losing the broken halberd and falling onto his back. He howled wildly.

The vile thing was on its knees, trembling, holding its bent arm.

More dead flooded the room and the three in the rafters put down a net of energy blasts, trying valiantly to stop them all. Pap ran forward, forgetting them and grabbed Grundy in an attempt to slide him further away from the fight. Jaka saw his intent and fell into helping him as the rafter team kept dropping the dead who got too close to them.

The two men still could not slide Grundy.

Candri Prentice swished her ignited whips about from both armbands. She struck one of the dead after another, dropping them in convulsions.

None of them noticed the creature standing once again, destroyed arm dangling. It stalked Candri Prentice from behind, patient and determined. The sword rekindled from nothing, back in its good hand.

Then Gideon Ridge reached them. He slipped between it and Candri Prentice. The right hand manipulated the white energies into a spiked mace while the left forged a shield from the light.

The thing struck out at Prentice but Ridge blocked the flaming weapon with his shield. He returned a strike and raked the thing's face mercilessly.

Paola Kett suddenly jerked back from Riker. His arm broke and twisted right before her eyes. One of his eyes burst into flame, only to go immediately out and turn to a blackened scar. He screamed, his voice his own again.

"I don't know what to do!" Paola screamed at Gideon Ridge.

"It's not you who has to do something!" he roared back.

The demonic creature lunged at Ridge, sword falling rapidly, but its arm stopped again and it began to convulse. Candri Prentice had lashed the arm with a whip again.

Ridge struck it twice with his forged mace. Black smoke trailed the weapon where it tore into the armor.

Baddenide joined again, his staff striking the thing's free arm.

Sylver Ridge jacked the lever on the sweeper. A shell kicked free but none replaced that one. He quickly groped about in his pockets and found...none. Tossing the sweeper aside, he jerked his venter to level.

Paola Kett leaned into Riker's face. She grabbed the last of the cords and cables interfaced with him, snatched them free then grabbed the skeletal man under his arms. She lifted him up onto his dead legs.

The lights in the chamber went out for a moment, coming back on in a dimmer shade.

"Riker, you did this! You have to be the one to stop it!"

Riker groaned and bobbed his head about.

"Pain...pain...transferring to me..."

"No! No pain! Resist it, Riker! Not the Psiborg, not Riker the slave! Andreas Riker, individual, human being, resist!" Kett shouted further.

Several of the dead broke through the raining energy of the Unity soldiers. All four ran at the Acolyte scholar, Paola Kett, from different directions.

Not many options available, she let Riker fall back into the chair. She leaped toward one of her attackers, aimed both staves downward and drove the electropulsed attack into the head of the corpse.

It went down hard.

A shot from the rafters dropped the second charger to the floor.

Kett then flipped into the path of another. She kicked its legs out from under it, struck it solidly with both staves then rolled to the side. She stabbed it in the spine with a staff, arcing blue voltage all over it.

The last barreled into her as she stood up and it drove her back onto the floor. Her staves fell free of her grasp and left her only bare hands to defend herself. She grabbed the thing's wrists and held it at bay.

Then the corpse's head exploded right off the rickety shoulders. The body dropped atop Paola, stone still. Old Pap Ridge twirled the light particle blaster around a finger and belted it again.

"Fight the evil, Riker!" Paola Kett shouted, running back to him.

"I don't know how…" he moaned.

"You made a choice to listen to the voice, to the whispers, to the lies! You've given yourself to that creature! It owns you but only if you don't take yourself back!"

"How can I-"

"You never believed in God, Riker, I remember from the old holofiles! It's time to believe! This creature is real, the evil is real! Don't you realize God is real?"

"I…yes, yes I do…I couldn't deny it now…how could I…"

"Resist the evil, Riker! Turn to God!"

"I'm afraid!"

The battle raged on behind the Acolyte and Riker.

"I won't lie, Riker; you're going to die here," the woman said with her jaw clenched. "There's nothing we can manage for your body. It's done and I'm sorry. But you'll live on! Not in some zombie ship and not in a mechanical disease but as a soul! All sentients do! Call out to God, call out to Jesus Christ! There's nothing to be afraid of anymore! When you die today you could experience paradise but you have to call on God! He wants you to, Riker. He stands at the door of the heart and knocks, hoping all will answer and invite Him in. It doesn't matter what your past is! It matters the state of your heart at this moment!"

"I…I want to do that…" Riker said finally. "I want to call on Jesus Christ!"

The demon, right in the shadow of an unsuspecting Candri Prentice, arced with pain and twisted itself, trying to free itself of the pain.

"I want Jesus Christ to save me from this evil, to forgive me of my past! I want to see paradise with Him!" Andreas Riker said, an undeniable joy spreading over his face.

The demon roared and spread out its arms in agony.

Candri Prentice spun at the sound and lashed a whip around the creature's legs. The energy smoldered against the coal black armor. She looped the other about its neck, smoldering against the armor there and the breaks in it, burning the thing's skin.

"Ask Jesus, Riker! That's all it takes! You gave yourself to enslavement but you can be free! Christ can break the chains that hold you! You can be free of them all!" Kett shouted. "In the name of Jesus Christ, I command all evil to loose you! Now make your own choice, Andreas Riker!"

Abruptly, the dead that had invaded the room fell to their knees. Puppets with cut strings, they were undead no more. They were simply corpses from around the cosmos, graveless and misplaced, but corpses nonetheless. They began to topple over for the last time.

The creature howled with pain as the armor split and fiery cracks appeared in it everywhere. The helmet shattered and fell off in lumps of burning coal. The arm folded over and one eye flamed then smoldered in smoke. It writhed in agony, tearing at both whips that burned it. With each struggle it dragged Prentice closer.

The lights in the room blackened again then returned even dimmer than the last shade.

"Oh Mighty God, Creator of the cosmos and all that is in it," wept Andreas Riker. His cybernetic parts whirred and rattled as his humanity returned with a vengeance. "Jesus Christ, Lord of all, I ask forgiveness... for my past, my arrogance...my sin...Please save me, take me to Heaven, to Paradise, to be with you...forever...I make You and only You, Jesus, the Lord of my life..." he wept.

Tears of joy and tears of abandon rolled and a soul was saved in one of the darkest moments the cosmos had ever seen.

The creature roared in utter torture and snatched Prentice from her feet. It grabbed her up by the whips and leaned in close to her face.

"At least I get to kill you," the creature spat hatefully. "Say goodbye, Acolyte!"

Pap Ridge could not get a clear shot.

Paola Kett was too far away, as was Jaka Baddenide, though both called out to Candri.

Grundy struggled to rise but could find no balance.

In a flash, faster than the eye could catch, the shield Gideon Ridge carried swept across the demon's face. The the mace did the same. Again, the shield. Again, the mace.

The evil head popped and bobbed all four times, black blood spraying every which way the weapons swept.

Candri fell to her feet and she backed away quickly.

Jaka and Paola rushed to her side while Pap stayed beside Grundy.

"In the name of Jesus Christ of Nazareth, I cast you back into fire and darkness!" Gideon shouted.

The mace and shield disappeared. Ridge, the white light smoking from his fists, clenched his hands tightly and drowned the creature in pure white light.

The giant creature teetered this way and that, screaming, smoking beneath the blistering brightness. It slowly began to topple then crashed onto its back. The armor exploded into loose, charred coals. Then the body burst into open flame all over, black fire mingled with the red and yellow…and white...

Then it burned into nothing, screaming still from some other horrible place into which it fell.

Gideon ran back to the Acolyte and Riker. He leaned down to Andreas Riker, prone where Paola Kett had dropped him.

"You did it. The voice is gone," Riker said softly, wheezing.

His eyes were very dull but no longer haunted, no longer afraid.

"No, Andreas. God did it. You called on Jesus. He did the rest. With you free, choosing God and not it, it couldn't stave off the effects of this physical plane and still exist in it. If you hadn't been free, it would've been draining your life still."

"Is it dead forever? Can it die? Is the voice silenced?" he asked.

"For a time...but not forever. Angels and demons have corporeal forms, though they rarely use them. Mostly, they remain in the spirit form. However, when a corporeal form is dealt too many wounds to hold together, the form dissipates and cannot be regained for a time…like a temporary death. It was using your life force to hold itself together, just as it was using it to hold the dead in action," Paola Kett gently whispered.

"I can see that…I understand it all…finally. I'm ready to go home."

"It won't be long now, Andreas," Ridge said, noting the man's wheezing and fading awareness.

He also noticed the lights failing further and the shuddering of the equipment that kept the life support going.

Paola Kett leaned down with Gideon and put a gentle hand on Riker's face.

"God the Father and God the Son and God the Holy Spirit bless and keep you, and make His face to shine upon you, and carry you to your reward," she whispered softly.

A trembling hand came up to grasp hers. "And you, Acolyte. You as well. Thank you."

"Uncle Sun," Gideon Ridge transmitted, holding the headset microphone. "Life support was being maintained for the Psiborn crew...but it isn't going to last long. We're done down here but we'll never make it back to the surface. Pull out, Uncle Sun. You need to go, now."

No response.

"Uncle Sun?"

"Allow…me…" Riker rasped, concentrating.

An odd flare of energy crackled and popped nearby, no more than the size of an average doorway. Light and color hummed and swirled about in a vortex, seemingly leading to some other place, an open portal or window.

"Spacefolding?" Paola Kett asked.

"Wormhole manipulation," Jaka Baddenide answered, "on a terribly small scale...one we'll likely never understand and never see again."

Pap Ridge was beside Gideon.

"Uncle Sun isn't answering."

"No time right now, son," Pap answered. "If we get back topside, we'll find out soon enough what's happened."

Andreas Riker coughed and struggled for breath. He pointed weakly to the glowing swirl.

"I am holding this for you...go through...you will be on the surface. Leave here...I will end this place."

"Andreas," Gideon started.

"I am weak," he groaned. "Waste no time..."

The Unity shooters ran into the room, having found a way down, and immediately fell into helping the others.

Grundy was helped into the light and everyone followed, helping each other as necessary. Gideon Ridge was the last to go.

Andreas Riker was barely holding on to life.

"Thank you, Andreas," Gideon Ridge said. "You rescued us."

"Thank you..." he whispered, unable to speak loudly. "Go...now. Will see you...again."

"Indeed," Ridge agreed, tears in his eyes. "Indeed. On the white shores of forever."

Then Riker was alone. He prayed to Jesus Christ that He would extend his life just long enough to hold life support and the dimensional rift for the raiders.

His prayer was answered.

Out of a disorienting, nauseating portal slipped the raiders, right at the landing gear of the *Spoken Word* and the *Belly Rub*. The team broke apart, rushing to where Uncle Sundar Ridge lay on a cargo ramp and where Cheyenne Winds lay beneath the ship's belly. Both of them were lifted and loaded aboard the ships.

Then the two ships soared away as the artificial world of the Psiborn exploded exponentially.

CHAPTER FIFTEEN : *Mourning, Victorious*

I t was an odd sight and that was in itself an understatement.

The two distant suns of the Dor Modros system angled for dominance. The competing white and yellow lights glittered over the thousands upon tens of thousands of starship fuselages. Many were no more than wreckage, no longer recognizable as any one particular type of ship. Many were still functioning, supporting life. All seemed to be smooth, shiny stones in the liquid sea of space, light dancing over them with no prejudice as to which side of the war they had supported.

Fires raged on in some of them where life support insisted on feeding the flame its oxygen. They burned like old Earth beacons lit high upon a hill as a warning…or a message.

Flee this place. There is death here.

Death did not rule the day, however. The ships of the living, some still mobile, proved that.

The battle had been catastrophic, yes, with the lost vessels and the lives aboard them a testament to the brutality of the engagement. And it was clear that sheer numbers would outweigh the living eventually, no matter their advantage with speed and teamwork and living thought for tactics. Given enough time, the dead would have rolled over the living like a wave of tragedy, all lives lost. It was clear to most of the living leadership that death was inevitable, the starmada of bones unstoppable.

Still they resisted, struggled, and held on to hope. Hope for a chance, hope for an anomaly. Hope for a miracle.

Then God gave them a miracle, a gift to all the living races. Suddenly and without any sort of warning, the dead simply fell silent and still, much like the husks of locust left behind after the shedding of their hulls. Those ships and the corpses within them dropped back into shadows and darkness, leaving behind the empty shells of a fleet, a bone starmada. In a moment of reckoning, the dead were dead once again.

The loss of life remained horrific but there was hope and light at the end of the battle.

When the *Spoken Word* and the *Belly Rub* broke from the edge of the Reaches, all the living ships within range began charging what weapons and shields they still had.

"More than two hundred weapons systems just locked onto us," Captain Joshua Brent noted. "Either that or just as many ships just doubled in size…it's hard to tell with this haphazard readout display."

He sat in the pilot's seat aboard the *Rub*. He was doing his best to piece together a very broken gaggle of translation codes feeding into three monitors.

Behind him, leaned over a shoulder, Paola Kett pointed to her forearm gear, projecting a translation matrix.

"Give me a second," she said.

"This is Commodore Wrigley Zeckinbridge," Wrigley transmitted from her position in the pilot's chair of the *Word*. "That's an unfriendly welcome I'm reading for a band of returning commandos. Acknowledged?"

Many voices answered her in many languages and the transmission came through garbled. Mind grinding static chased that confusion then more babbling and nonsense.

"What am I supposed to do with all that?" she asked Taylor Patrick.

Patrick sat in the copilot position and, from there, shot her a quizzical frown.

"I'm doing well just to be a copilot," he said. "I work Security, remember?"

Candri Prentice leaned over his shoulder.

"Those lights over there represent your Communications Translation mainframe. See how they're all different colors? That means all the languages coming in are unfiltered and non-prioritized. You're getting all the transmissions at once with no time, distance or language filters and prioritization."

Taylor Patrick turned to the Commodore with a straight face.

"What she said."

"You have to adjust it," Candri said with a sigh. "Be very gentle and patient; adjustments can be extremely finite with these older ships-"

Gideon Ridge stormed into the cockpit and reached past Candri Prentice. He slammed the mainframe access on the side and the innards rattled loudly. Everyone in the cockpit cringed.

The audio cleared immediately.

Ridge stole a headset from Patrick and tapped the earpiece.

"This the *Spoken Word*. I have wounded. Is there a medship here?"

A cacophony of unbridled happiness roared up from the Communications system. Cheers and congratulations rained upon the little ship's crew amid a pointed answer to the question.

"Captain Ridge, this is Commanding Surgeon Laura Prince of the former USAP vessel *McCoy*. We are closest to you of all our relief ships. We welcome you back and welcome you aboard. Plot a course and dock when ready."

"Acknowledged," Gideon said. He tossed his headset back to Patrick. "Take us there. Don't spare the thrusters."

He left the cockpit in a whirlwind.

"*Former* USAP vessel?" Zeckinbridge asked, firing the engines.

"You'll find Unity is a...struggling...alliance, now. There have been divisions, withdrawals and a lot more. Some are working to reshape its destiny. Some, like my ship, have simply declared independence until the direction of Unity is official," the surgeon Commander responded.

"I see. Well, maybe some of us won't still have a target on our backs for taking unauthorized actions. And ships. Taking ships."

Commanding Surgeon Prince answered, "No, I wouldn't think so. Not with all that has come to light."

"Good to know. I'm Unity Commodore Wrigley Zeckinbridge. I have, also, Unity Security Chief Taylor Patrick, of the *Corridor*. On board as well are two Acolytes; since we are all still in restricted, coded and short ranged communication, can you begin a relay to the rest of the fleet with that news?"

"It is done; I give you my word," Prince responded.

"This is Unity Captain Joshua Brent," the young captain added via communications, since Paola Kett had integrated her translation matrix with the ship. "I'm onboard the Starstalker vessel *Belly Rub*. With me is an Acolyte, daughter of one Jon Kett, if you could relay that to him."

"Happily, *Belly Rub*."

On the *Spoken Word*, Gideon Ridge stepped into the sleeping area.

"You okay, Big Man?"

Grundy perked up at his voice.

"Yes, my friend. You?"

Ridge felt sorry for the struggling friend who could not even stand.

Without the main horn, a Rothidai could not balance well, nor could he focus his vision. It was a physiological mystery as to why, though most medical studies agreed it had something to do with the eyes being set on opposite sides of the horn and horn ridge.

"I'm okay. Just rest, Grundy. We reached the survivors' fleet and we'll be in a medical transport soon."

"I'm not worried for myself," he grumbled. "I will persevere."

"Even without treatment, it grows back, I know," Gideon allowed. "But I want you to be seen by professionals."

"It grows back?" Jaka Baddenide asked, sitting near Grundy, watching over him.

"Yes. In just under a year," Grundy said.

"But how about you get some treatment anyway?" Gideon pushed. "You can be back on your feet in no time."

Grundy chuckled and said, "And miss a year of breakfast in bed?"

"Jaka will be going back to his Temple duties. Of course, I could ask Drea when I see her-"

Grundy snorted then grimaced in pain and clutched his horn nub.

"I'll take a doctor. You should, too, Gideon," he reminded.

Ridge touched his side then waved it off.

"Yeah, maybe. The Acolytes wrapped me up pretty well, though," Gideon said and turned back to Jaka. "If he needs me, I'll be with Pap."

"He already needs you. He's eaten almost everything in your galley."

Ridge shook his head as he moved further down the hall. At a very small room, one he never used, he paused and went inside. It was the Captain's quarters but he always slept in the crew accommodations with his crew.

The door swished closed behind him. It was dim, not dark, but the lights overhead were out. Two glowing rods on either side of the room gave subdued illumination in a soft, amber hue. The single bed, folded down from the wall, used most of the room except for the one portable chair and the folding desktop that dropped from one corner. On the desktop was Pap's Bible, open.

In the chair was Pap. The old man was asleep.

Sundar Ridge, Gideon's Uncle Sun, filled the narrow bed.

Gideon had never seen his old uncle look so...old. Makeshift emergency care had been administered and an improvised pulse charger and monitor had been attached to help regulate his failing heart. A case of too little, too late, the old man had not survived the run back from the Reaches.

Gideon wiped away tears, swallowed at the rage he felt for the woman responsible and tried to breathe.

"God, give me strength, please," he whispered.

Then, on his knees, Gideon Ridge began to pray in earnest.

When the *Word* finally joined at the airlock with the surgical ship *McCoy*, Gideon Ridge waited as Sundar Ridge was carted away, Pap at his side. Then others took Grundy away. The big Rothidai would be fine, the ship's orderlies swore. Grundy was already quizzing them on what food would be served.

Jaka Baddenide, Taylor Patrick, and Candri Prentice offered temporary adieus as Gideon Ridge remained behind.

"I need a minute or so," he told them.

Commodore Wrigley Zeckinbridge accepted an invitation to see the bridge of the *McCoy*, taking the young Captain Josh Brent with her. Paola Kett chose not to go, though she touched Brent's cheek affectionately and promised to catch up to him. She stayed behind and, in the quiet, prayed.

News came, messages from friends and loved ones. Celebrations called out and invited the newcomers to the victory parties. Communications relayed hope and comfort. They gave praise to God when they were relayed the information on the surviving ships, too. It seemed that several Acolytes had survived, though the message was not clear with names and identities. They did hear that the *Bloodwind* had outlasted the battle and so had the *Ferali* 5. Neither was still in fighting shape, however.

The Hotch twins, after their mission, had diverted to Drea Ridge's coordinates. They would rendezvous with the family later but sent word that there were things needing their attention.

Time crept onward. Hours passed.

Starship technicians and engineers crawled all over the *Word*, fighting with repairs. People came and went and the stalwart old ship stood faithfully in waiting. They told Gideon that Grundy would be just fine. The captain acknowledged it, adding that he had already known. He had faith in God, in Jesus Christ, to whom he had been praying fervently.

Gideon praised Him zealously. God is good, all the time, he promised them. Even if at first we cannot see it, God is working for the good in all things. Bad things can happen in the blink of an eye but, if one chose to hang onto Faith, he would find more Blessings than heartbreaks.

A messenger eventually came to Paola Kett aboard the *Belly Rub* to tell her that her father was en route. She jumped at their invitation to the mess hall to wait for him.

The day eventually passed into deep night as time marched on.

Many ships left the battle arena for their awaiting worlds and inhabitants. The rallied ships of the living that remained were giving repair and supplies to ships unable to operate on their own. Some were still giving medical help to those who needed it. Most, however, were going home to tell the cosmos about the unthinkable being true. The dead had waged war on the living. The supernatural activity was undeniable.

The physical world was not the only world, not the only truth.

Gideon Ridge waited in the cockpit of his own ship. Captain's chair leaned back, feet on the control console, he listened to the banging and the buzzing of repairs and technicians. After a time, the sounds seemed almost rhythmic, soothing. Eyelids heavy, Gideon Ridge drifted into sleep without even knowing he was going.

There he dreamed.

Clouds of all colors and shapes whipped across the sky overhead. It looked as though time was out of control, speeding away. Below that sky was the *Spoken Word*. Below it were the bodies of Sundar Ridge and Cheyenne Winds, both prone and as still as the dead.

Gideon Ridge, in a slumbering stupor, wandered to his prone uncle and dropped down beside him on his knees.

"What happened, Uncle Sun?" he asked emotionally, chest tight, heart breaking.

"Aw, boy, you know what happened. I told ya already."

Gideon stalled, quietly studying. The clouds distracted him.

"This ain't then," Sundar said. "I told ya then, when you found me. This ain't then. This is now."

"I don't understand," he admitted.

"It's like talkin' to your half deaf daddy," Sundar complained. Then he gestured to his right. "She shocked me, boy, and fried my ticker. Messed up my old, weak heart."

Gideon looked to Sundar Ridge's right. Cheyenne Winds sat on the loading ramp, leaning forward, arms braced on her knees.

"You..." he started, confused. He had not seen her move.

The woman bore five particle rifle burns on her jacket torso. She bore no serious wounds, however. The burns and the pain would have been enough to knock her unconscious and leave her in agony but her diffuser bands, on her wrists, would have prevented any severe injury.

Gideon looked back to Sundar. He would have known that.

"That's right," Sundar answered his thoughts. "I could've popped her in her cackling head and killed her. I'm a dead shot...if you'll forgive the pun. Diffusers wouldn't stop a particle rifle shot that far off from her armbands."

Cheyenne Winds cackled with laughter, saying, "True enough."

"But Uncle Sun-" Gideon started.

"Gotta tell ya everything twice?" he snapped. "I told ya then, when ya found me. Whatever. Listen, this time, boy. Ignore the slicker."

Gideon looked at Winds where she sat, shaking her finger at him, then turned back to his uncle.

"I chose mercy. My last act. I knew my time was up. I felt it, before she moved. Before I moved. I told her I was gonna kill her. But I chose not to. I chose mercy. And don't ask why. It was the right thing to do. I just knew it. And still know it. And you know it."

Gideon felt tears streaming down his face.

"I love you, too, boy," the old man answered Gideon's heart. "And your Pap. And Drea. And that Rothidai. And my twin boys; I'm so glad you and Sylver loved 'em into family after I adopted 'em. Orphans, no place to be...right thing to do. Just like not killin' Sparky. There's mercy in sparin' that slicker girl. Somethin' good, somethin' bigger than us. I want you to let go of your hate. That thirst for revenge. Ain't nothin' righteous about it. I'm dead; can't change it. All you can do is make the most of what I left ya. I left ya a challenge; choose mercy."

"I will," Gideon promised.

"I know, boy," Sundar chuckled, Cheyenne Winds laughing, too. "This is a memory. You already honored my wish. Already made your promise. Now keep doin' it." He reached up and patted the younger man's face. "Now, do yourself a favor and wake up."

Paola Kett was too excited to sleep. She could not even sit still. For her, it was a reunion.

"You should have seen it, Paola," Rabeau Loist said, his voice thick with his old world, Cajun flair. He angled his hand in the air and swept it about like a small starfighter, much as would a small boy with a toy, narrating, "I was all over the dead. I was rescuing this ship or that ship then flying off to defend another one. I have to hold the record for most ghost ship takedowns. I know one time-"

"One time he just talked a whole fleet to death," Taelynn Berreaux laughed, tossing back her thick hair.

Her face was tattooed on one side with electrical burns.

"Well, at least I didn't get towed out," Loist chuckled and pointed at Berreaux with both forefingers at once. "Yep, that would be you, towed by the *WildCard*."

David Rule cleared his throat and everyone shifted their eyes to him.

"A lot of us did not make it back at all. Remember to be grateful to God, each and every one of us who did," Rule reminded.

The gathering of Acolytes agreed. They passed around conversation, hugs and handshakes in the eating area of the surgical ship after a deep time of prayer. Paola Kett stood arm in arm with her father, Jon Kett. Taelynn Berreaux sat at one of the many tables with Candri Prentice and Rabeau Loist. Jaka Baddenide stood on the opposite side of the table with David Rule.

They were glad to have survived but even more grateful that the evil had been stopped.

The Hunon Pilot, Commander Wahll, reunited with his own people aboard a Hunon battleship. Other Interceptor Pilots gathered with him and they remembered the lost wingman of the good Commander. Afterward they told him how many Hunon had died in the conflict. It seemed that more individuals from every race had been slain than had even been counted so far.

The Starstalker's home world starmada left emissaries behind as well and on the mingling and meetings went.

In short, the living celebrated life itself in all the facets, shapes, races and species in which life comes...

...in unity.

"Captain Ridge."

Gideon Ridge stirred in his seat. It swiveled and dropped his feet from the console to the floor. The movement propelled the seat upward and forward and pitched him up to a sitting position. He winced and braced his side.

"Captain Gideon Ridge," a voice continued.

It was an incoming transmission.

Gideon rubbed his face. His eyes were still tired and burning.

"Captain-"

"Alive. Awake. Here. Yes?" he answered the page.

"Captain, this is Operations Director Garret, onboard the *McCoy*. There is a meeting taking place soon and your presence is requested.

Airlocked with us are several other ships, one of which is the Starstalker research vessel *Carnivore*. That ship is hosting the meeting on the surveyor deck."

"Ridge, en route," the young Captain said.

A quick change of clothing and a check of his bandages and Ridge wandered out of his ship. He had little trouble getting to his destination. It seemed everyone he passed surmised just who he was and where he needed to go, offering directions.

The major survey deck on board the research vessel *Carnivore* was not crowded. As a research level, it was home to many alcoves by the open view panels. Lining the whole perimeter of the rather large room were sitting spaces with computer consoles just staring into space, surveying the black tapestry upon which perched the stars. The center of the room had a massive table with seats all around for sharing of research and development as it was made. The meeting taking place took up many of the chairs at the table but not all of them; also, if the numbers increased, bodies could be directed to the alcove seating.

The one place with no view to space, the place with no alcove, was the rear point of the room. There waited the double doors, sliding aside to allow individuals off the elevator and into the room.

One of the latest arrivals was Gideon Ridge.

Several voices called out to him from the table. A handful called out from the Unity gathering at one end. Several Starstalkers hailed him from their position at the table. The Rothidai representatives at the meeting, sitting with a visibly nauseous Grundy, also greeted him. He waved to all who called him, nodding in respect to many. Still, he joined none of them. He wandered down the room-length table until he reached his father, a man holding him an empty seat.

"Where you been?" Pap asked dryly.

"I'm here, just late."

"You hate being late."

"I'm aware that I hate being late," Gideon Ridge muttered.

The Ridge son cocked his head to the side and raised one eyebrow. Stubble ran the gauntlet over his jaw line. He had not had time to shave.

"You should've used the Wipe. This meeting is important."

"Forgive me if I have no confidence in technology that uses sound waves and laser light to clean, burn away unwanted hair-"

"It's proven tech," his father argued.

"I don't care."

"So it diced up a couple of people ten years or so ago. That was before they worked the bugs out of it. I remember in me 'n' your Uncle Sun's day..."

Gideon felt the emotion choke him as his father's eyes misted over and his lower lip twitched his beard. He reached out and clamped a hand on the older man's shoulder.

"Can I have your attention, please?" a booming voice echoed in the room.

Everyone else quieted.

"I'm Arrou, Captain of this research and survey vessel, the *Carnivore*. I welcome each and every one of you here, on behalf of my own people, the Riistan, or the Starstalkers, as offworlders know us."

The speaker towered at the far end of the table, the point farthest from the doors. He was wide and powerfully built with a black mane, scarcely any darker than his complexion, that reached well down his back. The lines in his face carried many years with them, carving into his countenance the experiences, good and bad, for all to gauge. In his human form he still reached well over Gideon's height; the young captain wondered how tall the man would be in his feral form.

"My friends...something I feel I can call anyone who fought with us in this terrible conflict...I am glad you came to this meeting. Many races responded to this battlefront. Many armadas were represented here. Most of them left representatives; emissaries, if you will. We are here to talk about what has occurred, what came of it and how we will proceed, as allies. Allies of life. Allies of light."

"Alliesss are plentiful, Captain, and peacsse quickly found, when the enemy isss ssso vassst and terrible asss what we facssed here." The only Vipon at the table flicked his tongue. "One would wonder how long that will prevail."

Mumbling immediately spread through the gathering like a brush fire, small at first then blazing into arguments the next. Gideon Ridge looked at his father and the two shook their heads.

"Please," the Starstalker growled. His word was polite but his tone was authoritatively grave. "This is not why your peoples had you stay here. We can argue from a distance; let us work together to establish things since we are all together."

The rumble in the room died off again.

"Speaking as the Senior Officer here for the Unity Starmada-" a uniformed man began, rising to his feet.

His decorations displayed quite the service rank of an Admiral.

"There is no place for speaking as the United Starmada of Allied Planets," the host growled, interrupting him.

The somewhat rotund man lost all expression on his wide, flat face. He blinked several times rapidly as if his mind could not make sense of the words.

"I don't understand," he finally said. He rubbed his shaven head with a long wiping motion. "What do you mean?"

"Your people may not have informed you, as of yet, but my people have informed me. The decision was nearly unanimous throughout Unity membership. Until further notice, Unity is under reformation. There will be no hierarchy, no command structure, that supersedes the independent authority of independent, member-world governments."

"What does that-" the man began, grimacing.

"It means you don't get to speak for everyone in Unity," Wrigley Zeckinbridge snapped. "At most, as the highest ranking *Earth* Officer here, you could speak for Earth. Frankly, however, until things settle down, I'd stick to answering for just your own command."

In the ensuing silence, the Admiral looked about at the faces of the other Unity Starmada uniforms present. Most heads nodded his way. His face flushed with anger and embarrassment and the Admiral sat back down without another word.

"What is this then?" a grating Migroid voice queried. "Recruiting for a new starmada?"

"We are not here to discuss independent starmada fates," the host growled lowly, "We are certainly not proposing any new, centrally governed...dominating...alliances."

The black and gray, rocklike face of the Migroid opposition had no expression, of course, with blank white eyes and no discernible nose. It was especially expressionless since the voice box in a Migroid reverberated directly from the throat with no mouth involved. The tone expressed a lot, however.

The low scraping of a voice said, "We shall see."

"We need no opinions from the likes of you, vampire!" boomed a Rothidai in an eye patch. He nudged Grundy with an elbow as he spoke.

Grundy glanced his way and shook his head. Not here, not now, he seemed to be saying to his kinsman. There was no place, no time, for old prejudices.

"Stop this bickering!" shouted a Chabron.

Her golden skin glistened in the chamber light and the glow of twinkling stars outside, aside from the dark pigmentation spots over her bare shoulders and arms. She launched to her feet in a golden blur and drove her massive, two handed sword straight through the metal table. It seemed an angry gesture. In fact, it was a peaceful gesture...albeit an extremely demanding call for peace. Anyone else breaking peaceful procedure would potentially face battle with the mighty woman.

The room fell relatively quiet again, save a handful of muffled doubts about her ability. Though she would be a terrible enemy, those who doubted her abilities also doubted her authority. However, before any real comments could be made, the host, Arrou spoke.

"I am asking in all due deference to your cultures and your peoples, please keep the peace. Your own peoples had you stay behind here to work on our interplanetary cooperation."

A little conversation and consideration then quiet again.

Arrou continued, "I will say of Unity Command that it has been officially dissolved as you knew it. It was an organization that had taken itself to new heights of control and domination in the name of peace and unity. It is for mainly that reason that Unity is no more."

"I resent that!" the Admiral yelled, pointing a rigid finger at the host.

"Admiral Statham, I can appreciate your loyalty and your passion. For now, however, please silence yourself. This is not a Unity matter; you have no authority. You are an invited guest with all the rights and power of every other individual in this room…and no more of those than any one else."

Arrou let a growl emerge in his last phrase and the Admiral looked about in sudden concern. Their host then moved on.

"The Unity Starmada had taken the rights from all of its individual races and placed all the power in the control of a centralized command. In the name of equality they had crippled individual belief and thought for the 'greater tolerance', which was little more than only tolerating what the command allowed. It is a mistake in any governing body. Every world has seen it at one time or another in our individual racial and territorial and political conflicts. All of our races should have known better than to allow it in the vast freedom of space."

"Unity Command had reports and witness testimony squashed, witnesses harassed and worse, involving this massive starmada of the dead! That information could've saved countless lives, had it been shared!" Zeckinbridge shouted at the Unity Admiral. "How pompous do you have to be to wonder why it's being abandoned?"

"Why would anyone want to hide such?" the diminutive Hunon, Commander Wahll, asked exasperatedly.

"The Starmada regulatory commissions long ago banned belief in and discussion of the supernatural, among other things. With no one allowed to believe a certain way, there would be no division and no argument among members about what was 'right'. Instead of allowing true tolerance, where people could believe what they believed in peace, they attempted to force a 'code of tolerance' which was actually a code of allowed thought, whereby no one could express individual belief at all if any others were 'offended' at all. In a twisted attempt at peace, they created domination. That domination is now over," the Starstalker said.

"That's all fine, and good riddance, I say," a Toran lady sighed. Her lovely face was already pink, on its way to red. Apparently long conversations annoyed her. "Let's get to just what our kinsmen wanted of us by leaving us here to talk. Get to the meat of this meal, Captain Arrou."

"Indeed. What your independent worlds will do about a unified world fleet is outside my purview. I know that our own world will encourage freedom. Real freedom, not a controlled illusion. In that ilk, the peoples represented here were hoping all of us, together, could talk about what happened here and what to do now."

"Do about what?" Gideon Ridge asked.

"About this area of space and every other area, and how we, the races of light, can work together to protect all life in the cosmos."

"Another organization," an Octovoid babbled fluidly.

"No, not an organization, not a government…not a committee and not a commission." Arrou said and sighed. "As individuals, as races, as peoples, as worlds and as entire systems we can preserve real peace and lasting relationships. Then, when real evil arises, we can meet it as one."

"Under what world's control?"

The query was irritable and suspicious.

"Unity Command really did a number on the races," Gideon Ridge said. "No central control. No central command. Independent allies."

"And under what authority do you speak?" Admiral Stratham barked, mustering the courage again to speak. "A rogue pirate-"

The Starstalker captain slammed a hand down and roared and the room stiffened as one. Slowly, he swallowed his irritation, however.

"He speaks as Gideon Ridge, Captain of the *Spoken Word*," Arrou growled calmly, though his ire lurked close to the surface. "As part of the Raiders of the Stone Tombs, he deserves respect and a voice here." He cleared his throat and turned back to the Greshan woman to address her question. "No one world would have authority," Arrou answered.

"That is what Unity told our people, too," she countered.

Her voice was as velvety as her lavender skin. She brushed back her black, feather hair and blinked with yellow eyes that seemed to drink in the whole room as they glowed.

"And as they told our people, though we never fell for their tricks," a Lath man buzzed, his wispy wings fluttering all about his shoulders. Solid black eyes the size of saucers stared at the host. "Lathi remained free and independent."

"And you squeezed a fortune a shazbot times over from all the other races," accused a Rundoon woman slyly, her voice smooth and cutting at once. "Not being a part of Unity, your trade prices were not governed."

Her blood red hair fell about the equally blood red skin of her face, neck and one shoulder where her gown drooped. The gills on her neck flexed in irritation, belying her calm control.

"Lathi is a spaceport world. We make our commerce from traveling species. Is it our fault? We found ourselves in prime space routes, constantly playing host to those passing by us! We adjusted to make the most of our biggest trade!" the Lath buzzed, lifting from his seat a bit.

"You did not have to charge the way you did! You did not have to rob the races time and again!"

Before the Lath could argue with the Rundoon woman, another voice defended him.

"And why should they be controlled in what they charge for anything? Is it not freedom we are discussing? True freedom means not being told by governing forces what we can do, and how!" a Sabb female erupted, though it was difficult to tell the difference between their men and women.

Grundy found his feet and his halberd clanged down on the table. Every voice silenced as he turned to the Chabron woman and nodded. I am with you, his nod told her. They will be peaceful or they will answer to both of us.

The big Rothidai snorted, something their kind did as statements of certainty and emotion without words. The large horn of his face has been burned down to a nub, causing him a lot of trouble. Grafted to it, just until it could grow back completely, was a shining silver horn of Alloroia, a sound reactive and vibration absorbing metal of incredible strength. His snort was not only heard much more loudly with the horn but the ring of struck metal resounded in the room, too.

A few moments of silence passed before Arrou spoke again.

"Do you know how many of our people, all of our people, died in this expanse?"

"Too many," the lone Tressla spoke in a wavering voice, almost like a gurgle.

His people were known for wild behavior and for little words. For him to speak there, in front of a crowd, and to do so calmly, turned most of the heads at the table.

"Our single representative of Tressl spoke volumes in his two words," the patched Rothidai acknowledged.

"Not all of us are silent savages," the Tressla informed.

The Rothidai regarded the Tressla for a long moment with his one working eye.

The rough, sand-like skin of the Tressla reflected the lights unevenly over his bare chest. It did the same thing over his bald head and face from which very small, flat black eyes looked back at the Rothidai. In place where other races would have hair a tall, thin fin rose from the top of his head and went down his upper back.

His people and his world are still considered wild, the Rothidai thought somberly. Much like my own.

They nodded at each other.

It was an inspiration. Those two races, long enemies at one time or another, sharing a moment. Others began to soften in their rigid outlooks and, before most of them realized it, there was discussion and consideration of long lasting peace, as well as promises.

Promises of friendship, not regulated alliance. Something to admire.

"Let us name our dead, here, together. Let us share our mourning and our admiration of those who gave their lives here. There is much distance between us already, no longer than it has been since our victory over this wave of destruction. Let us draw closer by honoring the fallen, an act which I believe all would be willing to do."

"Amen," David Rule said, looking around at the other Acolytes.

"Perhaps you will begin, Krinn?" the host asked the lone Vipon, the individual present with the least interest in the idea. "Tell us of the heroes of your world, Casth."

The host was possibly attempting to move him with the honor. Either that or he was picking him first to make him be quiet.

Krinn flicked his tongue and hissed a long, long yes at the group. Then he began.

"Vipon respondersss left our home world of Casssth with four hundred unaffiliated Vipon vessssels. Thosse were all our governmentsss had…other than Vipon craftsss dedicated to Unity operation," he hissed lowly, staring at the pro-Unity Admiral Statham. "Thossse in Unity followed Unity Command." Then he swept his eyes around the group again. "When the battle ended, one hundred and ssseventeen of them were able to fly home."

"Would you like to announce the names of the lost and the ships they operated so valiantly?"

The Vipon seemed genuinely touched.

"I will speak their names," the Vipon hissed lowly from the shadows of his hooded cloak. A crooked arm slipped out of the garment and slid his goblet away from himself. "I have tasssted our wine in honor of their parting, just as bittersweet."

"Let us remember the dead, then."

Attendees contributed to the forum as Arrou led a remembrance of the dead. He nodded to the attendees at the table one by one, starting with the Vipon.

Krinn named his race's lost ships and Captains.

Then Arrou called upon others to do the same for their own kin.

Eventually David Rule ended the conversation with a recounting of the Acolyte losses and he even called for ending the meeting in prayer.

In the midst of them all, not a single attendant complained. No one was offended. Of the many, many religious backgrounds present, as well as the famed atheism of two of the races, not a single background caused any to storm out, nor did it cause rifts in the peace. All sat in harmony. It was a harmony of the knowledge that all were free, all were respected and all had their own choices before them.

When David Rule was finished, Arrou asked if anyone else wanted to pray in their own way. No one accepted other than the Hunon who wanted to offer their philosophical blessings on the peace.

Then the meeting ended. Companies parted and all started making their ways to separate ships. They left carrying the relief of a possible peace among the races and new freedom. They also carried the weight of the losses and the memories of friends and allies no longer with them.

As for the drifting wreckage in the graveyard of the arena, the plan was set. All the races would offer workers, attendants, caretakers and security to be stationed in the expanse. It had yet to be named but the graveyard would be preserved as a memorial just as it was and kept so by an allied effort of all the races.

The meeting closed but some of the attendees remained behind.

There were also some late arrivals.

Gideon embraced Commander Lorrayanka. He noted the new golden 'claws' on her insignia.

"You made Captain," he said with a wide smile.

"She earned it," Samara Garriton said, stepping around Lorrayanka.

Gideon and Samara embraced in a much different way. The hold lingered, the arms tighter, the faces pressed close, cheek to cheek.

Samara pulled back finally.

"Lorrayanka and her *Ferali 5* pulled us out of the fire more than once," she said.

"Not one little bit more than you did for us," the Starstalker countered. "What's left of her ship and what's left of my ship might actually make one whole ship if hacked together. Neither would have made it through without the other."

"I'm proud of you," Gideon said. "You deserve the claws."

"I don't celebrate it as much as some…it comes at the loss of a good Captain and friend."

She was speaking of Captain Prentia, lost in the war.

Wastasa Winds joined them, too, as did David Rule.

All of them took a seat at the table once again.

"Prentia was a warrioress without peer," Rule allowed. "She was valiance and loyalty and bravery personified. We will miss her."

"Indeed," said Arrou, lingering with them.

"And you, Captain Garriton," David Rule chimed. "Now that you have no fleet and no starmada, what will you and your crew do?"

"I can answer that," Wrigley Zeckinbridge interrupted, sauntering over and leaning against the table. "The crew of the *Bloodwind* has been hired to take on an independent ship in Earth's service. They also happen to need a Captain."

"What about its other Captain? Joshua Brent?" Gideon asked pointedly.

"Gideon, he's found another Calling. He and his comrade, Security Chief Patrick, have decided to become Acolytes." David Rule nodded, adding, "Good men, those two."

Samara Garriton paused, watching Gideon Ridge. Someone else had his attention and he was answering another question.

"I don't know…not yet..." she said to Wrigley.

Gideon glanced back at her and smiled but he looked away again just as quickly, answering something else asked by Wastasa Winds.

Samara Garriton excused herself then and walked away.

Wastasa Winds had asked Gideon to join him at an alcove seat, looking out at open space. Both missed Garriton's exit.

"Gideon," Wastasa began when both had seated themselves. "I don't know exactly what to say...there's so much..."

Gideon Ridge tensed his jaw at the wave of emotion. Then he moved just his eyes and found Wastasa's.

"Wastasa, you didn't do anything. You have to stop taking the guilt for your daughter's sin."

"But things I failed to do as a father-"

"Fine. Embrace that. Own it. Do better. She's a broken woman, Wastasa. There's something wrong inside her. Try to reach her. Do what you can. But just let go of all you can't do. You can't fix her. You can't make amends for her. You can't be good *for her*. That is, always has been and always will be required of her."

"She says Sundar could've killed her but didn't take a head shot. She thinks he let her live on purpose..." he muttered. "I talked to her earlier."

"It's true."

"The head shot could've saved his own life."

Gideon said nothing.

"I'm sorry, Gideon."

"Wastasa," the Ridge son sighed.

"I know, not my place to apologize. But I'm sorry. And confused. Why didn't Sundar take the shot? Why am I mourning an old man instead of my daughter? Why am I confused over how I should actually feel?"

"Because you love your daughter and because you're a good man, confused or not. I started telling you about my Faith, Wastasa. That's the answer to why Uncle Sun made the decision he did. He wanted Cheyenne to live, wanted his last act to be saving a life, not taking one. If you want a soul-searching explanation, explore the Faith."

"I will, Gideon, and sooner rather than later. This one act...it's a fork in the road. I can't understand it, wrap my head around it or even talk to my daughter about it unless I do understand your Faith...your uncle's Faith...and the reasons that led him to give mercy. This act changed everything. Everything."

They shook hands and Gideon smiled.

Inside, he was shouting Hallelujahs.

Praise God! Even in the storm! You sly old man, Uncle Sun. Reaching out, after death, with the Word of God and His message of mercy, love and compassion. Changing lives, the young Ridge thought. *Now I understand the why, too.*

The room talk continued even though Wastasa Winds had to go. A lot of information was offered and taken and shared among those remaining.

Gideon Ridge turned back for Samara Garriton and found her missing. He deftly escaped several more questions and suggestions, lost in his thoughts of the woman, until Pap slapped his shoulder.

"Go, boy, go after her," the old man ordered. "I'll fill you in on what you miss."

Gideon exchanged glances with Lorrayanka, Wrigley Zeckinbridge and David Rule, all of whom gave him a soft smile. He turned and left the room.

CHAPTER SIXTEEN: *Relationships*

A cross the cosmos, worlds promised to reach back to a time when they held their individuality precious. Earth was one of them. All realized that honesty and individuality were far better than pretending to be alike for the sake of conformity, a false unity. It was wrong, trying to form carbon cutter races with plasma copied ideals. The greatest respect for others was being honest about one's beliefs and allowing others to have their own ideas. Agreeing to disagree. Not all are the same nor should they be. Peace and unity could never be based on transforming everyone to be the same by force and calling that freedom.

The worlds agreed to try to work in unison, peacefully, starting with the expanse outside the Reaches.

The space graveyard would be preserved. Named the Front Line Memorial, the locale would include a visitor's space station with attendants from each and every race willing to help commemorate the battle...and remember.

Ships that could no longer operate under their own power after the war were left behind, donated to the memorial as landing points for people to explore the region. The *Bloodwind* was one of them, the bridge slated to become a great attraction.

Gideon Ridge's Bible was still on the console at the Command seat.

Samara Garriton looked through a docking field portal from the survey ship and let the image of the battered, shattered *Bloodwind* burn into her consciousness. It drifted just off the port side of the Starstalker vessel, at least one third of its form missing from the damage taken.

In the end she had been immobile, sensor blind and defenseless with the shields and weaponry all gone. The gravitonic reinforcement was gone from the hull and structural integrity had fallen into being a thing of the past by the time the enemy had been nullified. Pieces were literally falling off at the end and communications were down.

Her Captain had never stopped fighting, however, though she could not even call for aid.

Samara Garriton used the last hours of the war to fight the only way she could. She and her Chief Engineer and her Science Officer 'chopped and plopped' systems together, integrating working systems into functions outside normal parameters.

One of those systems was the highly powerful graviton beam. With use of deflector technology from shield projection and rerouted targeting systems, powered through dwindling life support, she had her exemplary crew use the beam to latch onto passing ships. Then they would let go and drift with the momentum, propelling the ship this way and that, giving it motion.

Garriton ordered the crew to project graviton fields as short lived shields to block limited attack runs. She even got them to utilize the energies to push targets instead of pulling them, sending ships with smaller mass ever so slightly off course, making them miss targets and often making them collide with other enemies, destroying both.

Samara Garriton had hardly considered herself a 'warrioress' in her own mind but the Chabron insisted she take the title. They had bestowed upon her the honor of adopting her into one of their clan families, the family of her dear friend, T'Leah. As T'Leah's sister, the family gave Garriton a family weapon to keep and bear.

Samara looked at the raekwin in her hands. It stretched out long and slender in its gentle, elegant curve. Forged of Mangalla alloys, the nigh weightless, shining blue sword promised to tie her forever to her lost friend, her warrioress sister. A tear dropped onto the sword and streamed down its length.

"They say you'd be an Admiral after your ship's performance, if Unity hadn't folded. Lorrayanka says she'd definitely vote for you."

Samara spun. Gideon Ridge stood behind her. She wiped her eyes.

"I hate seeing her that way," she said, gesturing back to the drifting ship. "She gave it all she had."

"I don't think she was the only one. Your crew was awesome."

"Thank you."

"Their Captain was...she is...inspirational," Gideon said. "One of a kind, truth be told."

Her big eyes drank him in. Soft pink lips parted but closed again.

"What?" he asked her.

"Nothing. Thank you again."

"What were you about to say?" he pressed, moving closer.

"Nothing, Ridge," she said, waving it away.

"Samara, tell me," he said.

"Everyone's talking about what they will do or want to do or got invited to do!" she snapped and propped a hand on her shapely hip. The other hand clenched the raekwin in the middle of the scabbard. "Here I am being honored by some, praised by others and probably even hated by some of Unity..."

"Samara," he said sympathetically. "If anybody can understand that, you know it's me."

"No, Ridge, no! You don't!" she shouted, face angry.

"What?" he spat, genuinely confused.

"During that whole conflict, I wondered if you were alright-"

"I worried for you, too!" he interrupted.

"-and wondered if I would ever see you again-" she continued.

"I wondered the same thing!" he half shouted.

"-and we get in that crowd and there's all this talk about honors, the future, plans and opportunities-"

"Well, of course there-"

"-and I think you might actually offer-"

"Oh, wait," he muttered, realization dawning.

"-to let me work with you, with Unity in the past! And-"

"Samara, I didn't even think-"

"-I'm a pretty deft Captain, if I say so myself-"

"Samara," he eased.

"-and a lot of others think that-"

Gideon Ridge grabbed her waist suddenly and jerked her forward. He kissed her, pushing his lips into hers passionately. For a moment, she pushed against him but she quickly relented. In a moment, their passions deepened and so did their kisses.

A long time passed before they parted slightly, still embracing.

Gideon had messed up her hair and still had a hand in it, behind her neck. He looked affectionately down into her bright eyes.

"Samara Garriton, will you travel with me?"

"I'm not giving up the title of Captain," she said breathlessly, her eyes big and glistening. Her lips were swollen from the rough, demanding kissing. "But...I can't think of many places I wouldn't go with you," she half whispered.

"I wouldn't ask you to give up your title, Samara. Besides, I like a woman with authority. And I can't think of any places I'd go and not invite you along." He leaned in and kissed her button nose, adding, "But what about your crew? A new ship? I thought-"

"No, you didn't," she said sarcastically. "You didn't think. Anybody even half way aware of their surroundings would've recognized my affection for you. I think I can leave the past behind if I have something better to look forward to...to work toward. And my crew loves me. I know they'll be happy for me. I would be for one of them."

Gideon smiled, squeezing her, and said, "Then come with me. With us. My family and I have this work that we do and we need all the help we can get."

"I can tell by your reputation. You're always getting into some sort of trouble," she teased. Then her eyes softened again. "By the way, I'm sorry, Gideon," she said softly, changing gears. "About Sundar, about the way you lost him."

"Samara, he made a decision that makes me very proud. I'm going to tell him so when I see him again, someday."

"Is that all you got to do, boy?" a voice snarled behind them.

Both turned to see Pap Ridge, encircled by a number of other familiar faces.

"Ain't there some work you could be doing down in the docking bay? That ship ain't going to prep itself."

"Relax, Sylver," Wrigley Zeckinbridge said.

The Commodore was in civilian attire and walked along with Pap, Grundy, and Jaka Baddenide. In another small clump, Paola Kett, Josh Brent, Candri Prentice, Taylor Patrick and Wastasa Winds strolled up to the group.

"What's this? The meeting was in the survey room," Gideon teased.

"This is good luck and farewell, for now," Winds said with a smile, shaking hands with the others. "For me, anyway."

Garriton kissed him on the cheek.

"I wish you well, Wastasa," she said.

"You too, Captain," he nodded.

"What are you going to do?" Ridge asked.

"I'm going to work with the Starstalker starmada effort for a while. They need good technicians and Lorrayanka says I can tag along on her vessel. She's going to put in a word for me. I like that lady Captain, I won't lie."

"She's a great lady," the young Ridge said.

"And Officer," Samara added with a succinct nod.

"Thing is, she can also help me another way. With the Unity Starmada gone, a lot of 'kill on sight' warrants my daughter earned will be dangerously active. In worlds that would have previously let her go because she worked with Unity, under contract, she's going to be a prime, lucrative target again."

The others nodded.

"I can't let her face justice on a lot of planets, just like her own, native Tongru. She's a 'kill on sight' target there, too. And, even on worlds that would have mercy on her and put her to a fair trial, bounty hunters will be coming out of the weldworks to catch her. Lorrayanka offered to take both of us back to her world. Cheyenne can be tried there for her crimes. They're fair and the fact is that most 'hunters are afraid to risk angering Starstalker governments by invading their system. For my girl's good and probably mine, too, we're going to their home."

"Be careful," Ridge said, shaking his hand a final time.

"You know me, Ridge."

"That's why he told you to be careful," Samara quipped with a grin.

"The other thing I wanted to share was about the Rothidai, Grockforth," he said, looking at Grundy. "He made it off that station in an Acolyte starfighter. It was designated the *Razorwing*. The big guy could've run for his life and no one would've ever known but he had too much honor for that. He stood with us, with all of us, against the dead. A valiant and loyal warrior to the end...he went down as our allies were fleeing the planetary atmosphere."

Grundy snorted and gave a Rothidai salute.

The others believed they could see a tear in his eye.

"One more thing," Winds said, pacing away slowly. "My daughter told me she shot Rala Kess off in a survival pod. I don't favor his chances...but his kind tends to keep on poppin' up like a Waddro beetle. They tend to survive everything. Keep your eyes open; none of us will be on his good side."

He took his leave and Grundy and Pap moved further along the bay.

"So long, everyone. Don't be long, son," Sylver called.

They cut a path through the walkways around the docking areas on their way for the shiny *Spoken Word*.

Gideon put on his headset from the ship in case the two needed anything when they got to it.

"Samara, I'm guessing you're done with big starmadas," Zeckinbridge said with a quick wink. "As close as you two seem, it looks like a given."

She stood close by Jaka Baddenide as she spoke.

"Yes," Samara said.

No explanations, no reasons, no justifications and no regrets.

"Well, it's going around," Joshua Brent said flatly.

"Brent is joining the Acolytes," Jaka said.

"I am, too," Patrick said. "I've had questions all my life. After what we saw in that chamber...in space...well, it's time to find the answers."

"I think a lot of people will find the Faith now," Paola Kett said. "They'll be forced to face what reality really is. There is more to existence than what we can sense here in this plane. The supernatural world and the beyond have been witnessed now. How could anyone ever doubt again?"

"You'd be surprised," Candri Prentice mused. "Signs and wonders have been given throughout time. They will deny this one, too. In time, they will say it never happened."

"We have to go," Paola said, shaking her head. "Rule and my dad are waiting. Farewell, Captain Ridge, Captain Garriton." She walked forward and kissed Samara Garriton on the cheek then did the same to Gideon. "It was an honor."

"The honor was ours," Gideon Ridge responded.

"Until we meet again," Candri Prentice said, kissing the duo, as well.

The group passed around gentle embraces and whispered hopes and dreams. Then most of the Acolytes were gone, taking with them Josh Brent and Taylor Patrick.

The only remaining Acolyte was Jaka Baddenide.

"Thing is," Wrigley Zeckinbridge said, "I'm done with big starmadas, too. I'm a Commodore with no fleet to command and no Captains to direct. My supervising Admirals are all dead...and so is Unity, for now. For the first time in a long, long time, I have no idea what I'm going to do. So, I'm going back home to Earth to see where God leads me."

"I'm going with her," Baddenide said. "I'm joining the Earth Temple. They need a martial trainer and Rule says I'm it. Plus," he grinned, looking at Wrigley, "I plan to get to know this fine Christian lady a bit better."

Wrigley grinned, too.

"What about your new ships and new Earth starmada plans?" Samara Garriton asked her friend.

Wrigley shrugged and said, "Let's just say, you and I both have better options."

The former Commodore looked fondly at Jaka Baddenide.

Then the last four parted.

Samara Garriton took one last, long look out through the open bay field at the old ship.

"You think we'll ever come back here?" she asked Gideon.

"I don't know. Maybe. Maybe not."

"Are you always so indecisive?" she teased.

"No. It just depends on where God wants us to go. I know I never make plans to go backward so I hope, in a way, we don't. I hope our work at the Reaches is done."

She smiled and touched his face.

"No going backward. I like that."

They leaned close for another kiss but Gideon's newly adorned headset squeaked. Both of them jumped, startled. Then the speaker came to life.

"Hurry up, boy, we ain't got all day."

Gideon sighed and rolled his eyes.

"You sure you want in on this paradise?" he asked sarcastically.

Samara gave him a soft, intimate smile.

"I wouldn't miss it."

The End